Maggie

A Journey of
Love, Loss and Survival

Vicki Tapia

Published March, 2018

Cover design by Robert Harrison

Cover scenery image courtesy of Lionel Tapia

Dedication

This work is dedicated to eight generations of strong women, beginning with my great-great-great grandma Margareta Mink Fries in the early 19th century and continuing onward into the 21st century, with the newest knot in an unbroken thread, Eliza Marie Chiasson.

Part One

All, as they say, that glitters, is not gold.
--John Dryden, *The Hind & The Panther*, 1687

1.

Lavina, Montana, October 15, 1941. I wake with a start, my nightgown damp with sweat. Dark memories from another life clamor for attention. For nearly fifty years the nightmare has played out, in an endless reverberation across my restless mind.

> *Sam dashes up the lane in his sulky, askew in the seat. He snaps the whip, altogether missing the horse's flank. I move to the side of our bedroom window, concealed by the lace curtain.*
>
> *Fear inches up my spine and creeps down my arms like hundreds of tiny pinpricks. Foreboding clenches at my insides.*
>
> *Taking a deep breath, I steel myself for his arrival. Spying the letter opener on my dressing table, I place it in the waistband of my skirt, but then reconsider. Slight of stature, I am no match for his brawn. If he manages to grab the instrument from me, there is no telling what might happen. Nausea sweeps over me.*
>
> *I risk another peek and shudder, my heart pounding. There's no time to bar the front door.*
>
> *How dare he come home in such a condition in the middle of the day!*
>
> *Shaking like a leaf in a windstorm, I step to the top of the stairs. He flings open the door, staggering into our entryway. I swallow the lump in my throat and stand my ground.*
>
> *"Maggie! What the hell are you doing up there?" Disheveled, his fair hair falling rakishly across his forehead, he*

tosses the sharp words into the air. His piercing blue eyes lock with mine and the hairs on the back of my neck stand on end.

With weak knees, taking one cautious step at a time, I begin a halting descent. My pulse racing, I stop halfway, feeling stronger and somehow larger standing above, peering down on him.

Gaping at me, he hollers, "Damn it woman, get yourself down here this instant and give me a proper welcome home!" He lurches toward the stairway, tripping on the umbrella stand, sending its contents clattering across the oak floor. He regains his balance enough to grip the banister, steadying himself and leering at me with eyes ablaze.

I stare back, my thoughts tangled, my heart twisted with emotion. Frozen, I am afraid to move forward, yet unable to turn away.

Then, mindful of our children napping nearby, I force myself down the steps. I hold my breath, bracing myself for what I know lies ahead. Fast and venomous as a striking rattlesnake, he grabs and overpowers me. With brute strength, he grips my backside and crushes me fully against his angry, unyielding body.

I roll over, hoping to lessen the ache in my shoulder, a persistent reminder of the time he shoved me down the steps. *Why had I succumbed to his malignant guile?* I will grant he *did* have a way about him which was exceedingly hard to resist, and in the early days we had loved each other with passion.

Through the open window, I see no hint of dawn. I breathe in the fresh night air, tinged with a scent of burnt leaves.

Well-acquainted with the wee hours of the night, I know sleep will elude me. I push back the covers and struggle to rise, placing both feet on the cold, wooden floor. My spine is now stiff with age and it resists as I bend down to pull on my cotton slippers. Grasping the bedpost to steady myself, I stand and ease first one arm, then the other, into my chenille housecoat, careful not to aggravate my shoulder.

In the front room, I pick up the faded quilt, cocooning it around me to still my shiver. Settling into my old rocker, the nightmare begins to soften, as the chair's lulling movement conjures soothing images of rocking my children.

But the groan and creak of the floorboards beneath me unleash a worn-out misery which wraps its tentacles around my heart, driving my attention back to Sam. After all these years, how can I still feel so conflicted?

In the end, it comes down to choices. Yet, how can I regret the past? Yes, they brought my greatest sorrows, but they also brought my greatest joys.

I clutch my chest and my heart stings. I tremble and take a few deliberate, calming breaths. The memories of Sam's cruelty and my lost children flood into my mind, creating a stream of unstoppable tears. The nightmare has had its way with me once more.

2.

Macomb County, Michigan, June, 1887. "Maggie," Mother called up the curved oak staircase, "Mr. Sam Jobsa has come calling!"

My eyes brightened as I eyed my older sister Lucy and two of my younger sisters, Edith and Janie. The four of us sat in the upstairs sitting room embroidering tea towels. A grin spread across my face, "Oh, sisters, did you hear? Mr. Jobsa's come calling!" Edith and Janie nodded and smiled.

Lucy raised an eyebrow. "Now, why do you suppose he has dropped by to see you yet again?"

I scowled at her. With no beau of her own, I sensed her envy.

There was no denying how his unannounced visits flattered me. Radiating an easy charm, William Samuel Jobsa, my heart's desire and the most handsome man I had ever laid eyes upon, stood more than a half-foot taller than myself, with wheat-colored hair and cornflower blue eyes. I couldn't recall a time when I hadn't been in love with Samuel. I prayed these frequent visits meant he entertained similar feelings toward me. I daydreamed of being a radiant bride, walking down the aisle to join my beloved at the altar. The mere thought filled me with joy.

Our families had known each other for years, linked by a common enthusiasm for harness racing Standardbreds around the county. My papa, James Perry, had made a name for himself winning racing purses. He had also developed a reputation in both the breeding and training of magnificent racehorses. Sam's father, Henry Jobsa, was likewise renowned in our region for his daring and cunning ability on the racetrack. Sam had recently begun harness racing, a bright new star on the horizon, full of bravado and confidence, decidedly like his father.

Mother's clear voice brought me back to the moment. "Maggie, did you hear me?"

"Yes, Mother, I'll be right down."

"How do I look?" I asked my sisters, tucking loose strands of hair back into my chignon, before brushing errant threads from my blue and white gingham-checked work dress.

"You look fine, Maggie, and you better hurry up before he leaves," Lucy admonished.

With a conspiratorial wink at my sisters, I withdrew to the hallway and down the stairs, pinching my cheeks to add color to the stubbornly pale, Irish skin inherited from my papa. Attempting to wipe dry my sweaty palms, I smoothed the skirt of my dress as I descended the final steps into the entryway, where Samuel stood waiting. He wore a cream-colored, tailored sack suit, complete with a wingtip collar and bowtie. Encircled by the sunlight, he appeared golden.

"Why, Mr. Jobsa, how lovely to see you again!" My pulse quickened as I cast my eyes downward and made a small curtsy.

"Miss Perry," lowering his head with a bow, "I'm charmed."

I need not have pinched my cheeks, as they had turned scarlet of their own accord. There I stood, staring at him most inappropriately. He matched my stare and our eyes locked. Seconds ticked by and Mother cleared her throat. Remembering my manners, I suggested, "Won't you join Mother and me in the parlor?" indicating the way with a turn of my hand.

Mother followed the two of us into this front room. Even though I considered it an outdated custom, my parents deemed a chaperone still necessary at seventeen, so I well knew the futility of asking Mother permission to meet privately with Samuel.

It cheered me to see the heavy brocaded drapes drawn back, allowing light to stream through the two large windows facing the front drive. The draperies, like the furniture in this room, were antiquated and horribly Victorian. I couldn't wait to have my own home, which would be decorated with more modern designs, like the Arts and Crafts style I had discovered in a magazine my oldest sister Ella brought home from the millinery shop.

"Why, Mr. Jobsa, might we offer you some tea or coffee this afternoon?" asked Mother, with a slight smile gracing the corners of her mouth. True to her Dutch and German ancestry, my mother, Mary Jane Fries Perry, was a tall woman. She always pulled her frizzy hair into a severely wound bun. Today, she wore a plum colored day dress, with a high-standing collar edged in a bit of lace. Her snug basque bodice fit her frame to perfection. All this might have given her the appearance of sternness, were it not for her warm gold-green eyes and her easily apparent zest for life, which everyone told me I had inherited.

"Mrs. Perry," responded Samuel, his lithe body draped across the settee in a relaxed manner, "I've such an affinity for an afternoon cup of coffee and don't often have the opportunity. Thank you for your hospitality!"

Mother acknowledged him with a polite nod, before addressing me, "Maggie, why don't you see to that?"

"Yes, Mother, of course." I fumed silently, yet smiled sweetly, and hurried off to the kitchen to make coffee. Without hesitation, I pumped some water into the kettle and set it on the stove, still warm from earlier cooking. Next I stoked up the fire with scraps of kindling. The few minutes I waited for the water to heat seemed an eternity, when all I really fancied was gazing upon Samuel's fine countenance. Yet, here I idled like a servant in the far corner of the house making coffee. *Why couldn't Mother have done it?* I pouted, even as I distracted myself with thoughts of Samuel's full lips touching mine.

At last the water bubbled in the kettle, so I slowly poured the perfect amount over the muslin bag holding the coffee grounds. After the water had filtered through and the liquid below looked a deep brown, I poured the coffee into one of our finest mugs and set it on a tray. To this I added some leftover biscuits from our noon meal, along with a tin of spiced jelly preserved last summer from our apple orchard.

The aroma of roasted coffee beans wafted behind me as I carried the tray into the parlor, where all was quiet. I briefly pondered what they might have talked about while I had been in the kitchen.

"Miss Perry, now *there* is a sight to behold!" His sparkling eyes suggested he meant something more than coffee and biscuits. Even before I had time to place the tray on the side table, Sam had reached for the steaming mug. He sipped a generous amount, exclaiming, "You truly make the best coffee that's ever crossed my lips."

I smiled in satisfaction, my irritation evaporating as I recognized Mother's wisdom in asking me to make the coffee. She appreciated my skill at brewing a delicious cup, and when you have six daughters for whom to find husbands, wisdom was imperative.

My confidence improved and I met his ardent gaze head-on. "Will you be racing this weekend?"

"Yes, of course, and I can't help but conjure visions of you on the sidelines, cheering me on!"

Mother nodded, which to me implied affirmation. "You *will* see me! Papa will be racing Toby, too. Will your father compete?"

"It's possible, although Alba has developed a slight limp in recent days. It'll depend upon her stamina and strength by Sunday afternoon. She is tenacious, but Father won't risk damaging her leg if she isn't in tip-top shape."

We talked on of inconsequential matters, until all that remained on the tray were a few errant crumbs. He stood, along with Mother and me, as the time had come for him to depart.

We showed him to the door where, in a flourish, he bowed, took my hand in his, and brushed his lips across it. A tingling sensation rose up my arm and I imagined myself swooning with delight, but the scowl from Mother quickly stifled any such notion.

I stood in the entryway, my hand over a trembling heart, and watched as Samuel loosened the reins from our cast iron hitching post and gracefully mounted his handsome harness-racing horse Absalom. What a picture they made, Samuel luminous atop the velvety black stallion. With a snap of Samuel's crop, the steed released an explosive snort, shook his mane and pranced in a half circle before cantering down the lane, his tail flicking back and forth in flawless harmony with his trot.

I dreamily closed the front door while my heart settled back into a normal rhythm.

"Maggie." Mother startled me out of my trance. "I'll clean up here and you go on and join your sisters to finish with the embroidery project. It's almost time to start supper preparations."

"Yes, Mother." I abandoned my reverie of magnificent horses and suave suitors and sprinted up the steps. Bounding onto the landing, I bumped square into Janie and Edith, toppling us all to the ground. They had been peeking around the corner and I'm quite sure they caught a glimpse of Samuel kissing my hand.

"Oh! Sisters!" I cried as we fell into a heap of arms, legs and dresses.

"Maggie! Slow down and move with decorum." Mother's firm voice suppressed our giggles, but we couldn't disguise the merriment in our eyes as we scurried back toward the sitting room to gather our embroidery.

In the midst of our supper preparations, the front door slammed and Ella burst into the kitchen. At 29, others considered my favorite sister an old maid. I dismissed such reasoning, even though it was unfathomable why her knight in shining armor had not yet found her.

I concluded it might be a good idea for her to quit waiting and begin searching for him herself. Though bright and sweet-tempered around family and friends, Ella was uncommonly shy and hesitant around menfolk. She cheerfully worked in Mt. Clemens as a milliner, where she safely spent her time making hats for women. Patrons regularly commented on her talent for the profession. She had the ideal eye for fashion, as evidenced by her ability to also design and sew women's clothing.

Addressing no one in particular, Ella announced, "You'll never guess what happened at work today," her demeanor uncharacteristically jubilant. In fact, I couldn't recall ever having seen her quite so exuberant. What could it be? *Maybe she had met her knight!*

"Well, I have no doubt that you'll tell us," Lucy said.

"Tell us, tell us!" shrieked 6-year-old Eva, as she jumped up and down.

"Of course she'll tell us," intoned Lucy, "but you must be quiet, little sister."

Ella had a twinkle in her eye as she chirped, "Today, Mr. Whitworth announced he will open a second millinery shop and he's asked me to manage it." She regarded the five of us, each in some stage of cooking or assembling our supper. Well, at least *some* of us still worked at making ready, I noted, as Lucy perched on a kitchen stool with Eva sitting on her lap.

Ella said, "I feel so fortunate he considers me up to the task. It's nothing short of extraordinary!"

"Mercy, Ella, what did you say to him?" Lucy demanded.

"I said yes!"

"How marvelous for you!" How splendid to see my Ellie so over the moon for a change.

"Mt. Clemens isn't that large. Where would the second shop be located?" Lucy asked.

"Detroit," Ella answered.

"Detroit?"

"Detroit? Detroit isn't in Mt. Clemens!" We all talked at once.

"You can't move to Detroit."

"Alone in Detroit?"

"Where would you live?"

"How would you even get there?"

"I can imagine what Mother and Papa will say," I commented, as Mother walked into the kitchen.

"What's all the shouting and carryings-on about? What are we going to say about what?" asked Mother.

"I've been offered and accepted a job opportunity in Detroit!" Ella's face glowed.

I feared Mother's eyes might pop out of her head.

"Lo and behold, Ella, *that* is startling news. Although by now, I'm confident you know your own mind. Let's see what your papa has to say." She turned just as Papa walked in our back door, followed by two of my brothers, Louis and James.

"Did I hear my name being mentioned, then?" said Papa in his lilting Irish voice. A man of moderate height, with dark hair and memorable blue eyes, he encompassed a myriad of talents. His cheerful disposition, kindness and intuitive nature drew others to him. Yet, even though he delighted our family, he also had a fondness, as many Irish do, for strong drink.

Our kitchen erupted into a cacophony of voices.

"Give Papa some space!" Born five minutes before her twin, Louis, Lucy reveled in being in control of the situation. She routinely accomplished this by being the loudest.

Nine abruptly silent people all turned to stare at her, still sitting on the stool. Though not classically beautiful like Ella, Lucy had inherited Mother's brilliant green eyes and thick chestnut hair. I pondered why I appealed to Samuel, when he could be pursuing my vivacious sister. I concluded he had already determined her too bossy for his tastes.

I had to admit her loud voice commanded enough quiet for Ella to relay her news once again, which she did forthwith. Papa nodded his head and addressed his eldest daughter. "Well, bully for you, Ella." His bright eyes twinkled and she beamed. "We'll talk more about this remarkable news later, daughter."

3.

June 12, 1887. It was true. My dearest Ellie would soon be off to Detroit. From my perspective, the city of 100,000 residents, 26 miles away, might as well have been 260 miles away. On any particular day, my family alternated between bewilderment and apprehension. Where would she live and how would she manage on her own, after living at home these last twenty-nine years? She had seemed so satisfied with that arrangement.

Oh, how I would miss her, I ruminated as our family walked together on our way home from the Presbyterian Church on a breezy Sunday in June. Still well before noon, people appreciated the early summer services to avoid the midday furnace-like heat of the building. More importantly, the earlier service freed us up to attend afternoon harness races. Not all congregations could be regarded as progressive, like us Presbyterians.

With a light heart, I put aside thoughts of Ella's impending departure and called to my two younger sisters, "Eva! Edith!" clasping their hands. We skipped together up the lane, while Ella and Janie smiled at us, and Lucy shook her head with disdain.

The farmhouse in sight, our skip turned to a saunter and we walked arm-in-arm the remaining short distance home. I regarded the fields, robust with recent growth. The corn stalks were beginning to poke out of the ground, resembling little soldiers all in a row. I breathed in the fresh earthy smell of the season.

A small fruit orchard stretched across the field beside our house, lined with apple, pear, cherry and pawpaw trees. Our farm sat nearby the Clinton River, about a half-mile from where it emptied into Lake St. Clair. The warmth of the sun upon my back reminded me of all the summer days to come and I imagined myself sitting lakeside, on the sand, holding hands with Samuel.

For a brief moment, my sisters and I stood at the edge of our yard. My heart skipped a beat as I beheld the only home I had ever known, wondering how much longer I might live there. With all the commotion created by our arrival at home, my fanciful musings soon dissolved. The men headed to the barn to do midday chores, while we women divvied up kitchen tasks in preparation for Sunday dinner.

"Ella and Maggie, why don't you see to the table?" Mother suggested.

I decided Mother favored her oldest daughter with this plum assignment because of her impending move. I smiled, pleased to be included, as Mother surely identified me as Ella's favorite sister.

"Too many cooks!" Both our heads popped up from retrieving our Sunday best white linen tablecloth from the sideboard in the dining room. There stood Lucy, escaping the chaos of the kitchen. Before we could say a word, she moved toward the windows, "Why don't we open these to bring in some fresh air?" She unlatched and opened them both.

Lucy did enjoy being in charge, and even I had to admit her idea was first-rate, as a soft breeze drifted across the room, bringing with it the fragrant scent of the meadow. This spacious room, covered with a solid oak flooring, took up almost one-third of our main floor living space. The saffron yellow tapestry overlay drapery had been pulled to the side for the season to reveal two large windows, each semi-hidden under a veil of dainty lace curtains. Embellished with miniature matching saffron and jasmine-colored baby roses, the cream-colored wallpaper added to the sunshiny aura of this cheerful room.

Arranging the place settings, I reflected on the multitude of chips around the edges of some of the dinner plates. Those signs of wear evoked an instant melancholy, as I reckoned, like Mother and Papa, the Blue Lily patterned ironstone was growing old. A wedding gift from Mother's family when my parents married in a village near Rochester, New York, it was one of the few possessions accompanying them to Michigan when they migrated here that same year, more than thirty years ago.

And now, the time had come for Ella to move away. I realized life was full of endings and beginnings. Coming and going. Leaving and staying. Would I ever be the one leaving, or always be the one staying behind? I supposed Papa understood better than any of us about being left.

How many times had he told the story? I could recount it by heart.

Papa's parents, John and Mary, left him behind with relatives when they immigrated to Canada from Ireland. I can't even imagine what that must have been like for all three of them. He says they shared their worry about the crossing, not to mention finding their way in North America, and stayed in touch with occasional letters. Still, it must have been terribly sad to wave goodbye to his Mama and Papa from a dock in Cork as a five-year-old. In 1848, before he turned thirteen, he had bravely come over shipboard and reunited with them in western New York, where they had relocated from Canada.

Lucy's lament, "Oh, Ella, I wish I were coming with you," drew me back to the present.

"Well, you know, Lucy, Mr. Whitworth may be hiring a second milliner. Even though you're just nineteen, he'd probably consider you simply because you're my sister. Too bad you don't have any experience, though." With sudden inspiration, she proclaimed, "Lucy! You can apply for my job in Mt. Clemens, and after gaining the know-how, you might join me in Detroit!"

"Oh, Ella, do you think so? If only Mother and Papa might agree. It would be such a welcome improvement over my current tedious life." I surmised she was already concocting a scheme to convince them to give her permission to apply for Ella's old job.

The longer I listened to my sisters' conversation, the more the notion of moving to Detroit sounded like an extraordinary adventure. No one loved adventure more than me, but I kept my yearning well hidden. What might it be like to live on my own in a big city? All the people and excitement! My imagination sprouted with prospects. I had read about the new electric streetcars and fancied myself taking one to visit the Zoological Gardens. Or, possibly I would ride it to Belle Isle Park. I would go shopping at J. L. Hudson's, buy a new ready-made gown and attend the Detroit Opera. So many possibilities awaited me. *But, no, that would never be. My destiny lay here.* I was convinced *my* future was in Mt. Clemens as the wife of William Samuel Jobsa.

Still deep in thought, I helped my sisters finish up setting the table.

"Please pass the stew," requested James, an eighteen-year old with an enormous appetite. Dinner had commenced.

"Besides James and Louis, who else would like to come cheer for Toby and me this afternoon?" asked Papa.

"Oh, Papa, I would love to come!" I grinned at him.

"Yes, I'd also enjoy the outing," agreed Ella.

"James, as much as I fancy seeing you win a good race, I think I'll stay home this afternoon. I'm weary from the heat and find it's affected my appetite, leaving me with little energy."

Mother did look a little peaked.

"Of course, Mary Jane. Stay home and rest," Papa agreed.

"I believe I'll stay home too," Lucy said. She didn't enjoy harness racing, having told me ages ago, "I'm not going to stand in the hot sun and watch men in carts whip horses." I doubted she would ever admit such in front of Papa or our brothers.

"Since your mother isn't going, I'd like you three youngsters to stay home, too," Papa said. My three younger sisters nodded, not unhappily. "Ella and Maggie, you may ride in the buggy with James and Louis, and I'll drive my racing cart."

Talk turned to Ella's proposed move. "Ella, did Mr. Whitworth give any indication as to when he expects you to begin your new job?" inquired Papa.

"He hopes to have the new business open by the end of next month."

"Ella?" interrupted our youngest sister, Eva.

"Yes, Eva?"

"Can I have your bed when you leave?"

We all erupted into laughter at my little sister's request.

"Oh, my darling Eva. You'll need to ask Lucy. She's next oldest and I imagine it's *her* turn to have her own bed."

Attention had turned toward Lucy and Eva, which Lucy used to her advantage.

"Papa? Mother? I'd like to make a proposition."

"Yes, Lucy?" Mother arched a brow.

Lucy leaned forward in her chair and smiled charmingly. "What would you say to my petitioning Mr. Whitworth to replace Ella at her current job in Mt. Clemens?"

Please, let her go! I'd had quite enough of my sister's sharp tongue.

Neither Mother nor Papa appeared startled by Lucy's idea. Papa said, "Well now, Lucy, what an interesting proposal! You're almost twenty, so maybe it is time to consider employment opportunities."

"It would shift some housekeeping burdens to the younger children," Mother remarked, "but it might provide opportunities for you, if you're interested in such a trade. I haven't heard you ever mention an enthusiasm for hat design."

"Oh, yes, I'm confident I'll adore the art of hat design. I'm a quick study, so if Mr. Whitworth might take a chance on me, I have faith I wouldn't disappoint."

With that, Mother and Papa nodded their consent.

"Thank you! Oh, thank you! You'll not be dissatisfied with this decision. I'm quite sure I'll be a first-rate employee and will still do my part at home."

"Well, you haven't gotten the job yet," I pointed out.

Lucy eyed me, and with an underlying tone of challenge, stated emphatically, "No, Maggie, you're right. I haven't. I predict I *will* have the job, before the month is over."

My sister didn't lack for confidence.

After we left the table, I raced upstairs to our dressing room to change out of my church gown. Lucky that my older sisters and I were near enough in size to share clothes, I chose the sky-blue Florentine silk to wear to the races, wanting to look my best for Samuel. After tidying my hair, I dashed back down the stairs, hearing the others laughing and talking as they stepped out onto the back porch. I caught up to Ella and we followed Papa and my brothers toward the barn.

"Ella, are you worried about Mother? It appears to me she hasn't displayed her normal spunk of late."

"Hmm . . . now that you mention it, it may be true." After a momentary silence, she said, "I'm not sure what to think, Maggie. She's always been such a strong woman. I pray it's only a touch of malaise."

"It's really no wonder, though, after birthing so many children and keeping house all these many years. Poor Mother. I certainly intend to have fewer children."

Ella chuckled. "Perchance you'll want to find a husband first?"

Blushing, I speculated about how many children Samuel wanted.

Papa was waiting in his sulky, with Toby high stepping in a circle, snorting at the air, anxious to be off. Ella and I climbed into the back seat of the buggy hitched to two of my equine favorites, Billy and Blackie, while James sat beside Louis, who called, "Giddy-up!"

I stared at the back of my brothers' heads. They were as different as their complexions. James and Lucy, with their chestnut hair and fiery tempers, acted and even looked more like twins than Louis and Lucy. Louis, with his calming influence, was fair of hair and mind. I grabbed Ella's hand and smiled, happy to be sitting beside her.

Located near Mt. Clemens, the track had no official designation as a racetrack, but nonetheless maintained a sense of local pride. An appeal spread by word of mouth throughout our county several years ago to develop a racetrack for harness racing. A wealthy landowner, who enjoyed watching the sport, had stepped forward for the cause and donated an unfarmed section of his land, which included an old outbuilding. Prior to this, the races had taken place on a country lane which, by comparison, seemed quite backward.

A dozen or more enthusiasts in our township, including both Papa and Mr. Jobsa, came together, and over time, built the half mile-long, almost circular track. They had repaired the outbuilding and constructed a fence rail around the perimeter, which offered some protection and separated the carts from the spectators. The course was quite professional with its raised judges' platform at the starting line. The most popular way to spend a Sunday afternoon, the races garnered much local interest--sometimes even in winter--when the men used cutters instead of sulkies. Were I a man, you'd see me in a sulkie racing a Standardbred, that I knew.

Our buggy pulled to a stop close to the track. Nearby, people were milling around, exchanging pleasantries. The anticipation of today's races was palpable and the air buzzed with expectancy. I smiled with delight as I inhaled the scent of dust, horses and sweat, all the racetrack smells of summers past.

To win the purse, a horse and cart must secure first place in three different heats. This could last hours, sometimes taking a dozen of the one-mile races to declare the winner. Hence, it often became a test of the Standardbreds' strength and stamina rather than the horses' skills.

Pandemonium greeted us. The first heat of the afternoon was in the process of assembling, with the sulkies jockeying for position at the starting line. With a nod of his head, Papa drove his cart directly to the track. I couldn't help but scan the crowd before me, seeking a glimpse of Samuel. Ella and I stood beside our buggy, waiting patiently while our brothers searched for a satisfactory vantage point. Even with the crowds, I trusted they would find space near the finish line, where the thrill of watching the sulkies come down the home stretch was unmatched.

My stomach overflowed with butterflies. Oh, where was Samuel? Would he wave when he saw me? With my short stature, I found it nigh on impossible to see much of anything, as spectators bustled about on the sidelines, shouting boisterously, placing bets on their favorite contenders.

I bounced on tiptoe and craned my neck in every direction, hoping to locate Samuel, but with no success. I had an idea that I could likely see better from the buggy seat, so without a moment's hesitation, I hoisted myself up. The inordinate amount of dust in the air didn't help my line of sight and made my throat dry. I sneezed, which caught Ella's attention.

"Maggie, *what* are you doing?" asked Ella in a bewildered voice, as she turned to look up at me standing tall in the buggy, my shadow bearing down upon her.

"Er . . . oh, surveying the crowd," I squeaked, as I quickly, and dare I say, desperately, scanned the track for Samuel and Absalom.

"Good heavens, Maggie, are you looking for Samuel? That is most unbecoming. You come back down here this instant."

Scowling at her, I climbed back down. Soon after, Louis came back to fetch us.

"Sisters, we've found a suitable viewing location over there," he pointed off to the left where James stood, nearly twenty yards in front of the starting line. My heart swelled with love for my unassuming and gentle brother. Ella and I each took one of his arms and I attempted to calm my jitters by matching their stroll as we approached the perimeter fence.

Why couldn't I see Samuel anywhere? I did see his father, Mr. Jobsa, in his sulky, with a skittish Alba prancing in circles. So, he *would* race today! I spotted Papa and Toby, but no Sam. *Where was he? Had some mayhem befallen him or Absalom?* I beseeched my imagination to cease such pointless speculation, in the uncertain hope he would show himself.

The judge shouted instructions to the drivers, as each attempted to navigate toward the best patch of turf from which to launch their carts. I finally spotted Samuel driving his sulky, rushing out of the old building where they did repairs. At the last minute, they raced to the starting line as the judge shouted final instructions.

In a moment of breathless fury, they were off! I beheld the scene of these magnificent creatures straining so splendidly in their efforts to dash around the track, the earth reverberating under pounding hooves, the air thick with grit and flying clods of dirt. Intermixed with the deafening thunder of hooves was the unmistakable crack of the drivers' crops, and the surging cheers of the crowd. Ella and I jumped up and down, shrieking with delight, as Papa won the first heat.

To be called a Standardbred, a horse had to run the mile in two and a half minutes or less. After two times around the track, the race was at an end. Between races, cart drivers focused on small equipment changes or repairs and calming their horses.

Because we stood close to the finish line, I at last succeeded in catching Sam's attention with a cautious wave. He smiled broadly and nodded back. My heart did cartwheels, while a familiar warmth seared my cheeks.

The second heat did not proceed far, as the judge pounded his bell, which indicated an imperfect start. These false starts always frayed the nerves of the drivers, horses and spectators alike. His jaw clenched and beads of sweat trickling down his face, Sam expertly navigated Absalom and his cart back into the starting position.

Race after race flew by our vantage point on the sidelines. We all cheered wildly as Sam and Absalom won by a nose in the third heat and Papa, hands down, the fourth. Mr. Jobsa came right back in a burst of speed to triumph in the fifth race and other carts won the next several. The finale included four sulkies, each driver having won two heats. This included both Papa and Sam, but not Mr. Jobsa, who won just the fifth heat, so unlike him as he was nearly always in the final. In the back of my mind, nagging worry lingered as to the true extent of Alba's injury and if his unrestrained burst of speed had perhaps re-damaged the leg.

The racers maneuvered into position for the grand finale. Hopelessly torn between cheering for Papa or Sam left me unable to cheer for either. The crowd hollered with vivacity and spirit, as I stood silently watching the horses race by. On the second lap, a short distance past our vantage point, Sam's sulky, which had been third on the rail--a dangerous and undesirable position oftentimes called the "death hole"--suddenly careened off to the left of the track. I heard a shrieking sound I at once identified as my own voice, and watched in horror as the scene before me unfolded. *Oh, mercy! What was happening?* Still traveling at a furious speed, his cart tipped sideways onto one wheel.

The high wheels of a sulky are quite fragile with their wooden spokes, peril always near at hand. The frightening unpredictability of crashes demanded both drivers and spectators be alert at all times, particularly near the perimeter fence.

For a moment, it appeared Sam's skillful hands would steady the sulky and keep it upright, but with an unmistakable splintering sound, it overturned, scarcely past the half-mile mark. Sam flew from the cart and landed with an audible thump. He lay motionless on the ground. I couldn't breathe or see straight, as I feared the worst.

Cheers dissolved into shrieks, as men descended upon the crash site in seconds. Absalom stayed upright, though visibly agitated.

"Maggie! Oh, Maggie!" My sister's shouts brought me to attention.

"Oh, Ellie, I must . . ." My sentence left unfinished, I ducked under the fence rail and ran across the track, satin shoes be damned. I found myself among half a dozen men surveying the damage. Several of them were moving the damaged sulky off the course, while one grabbed the reins of Absalom, who stomped his front hoof and whinnied loudly. Sam lay perfectly still. Was he dead? I wanted to see the rise and fall of his muscular chest. Oh, how many times had I imagined myself resting my face against that same chest? Had I missed my chance forever? I couldn't bear it! Two men bent over him, while I gaped at his prone figure.

Without preamble, Sam sat up and swore vehemently, "What the hell?" His mother, a devout Christian Scientist, wouldn't like to hear such language coming out of his mouth.

Overcome with relief, I dissolved into tears. Sam sizzled with anger, but was otherwise apparently unharmed. Dusting himself off, he stood and shook his head, and looked directly at me.

"Why, Miss Perry, I'm speechless! What are you doing on the racetrack?"

All the other men turned their eyes toward me, startled by my presence. *Oh, dear, what was I doing on the racetrack?*

My face colored scarlet yet again, and I found I had no voice. Regretting my impulsiveness and lack of propriety, I wished to disappear. Without further adieu, Papa's friend, Mr. O'Brien, snatched me by the arm and hurried me back to the sidelines, where Ellie, James, and Louis stood, looking stunned. Once on the other side of the fence rail, Ellie reached out her arms and pulled me to her.

"Maggie, what were you thinking? You could have been injured! I was so worried."

"Maggie Perry, are you ever in a bucket of trouble," James pronounced. *Did I detect a sparkle of humor in his eyes?* It all happened so quickly that before I even fully comprehended this turn of events, Papa and Toby dashed into the lead on the last leg to cross the finish line, winning the day's purse. My siblings and I rushed to congratulate Papa on his superbly timed win, my transgression temporarily forgotten.

4.

July, 1887. "Wake up! Time's a-wasting . . ." called Lucy at the door of our sleeping room.

"What time is it?"

"Time to get up!" she retorted.

I rolled over, looked out the window and groaned, "It's barely light outside."

"We've berries to harvest and jam to preserve."

There was no getting around Lucy. Janie, Edith, Eva and I reluctantly left the cozy nest of our beds, slipped on our dressing gowns and made way for the privy.

Mother and Ella stood in the kitchen preparing us a second breakfast of oatmeal, eggs, toast, and milky coffee. The men were already in the fields, getting a head start on the day.

"Morning, sisters," greeted my ever cheerful sister, Ella.

The three of us nodded as we trailed past her and out the back door to the outbuilding, for our morning constitutionals. A chattering blue jay scolding another bird put a smile on my face, reminding me of Lucy. An orange sun had begun its climb, sending streaks of shimmering light radiating across our faces as we stood waiting for our little sister. "Hurry up, Eva!" I called, already sticky from the humidity.

Back in our dressing room, I searched and found a suitably lightweight frock, an olive-colored gingham, and hurriedly dressed, as the aroma of morning coffee beckoned me back to the kitchen.

My sisters and I worked with diligence, plucking berries from the multitude of strawberry bushes lining our garden, hurrying to finish before the sultriness of midday. I straightened up, finding the chore back-wrenching, and smiled at Eva. Judging from the trail of berry juice ebbing from the corners of her mouth and the new pink splotches dotting her yellow frock, more berries were entering her tummy than her basket.

We accomplished our task before noon, but not before beads of sweat trickled down my face and inside my dress. After being rinsed of dust under the barnyard water pump, the five buckets of wet, crimson berries looked luscious, glistening in the sun. Lucy, Janie and I sat on the back porch sorting and removing stems before slicing the strawberries in preparation for the jam. The little girls played nearby, while Mother retired to her bedroom, claiming vertigo. The heat seemed to bother her more than usual these days. She dismissed it as "old age." I supposed, with her fifty-first birthday coming up next month, she would know. This meant the jam making fell to Ella. I did not envy her standing over the hot stove stirring berries.

"There's a big harness race tomorrow," announced Lucy, as if I wasn't already aware of this.

I sulked. She well knew my banishment lasted another two weeks. I deemed it an unfair punishment, but Papa wouldn't budge, calling my behavior at the first race "impulsive and reckless."

"I think I may go tomorrow," she went on, "with the holiday and all, I imagine there'll be a lot of eligible men out and about."

I held my tongue by biting the inside of my cheek, knowing she said things like this simply to aggravate me. As much as I didn't want to let on it bothered me, I found her hard to ignore. "Well, I'm looking forward to the Independence Day celebration in two days' time. In fact, I think we should make strawberry ice cream for the occasion."

"I'll probably see Mr. Samuel Jobsa and Absalom tomorrow, don't you suppose?"

"Harumph." I stood, grimacing, and took my portion of the berries into the kitchen. I could tolerate only so much of my sister and her pointed tongue. Since she had gotten the millinery job in Mt. Clemens, she had become even more insufferable, with an unearned air of superiority. I took solace in recognizing that, if not for Ella, she wouldn't have this job. The screen banged behind me. I wished it could have been even louder, for effect.

"Are you excited for Tuesday?" I asked Ella, who stirred the jam bubbling in the huge pot.

"I am! But I also feel apprehension. This will be such a life change for me. I'm too naïve to even know what to be frightened of."

"Oh Ellie, I'll miss you so much!"

"Maggie, oh Maggie! I'm not going away forever, and you will certainly come see me in the city. Besides, I'll be back here to visit too."

"I really am glad for you, Ella, but you and I see eye-to-eye better than anyone, so who will I have to talk to after you leave?"

"We could write to one another, if you'd like."

"Why, that's a capital idea!"

We would become correspondents to share our heart of hearts. I supposed I could live with that.

⸻

The day of the race Ella elected to stay home with me, to organize and pack her few belongings. The house radiated a stillness and quietude. In our large family, I had little experience with silence and found I rather liked it.

The two of us stood in the girl's dressing room looking at clothing possibilities.

"Hmm. I think I'll leave the blue Florentine dress behind, Maggie. It's easy to see how much you love it!"

"Ellie, it was yours first, so I'd understand if you chose to take it, but if you do leave it behind, I'll be very grateful!"

Ella smiled back. She was so pretty. I imagined her knight waiting for her in Detroit.

"This has been the best afternoon ever, spending time with you. I do have faith that Papa will agree to bring me along on his next business trip to Detroit."

"I'm sure he will, Maggie. You'll see. The time will soon pass and you'll hardly have time to miss me, dear sister."

The afternoon waned, and Ella and I began supper preparations. While we were setting the table, everyone clattered in the back entry. Our peacefulness at an end, Ella and I hurried into the kitchen to hear about the afternoon.

"Where's Papa?" I inquired. Lucy wiggled her head back and forth. Louis put his finger to his lips to shush me, and James shook his head, tipping it in Mother's direction.

"He stayed behind with friends," Mother said sharply. She offered no opportunity for questions.

Mother left the room, after which Louis explained, "Things didn't go his way today. Papa lost the purse in the championship heat by one cart-length. He stayed behind with friends to drown his sorrow." No wonder Mother sounded terse.

Papa's absence, combined with Ella's looming departure, cast a somber tone at the dining table. Mother again had no appetite. She barely picked at her food and excused herself from the table minutes after the meal began, noticeably upset by Papa's choice. Eva and Edith provided our suppertime liveliness, arguing over a chicken leg.

Not surprisingly, Lucy piped up, "Listen you two, work it out or you may leave the table and go straight to bed."

"You can't boss us!" protested Edith. An eleven-year-old spitfire with red hair and freckles, she had a mind of her own. I likened it to Lucy's own determined personality. Neither of them backed down without difficulty.

"Well, young lady, we'll see about that," said Lucy, rising from her chair and walking around the table toward Edith.

"All right! Eva, here," said Edith, handing her sister the drumstick. "Take the old chicken leg. I didn't want it anyway."

Even with this frivolous distraction, an escalating undercurrent of apprehension rippled through the room. None of us could predict what the evening might bring. My sisters and I tidied up the supper dishes in silence, while James and Louis went out to do chores. Later, as we sat reading by lamplight, I could feel the lingering tension. When my sisters and I retired for the evening, my brothers remained in the parlor, awaiting Papa's return.

I'm flying, not very high, above the treetops of our fruit orchard. A glorious freedom and lightness saturates my senses. Long, undulating grasses stretch toward the horizon, beckoning me on. Buoyant, I dip and bend, riding the air currents with graceful fluidity.

Suddenly, someone screams. Beneath, I see Mother struggling to climb out of a water-filled stream. She's screaming for help, clawing at the brush along the water bank. I watch helplessly from above as she starts to lose her grip, and is pulled backward into the fast-flowing water. I realize she can't swim and it's up to me to rescue her, yet I don't remember how to land. My overwhelming fear is crashing headlong into the ground.

What was that high-pitched, angry yelling? In seconds, Eva and Edith, both shivering, crawled into bed with Lucy and me, as the enraged shrieking continued. Mother! Ella and I jumped out of our beds and slid her single bed in front of the door. The glow of the moonlight streaming into our room reflected off four ashen faces.

Mother's cries sounded more angry than scared. My imagination ran amok wondering what had happened. Was there an intruder? Had Papa attacked her? I trusted James or Louis would come swiftly to her rescue. We heard a huge thud, and then silence. What now? We stared at each other in wide-eyed terror, petrified. In the ensuing stillness, we recovered ourselves enough to shove the bed out of the way, and dashed down the hall to crowd into our parents' room. James and Louis, still dressed, knelt over our Papa, who lay sprawled out cold on the floor beside the bed. Mother loomed over all three of them, gripping her cast iron frying pan in both hands.

She looked at the five of us with remarkable calmness. "Go back to bed, children. Everything's fine."

"It doesn't look fine, Mama," countered Edith.

"Your Papa had a small accident. He'll be all right." Mother had the ability to communicate well with a look. This look left no recourse but to pad back down the hall to our room, where speculation ensued.

"Why did Mama have a big frying pan in her hand?" Edith giggled nervously.

"Well, that's obvious," Janie said, "it was to guard against Papa's dark side."

"Do you think he's dead?" Eva's voice quivered.

"Oh, lovey, come here," called Ella, "of course not. Papa will be fine. He's taking a little nap."

I hoped she was right. In Mother's hands, the frying pan seemed ominous.

After a light rap on the door, Louis poked his head in. "Sisters, I don't want you to be worried. Papa is awake, and as I speak, James is helping him into bed."

"Louis, why did Mama hit Papa with a frying pan? Was he bad?"

"Sweet little Eva. Papa had had too much of the strong drink and scared Mama. Everything will be all right. Let's everyone crawl back into bed, and get some rest. We have a big celebration day tomorrow!" With that, he soundlessly disappeared down the hall.

I wanted to see for myself Mother's state of mind, so when I perceived my sisters had fallen asleep, I eased out of the bed and tiptoed to the door, turning the brass knob and peeking out into the hallway. I made my way down the darkened corridor in silence, to my parents' room. I heard Mother softly crying and debated the wisdom of my actions, but in the end, decided to proceed.

"Mama?" I whispered into the dark room, "are you quite all right?"

One generous snuffle and a muffled "Yes, Maggie, I'm all right."

I could hear her still sniffling, so I kneeled beside her, vigilant. I contemplated her life with Papa. The story they had always told of their meeting and courtship back in New York caused me to wonder, and not for the first time, how their life together could sometimes turn so inside out.

Papa claimed he first laid eyes on Mother, who he always described as the "dark-haired beauty with emerald eyes," in the Lutheran Church. Raised a Presbyterian, he said he had needed fellowship, but with no Presbyterian Church in Sodus, he decided to mingle with the Lutherans.

I still marvel today how events aligned to perfection, for Papa and Mother to meet.

"'Twas a fine day . . . a cloudless spring day, it was. Church services had concluded and we congregants stood in the courtyard visiting, aye. I still recall the insistent calls of a flock of wee black-capped chickadees in a nearby red oak vying for your Mother's attention." He liked to wink at her when sharing this part.

"Emboldened by the pastor's inspiring sermon, I walked straight over to where your Mother stood with her family and struck up a conversation, I did. She looked me square in the eye and radiated such self-assurance, I knew then and there she was the woman for me, so I asked for her name." Mother always confirmed this with a smile and nod of her head.

"Aye, what a beauty . . . and so soft spoken." He invariably smiled at her when he said this, causing her to blush.

It took all his Irish charm to bring her parents around to the idea of a courtship, as they had set their sights on a hard-working German or Dutchman for their daughter--definitely not an irresistibly jovial Irishman.

Mother liked to add, "Yes, I was stubborn. I dug in my heels. It was my decision to marry Papa and to this day, I've no regrets." Yet tonight, I couldn't help but find this remembrance peculiar.

When her breathing grew more regular, satisfying me she had gone to sleep, I tiptoed back to our sleeping room, thinking of my Papa, ordinarily as gentle as a newborn lamb. While he had mostly managed to stay away from liquor in recent years, I held shadowy memories of his past rages and Mother's unmentionable bruises. I loved him so much, but could not comprehend such wretched behavior or whatever possessed him to attack the one he loved best.

Perhaps I had two Papas. One a lamb, the other a ferocious sleeping dragon which lay dormant deep inside. Yes, that could explain it. Unleashed by whiskey, this beast roared to the surface and attacked the person closest at hand, typically, Mother. Poor Mother. I would never put up behavior like Papa's earlier this evening, but she seemed to love him so and anyone could easily see how much he cherished her. And yet, what choice did she have? Life could be so confusing.

I tossed and turned on my side of the bed, listening to the soft snores of my sisters. My mind had tremendous difficulty calming itself and I found no slumber until the sun peeked over the horizon, hinting of sunrise. What an inauspicious start to the 111th birthday of our country!

Mother was in the kitchen making pies, as I walked through on my way to the privy. "Morning, Maggie. Did you sleep well last night?" she asked, smiling at me.

"Yes, Mother." *Had she forgotten I had been in her room watching her cry herself to sleep? Or was she trying to pretend nothing had happened? And, why was I perpetuating this untruth?*

After breakfast we scurried in all directions working on projects for the annual celebration. We would be departing late morning for the gathering spot on the outskirts of Mt. Clemens, and each of us had a job to do. Mother had already baked two-dozen biscuits and put three cherry pies in the oven. The aromas emanating from our kitchen smelled nothing short of heavenly.

By mid-morning, we had assembled our offerings for the community picnic and prepared to load the buckboard. James and Louis had loaded a big block of ice from the pump house into the wagon box to keep the food cool. They collected some empty gunny sacks for the sack races and a bunch of old, dried-up potatoes for the potato race. I wondered whether Papa would join us today for the festivities.

It was but a short time before our planned departure when at last he nonchalantly strolled into the kitchen. *Did he even remember last night?*

"And how's my favorite little gingernut?" He bent over and hugged Edith from behind. She squealed and ran outside, Eva on her heels. I couldn't tell if her reaction was fearful, playful or a tad of both. Papa smiled at the rest of us before proceeding on to the privy.

In the other room looking for a platter, Mother missed the entire exchange.

"Papa's up and about," Lucy relayed to Mother when she reappeared in the kitchen doorway.

"I wondered why I heard all that squealing."

We persisted at our tasks, offering no further comments. Sometimes no words were the best words.

The Independence Day celebration drew a huge crowd, second only to the county fair. With no one laboring to plant or harvest, it was a welcome mid-summer diversion where people could relax and be neighborly.

"Whoa, now," shouted Papa, pulling the horses' reins taut, as the buggy carrying him, Mother, Ella and Lucy came to a halt. The rest of us pulled up beside the buggy in the buckboard and all clambered out. The open space in the center of the community meeting grounds was crowded with a number of wooden picnic tables and encircled by a grove of birch trees. Soon these well-weathered tables would be overflowing with mountains of food. Off to one side, nestled in a small grove of trees, stood a white Gazebo, from which an enormous American flag swayed in the breeze.

Soon, everyone except James, Janie and me had wandered off to explore the grounds. In the distance, a speaker inside the gazebo recited what sounded like the Preamble to the Constitution. We had probably missed the reading of the Declaration of Independence, which didn't bother me, as I calculated I had most likely been in the audience on at least sixteen other occasions. There would also be a political speech or two before the meal commenced. A brass band assembled nearby, which always added merriment to the festivities.

"Janie, let's take a stroll and see who's here, shall we?" With a sharp eye, I had already ascertained the location of Samuel's family.

"Shouldn't we ask permission from Mama or Papa?"

"I think they're off to visit with Uncle Andrew and Grandma Margareta over yonder," James said. "Go ahead, girls, I'll take responsibility . . . as long as you stay out of trouble," his voice serious.

I asked myself what trouble he imagined the two of us might find. Janie and I nodded in agreement with our brother, opened our ruffled-lace parasols, and strolled off in the direction of the Jobsa's encampment. My heart was in my throat. While nervous Samuel might be peeved with me for my misjudgment at the cart races, my pulse still raced at the prospect of stealing some time together today. A pleasant shudder ran through my body, as we came closer to the Jobsa wagon.

"Why, Maggie, you're trembling!" Janie exclaimed.

"Excitement, I suppose."

Mr. Jobsa promptly took note of our presence, "Misses Perry, gazing upon you two is like nectar to my soul! Veritably, a sight for these sore, old eyes!"

Mr. Jobsa had a well-earned reputation for flirting. We blushed and stared at our shoes. Uncertain how to respond, I wondered about the whereabouts of Mrs. Jobsa. Before either of us could offer a reply, Sam appeared out of nowhere and gave a slight bow. "Ladies, how delighted I am to see you both!" He was smartly attired in his cream-colored suit, sporting one of the newly fashionable boater hats.

Like father, like son. I smiled demurely and Janie giggled.

"Will you do me the honor of promenading about, while we listen to our neighbors recite patriotic words?"

Relieved he made no mention of the cart-racing incident, the three of us proceeded to parade around the perimeter of the grounds, stopping along the way to visit with other neighbors, friends and relatives. Ah, it was pure ambrosia to be out socializing again, especially on the arm of Samuel. Even though I had to share his other arm with my younger sister, I delighted in the looks of envy from all the other marriageable girls along our path.

After the speeches ended, and while the band entertained, Janie and I returned to our wagon to help carry food to the picnic tables, where everyone congregated for the shared feast. What a spectacle to behold! Mounds of potato salad, smoked ham, cold chicken, new peas and baby green onions, along with string beans and asparagus, biscuits and breads galore, strawberries, pickles, and even deviled eggs. Someone brought kegs of beer, which I noted with relief Papa had thus far avoided. For those of us who didn't imbibe, jugs of water and iced coffee, cooled with chips of ice from someone's icehouse, waited on the picnic table, ready to quench our thirst.

"Maggie, did I just see you and your sister, each on an arm of the divine Mr. Samuel Jobsa?" Emma Martin, an acquaintance from our schooldays, tugged my sleeve as I sat down at the table.

"Why yes, Emma, it *was* us. We quite enjoyed promenading together, Samuel and I. Well . . . and, of course, Mary Jane."

"Julia and I were just discussing how lovely it would be to pass some time with him. He's ever so handsome and well-spoken."

I smiled, particularly self-satisfied to hear her say these words.

Predictably, everyone ate too much and afterwards, I didn't look to be alone in my sluggishness, though the children didn't appear fazed in the least. My brothers, along with Samuel and a few of the other young men, managed to herd the children toward a grassy section under the trees set aside for the games. Animated by the promise of prizes hinted to be either lemon or lime-flavored wafers, candy corn or chewing gum, they ran circles around everyone else. While they participated in the sack and potato races, the families who had ice cream buckets began the process of turning the cream, sugar and eggs into iced cream. We each took a turn cranking the churn, until our arms grew weary. When at last the handle was next to impossible to move, I lifted the lid off our bucket and dumped the fresh strawberries into the mix for a final few turns, convinced ours would be the most delicious ice cream of them all.

After we polished off all the pies and ice cream, the late afternoon languorously dissipated into early evening. God had painted the sky with brilliant streaks of rose and apricot, like bursts of natural fireworks illuminating the fading day.

In the long tradition of waiting for darkness before setting off the fireworks, people found time to relax, the tasks of the day complete. For some, the time had come to return home for the evening chores which couldn't wait. Louis volunteered to take the buggy on home to do ours, leaving the rest of us to squeeze together into the buckboard, come our departure time.

The sun dipped lower and many of the adults relaxed on blankets, leaning up against their wagons, while a few of the men gathered to socialize at the beer kegs. It eased my mind to see Mother speaking to Papa again. Along with Janie, they sat next to each other on a blanket, near Mr. and Mrs. Jobsa. The sound of Mr. Jobsa's voice droned on, his words no longer crisp, leading me to believe he had partaken more than a little of the brew. Poor Mrs. Jobsa. A religious woman, I was certain she had taught her children in a different manner and felt relieved Samuel would never overindulge like his father.

The youngsters played, while people my age stood together in several small groups chatting. Opportunity blossomed. I casually strolled over and joined the group that happened to include Samuel. Most of them stood near the beer keg, laughing and drinking. He winked at me and meandered closer.

"Miss Perry, how lovely you appear in the twilight."

Beaming, I did my utmost to appear modest. The catch of Mt. Clemens, this man had snared my heart. Plenty of other girls would give their eyeteeth to stand in my place next to him.

"Would you like to take a stroll with me?" His lopsided smile made him even more attractive.

"Mr. Jobsa, I'd be delighted." I looped my arm through his and we strolled away from the small group, this time without Janie, and unnoticed by Papa and Mother. It was risky to be seen without a chaperone, but I deemed it a chance worth taking. Eventide descended as we walked arm in arm toward a modest stand of white birches, south of our families' wagons.

"Oh, Mr. Jobsa, look at the fireflies!" They darted all around us, adding a magical aura to the moment.

"Who needs fireworks when we're surrounded by all these astonishing creatures?" He swayed ever so slightly as we edged our way closer to the privacy of the birch trees. I drank in the evening air, its coolness caressing my face.

"Miss Maggie . . . may I call you that?"

"Yes, of course. Call me Maggie!" I had a queer sensation in my stomach. What might he say?

"Please, call me Sam. Mr. Jobsa is my father's name," he chuckled. Perhaps emboldened by the drink, he stopped, turned toward me with a serious expression and spoke frankly. "Maggie, then, I have witnessed you blossom into an enchanting woman over the past few years."

Grateful for the twilight, I blushed, as our eyes embraced.

"Maggie, you captivate me. My mind is consumed with thoughts of you, both night and day. You may find me a bit on the elder side at twenty-three . . ."

"Oh no!" I shook my head. "Twenty-three is not too elderly for me, whatsoever!"

In a voice tinged with mirth, he declared, "Miss Perry--Maggie-- my intentions are honorable, as evidenced by all my unannounced visits and I'd very much like to ask permission to court you. I think it's time we made it official. Of course, I understand I must also ask your father for his consent, but it is important for me to first inquire if you're merely dallying with my affections or if you're sincerely interested in my proposition to ultimately make this flirtation a more permanent relationship?" This all came out in a rush, with an engaging smile and his eyes agleam.

Had my ears truly heard what I had longed to hear? Was this a proposal? "Mr. Samuel Jobsa, let it be known I carry a torch solely for you and can't imagine spending my life with another." *Good gracious! Was I too forward?* I watched for his reaction.

His face brightened, "Maggie, your words are but a sweet melody to my unworthy ears. I shall cherish and hold them close to my heart til the end of time. It will come as no revelation, therefore, that I harbor similar feelings toward you."

Such talk took my breath away! *Samuel Jobsa did have strong feelings for me, as I had long dreamed.* I pressed my palms together. *My knight in shining armor.* Displaying a broad grin, his white teeth flashed in the darkness.

He had taken off his suit jacket earlier in the afternoon, so his strong, well-defined arms were visible through his white and tan pinstriped shirt. I held my breath as he took a step forward and encircled me with those arms, caressing me, sending shivers down my spine at the same moment the first of the fireworks exploded above us in a dizzying array of color and cacophony.

I lifted my face and gazed at him adoringly, believing I might dissolve with joy. Desire rising, my shoulders and neck tingled, as the moment I had long anticipated had arrived. In breathless expectation, I inhaled his scent of leather and--was it cinnamon? I purposefully shut my eyes, and my lips parted as he leaned into me. I smelled a whiff of stale beer and the next thing I knew, I was sitting on the ground, Sam flat on his back in front of me.

"Margareta May Perry!" roared my brother James, his speech slurred, "just what are you up to?"

Adroitly rising from his prone position on the ground, Sam rubbed his chin. Without warning and acting completely sober, he lunged and grabbed my inebriated brother around the knees. James hit the hard dirt with a thump and the air whooshed out of his lungs. James rolled over and as he struggled to get up, Sam began to punch my brother with a zealousness I found disconcerting.

Terrified, I began screaming, "Help! Help me!" the moment another cluster of fireworks exploded far above us. The sound of my voice had been swallowed, and no one heard my shrieks for help. James had recovered, returning blow for blow as the fight escalated. In desperation, I leaped between them shouting, "Stop! Stop it this instant!" We all tumbled to the ground. This time, the ferocity of my distraught voice carried into the night and several people, including Papa, sprinted towards us like wildfire. He found us in the process of disentangling ourselves from each other.

"What in the Sam Hill is going on here?" He yanked James and Sam apart.

The three of us sat mute before him. I peered up at him with as much innocence as I could muster. A small group assembled around us, staring with interest at the goings-on.

Sam reached up, took a handkerchief from his pocket and wiped the blood off his mouth, while his treacherous eyes shot daggers at my brother. His mouth set in a hard line, he stood, dusted himself off, and ignoring me, turned on his heel and strode back to his family's wagon without a backwards glance. James leapt up, an angry glower slicing Sam's back, and ambled off unsteadily in the other direction.

"Margareta Perry, what's this all about?"

"Oh, Papa, James spied Mr. Samuel Jobsa trying to kiss me and must have concluded he needed to defend my honor."

Papa, along with several of the bystanders, whooped with laughter. "Oh daughter, what would I do without you and your shenanigans? Come on back now, and watch the rest of the fireworks with your Papa."

To say I was relieved would be an understatement. I deemed it best to follow his instructions, keep a low profile for the remainder of the evening, and pray no one mentioned the word "chaperone." The commotion over, the curious crowd dispersed, and I meekly followed Papa back to where he and Mother sat near our wagon. On the walk back, I wistfully recreated the thrill of Sam's touch, and dreamt about our lips meeting. Abruptly, I was struck by another thought. *What if Sam never spoke to me again? What if James had ruined everything?*

5.

Mid-September, 1887. Alone in the parlor, I watered Mother's potted philodendron plant resting atop a wooden pedestal near the settee. Lost in a daydream, I was startled to spy a horse and carriage approaching up the lane. I recognized the buggy as old Doc Brockton's. It came to a halt and I watched with curiosity as the doctor stepped down, walked around to the other side, opened up the door, and extended his hand to a passenger. Nonplussed, my Grandma Margareta Fries gingerly stepped down. I hurried to open the front door.

"Maggie," Grandma Margareta acknowledged me, "even though your mother insists there's nothing wrong but a slight 'womanly problem,' I find I can't endure this nonsense for one day longer, so I've asked the good doctor to examine her." Grandma could be counted on to move directly to the crux of the matter.

"Hello, Grandma." I nodded my head. "Doctor Brockton, welcome." My brows knit together, I asked, "Is Mother expecting you?" Both strong-willed, Mother and Grandma often had conflicting opinions.

"Of course not! She would have dismissed the idea entirely," said Grandma with a wave of her arthritic hand, "Where is she?"

This could prove an interesting morning. "She went upstairs to rest after breakfast. I'll go inform her she has visitors."

"Land sakes, no, child. She would simply tell us to go away. Step aside and let us pass." She turned and gestured towards the stairs, "Doctor, shall we proceed?" And with that, in a flourish, they swept past me.

I trailed along behind to watch the confrontation unfold.

"Mary Jane! You look god-awful. Good Lord, your hair is falling out! You tell me it's 'the change of life.' I can plainly see it's something more. It is high time we get to the bottom of this ailment of yours. Dr. Brockton has come to examine you." Even though her words sounded severe, I heard the concern in her voice.

Sluggish, Mother rolled over and sat up in bed, her pale face expressionless, her stare vacant. Seeing her through Grandma's eyes, I confronted a grievous truth. What had happened to my steady and tireless mother? Haggard, her bulging veins formed hills in the uneven landscape of her hands, near to bursting out of her wizened skin. Her once thick hair had lost its sheen, her eyes were dull. My mother had grown frail.

Despite my speculation about her health these past few months, it had been easy to chalk up the changes to overwork, summer heat and normal aging. *I shuddered, realizing we were all guilty of turning a blind eye to Mother's ill health.*

Had Mother been acting more like herself, I was positive she would've had a thing or two to say to *her* mother about bringing the doctor unannounced. As it was, she seemed to have only enough energy to stare blankly at the three of us.

"Hello, Mrs. Perry," Dr. Brockton spoke with a soothing voice, "It's been quite a while since we've seen each other, hasn't it?" He turned to us, "If you'll excuse us, Mrs. Fries and Miss Perry, I would like to speak with Mrs. Perry alone," motioning with his head toward the hallway. Grandma and I respected the doctor's request, withdrawing. With a certain finality, the doctor closed the door behind us.

Grandma and I proceeded into the sitting room, where we sat side-by-side, our hands folded in our laps. With Janie, Edith and Eva at school, Lucy at work, and the men all out chopping and binding the last of the corn stalks into shocks, an eerie stillness filled the room. To pass the time, I counted the tiny vermillion roses on the sitting room wallpaper until my eyes were crossed.

I contemplated the framed family portraits on the wall across from where Grandma and I sat on the loveseat. My gaze landed on both the wedding picture of Mother and Papa and a photograph of Mother's extended family taken in Sodus, before everyone journeyed west. In the family photo, Mother appeared close to my age, so it had probably been taken a couple of years before she and Papa wed. It came to me that photographs or portraits presented the one clear way to remain forever young. Without question, time took our youth and eventually our health.

I glanced over at Grandma, who sat with eyes closed, her head resting on the back of the loveseat, taking a catnap. She was my namesake, a woman whose short stature belied her considerable strength of will. Even though it was hard for me to imagine Grandma Margareta ever being my age, I chose to believe I had inherited her persistence and tenacity to make the best of what happened along life's path. She liked to say, "Life's not about what happens, it's about what you do with what happens." I considered this a sound philosophy of life and intended to abide by it.

We heard a muffled cry, yet there was naught to do but continue our vigil, waiting for the doctor to emerge. More time slipped by, before he at last invited us back into the bedroom. I could tell by Mother's expression that I did not want to listen to the results of the doctor's exam. She had been crying, a rarity, in my memory. Tears welled up in my own eyes.

"Maggie. Mama. I asked Dr. Brockton if I might share his findings with you, myself." He stood in the shadows, his face hidden. Mother spoke quietly, but succinctly. "Over the past many months, I told myself if I just ignored my maladies and went on with my life, whatever ailed me would eventually resolve with time and prayer. If I relented and let the doctor examine me, I risked the possibility of him finding something I might not want to know. For so long, I have preferred ignorance.

"I now find the time has come to face reality. So, to begin with, thank you, Mama, for bringing the doctor to me today. I . . . need to tell you myself." She let go of a sigh. "This must be said, but I find it difficult to find the words." We stared at her anxiously. "Dr. Brockton is reasonably certain . . ." Her voice faltered again and went silent.

Grandma and I both held our breath, helpless, while Mother wept. Mute, we watched as she dabbed at her eyes with a hankie.

In a quivering voice, she finished ". . . of his diagnosis of a cancer spreading throughout my female parts." Grandma sat down wearily in the chair next to the bed. Somehow I remained upright, trying to make sense of these words.

Collecting herself, Mother's voice grew stronger. "I imagined the cramping in my stomach and continual womanly bleeding was merely a normal part of the change of life. I dismissed the ever-increasing pain in my hip as the result of too much heavy lifting over the years. It seems this is all related to the rapidly growing cancer." Her voice trailed off.

My ever-practical Grandma turned to Doc Brocton and asked, "Doctor, what can be done?" I heard the fear in her voice.

"Mrs. Fries, I'll prescribe laudanum for her pain," he said in a kindly voice, as he reached into his black bag for the little blue bottle containing the narcotic. "I'll return in a few days to see how the laudanum is working. We may have to adjust the written dosage on the bottle. It should help her feel more comfortable."

"But, doctor, how long before she'll get better? Won't she need an operation," I asked, "to remove this cancer?"

My entire body began to tremble, as my mind raced madly. *What was this cancer illness, anyway? She was bleeding? None of us knew! Had she told Papa about the bleeding? Surely an operation could eliminate this cancer.* Dizzy, my fingers began to tingle.

"Maggie, I'm not going to get better." Her words leapt out and scorched me, like an errant flame from our wood stove. "There is *no* operation for this." It was then I understood the meaning of stoicism.

These were words no one would ever want to hear or say. I looked first at my mother, then the doctor, and finally my Grandma, who had pulled out her own handkerchief to pat at the corners of her eyes.

Unable to bear all the words hovering bleakly in the room, I turned and fled downstairs.

I dashed out the front door and down the steps. Heedless, I ran. I ran away from the room, the doctor and his horrifying conclusion. He was wrong! He had to be wrong. That was it; he had simply made a terrible mistake. Mother would recover. I knew she would.

My mind gradually calmed, as did my pace. How could I sort out these distressing words? It simply made no sense, as Mother still acted as our mother, cooking and cleaning and taking care of our family. I flatly refused to believe the doctor. My gait slowed and soon, my feet had carried me to Mt. Clemens. Shaking, I stood in front of the millinery shop where Lucy worked. She happened to look up from her workstation and notice me on the wooden walkway. She jumped up, opened the door and gawked at me, hesitant.

"Maggie? What are you doing here? Look at you! There's dirt all over the hem of your dress."

Still trembling, I ignored her comments and stared at her.

"Maggie, what's going on? Speak!" What next transpired could not be called part of my nature at all, as I rather liked keeping things to myself.

Crying, I began to tell Lucy the distressing news, but it came out garbled and she soon interrupted me, "Maggie! What are you saying? Come into the shop this instant. You're causing a scene!" She hurried out, took hold of me by the arm, yanked me inside, bolted the door and turned the sign over to "Closed."

"Maggie, start again and speak slowly," she commanded.

I repeated what the doctor had said and all the color drained from Lucy's face.

"No! This can't be true." She shook her head, clutching her arms to her chest.

⸎

Doctor Brockton had gone, but Grandma Fries still sat in the bedroom chair beside the bed, holding Mother's hand. "Oh, there you are, Maggie. Why, Lucy, where did you come from?"

"Maggie found me at the shop. It's nice to see you, Grandma Margareta," she bent over and brushed Grandma's cheek with her lips.

"Dearest Mother," Lucy gave her a gentle hug.

"My precious girls. I've been the most blessed of mothers to have so many loving daughters and sons." Mother had regained her composure. "I will make my peace and take delight in my remaining time by spending it as I always have; with my family." Tears crept down her face.

Mother sounded so brave, but her trembling lips and chin said otherwise. Her eyes drooped. I wanted to hide somewhere, to do anything other than face this. Without words, Lucy and I both kneeled bedside, and I took her hand in mine.

After a time, Mother again reclaimed her self possession. "Girls, I'd like to tell Papa next before anyone else, so I need your silence on this matter."

"Yes, of course," we both nodded in unison.

The men had taken their lunch along to the fields today, creating space between now and when Mother would face more family with her revelation. Low spirits crowded into the room, our moods grey. No one seemed quite sure what to say or do next.

Lucy broke through the heaviness. "Mother, could we bring you something to eat or drink?"

"I might try a cup of weak tea and a piece of toast," she said with little enthusiasm.

Lucy and I retreated to the kitchen. While she rummaged around in the pantry, searching for bread and tea, I looked out the window to see Papa walking across the barnyard.

"Papa!" I called to him through the open kitchen window.

"Hi darlin', I've come back to do a quick repair on one of the corn choppers." He stopped in his tracks and searched my face through the window. "Maggie, what's wrong? You look as though you've seen a ghost!" He changed direction and walked toward the back porch.

If I even came near him, I would dissolve into tears. I turned and ran upstairs to my bedroom and hid in the dressing room. I heard muffled voices in the kitchen, followed by quick footsteps on the stairs.

I poked my head out into the hallway moments later, and found my forlorn Grandma back in the sitting room, wearing a grim expression. I sat down beside her, put my arms around her and we hugged. Lucy came upstairs with a teapot, cups, and buttered toast on a tray.

"Hi, Grandma, how about a cup of tea?"

"Land sakes, yes. Thank you, Lucy."

We drank our tea in silence. My reflections ran dark, as dark as the tea itself. I examined the leaves in the bottom of my cup, wishing I had the ability to read them, wishing I could change an impending sense of doom lurking deep inside me.

6.

Wednesday, November 9, 1887. Eva sat snuggled beside me, emitting intermittent sniffles mixed with uncontrollable hiccups. How effortless it would be to join in her sorrow had I not already exhausted my own reservoir of tears. I was but an empty vessel, devoid of all emotion, my body numb and unfeeling. I understood no one escaped loss in life, but how could I reconcile losing my mother?

My arm around Eva's thin little shoulders, I pulled her closer to me. We sat in the front parlor near Mother's body, the body she no longer had any use for and had forever left behind. We awaited the arrival of Grandma, my eldest brother John Henry and his wife Abi, and the hearse carriage that would carry our beloved mother to the church.

A heaviness had settled upon our house. Even the stale air carried weight, pressing against me until my heart clenched. Three days had passed since Papa stopped the grandfather clock in the front hall at 2:15 p.m. The mantels and windows were draped in black crepe in both the parlor and dining room, along with the windows in Mother and Papa's bedroom. Black muslin covered the mirrors, as well as all family pictures. The funeral invitations had been written and delivered to friends, neighbors and extended family. We were a family in the depths of mourning. Like the grandfather clock, time had stopped for us all.

The day matched my mood, wearing its dreary, ash-colored coat, much the same hue as my drab grey skirt. The drawn shades and shuttered windows intensified the oppressive aura. I listened to the wind with its woeful cry, imagining the last of the autumn leaves furiously twirling into countless, miniature cyclones. Rain sprinkled the earth, grieving our loss with tears of its own making.

The previous Sunday morning, Mother had awakened everyone before sunrise with a loud wail, flinging herself about with an uncommon strength, astonishing us all. Moaning, she experienced a horrific loss of control of bodily functions, and vomited what little was left in her stomach. Panic stricken, Papa had sent Louis off in the buggy to fetch Dr. Brockton.

Papa had waited with her while the doctor did his exam; the rest of us had crowded into the hall. Those of us closest saw the doctor administer morphine in a syringe. He then propped Mother into a more upright position against her pillows, to assist her airway. Even in the hallway, her jagged breathing overshadowed our whispers.

Her agitation, which must have utterly depleted what little energy she had left, subsided as the drug took effect, and her breathing calmed. At last she lay still, her eyes closed. After a time, Dr. Brockton had joined us, saying, "I believe the time's come for each of you to spend a few minutes with her." The hour we had long feared had arrived, uninvited. She had embarked upon her final journey in this realm.

Distraught, my chin trembled as I struggled to remain calm. I squeezed my eyes shut and covered my face with my hands, but it did nothing to slow my tears. Why, oh why, was this happening? *Was what Papa says true? Was God punishing him?* I heard Papa's voice in my head, repeating over and over, "It's my punishment for imbibing in the drink. Aye, God has chosen to take her from me." Nothing we said consoled him. It was the darkest of times.

"Maggie," Papa had motioned me into their room. My turn. I tiptoed over to the bed, kneeled down and clasped her hand. I had never watched someone die before. Tufts of thin grey hair poked out of her nightcap, wispy around the edges of her translucent skin. Her hollowed eyes were closed, her breaths shallow and her body tranquil.

My voice had quivered as I whispered, "Mama, I will never forget all you've taught me." I had hoped to be braver, but found I had to stop speaking. I bit my lip hard, in hopes of regaining control of my voice.

I looked at the only mother I would ever have. *How could I let her go without it hurting so much inside?* Oh, how I loved her. Mother meant so much to us all. She was the fabric which held our family together. Had she already departed into some twilight world between life and death? I prayed for strength. I hadn't wanted her to worry about us. *If she could hear me, what might I say to comfort her?*

"Mama, I'll take care of everyone, I promise." I paused. "You will live in my heart forever. I love you so much!" With great tenderness, I had kissed her cheek. ". . . Godspeed." I had choked on that last word and went silent, my face wet with tears.

She had squeezed my hand weakly and opened her eyes. Oh, the effort it must have taken for her to do that, however imperceptibly. She gazed at me and smiled for a few short seconds, before her eyes drooped shut once again.

My heart rested, knowing she had understood my words. A buzzing sensation had erupted inside my head and an agonizing nausea threatened to overpower me. I sat beside her in silence, holding her exquisitely fragile hand and trying to commit her face to memory, while contemplating how life could conceivably go on. Too soon, Papa had nudged me. *No, please! I'm not ready to leave her.*

"Don't make me leave!"

"Shh, come on now, lass. Your brothers and sisters deserve a little time with her, too." My legs leaden, I needed help to rise up. I remember he gently hugged me and walked me to the doorway. What would become of us all? Nothing would ever be the same. My vision clouded, I faltered as I struggled to move past the others still waiting in the hallway.

It had not been long until Papa called us all back into their room. "She's gone off with the angels. She left tranquilly, with no pain." His face drained of color, he recounted how he had held her hand, and how her breaths came further and further apart. Untroubled, she had breathed her last breath, and eased from this world to the next. Broken, we all mourned, holding fast to each other, drowning in the tears flooding the room.

Louis had courageously gone to bring the undertaker, and the others assisted Papa to the parlor. According to tradition, as the three eldest daughters, Ella, Lucy and I had stayed behind. We discovered our own courage as we compassionately washed our dearest mother's cancer-ravaged body, our overflowing tears blending with the warm, clear water.

Skin covering bones, she was a mere shadow of her former robust self. I worried our touch might cause her to dissolve. Witnessing the profound peacefulness she radiated, I told myself we should all be rejoicing; she had at last been freed from the pain of this life.

We tenderly patted her body dry and covered her delicately with the indigo blue and white star quilt, transported all the way from New York so long ago, a wedding gift from Mother's sisters.

The three of us had then sat beside her to await the undertaker.

After he had performed the embalming, we clothed her in her grey and burgundy gown, one of her favorites. Then, she was moved into the casket waiting in the parlor. Three days later, this was where we now sat, waiting.

"Maggie, when will *we* die? Will it hurt a lot?" Eva emitted a vigorous hiccup.

Deep thoughts for a small person. "Oh, Eva, no one is privy to that answer. We die only when it's our time to die. It will be a long time from now." I hoped this last assertion reassured her.

"When will it be time to go to the funeral?"

"Soon after Grandma, John Henry and Abi arrive." I discerned no reason to acknowledge the hearse's impending arrival, as well.

Papa had fashioned Mother's casket out of maple, pine, ash and oak hardwoods, staining, sanding and sealing the wood to a glossy, golden perfection. These past weeks, when not at Mother's bedside, we frequently found him in his workshop next to the barn, where I believe he found solace in constructing Mother's final resting place. We all agreed it was an exceptional work of art. I couldn't understand why something so exquisite would be put into the ground, but knew it was important for Mother's crossing into eternity.

At last, the undertaker arrived with his hearse. In preparation for our departure to the church, our family gathered in the parlor to perform the last ritual before closing the lid of the casket. Holding hands in our fog of grief, we stood in a circle, surrounding our beloved Mother, consumed by our misery. Grandma, especially, seemed to have shrunk perceptibly in the past three days.

Our communal breathing was the only sound in the room. We each placed a small memento next to Mother to surround her with love from our family as she entered into the hereafter. I had chosen a dried red rose, along with a handwritten note expressing my affection and devotion.

Papa carefully removed Mother's gold wedding band. Next, he removed the locket from around her neck, placing both into a small velvet bag. The locket, his gift to her on their wedding day, held a picture of the two of them, along with miniscule locks of hair from her babies that died in infancy. Perhaps she was already in heaven holding those lost children, yet this thought gave me little comfort. I instead selfishly longed for her to be here embracing us, healthy and whole.

We stood back while the undertaker stepped out from where he had been waiting in a darkened corner of our parlor. After the lid was in place, he nailed it shut, portending the situation's hopeless finality, jarring my very being. I stood frozen in place until Lucy nudged me to move forward. The undertaker, along with Papa and my three brothers, carried the casket out the front door. My sisters and I followed as they somberly loaded it into the hearse. Two black Arabians awaited to draw the hearse, both whinnying, one of them pawing the ground in seeming impatience. Steam emanated from their flared nostrils in the chilly November air. Ready to be off, unlike us, the stallions evinced no need to brace themselves for what lay ahead.

We trudged down the lane behind the slow-moving hearse, my Grandma, sisters and I clothed in various shades of black and grey, following Papa, John Henry, Louis and James, somber with their black armbands and the weepers wrapped around their hats. A few others who lived along the pathway joined us, as we walked solemnly together as a group, towards our little church.

The wind calmed and the rain diminished. Thankfully, the neighboring brushfires threatening the township these past few days had been all but extinguished, leaving behind wisps of smoke, lingering in a slow dance toward heaven. I appreciated these distractions, which kept me from falling to the ground keening for my lost mother. I darted between fantasy and reality on an interminable walk.

We arrived to find the church nearly filled. This came as no surprise, as Mother was well respected in our community. Our family crowded together onto the benches up front. Eva sat next to me, and I gently patted her back when she began coughing, probably caused by latent smoke in the stale air.

Absorbing the chill which seeped into my skin from sitting on the cold, hard stone bench, I somehow endured the funeral service. Our family openly wept; new casualties of heartbreak in an unexpected passageway of life.

After the service, as we walked through the vestibule to the graveyard, Samuel approached and attempted to say something comforting. In my current despair, the words sounded muddled and I knew I'd lost their meaning.

I found the internment even more painful to bear. Burying her in the ground became another sign of an irrevocable ending. I think we all hoped, beyond hope, she would rise up out of the casket at the last minute and this entire episode would be nothing more than a ghastly nightmare from which we all suddenly awakened. The minister read the 23rd Psalm and I heard nothing past the *"Yea, though I walk through the valley of the shadow of death, I will fear no evil . . ."*

We formed a circle around the casket, as each family member placed a flower taken from a basket of fall blooms on our front porch.

"Open wide, O earth, and receive her that was fashioned from thee by the hand of God aforetime, and who returneth again unto Thee that gave her birth. That which was made according to his image the Creator hath received unto himself; do thou receive back that which is thine own."

The words of the minister rang in my ears as Mother's burial box was lowered into the ground. He scooped the first shovel full of dirt on top, with a somber, "ashes to ashes, dust to dust," then passed the shovel to Papa, who repeated this ritual before handing it to the next family member. Louis helped each of my little sisters accomplish this symbolic gesture, which I, in truth, understood as the ultimate act representing closure for us. I would never forget the thump of the dirt as it struck that wooden box, its very sound echoing within my soul. It marked a finality, leaving our family to find our way without her.

7.

November 25, 1887. In the week following Mother's funeral, Ella returned to Detroit, quit her job, collected her belongings, and moved home to help Papa manage our household. I admired her self-sacrificing nature, while admitting to myself I felt no certainty I would do the same.

By the end of the next week, an ingenious Lucy, impressing even me, had maneuvered herself into Ella's old job in Detroit. Still underage, Papa would forbid her living in the city without a chaperone, so she orchestrated the move with the knowledge that her twin, Louis, had long aspired to study the barbering trade and there was a barbering school in Detroit. It also helped that, in Papa's eyes, the proposal was an opportunity for the both of them to develop skills to better themselves in the working world.

"Hurry up, Maggie, we don't want to miss the train!" Lucy scolded me impatiently. I gave her my best evil eye as I pulled on my boots, wishing I had never agreed to accompany the twins and Papa to the station, yet desperate for any variation in an otherwise mundane life. We had somehow muddled our way through Thanksgiving yesterday, in a futile bid to find reasons for gratitude.

I heard the tinkling of sleigh bells, signaling Papa's arrival out in front of the house. I opened the door and gasped as a gust of wind assaulted me. I took a quick breath as the twins dashed by, sprinting down the front steps, their excitement obvious. Louis loaded both their satchels into the sleigh and the three of us climbed aboard.

Billy and Blackie snorted wisps of vapor into the frigid air as we set forth into the cloudless, blustery day, swirls of snow blowing willy-nilly across the road. Settled next to my sister in the back of the sleigh, I snuggled deeper into the wool blanket and longed for something exciting to happen in my life. Even though Samuel and I were formally courting, there had been little forward progress since that day last summer when he had come to speak with Papa.

In opposition to today's frostiness, my heart warmed as I went back in time and revelled again in the memory of an unforgettable afternoon. I had been sitting on the front steps with my sisters, sweltering in the stifling humidity as we chattered and snapped green string beans. The sound of a horse's hooves interrupted our conversation and my heart skipped a beat when I saw Sam atop Absalom, prancing up our lane.

I wasn't privy to the conversation between Papa and him, but deduced it favorable when Sam doffed his hat and flashed me a broad grin as he took his leave, a spring in his step. He whistled a nameless tune as he approached Absalom, who, tied to the hitching pole, calmly waited for his master. Not long after Sam and Absalom trotted away, Papa had called me into his office.

"Well, my sweet one, it looks as though you have a suitor, all right and proper! Mr. Samuel Jobsa has asked my permission to court you in anticipation of a subsequent engagement. I judge Mr. Jobsa a fine young man with a promising future, both as a farmer and horseman, and found no reason to be disagreeable. Based on the July Fourth kissing incident, I surmise you might harbor similar sentiments, aye? I'm not certain about your brother James' views on the matter, however," he joked.

"Oh, Papa," I laughed, giving him an exuberant hug. "You're most discerning!" I always appreciated Papa's sense of humor. My feet barely touched the ground as I rushed to the kitchen to share my momentous news with Mother.

Recalling my conversation with Mother that day still perplexed me, months later. Her reaction made it evident she didn't seem quite as taken with the proposed arrangement as I had expected.

"Maggie, please be sure this is the right man for you before you sign up lock, stock and barrel," she cautioned in a serious voice as we embraced, standing there beside the kitchen sink.

"Oh, Mama," I said, pulling away from her, "I find Samuel so divinely intriguing and appealing. I'm certain he'll make me happy for the rest of our lives!"

"Maggie," she gazed deeply into my eyes, "sometimes what we see on the outside has little to do with what's on the inside. Take this into account as you move forward in this courtship."

"Whatever do you mean?"

"Only that the chestnut does not fall far from the tree. Observe his father and that will tell you what Samuel may be like in later years."

"Sam would never be like his father! That old man is overly flirtatious and he often drinks too much. I would *never* be so meek as Mrs. Jobsa, and tolerate such a situation."

Mother seemed to hesitate then, and stared at me thoughtfully. I couldn't let her dour response ruin my expectations for my future, so I went back outside to bask in the company of my sisters, announcing that I officially had a suitor.

Summer turned to autumn, and the focus of our family's existence shifted to Mother's illness. Ofttimes when Sam came courting, he delivered zinnias, sunflowers or mums from their family garden, one bouquet for me and one for Mother. I found this gesture incredibly generous and considerate, and hoped it encouraged Mother to see him in a different light. Just thinking of Mother brought me back to the present and I dabbed at tiny, icy tears. *Oh, Mother, how we all miss you.*

The train pulled into the station as we unloaded the twins' satchels and hugged them goodbye. "Children, take heed of your surroundings. Detroit is a big city and I want you two to watch out for one another."

"Yes Papa," Louis said, giving a half smile, while Lucy nodded her head with enthusiasm. Papa gave each of them another hug, after which he patted my brother on the back. Dear Louis, my favorite big brother. He would have his hands full watching out for my impetuous and dare I say, ill-tempered, sister.

"Goodbye, fare thee well, don't forget to write!" I called to them as they climbed aboard the train. Papa and I turned to walk back to the sleigh. He took hold of my hand, squeezing it before he slipped it under his arm.

May, 1888. Six months passed, marking the official end of our family's mourning period and the reappearance of color into our wardrobes. That, and the emergence of spring brightened everyone's spirits. Though the winter had been distressingly long and bleak, Sam had never missed our weekly courting time, regardless of the temperature.

I believed Mother's death had drawn us closer. Extraordinarily kind and chivalrous, with only a rare dour mood, he would sit with me and hold my hand when I cried or tell me funny stories to lift my spirits. He had taken Ella and me on sleigh rides and brought me sweets. One day he had come bearing wax crayons for Edith and Eva and a checkers game board for Janie and me.

I eagerly anticipated his afternoon visit today, delighted we would be unchaperoned. Perchance we would take a buggy ride or a stroll through the meadow. The warmth of the past several days had unleashed a multitude of blooms, bursting with vibrant shades of yellow, pink, magenta and crimson, all framed by the soft green of spring.

Scandalously, on several occasions over the past few months when Ella was busy with some household task, Sam and I had spent time by ourselves in the parlor. In five short days, I would at last be eighteen; and while Papa had been rather unpredictable with his rules, I believed and hoped he would consider age eighteen to be past the time of needing a chaperone. Freedom would be the best birthday gift I could ever receive.

Since Independence Day, I had become more proficient at romance and was convinced that among my unmarried siblings, I had the most practice with kissing. Sam had vastly more experience in this sphere and I became his eager and willing pupil. I found his kisses exhilarating, verging on provocative, especially when his tongue searched out mine. Yes, I considered myself quite teachable, and looked forward to more instruction on this glorious afternoon.

"Maggie! Mr. Sam's coming up the lane!" called Eva from the front steps, where she sat playing with her dolly. Lost in my musings, I had ignored my messy hair. Hastily, I attempted to tame my curls into a smooth chignon, quickly realizing it hopeless. Instead, I wound it into a slipshod bun, stabbing it with hairpins, before dashing down the stairs. I didn't want to waste a minute of our time together on my unruly hair.

I rushed outside as Sam dismounted Absalom, tying the reins to the post. He gazed at me and, as always, his broad smile disarmed me. I found him irresistible.

"How's my Maggie May this fine spring day?"

With my most beguiling smile, I answered him with my own question, "Are you growing a moustache?"

"Ah, so you noticed! My fair hair doesn't make it apparent, but yes, that is my intent!" Somehow, his smile grew more enormous, practically obscuring his somewhat meager attempt at a moustache. Moustaches were all the rage these days.

"Shall we take a walk through the meadow? It's so alive with color!" I proposed.

"Marvelous idea!" A crease ran across his brow. "Where is Miss Ella today?"

"She's with John Henry's wife, Abi, helping with the new baby, so I suppose we'll be forced to get along without her this afternoon." I smiled conspiratorially and held out my hand to him. I had kept quiet at breakfast when Ella mentioned she had volunteered to help our sister-in-law today.

Off we went, hand in hand, to stroll through the field. It took but one sidelong glance at Sam to fill my heart with an unbridled yearning. I shivered with desire as we walked in silence.

Partway across the meadow, Sam's attitude shifted. "I find I'm in a bit of a snit today, Maggie. Father and I repeatedly fail to agree about plans to improve the farm. Just between you and me, he's far too set in his ways and not eager to embrace new ideas, so we're at loggerheads."

He sucked in a long breath and slowly exhaled, giving me a moment to consider his admission, before he grumbled, "Our arguments are becoming more heated and I'm uncertain how much more squabbling I can withstand. It's obvious to me he's *not* forward thinking, so I find I may have to strike out on my own."

Another lull. My heart beat a little faster, apprehensive at what might come next.

"There's a seventy-acre plot down Sugarbush Road which our family leases to the Hendriksen family, and of course, I wouldn't want Father to push them out, but I can see myself . . . er, us, on that property."

I smiled, relaxing a little, to hear him making plans for our future.

"I'm formulating a proposal to convince Father of the wisdom of letting me take over this section of land when the lease runs out. Many days, I feel I'm almost at the end of my rope with his stubbornness." Angrily, he spat on the ground.

Before I could offer any comment or pose any question about this unexpected development, his one-sided conversation took an unexpected turn when he stared at me quizzically, as though noticing me for the first time today. "What the dickens have you done to your hair?"

The ever-faithful scarlet blush crept up my cheeks. "Well, I was attempting to bring it under control when Eva called to me you'd arrived, and I didn't want to miss . . ."

"Yes, yes. Next time you should plan your time better, so you don't appear so unkempt."

His words stung and silenced me. I chalked up his callous remark to his frustration with his father. Nevertheless, I could not deny an uncomfortable twinge in my chest. Though bursting with questions, I did not want to arouse his frustration and anger again and decided this was not the time to raise them.

We walked on, and with each passing step, the friction brewing between us dissipated. "I'm sorry, Maggie, I didn't mean to sound harsh. My father has gotten my dander up and I'm afraid I've been taking it out on those around me."

"It's all right, Sam. I understand." I didn't really, but decided it best to ignore the strange flutter in my stomach and move on.

We found ourselves standing beside a massive oak tree, on the far side of the field, where the wild poppies grew. Overtaken by the vibrancy of the flowers surrounding me and the earthy scent of Sam as he moved close, I was swept away. He leaned up against the tree and took my hands in his, pulling me toward him and kissing both my palms. I effortlessly fell into his embrace and lifted my lips to meet his. Seconds later, with the aid of several fiery kisses, the memory of Sam's harsh tone softened considerably. The intensity of his ardor startled me, and in my muddled mind I wondered if we might not ignite into a ball of flame, as the intense passion crushed us together.

"Oh my God! Maggie!" He moaned, and his lips devoured mine. All of a sudden, he pulled away, searching my face with his smoldering eyes. He grasped the back of my head and yanked out my hair pins, so that my loosened hair tumbled down with abandon.

A tingling started at my shoulders and spread downward toward my groin. "Sam, oh, Sam!" I whispered, as he pulled me back toward him. What had come over me? I melted into his arms, and as he held me close, his growing manhood pressed against me. He clasped my shoulders and gently pushed me away from him. One hand cupped my breast as his fingers lightly rubbed the nipple through the fabric of my frock. With his other hand, he unbuttoned my bodice. Waves of pleasure crashed over me, and I trembled with pleasure, moaning softly.

Suddenly, sanity prevailed and I jerked myself away from him, shaking my head to clear it. Heart pounding and barely able to breathe, I turned without a word, hiked up my dress, and set off at a swift pace back toward the farmhouse. I was certain my actions had *not* pleased him, and soon found out I was right. He caught up with me and gripped me by the shoulders, shaking me slightly.

"What the devil? How can you lead me on like that and then turn your back on me and run away? What's wrong with you, woman?"

Without words, I looked at him and he turned blurry as my eyes pooled with tears. *Was* there something wrong with me?

I stood mute, while he shook his head in disgust and pushed me away. I stumbled backwards, before regaining my balance and continuing my march homeward, my jaw clenched. He paced himself several steps behind me, giving us both time to gather our tempers.

In sight of the farmhouse, I hastily finished buttoning my bodice and he caught up with me. "Maggie, forgive me. Perhaps I was out of line back there, but you bring forth such a raging fire within me, I find it difficult, almost impossible, to maintain any sort of respectability. And when you returned my ardor, well . . ."

Dare I tell him I felt that same desire? My mind in turmoil, I did naught but frown.

"Please, Maggie!" Desperately, he reached for my hand. "Please say you'll forgive me for my lack of propriety," he added earnestly and, it seemed, rather apologetically.

I considered him, still unsure how to respond. Maybe we did need a chaperone, after all.

Summer, 1889. "Maggie! I can't make my hair behave!" An exasperated Edith handed me the brush.

With the brush in hand, I said, "Sit down and let me see what I can do." She had a mane of unmanageable red hair and I saw her point. It verged on wildness, much like *she'd* been for the past year.

"Girls, it's almost time for them to arrive. Are you ready?" asked Ella, as she came around the corner of our sleeping room into our dressing area. She looked so fetching in her stylish dove grey skirt, with its upswept cotton challis overskirt exposing the crepe skirt underneath. Her pale pink-colored blouse, sewn from a Dresden-style lawn fabric, had fashionable puffed sleeves and complemented her skirt impeccably. I wished I looked like her.

"Everyone's already in the parlor," was a hint from Ella we needed to hurry, as we most certainly did not want to be upstairs when they walked in the front door. To my credit, I succeeded in smoothing Edith's hair into a clip and tied the bow on the first try. Her dress, a pale lavender high-waisted empress style frock sewn from a dimity fabric, reflected that awkward stage between child and woman.

I wore an aqua-colored gown stitched under Ella's guidance, made from a thin cotton dimity over Swiss taffeta. It was a perfect fit and I was proud of the result.

The three of us scurried downstairs, joining Eva, Janie and James. Eva walked over to where I stood and took my hand in hers, as I attempted to bring my emotions into order.

Scrunching her face into a little frown, Eva peered up at me and asked, "Maggie, where will Mrs. Lizzie sleep?"

"Well, Eva, she'll sleep with Papa," I replied, unsure how much information to share with a nine-year-old.

"She will? Why? Why would she do that?" She stomped her foot.

"Um, well, because yesterday she became Papa's wife, and husbands and wives usually stay in the same room together during the night."

"But, that's Mama's bed!"

"Yes, well, that *is* true, but Mama has no use for that bed any longer. She sleeps in her heavenly bed where she can watch over us!" Evidently this satisfied her, as no further questions arose. She let go of my hand and walked back over to the window to watch for the newlyweds' carriage to come up the lane. They had been married in Detroit two days earlier, returning to Mt. Clemens by train around midday.

The skies were overcast when I awakened this morning, and although the clouds had dissipated and the July day had turned out to be pleasant, it was still stuffy and muggy indoors. I was grateful our celebration would be out-of-doors.

I had mixed feelings about what might happen after Lizzie came to live in our home. What would she be like? Would we get along? I questioned what my place would now be, with the acquisition of a stepmother, as I had held the official title of "eldest daughter" in the household for several months. With Ella moving into Mt. Clemens and Lucy living in Detroit, for all intents and purposes I ran the household and all it entailed.

If it hadn't been for Papa's rheumatism, we probably wouldn't be waiting in the parlor today. When his rheumatism acted up, he'd often take a trip into Mt. Clemens to partake of the healing mineral waters at one of the local bathhouses. It was at the Medea Bathhouse where Lizzie came into his life, and ultimately, ours. After he soaked in the restorative black waters, her job as a rubber gave the two of them ample time to talk as she massaged away his aches and pains. While Papa seemed quite old for such antics, over time, a romance had blossomed. Now and then, over the past months, Papa had brought her out to the farm on her day off to share a meal with our family.

Elizabeth "Lizzie" Bond had escaped a dangerous marriage. She had endured many years of abuse before divorcing her husband, a house painter by trade and a drunkard by choice. Sadly, with no means to support her children, she had been denied custody of her two sons. Furthering Lizzie's misery, her third son had tragically died in an influenza outbreak a few years prior. We called Lizzie a lonely woman who had put the sparkle back in our Papa's eyes.

Ready and willing to give her a chance, I couldn't help but be pleased for the two of them. I did find it difficult not to feel a touch of jealousy and impatience with the lack of progress in my own life. At nineteen, only the fact that neither Lucy nor Ella had yet wedded kept me from feeling like an old maid. I had learned early on it was useless to prod Sam with hints of marrying. He apparently had his own private timetable and didn't take kindly to my purported "interference." I allowed myself to daydream a moment or two about my wedding until the noise level in the parlor increased, ending my reverie. A coach had been spotted coming up the lane, so we all gathered on the porch to form a welcome party.

"What's all this about?" Papa smiled innocently, as he climbed down from the carriage.

"It's your surprise party!" squealed Eva.

"Well, this *is* a grand surprise! Thank you, my dear children!" He turned to smile at his bride, as he helped her step down from the coach, proclaiming, "I'd like you all to greet my new wife, Lizzie!" I suspected he had purchased her a new gown, crepe de chine in a pale orchid and simply gorgeous. Tall as Papa, and slender, her calm demeanor charmed me. Her light brown hair was piled into a topknot, curls spilling over on her forehead.

"How do you do?" she asked, as she greeted each of us with a soft handshake, and no sign of being overwhelmed. When she stood before Eva, Lizzie bent down on one knee, looked Eva in the eye and gently clasped her shoulders. "Eva, I am so pleased to see you again! Your Papa told me how you love to help with the baking."

Eva smiled bashfully, staring at her shoes.

"How would you like to be my helper in the kitchen and learn to bake bread?"

"Okay . . ."

Well, it was a start. It occurred to me that I just might grow to love this sweet-tempered woman.

"Welcome to your new home, Lizzie." I gave her a hug, as did Ella and Janie. Her kindly blue-grey eyes filled with tears of happiness or relief, or possibly both. Somehow, I had a hunch Mother would approve.

8.

Early September, 1889. I sat on the front stoop waiting for Sam, brooding about relationships and the complications they involve. Sometimes I wished I could be a self-assured man like my brother, James. Deciding he didn't want to farm, he moved to Mt. Clemens, took training as a tailor, and met and married Grace, all within the last year. Yet here I sat, yearning for Sam to ask for my hand in marriage. On top of that, Lucy unexpectedly moved home two weeks ago, after her employer, Mr. Whitworth, was killed in a ghastly accident. Stopped at a train crossing, the train whistle startled his horse, who reared up and tipped the buggy, crushing Mr. Whitworth. Posthaste, his widow shut down the Detroit Millinery Shop, and Lucy unexpectedly found herself without employment.

Lucy maintained her move home would be temporary, insisting as soon as she found work in Mt. Clemens, she would move into town with Ella. From my perspective, the sooner the better, because it took but a few hours for me to recognize she hadn't lost her bossiness and Papa's house was no longer big enough for the both of us. We got on much better when we lived in different households.

I contemplated Ella and Lucy's overriding interest in working and living on their own. Finding a husband did not seem high on their list of priorities and it puzzled me.

Where was Sam? He was late. I blamed my impatience on my frustration that my family had moved on. Papa had remarried, Lucy, Louis and Ella were pursuing careers, and James had married and moved to town. It seemed life had left me behind. Yet, if I were completely honest with myself, it was more than just circumstances.

Nearly two years had passed since Sam had come courting. Our passion for each other hadn't diminished, but I sometimes worried Sam's enthusiasm for marriage had waned. He had been extremely distracted by harness racing, traveling to events around the area. Winning or placing with an increasing frequency, he had been saving the money to start building his breeding stock.

Reconciling this as the male version of a hope chest, I applauded anything which might help us move in the direction of marriage, even though all this travel meant we hadn't courted as often, of late.

At times, my heart physically ached; I missed him so much. Marrying Sam would fulfill my long-held dream of marrying well, creating a beautiful home and filling it with his fair-haired children. I had a cast-iron certainty I would be the envy of all the unmarried girls in Mt. Clemens.

Glancing up then, I saw Sam riding up the lane in a buggy, and stood to greet him. "Hello!" I called and waved, proud to be courted by such a nattily clad, attractive man, despite last year's failed moustache attempt. I smiled at the remembrance, a topic best left unspoken.

I wondered why he had the buggy today. He jumped from the carriage and moved toward me, grabbing my hands in his. "What would you think of taking a carriage ride with me on this fine September afternoon?"

The warmth of the sun seeped into my skin on this blue-skied late summer day, one of my favorite times of the year. A carriage ride with Sam sounded sublime.

"Sam, what a splendid idea!" We sat together on the steps, my leg touching his, creating the familiar tingle, and I shivered.

He pressed it closer, turned and smiled his beguiling smile. "I have a special surprise for you today, Miss Maggie May!"

"Do tell! Where are we going?" I laughed, as we both stood and walked toward the buggy.

"Ah, well now, that's part of the surprise! Patience is a virtue, you know."

Lighthearted, I eagerly climbed up to the seat. We traveled north for less than a half hour, when Sam turned down a lane. It occurred to me we had turned onto Sugarbush Road and I couldn't quell a growing expectation. I squeezed my hands together, finding it hard to keep calm.

He stopped in front of an empty, dilapidated two-story farmhouse with peeling white paint and an old, faded red barn, which looked to be in better condition than the house. I also spotted several small outbuildings near the barn.

"Maggie," he turned toward me, "The house isn't much, but Father has at last consented to let me try my hand at farming. I think we can rehabilitate the house and property. That means we'll have a place to live after we are married."

I idly speculated about what had happened to the Hendriksen family, who used to live there. This was not exactly what I had dreamed of, but hearing the word "married" overshadowed all other considerations and any disappointment with potential living arrangements. "Sam! Oh, Sam!" I threw my arms around him and he pulled me into a warm embrace.

With his hands on my shoulders, he pulled away long enough to look me in the eyes and proclaim, "I believe the time has come to marry."

At last! The words I had been waiting so long to hear! Before I could answer, he ardently grasped my face between his hands, bent down, and kissed me with such fervor that the force of his kiss bruised my lips. I didn't care. It was the happiest moment of my life. I caught my breath and the word "Yes!" burst out of my mouth as we kissed. Both laughing and crying, the world seemed too small to contain my joy. Sam laughed with me and we began to talk non-stop of our future, all the way back home. "Of course, I must first ask your father for your hand in marriage, before we make it official, but I discern no good reason he might reject the offer," Sam chortled.

I chuckled too, thinking Papa would be relieved he had at last launched a daughter into wedded matrimony!

"I realize the house needs some work, but structurally it's sound. I'm confident that with your touch, it will be a showplace in no time," he winked at me.

We rode along in companionable silence for a few minutes before I ventured to ask, "Oh, Sam, when will we marry? Might it be this autumn?" Belatedly, I realized how overeager I sounded.

The muscles in his face tightened as he answered evenly, "Well, Maggie, I haven't settled on a date yet."

Not infrequently, his moods fluctuated between tenderness and irritability. I chided myself for my impertinence. Of course he didn't have a date in mind. It had been only moments since he'd asked me. What might my dear Mother say? Would she approve? Would she be happy for me? Oh, how I ached to talk to her.

We arrived back at the house near suppertime, so I invited Sam to join us. He declined, saying his mother expected him for supper, and he had plans for the evening. Wondering what those plans might be, I nodded and gave his hand a squeeze before climbing out of the buggy.

Chaos reigned. I walked inside to find Janie and Edith had accidentally started a fire in the kitchen stove. Lucy and Lizzie, each carrying a bucket of water from the barnyard pump, shouted at me to stand back as they tossed the water, dousing the flames licking up at the ceiling. The pandemonium lasted less than a minute, but quashed my euphoric spirit. I decided to wait until a more opportune time to make my joyful announcement.

"Lucy?" I whispered, "are you awake?"

"Mmph," came her muffled reply, "I am now."

"Guess what?"

"I guess it's around midnight and I have to get up early tomorrow. Couldn't this wait until morning?"

"No, I'll burst if I don't tell someone."

"What, then?"

"Sam asked me to marry him this afternoon."

"What?" she spoke crossly, as she sat bolt upright in her bed, causing a loud squeak in the bed frame.

"Sssh! Don't wake up the girls!" I frowned at her in the darkness, but of course she couldn't see me.

"Why are you telling me this in the dark of night?"

"Because I'm so happy I had to tell someone! I beg your pardon for bothering you."

"Oh, I'm sorry, Maggie. I'm still half-asleep. I'm happy for you!"

There. She had done it! She had given me a more proper answer. "Thank you! It seems like so long ago we began courting, I was unsure if I would ever have a chance to say those words."

"Well, I'm glad you're happy, Maggie. I wish you and Mr. Jobsa the best, but I have to get back to sleep. We'll talk more tomorrow, if that's all right with you?"

I lay awake contemplating life. Nothing ever seemed to turn out as I had imagined. Why was everyone so irritable?

⁘

November, 1889. With the harvest complete, Papa's approval secured, and cart races all but over for the season, Sam had time on his hands and so did I. We began in earnest to repair and refurbish the derelict farmhouse on Sam's new property.

In the absence of people, the dwelling housed all manner of critters. With winter approaching, the mice ran rampant, scurrying about in their haste to build nests. Ridding the house of these varmints was our first priority. This involved either trapping or shooting the larger rodents, and laying out dishes of poison for any remaining. I couldn't bear to set foot inside the house until Samuel bagged up and disposed of their remains. A few wily mice avoided capture or extermination, clearly expecting it their due to take up residence with us.

The list of tasks required to make the house habitable seemed endless. Yet, I honestly began to see some progress in the restoration, especially on the days Sam's father lent us his hired man to help with the more burdensome tasks. By early November, after more than a month of intense cleanup, it had slowly begun to look habitable.

On an unremarkable late autumn day, I rolled up my sleeves as I worked upstairs, crouched on a folded blanket to protect my knees from splinters in the rough hardwood flooring. I was focused on washing the lower part of the wall when Sam came bounding up the stairs.

"Maggie, I've figured out why the house keeps filling with smoke whenever I light the fireplace! It wasn't a problem with the damper, after all."

Wrinkling my forehead, I turned my head toward him, seeking enlightenment. "Yes?"

"A large chimney swift had made a nest near the top of the chimney."

"Ah, so I did hear you up on the roof!"

"Once I cleared it away, I was able to light a fire and voila, the smoke went up, not in!" Sensing my apparent lack of enthusiasm, he asked, "I believe you'll agree we will need a functional fireplace as the weather worsens?"

"Of course. Yes! I'm so glad you figured it out." I attempted to match his elation with a fervor I did not necessarily feel. Tired of scraping, sanding, sweeping, washing, and disinfecting, I had steeled myself to finish washing the walls of this room, our future bedroom, today. I then planned to wallpaper, and Ella said she would come help me on her next day off.

I hadn't appreciated how important such small victories were for Sam. He seized me under the arms from behind and swung me up to my feet, turned me around to face him and began to kiss me with increasing intensity. His lips first brushed each eyelid, followed by several soft, moist kisses on my nose, my cheeks and my ears, leading to my lips. Soon, Sam was no longer the only stimulated person in the room. Before I knew it, we lay entwined upon the now unfolded blanket. While we had experimented and explored each other's bodies to some degree on previous occasions, my instincts told me today would be different.

His hands languidly caressed my skin near the neckline of my bodice and presently found their way to the tiny buttons of its front. My fingers wiggled under his to help with the process of unbuttoning and then, in like manner, my hands undid the larger and more easily accessed buttons of his shirt. With fleeting misgivings about how rough the edges of my fingers must feel, I stroked his nearly smooth chest, in a fluttering, tickling motion. His breathing grew faster.

Consumed by desire, I allowed him to relieve me of my corset. Somehow my camisole also vanished. His hands cupped my bare breasts, his thumbs rubbing my nipples as a smoldering flame ignited within me. He shifted his head downward to lick my nipples slowly and deliberately. Aroused by his hot breath, a familiar tingling spread throughout my body, increasing with a throbbing intensity.

"Oh, Maggie," he moaned, "I can't wait for you! One. Moment. Longer." In the blink of an eye, he had doffed his pants and undergarments. Shocked, my eyes opened wide and I misplaced my voice. He pushed my skirt up and my pantaloons down, but the fabric in my skirt bunched uncomfortably between us. After a momentary hesitation, I unbuttoned the offending article of clothing and he pulled it from me. I was in a trance, suspended in time. Up on his knees, he straddled me, his hand caressing my face, tucking my hair behind my ears. Carefully, he moved closer to lie on top of me and resumed kissing me with increasing fervor.

My body responded as he rubbed against me and I could feel his member enormous between us. I pulled his head toward my breasts, and as his mouth enveloped my nipples, I gasped, overcome by an exquisite euphoria. My head tipped back and I thought I might explode as wave after wave of pleasure cascaded throughout every fiber of my being.

He took my hand in his and together we stroked his manhood until it swelled to fullness and, with his help, found its way home. The further his hardness slid inside me, the more discomfort and pressure assailed me. I consciously dismissed these sensations, feeling as though I was hovering outside my body, watching from above.

Our bodies pulsated together as one, faster and faster, up and down. Over and over, we moved in unison, both of us sweating and groaning aloud, until at last, he gave a giant shudder and cried out. Despite his ragged breathing, he lay still upon me. The encounter was not without delight, not by any means. What would happen next?

Physically drained, Sam shifted himself to rest beside me. Both on our backs, we contemplated the paint peeling from the ceiling. We lingered; neither of us spoke. A myriad of emotions rushed through me while I waited for my body to calm. Passion was a curious experience. I realized it had obliterated my sense of decorum and in the heat of the moment, I had abandoned all reason. I could not take the moment back.

Sam seemed so accomplished, so skillful in his knowledge of what to do. I turned my head toward him and another much more troubling notion invaded my mind. I had clearly not been his first. Without warning, my passion crumbled, and an emptiness invaded my soul. I could not reconcile this new awareness, let alone all the other overwhelming sensations. How could this union, this coming together, now create such a hollowness? My private place pulsed with pain.

I surveyed the room, noticing our clothing scattered about in utter disarray. A lone tear rolled out of the corner of my left eye, gliding unhurriedly down my temple, into my disheveled hair. *What had I done? Oh Mama, will you ever forgive me?*

Still looking at the ceiling, he breathed, "Maggie, you were magnificent!" He turned to me, "What? Why do you cry? Don't worry, we are betrothed, so this is expected." He studied me more intently. "Dearest one, are you all right? Whatever is the matter?"

"Sam. Oh, Sam. What have we done?" I didn't know what else to say. How might I have explained it to him? Should I have told him how I hurt . . . both in my mind *and* my body?

"Truthfully, darling, it will be fine," he went on. "Do not trouble yourself. Soon we'll be wed. Yes? Please don't cry. You have made me so happy. Come, let me help you." He rose to his knees and extended his hand to help me stand. Something on the blanket caught my eye. Blood. My blood.

We collected our clothing in silence, departing soon after, my walls unfinished.

⌒〜〜つ

Telling Sam went poorly, as my suspicions collided head-on with his grand plans. Ofttimes irregular, I missed my flow, due mid-November, yet sensed no concern. When I began to retch every morning at first light, a startling realization began to take hold. Awareness dawned, calling forth memories of stories my sister-in-law Abi had told when she was with child.

"What? What do you mean, you're retching every morning?"

"Sam. I believe I'm with child. That's what I mean."

We stood in the main floor living area of the farmhouse, waiting for some warmth to take hold from the fireplace before we installed the shelving in the kitchen.

He glared at me with an inscrutable expression before exploding, "Well, how the hell did you let *that* happen?"

My eyes shot daggers at him; my voice failed me. He considered this *my* fault?

He stomped out the front door, leaving it open to the wind. With as much force as I could muster, I pushed it shut behind him. For good measure, I hauled off and slapped the massive, oak door, causing a nasty burning sensation in my hand. Unsure of what stung more, the truth of his words or my throbbing palm, I chose to ignore my own complicity and lack of sound judgment.

How *dare* he call this predicament my fault? How *dare* he stomp out of the house like that, behaving as a child? I didn't want it to be true either! I kicked the wall, shrieking "Ow!" My thin boots offered little protection from my fury. With a stinging hand and a throbbing foot, I hobbled over to the fireplace, rubbing my hands together in an effort to warm myself in this chilly room. Sam had been clear in his plan to wait to marry until we had completed the house repairs, but with the colder weather upon us, those repairs had slowed to the pace of a turtle with a broken leg.

Within seconds, he flung the door open and stomped back in.

"Fine. We'll get married next week." He turned around and stomped back out.

I slammed the door behind him for a second time. Returning to my place near the fireplace hearth, I sat down and wept, overcome by my raging emotions.

How had this happened? Well, I *knew* how it happened and it had *not* been my plan either. Under no circumstances did I want to be with child. Not now!

What about my dreams for a wedding in the springtime? What about my vision of our church filled with family and friends, sunshine streaming into the sanctuary through the narrow slit windows high above everyone's heads? A glorious processional would resound from the organ as I glided down the aisle arm-in-arm with Papa, wearing an elegant gown adorned with delicate French lace. In my vision, I would move toward Samuel, awaiting me at the altar. After a joy-filled ceremony, there would be a memorable party to celebrate my long-held dream come true. A dream that had now crumbled into dust.

Life was unfair. We had only crossed those forbidden boundaries one time. What would I do with a child coming in a matter of months? How could I prepare for something I wasn't yet ready for?

A couple of days after our tumultuous row, Sam located a pastor in Mt. Clemens, the Reverend J. L. DeLand, available and willing to perform our marriage on Wednesday, the eighteenth of December. Lucy and Ella agreed to be our witnesses.

～

Ella and I stood in the girls' dressing room next to the sleeping room, inspecting the dress I would wear for tomorrow's ceremony. "Oh, Ella! You have fashioned a miracle!" I stood before my best wool frock, which she had managed to turn, with her sewing acumen and very short notice, into my wedding dress. Using a needle and thread, she had attached some exquisite four-inch wide decorative lace trim down either side of the front pleat of my grey skirt, and a much daintier French lace along the neckline of my matching bodice. Her talent evident, she had also made an exquisite lace headpiece, which would encircle my head and cascade down my back, woven with dried baby's breath.

"Hi girls, hope I'm not interrupting?"

"No, of course not, Lizzie. I was admiring Ella's handiwork. Her work is topnotch!"

"She is a remarkable seamstress," Lizzie concurred, smiling at the two of us. "Maggie, even though we won't be attending the wedding, I have a little something for you." She handed me a small velvet-covered box. I raised both brows in question. "Yes, you may open it," she nodded.

I opened the lid and found a dainty pearl brooch in the shape of a heart. It somehow seemed familiar to me. Confused, I studied her face. "Lizzie, isn't . . ."

"Yes, it was mine. Wore it on my wedding day, I did. I'm done with weddings and I'd like it to bring you the luck it has brought me by marrying into this family."

Touched, I hugged her close to me. "Oh, Lizzie. You are such a special mother. Thank you. How I wish you were going to be at the ceremony."

"You know, dearie, I'd love to be there, but it's not my place to cross your Papa's choice to remain home."

I loved her for saying that. Words could not describe my disappointment when I learned Lizzie and my own Papa would not attend the ceremony. With a sense of shame, I well understood I had let him down, so I chose not to beseech him to be present. Their absence would be my burden to bear.

Sam's parents also chose to be absent. Sam said his mother, with her devout religious beliefs, found the whole situation abhorrent, which led me to question if she would ever speak to me again. She regarded me as Jacob's Leah, tricking her "innocent" son into my bed to secure the marriage. Until this happened, she had always acted favorably toward our union, and the current situation left a disturbing knot in the pit of my stomach. Still coming to terms myself with this ill-timed plight, I hoped a grandchild might soften her resolve. Time would tell.

Ella and Lucy both accepted my confession with equanimity, standing by me through this trying time. Once he got used to the idea, Sam came around and, to my immense relief, acted excited by the prospect of fatherhood. In fact, he seemed undeniably more excited than me, but he wasn't retching daily, either.

9.

December 18, 1889. After several inches of fresh snow, the day had dawned crisp and cold, with gusty winds. Snow devils danced fancifully beside our carriages. I imagined that since I wasn't able to dress in fashionable white for my wedding, the world dressed in white for me.

My first-rate sisters, Lucy and Ella, had decorated the small rectory with evergreen branches and holly, which accorded a festive air. They wore their best wool dresses, Ella's plum and Lucy's grey, each adorned with a fringe of lace around the neckline of its bodice. Sam wore a dark grey sack suit with a sprig of baby's breath in his buttonhole, along with his father's black top hat.

"Are you all ready, therefore, to begin?" Pastor DeLand quizzed the four of us, standing in a semicircle before him. The overall mood of the room was anticipatory, but I could sense a hint of nervousness, as well. The actual ceremony took less than ten minutes and by 10:15, our fates were sealed together.

I sincerely wanted to feel somehow different. I did not. All my hopes and dreams for the past several years had revolved around this event. I listened for some brilliantly exploding fireworks and pealing church bells, but heard only silence.

If Mother had been alive, would she have compelled Papa to reason? Would they have attended the ceremony? Would she have been proud I had married well?

I glanced down at my left hand, staring for a moment at the thin, golden band he had slipped on my finger a few minutes earlier, gratified I had at last become Mrs. W. Samuel Jobsa. It no longer mattered that it had not been the wedding of my dreams.

Sam and I began our wedded life with a sleigh ride to the largest hotel in Michigan, the Avery. My sisters had planned a buffet at this lavish location as their wedding gift. We had invited the widowed minister, so we rode in two sleighs, warmly wrapped in wool blankets. Gliding along, I couldn't help but admire all the tree branches dressed in their frosty white cloaks.

I snuggled closer to Sam, who, gripping the reins with one hand, put his other arm around me and pulled me close under the wool wrap we shared. Still several streets away, I spotted the majestic Victorian-style Avery building, rising above the tangle of dark, leafless branches. I spotted its French mansard roof, the corner towers topped by American flags, which fluttered in the gentle breeze.

Sam helped me descend like a princess from the sleigh, before handing the reins over to the attendant. Taking my husband's arm, I stared ahead, observing the hotel's spacious veranda, eager to see what lay beyond. My eyes feasted on the opulent decor as we walked through the ornate lobby. Covering the dark oak flooring, two Turkish carpet runners swathed eight-foot wide end-to-end sections of the lobby. I spied more pedestal tables than I could readily count, upon which rested multifaceted, multicolored leaded glass lamps. The plush burgundy velvet wingback chairs added a tangible richness beyond anything I had ever seen. I peered heavenward, awed to behold the lofty embossed tin ceiling.

A doorman led the five of us through the lobby to the restaurant. Seated near the window, we overlooked the hotel courtyard, blanketed with the freshly fallen snow. The sun poked its nose from behind a cloud, shining on the pristine white landscape, giving it a glazed appearance. Beyond the courtyard and connected to the Avery stood the original Mt. Clemens bathhouse. Arriving for treatment in the rich mineral waters, several patrons walked arm in arm toward the entrance. I said a prayer they would find the healing Mother had not. How many times during her illness had we carried her into those healing baths in hope of a miracle? Countless.

Sighing, my attention shifted back to the dining room and the many tables topped with fresh, white linen tablecloths and set with fine white china, edged in gold. More elegantly fringed Turkish carpeting concealed the golden oak flooring in this immense room. So shiny it glistened, a rich, dark oak wainscoting covered the lower portion of the wall, while the upper half was overlaid with an embossed cream-colored wallpaper.

What an extraordinary room! Hopefully, no one noticed my mouth hanging agape.

Gazing around the room, the smile on my face began to fade as an unpleasant, familiar queasiness began to grip my belly, caused by the pungent aromas of the fare being served. All manner of odors could send me running outdoors, where I would lose the contents of my stomach. I prayed the smell of food *this* morning would not do so.

Our buffet commenced with a flute of champagne and toasts from both Lucy and Reverend DeLand. I did my best to ignore the ominous queasiness.

"May all your hopes take flight and your dreams come true; may the memory of this day become dearer to you both, with the passing of every year."

"Thank you Lucy. Your toast was lovely." I nodded my head and took a sip, which sent bubbles into my nostrils, a most strange sensation. I had never tasted champagne before and found it to be both sweet and tart, quite a paradox! I gazed at the others smiling, laughing and sipping their drinks. It was almost as if I had been thrust into some sort of stage performance. My innards gurgled in response to the bubbly spirits, and the first hints of nausea began pulsing in tiny waves of discomfort.

Reverend DeLand stood and held his glass out toward Sam and me. "Cherish the love you feel toward each other this day." We beheld one another, smiling, as the reverend continued, "And, look back often and measure how much it has grown." Then, another toast, along with another sip of champagne. The only thing growing at the moment was the turbulence in my stomach.

"Thank you, Reverend DeLand," said Sam, as he stood and turned toward me, holding his fluted glass high. "And to my beautiful bride, may today be but the first of many joyous days together as man and wife." My stomach was officially in distress.

Everyone clapped and Sam sat back down, leaned over and kissed me soundly on the lips. My face turned scarlet, my mind distracted by more intimate thoughts. Should I toast him in return? Ill prepared, I let the moment pass, in an effort to bring my nausea under control.

The waiters made an unforgettable entrance with our first course, the soup du jour, a tomato bisque served with cold calf's head. After one glance at the calf's head, I knew my struggle against nausea was destined to fail. I grabbed my linen napkin, covered my mouth, stood and attempted to make my way outside as quickly and with as much poise as possible. I made it as far as the arches of the entryway before losing the contents of my stomach. My sisters and one of our waiters soon surrounded me speaking all at once to offer apologies, while Sam stood dumbfounded.

I looked up long enough to croak, "calf's head," and gagged.

"My dear lady, the offending dish will be removed at once," stammered the waiter.

"Oh, sister, we'd no idea the calf's head would affect you this way!" exclaimed Ella. Upon even hearing those two words, I began to retch again." Oh, Maggie, we envisioned it as a splendid treat!" Lucy looked crestfallen. Obviously, neither Ella nor Lucy had ever experienced being in the family way.

Looking up, I saw everyone in the dining room openly gawking at our little gathering under the archway.

What was that odor? Smelling salts waved under my nose. *Oh, no!* I had fainted, and the crowd of diners now surrounded me, staring with fascination at the woman lying on the ground in her own spittle. I hoped the incident would soon be forgotten, but that was evidently not to be the case. After being sponged clean with a damp cloth and reseated, I looked around the room and observed other diners gaping back with a discernible curiosity.

"Madam, if you are quite recovered, we should like to continue with your banquet?" asked the maître d', who had come to stand beside our table.

"Yes, please do," I answered in my most dignified voice, feeling anything but.

I believe my sisters paid more than fifty cents apiece for our celebratory feast, and extra for the champagne and wedding cake. I recognized this as a huge sacrifice on their part, and my heart filled with gratitude for Ella and Lucy's generosity. There was no escaping my disappointment, though, that I couldn't quite enjoy the lavish buffet. Sam's zeal as he set upon *his* plate of food assuaged to some degree the guilt I felt about my own lack of appetite.

The rest of the meal passed without incident, the brunch ably served by skillful waiters. They offered banquet omelets, fried potatoes and sausage. Brown bread with butter and jam accompanied this course. A bit of the omelet and bread settled well. Next, our wedding party tried grapefruit, a delicacy shipped in from the Deep South by train, along with pecan muffins and smoked fish. My stomach had calmed, so I felt safe in sampling the palate cleanser brought to each of us by the waiters. It reminded me of sherbet and soothed my irritated innards.

The waiters made a fuss over bringing the bride's cake to our table, clapping and creating a stir in the spacious room. We all laughed, accepting this more positive attention from the other patrons.

The traditional plum cake, all I could have wished for, had white butter-cream frosting with a satin sheen, reminding me of the shimmering snow beyond the restaurant window. In keeping with tradition, I cut the first piece with Sam's assistance and daintily fed it to him. He returned the favor before we cut slices for the rest of our group. While our little gathering enjoyed a cup of tea or coffee with the cake, I told myself I would remember this as a perfect ending to our banquet, setting aside the disastrous calf's head debacle.

⁓

"Sam! This is wonderful," I enthused, admiring the interior décor of our room at the Avery. "I had no inkling we'd spend the night. Oh, this is most exciting!" I had never stayed in a hotel before. Surely my eyes sparkled with unanticipated joy.

Sam smiled, "With any luck, you won't find it necessary to retch on the bedspread."

Ignoring this poor attempt at humor, my attention turned to the valise sitting beside the small corner table and I regarded Sam questioningly.

"Oh," he said, following my gaze, "Your sisters were apprised of the plan."

I smiled, nodding. Timidly, I opened the drawstring of my cloth handbag, reached in and took out my gift for him, wrapped in tissue paper and tied neatly with a red bow. "It isn't much," I offered in apology, "but . . ."

"I'm certain it will please me!" He tore off the tissue. "Oh, Maggie! It's splendid. Thank you, dearest. You've even embroidered my initials on it. Capital!" He folded the white linen handkerchief with "WSJ" embroidered in grey thread into thirds, positioning it in the breast pocket of his suit to reveal the initials.

"I have a surprise for you as well." His eyes danced, as a smile pulled at the corners of his mouth. He removed an envelope from his jacket pocket. I excitedly tore it open to reveal two tickets.

"Those are for the mineral baths. I was able to secure tickets for each of us, though we can't do it together, as you would know," his voice trailed off.

Yes, how could I ever forget the segregated baths? Oh, my beloved mother. I turned my back to him and looked out the window, struggling to veil my sorrow at this reminder of our loss.

"Shall we use our tickets to soak in the baths now?" I turned back to face Sam. One look at him answered my question. He stood before me, stripped down to his undergarments. Could I say I lacked the proper mental attitude, my stomach still somewhat queasy? But before I could say anything, he was standing before me, wearing nothing but his socks, grinning from ear to ear.

"Mrs. Jobsa, will you do me the honor?" he asked, as he waved his arm toward the bed.

I smiled, swallowed any misgivings, and began to disrobe, as he pulled back the bed's coverlet. Wearing only my gold wedding band, I joined him in bed, with an undeniable sense of relief that this time it would be all right.

Admittedly, I found the experience a lot less painful than the first time, yet afterward I experienced that same small pocket of emptiness. I couldn't quite put my finger on it, but something was missing. Putting this notion out of my mind, I soon drifted off. I awakened with a start, immediately noticing how much lower in the sky the sun had dipped. The second thing I noted was Sam's absence.

"Sam?" I called, looking around the room. Unless I found him under the bed, it was evident he had left the room.

I arose, cleaned myself and dressed. Four o'clock. Where could he be? It would be unseemly for me to venture out in search of him, so there was naught to do but wait. After nearly an hour, twilight fell and still, no sign of Sam. Moments later, there came a rap at the door.

"Yes?" I called out. *Had Sam forgotten his key?*

Through the door, someone said, "Yes, ma'am. Would you like anything? Might I light your lamp?" I opened it to find a maid making her evening rounds.

"Oh, yes, of course." Embarrassed, I realized she would see the total disarray of the bed. Well, there was nothing to be done for it.

What must she think? The maid bustled around the room, showing no reaction as she straightened the room, replacing the coverlet, lighting my lamp and bringing me some fresh water.

"Thank you." I handed her a small coin from my handbag, having no idea of the proper amount to tip. She smiled, curtsied as she backed out of the room, and closed the door quietly behind her.

5:05 p.m. I sat down, took a small book from my handbag, and began to read. After rereading the same page for the fifth time, I shut the book and stared out the window, watching as the gas lamps flickered on like little stars, each a guiding light for a weary traveler. I could still distinguish shadowy figures walking about, intent on their purposes as they moved toward their various destinations.

5:30 p.m. The door banged against the wall as it flew open and Sam walked in, tie missing, shirt askew, and a glint in his eye. His boisterous entrance told me he had been in the hotel saloon too long. Far too long.

"Maggie May! Well, aren't you delectable?" He lunged for me and yanked me toward him. After a sloppy kiss, he pushed me toward the bed.

"No, Sam! Not like this."

That stopped him in his tracks. A shadow crossed his face, and his mood instantly darkened.

"Do not ever speak to me that way," he spoke gruffly and gripped my arm, twisting it upwards behind my back. I tried to pull it away, but his brawn placed me wholly at his mercy. He shoved me on the bed.

Without even removing the coverlet, he pounced on me, attempting to have his way. His member refused to cooperate, which offered me a reprieve, but infuriated him even more. He reared away, dressed in a hurry, and fled, leaving me a sobbing heap in the center of the bed. I curled into a ball, shivering and shaking.

Some minutes later, the door flew open, banging the wall for a second time, causing the chandelier to rattle and shake. This time,

Sam acted completely sober and apologized in a remorseful voice. "Maggie, I am *so* sorry. I don't know what came over me! Not wishing to offend all the patrons of the saloon who bid me congratulations with a toast, I find I may have overindulged. Please, I beg you to forgive me. Please?"

When I didn't answer, he expounded, "My darling wife, you bewitch me whenever I gaze into those luminous eyes, the color of the sea. Your face enchants me whenever I behold that little turned up nose and those adorable dimples, framed by your delicate smile. I find it nigh on impossible to resist your charms, Maggie, but I can promise you such contemptible behavior on my part will never happen again." After a pause, he ended his speech with, "Can you ever forgive me?" and stared at his shoes contritely.

I hiccupped and sat up, not responding for several moments. "I'll forgive you," I finally murmured, gazing down at my clasped hands, no smile or enchanting dimples in sight.

He approached the bed, took my chin gently in his hand and lifted my face to look up at him. He sought out my puffy, red-rimmed eyes, and said, "Maggie, I love you with all my heart and would never, ever intentionally hurt you. Please believe me. I blame this all on you for being so beguiling." A smile accompanied his earnest voice. "Let's get you up and dressed and have our wedding supper. Afterwards, maybe we will take in the mineral baths. What do you say?"

With a hesitant "Very well," I slid over to the edge of the bed. He found a cloth, moistened it, and dabbed at my splotchy face. He then helped me dress and even attentively brushed out my tangled hair. I wound it into a topknot, holding it in place with my tortoiseshell comb.

"Your appearance suggests a radiant bride, for whom I have one last gift." He reached into his jacket pocket and withdrew the tiniest of tiny wine-colored leather purses, and presented it to me. I unsnapped the purse to find a dainty locket, hanging from a golden chain, with a cleverly intertwined "M" and "S" engraved on its face.

He took it from me then, opened the clasp and placed it around my neck, before turning me to face him. He took me into his arms, pulling me toward him into a warm embrace. After a moment, he cupped my chin in the palm of his hand and gazed into my wistful eyes, before leaning in to softly caress my lips with his.

He offered me his arm and we proceeded to the dining room, newlyweds. Still shaky from recent events, I was thankful for his support. I told myself all would be well, and believed it. I would learn to be a good and proper wife, so nothing like this ever happened again.

Supper passed much more smoothly than the morning buffet and I gladly ate some mutton, potatoes, and bread, with an orange for dessert. Sam's appetite appeared no larger than mine had been this morning. Following his afternoon in the saloon, perhaps he was now the one with a tremulous stomach.

The despondency I had worked so diligently to cast aside returned as I walked into the baths. My mind wandered unintentionally to grievous memories of bringing Mother here, and how we had prayed for a miracle cure. Lucy or I had often accompanied her and I recalled how sensitive the bath attendant had been, massaging Mother's fragile body after her soak, treating her with such tenderness. I also remembered how often I had turned away to hide my tears.

Refocusing, I forced myself to muse on other, more positive reflections. I luxuriated in the bath, after which I relaxed into the skilled hands of the rubber, who was pleasant and courteous, massaging my body with an accomplished thoroughness. After the difficult day I'd had, it felt blissful. My mind drifted to images of our new home and the experience of sleeping in a hotel for the first time, and I smiled with contentment.

My thoughts turned toward Sam. With a start, I realized I was no longer so confident in my choice. A new anxiety blossomed, circling back to Mother and her admonition on the day Sam asked for and received permission from Papa to court me. *Oh, Mama, how do I know if I chose wisely? How can anyone know?*

Lying on my back, my body stiffened, my eyes popped open and I bolted upright. Disconcerted, the attendant looked at me with uncertainty. "Oh! It's all right." I reassured her and forced myself to lie back down in an attempt to regain my composure, while the uneasiness seeped deeper into my being.

Feeling as relaxed and limp as one of Mother's homemade noodles, I appreciated the attendant's assistance with dressing after my session ended. She walked with me into the foyer, where Sam sat waiting.

Every bit the solicitous groom, he leapt to his feet and reached out his hand to me, "How did you like the baths, my darling?"

"Fine, Sam . . . I'm so . . . relaxed." Exhausted, I was most anxious to return to our room.

Perceptive enough to recognize my weariness, Sam kindly helped me to undress, tucked me into bed, kissed me on the forehead, and sat down in the wingback chair beside the bed to read.

"I'll join you shortly," he affirmed, "as soon as my euphoria over this momentous day calms."

Part Two

Very few of us are what we seem.
--Agatha Christie

10.

Lavina, Montana, October 15, 1941. After a time, the stream of relentless tears slows and I wipe them away with the back of my hand. I remember many long years ago, in the naïveté
of my youth, when I believed if you loved someone and they loved you, everything would work out in the end. If only it were that simple! My eyes drift shut and I lean my head back against the chair and begin to rock. I must have dozed, as when I open my eyes again, I see some light creeping onto the horizon. It's probably about 6:30, yet I hear no twitter of birdsong to greet the day. I suppose they've mostly all flown south for the winter.

In the shadows, I look down at the red and white star quilt covering my lap. *Didn't Ella help me cut all the squares?* I can't recollect now. So well sewn, I imagine it will endure long after I have gone. *All that hand stitching. Mercy!*

Setting it aside, I stand, and too quickly, for I feel a moment of light-headedness. Steadying myself, I pad into the kitchen and, in the near darkness, reach for the tea bags in the cupboard to the left of the sink. I turn on the tap and run water into the teakettle, recalling the words of my mother: "Fresh, cold water makes the best cup of tea." I place the kettle on the burner and switch on the gas. In no time, I'm back in the rocking chair under the quilt, sipping a hot cup of Lipton's, with a touch of milk and a spoonful of sugar, witnessing the dawn of a new day. I love waking up with the day. Colors streak across the sky in dazzling shades of marmalade. The darkness begins to dissipate, and I am buoyed by the air of promise which arrives with each new sunrise, offering fresh possibilities a sunset can never claim.

Why, maybe I'll make a pie this morning and take it next door to the cafe. Yes, that's what I'll do! After finishing my tea, I find my apron, tying it over my housecoat. No one will see me and there is little motivation to get dressed for the day quite yet. It can wait. The blush of daybreak illuminates the kitchen with a warm glow. In the pantry, I locate the sack of apples picked from the tree out back, most of which need to be used before they spoil. I sort through and select the firmest ones for my pie and set to work peeling. Before I dust the apples with sugar and cinnamon, I cut them into thin slices, wishing for a bit of lemon juice to keep them from turning brown. Well, I will make the crust before it can happen. I taste one of the raw, tart pieces, and smile to myself, savoring the flavor.

Next, I light the oven and adjust the temperature before reaching into the lower cupboard to pull out my blue mixing bowl. I scoop some flour and a little salt into it and then mix in the shortening. From long experience, my fingers sense through touch when the dough has the right amount of each ingredient. I add a bit more flour. I well know the importance of not over-mixing, or the crust will be tough. Once it resembles little round peas, I turn on the faucet and let the water run. I want the small measure of water to be ice cold. It takes but a mere three or four turns with the fork to blend and then I divide the dough into two sections, satisfied it's ready to roll out. Making pies remains one of life's great pleasures. A skill developed at my mother's elbow a lifetime ago, baking a pie is a relaxing distraction from the complexities of life. The Good Lord knows I made hundreds of them during the time I operated the home station.

Once I roll out the bottom crust and place it in a ceramic pie plate, I add the apples and several tiny pats of butter. I then carefully roll out the remaining crust, fold it in half on my pastry cloth and cut a few vent holes near the center to allow the fragrant steam from the cooking apples to escape. Wetting the rim of the bottom crust helps to seal the crusts as I pinch them together with my thumb and finger. *Too bad the sealing of marriage vows doesn't work the same way.* I sprinkle a few drops of milk and sugar on top, before placing the plump concoction in the oven. The kitchen fills with aroma and anticipation.

11.

Sugarbush Road, Late Spring, 1890. After a mild winter, the fields stood soggy throughout April and into May. Farmers welcome moisture, but the unremitting downpour made tilling the earth and planting crops impossible.

When the showers fell gently, I slipped into lethargy, vapid from the ceaseless pitter-patter on the window pane. But, when the wind reared its blustery head, giving rise to a constant rat-a-tat-tat of pelting rain, I worried I might go daft. The longer it rained, the more irritable Sam became. I did my best to be agreeable and, for the most part, stayed out of his way. He spent much of his time in town on business or in the tack room, while I endured the tedium of staying in the house, a captive of the weather and Sam's mood.

Then, without fanfare, the rains ended, the fields dried out, and cultivation was underway. With the midday meal and cleanup finished, the warmth of the sunshine beckoned me onto the front porch. My ever-expanding bulk left me weary, so I told myself it was acceptable to sit for a spell and rest. I planned to put the time to good use by studying the book Sam's mother had given me. From what I had read thus far, I gathered the gift of *Hill's Manual of Social and Business Forms, 1888* was my mother-in-law's attempt to turn me into a suitable wife. Although somewhat chagrined by the possible implications of her gift, at least she was speaking to me again.

Whatever have been the cares of the day, greet your husband with a smile when he returns. Make your personal appearance just as beautiful as possible. Let him enter rooms so attractive and sunny that all the recollections of his home, when away from the same, shall attract him back.

I laughed out loud. Whenever I stared at the reflection of my body in our mirror, I saw a bulky, ponderous bovine, making it difficult to view my appearance as anything close to *beautiful.* I had to admit, however, that my husband saw my fullness of figure differently. Throughout these past months, he often took my hand and led me to our bed, a gleam in his eye. I grew more and more uncomfortable as time passed, and I began to dread the frequency of his overtures.

My growing awkwardness did nothing to improve my oft-sour attitude. At times I couldn't help but worry and feel trapped. What if I didn't like being a mother, or worse, proved to be inadequate? I barely knew how to be a wife, much less a mother. Fearing Sam's reaction, I had been careful to keep such discordant thoughts to myself.

The manual suggested a virtuous wife should endeavor to make the rooms in a house *attractive and sunny.* We had made progress over the winter with some fresh paint and wallpaper. Thank goodness for Ella, who had offered me a hand whenever she could.

I read further in the instruction book and learned it my *responsibility* to provide my husband with *a happy home . . . the single spot of rest, which a man has upon this earth for the cultivation of his noblest sensibilities.* The word *cultivation* drew my attention back to our fields. I had begun to feel more relaxed these last few days as the soft, muddy ground began to dry and Sam's mood improved. Were I not with child, my place would be in the field as his helper. We'd had another conversation about it earlier today, as I had sensed his exasperation with the delayed planting.

"Sam, please let me lend you a hand this afternoon."

He shook his head, "No, Maggie, having you down in the field would only serve to increase my anxiety, as I'd be in constant fear for the baby's safety, should you fall or overexert yourself in some way. You'll remain here in our house, where I can be assured you're safe and secure. Even without help, I believe I can finish up the tilling before nightfall, so planting can begin tomorrow."

"All right, Sam, you know best." I agreed with his assessment and felt relieved by his answer. Not that I shirked duty, but my increasing size did limit mobility and affect my balance.

Sam now strode across the yard toward the house, his jaw set. He called to me, "The damn bolt came loose and fell from the tooth beam on the harrow. I've spent far too long searching in the soil for it, without success. I'll have to make a trip to town to get a replacement."

"Oh, dear! I am sorry, Sam."

How I wished I might go with him. In fact, I *needed* to go along, if only for a diversion. In January, Ella had begun working in the dry goods area of the mercantile, and through this, had acquired additional outside work as a seamstress, which meant Lucy regained the position at the millinery shop. They lived together in a small cottage in Mt. Clemens. They visited when possible, but I wished I were able to see them more often. A trip to town with Sam would provide a perfect opportunity to do so.

In my current state, however, it would make heads turn and tongues wag, plus it would take him longer to hitch the buggy than to saddle his horse. I satisfied myself with, "Would you please greet Ella for me?"

"Yes, if I think of it, but I am in a hurry." He brushed my lips with a kiss, and headed back to the barn to saddle up Absalom.

A growling stomach turned my attention to food. I had finally overcome my queasiness and hunger now accompanied my every waking moment. Sam would be late for supper. What might I eat in the meantime? I took stock of our larder. We still had some of the butchered hog Papa had given us at Christmas. I perceived this gesture as an olive branch and the beginning of a shift in attitude with regard to the circumstances of our wedding. I imagined the impending arrival of a grandchild would continue to thaw the chill in his heart.

I missed my family, often feeling cooped up and isolated. Sewing and embroidering baby clothing occupied a portion of my spare time, reminding me how dramatically my life would change in a few months. I persisted in developing my patience and biding my time with as much equanimity as possible, praying I would be able to find love in my heart for this unknown child.

August 11, 1890. I lie in a small cove along the slow moving river's edge, the lower half of my body partly submerged, the cerulean-colored water pleasurably warm. I bask in the sun's rays, and my eyes drift shut. I brush one of my hands through the rushes surrounding me, the grasses soft and lush. Uninvited, a dark cloud passes overhead, and I feel cool and damp in its shadow.

A light pulsing pressure below my waist awakened me and I sat up, wondering the time. Groggy, I opened my eyes to the silent darkness, realizing both my bedclothes and the bed linens beneath me were wringing wet. Sam lay snoring softly beside me, so I laid back down, not wishing to disturb him. After a couple of minutes, I abandoned this tactic as my discomfort increased, along with the beginning of a chill, lying on soaked sheets in a sodden nightgown.

"Sam?" I whispered. No response. I tried again, but this time, I spoke aloud, "Sam?"

He bolted upright, and leapt out of bed. "Maggie, what's going on? Is it time? Is the baby coming?" in a low, raspy voice.

"My waters have broken." I pointed at the bed. We had both seen enough animals birthed to know the child would come next. My back developed a spasm and, with a gasp, I lay back down.

Without delay, he leapt up, grabbed his pants off the chair and hopped around in an attempt to put them on. He lost his balance, tumbling backwards onto the bed, jolting me. I whimpered in response to this unexpected jarring.

"Calm down, husband, so as not to break your leg! I don't think it's urgent. The pain is mild."

Mumbling curses, he steadied himself and managed to pull up his pants, tuck in his nightshirt and button the fly. He grabbed his boots, ran toward the door and turned to declare, "Dear wife, I've no wish to place you *or my son* in any peril! Stay in bed and I'll be back with the midwife, directly."

I laughed, loving him for his over-concern. Under the circumstances, there was little chance I'd venture very far. *Well*, I told myself, *I'd certainly found a way to avoid canning all those vegetables I picked from the garden yesterday, hadn't I?*

On his way out, he turned to look at me, hesitating, before he walked back and gathered me in his arms to lay me on the dry side of the bed. I appreciated the gesture, but my nightgown remained soggy. With uncharacteristic tenderness, he kissed my forehead before disappearing down the stairs.

The front door closed. Despite the mild cramping, I stood and found my other nightdress on the wall peg. I peeled off the wet one and replaced it with the dry. My attitude improved, and even though the contractions felt uncomfortable, I could cope.

I laid back down and the back spasms subsided. Breathing steadily, I moved not a muscle, hoping to evade the distressing sensations as long as possible. Although my body was still, my mind could and did move, wandering from thought to thought. Sam's comment about "his son" replayed in my head. Convinced from the beginning that I carried a boy, I recognized how much happiness this belief brought him, so I had done little to dissuade him, which caused me some uneasiness in the event it was a little girl child. Oh, I prayed he was right and the baby *was* a boy, as I suspected he would blame me were it not.

I allowed a small seed of eagerness to take root. Startled by this new awareness, I began to muse about what it would be like to hold this tiny, helpless being in my arms for the first time. At last I relaxed and my final, lingering thought before nodding off was a fervent desire to avoid what lay ahead.

⁓

"Maggie?" I awakened to Sam's call from the bottom of the stairway. In the time he'd been gone, I had drifted nebulously between broken slumber and wakefulness. I had no sense of how long he had been away, although the room had begun to glow golden, proclaiming day was upon us.

"Sam, I'm here, right where you left me," I called back to him. He trudged up the stairs and into our bedroom, followed by the midwife, Sarah Kelly. Grandmotherly, round and jolly with a neat grey bun, loved by all, she beamed at me. "Well, now, lovey, how're you doing?" She spoke with an Irish lilt, signifying her arrival in this country by boat, not birth. She moved toward the bed and knelt beside me.

"I'm coping. It's mostly cramps, with some back spasms," I relayed in a normal tone.

"Sounds like you're holding your own, then. Let's take a look-see at what we've got going, shall we? Kind sir, why don't you wait a spell in the hallway, while the missus and I get better acquainted, if you catch my meaning." He backed out of the room without another word.

"Now, ma'am, I'm going to take a gander and see what's what." She patted my arm. "Judging from your look, I'd say you're having little pain, aye?"

Now safe in her competent hands, I nodded, at ease, at least for the moment.

"Dearie, we're gonna take a look. Hmm . . . hmm." The sensation distinctly uncomfortable, she manipulated my female opening. "Well, pet, you're about a finger wide, meaning you're getting started, but there's a ways to go."

I made a noise, vaguely sounding like, "Ooomph . . ."

"Mr. Jobsa, you're welcome to come back."

"How is she?"

"Aw sure, look it. She's coming along."

"How long?"

Her eyes twinkling, Sarah chuckled, "Well now, if I could answer that, people'd be making tracks to my door, now wouldn't they, hmm? My hunch is less than donkey's years, but I'm no eejit, so will make no promise." She glanced at my stricken face and relented somewhat, "If I *were* to make a wager, I'd say before the morrow."

Through the open window, I glimpsed brilliant ribbons of crimson and gold stretching across the far horizon, foretelling a new day. My intuition told me her pronouncement true and that before I witnessed another dawn, I would be a mother.

"Is there anything I might do?"

"Sam, Ella said she would come. Could you fetch her?"

"Of course, my dear. I'll attend to it ."

"Might there be some coffee for an auld midwife?"

He nodded, bowed and retreated downstairs, where we soon heard him clattering dishes, making us both cringe.

"Mayhaps I'd best check on him."

I gave her a half-smile and a nod, aware Sam was out of his element when it came to anything in the kitchen.

By midmorning, the room had warmed considerably and beads of sweat formed above my lip and on my brow. Though still irregular, the intensity of the contractions had increased.

"Let's get you up from the bed and take a little stroll."

Most content to lie in bed, it sounded like a ghastly idea to me. Without waiting for my answer, she confidently sat me up, before lifting my legs, rotating my feet to the ground and assisting me to stand.

"Ouch! That hurts."

"Well, lamb, the more we move you around, the faster we'll meet your young'un."

"All right, let's get on with it." I complied and she helped me take small steps around the room, which lasted far too long. I asked to lie down again.

Sarah massaged my belly with jasmine, lavender and cedarwood oils to calm and relax me. Her touch somehow soothed me and I felt less alone in my blossoming misery.

"Maggie, Maggie," Ella's familiar voice called from the stairway. "Hello, Sarah. Oh, dear sister, whatever might I do to help?" she asked as she rushed into the room.

"Oh, Ellie, I'm so happy to see you." She kneeled at the bedside, and I relaxed into her gentle hug. "Would you like to braid my hair?" A memory from when Mother had children told me braiding would keep my long hair from knotting and tangling during the coming hours.

Midday arrived and with it, the stifling summer heat. In a rather fruitless effort to cool me, Ella first fanned me and then sponged my skin with a wet cloth, while Sarah gave me sips of water. Sarah also offered me bits of food, although I had little appetite. "Angel, we need to keep your strength up, so please try to eat a bit," she urged me. "The real work is yet to come."

The day wore on and the tenor of my mood gradually changed. I no longer felt like conversing. Suddenly incapacitated by a cascading wave of pain which began under my ribcage and radiated downward, Sarah immediately noticed and declared active labor had begun.

"Ohhh . . ." Not too many minutes later, a fresh wave of cramping assailed me. I absorbed the discomfort, breathing as slowly as possible. I focused on my breath as a distraction from the misery and an overriding sense of a loss of control over my own body.

My contractions began arriving with increasing regularity, and so did visits from Sam. "Maggie, is there anything you would like? How are you feeling, darling?"

On some level I sensed him doing his best to be kind, but he had absolutely no notion of the agony of childbirth. Eventually I reached my threshold of patience and stopped responding to his persistent queries. When I didn't answer, he came closer to the bed. "Maggie? Can you speak?"

Stifling an urge to shout at him, I nodded my head.

"Why don't you answer me?"

I groaned. I found the struggle to form a sentence too much to bear.

"Sir, might it be best to make yourself scarce? The missus is having some misery, as you can see, getting this babby into the world."

He took the hint, no further encouragement necessary, and disappeared. I imagined he had gone to the barn to wait, beyond earshot of my intermittent screams.

<hr />

I howled to the heavens, as another surge of cramping racked my body. The contractions were now coming one on top of the other, with throbbing spasms unleashed in waves of pure anguish. I writhed in misery. *How did my dear mother do this twelve times?*

Sarah alternated between coaxing me to sip water, walking me about the room, palpating my stomach and checking my privates. All her interventions were interspersed with my own suffering, the pain more violent and relentless with each passing hour. On the edge of my awareness, I discerned Ella lighting the lamps in our room, as the sun began its descent toward the horizon. How much longer could I endure?

"Are you feeling a bit knackered?" Sarah touched my forehead gently.

"Uh, a bit, but I'll see this through."

"Aye, that you will, dearie."

I sobbed, as another spasm gripped my body, wrenching it like someone squeezing water from a wet rag. In the fading daylight, time ceased to exist. All that remained was me and my pain-ravaged body.

"Honey, you are getting closer."

At that instant, something changed. Even with my inexperience, I knew I *was* getting closer. I had an unbearable urge to push. "Sarah! Oh! Oh! Oh!"

They both descended upon me. Ella took my hand in hers, but I didn't feel like holding anyone's hand and yanked it away. In fact, I was irritated, having had about enough of this whole affair, when Sarah affirmed, "Aye! You're opened to a fist-size! Time to push, pet. The babby's head is beginning to crown. You can do this, Missus! Breathe! Breathe!"

From somewhere deep inside, I know not where, I discovered a hidden reserve of determination. I *could* do this.

"Grand!" The rolling pain subsided.

I *would* do this!

"Rest a moment, while we wait for another push. The pushing helps the babby to move, so you're doing first rate."

The agony of pushing, then waiting for the next spasm of torture went on for what seemed like a lifetime. I wailed. I screamed. I shrieked, "Go away! Everyone go away!" No one listened to me. How could I withstand this torment?

"Work with me, lovey. You have courage. Now come on, take a deep breath and push. Aye! That's the ticket, girl. You can do it."

With one last breathtaking push, my life forever changed. The chaos and fog of labor cleared and the world stood still as I beheld the sight and first wailing sounds of my newborn son. Sarah deftly lay the baby on my stomach, where he began to root around. Experienced and confident, my midwife clipped the cord and tied it off before holding him up for all to see.

In a voice brimming with awe, Ella marveled, "You did it Maggie! You did it!"

I smiled, no words necessary. I had participated in a miracle.

Sarah took a soft, clean wet cloth and wiped him off. Ella helped me pull off my nightgown, drenched in sweat. Sarah placed my baby skin-to-skin on my chest, covering the two of us with a blanket.

My irritation had vanished, replaced by overwhelming fatigue and the most intense sense of accomplishment. Twilight was upon us. My instinct and Sarah's wager had come to pass. She focused on delivering the afterbirth.

Oh, the unexpected agony! Even this wee little babe, bundled on my chest, sticky and tinged with my blood, couldn't provide enough distraction.

"Ohhh! Oh, my God!" I stifled a scream. Overcome by an intense, throbbing misery, I imagined my insides being ripped from me. Did it go on for minutes or hours? Ella took the baby from me, as I wailed and moaned, begging for the nightmare to end. I would never have another child. Never!

Sarah palpated my stomach, saying nothing.

"Let me die! Take away this wretched pain!"

"Maggie! Sarah, oh Sarah, *is* she dying? What's happening?" From some distant place, I sensed the naked terror in Ella's voice.

"Sometimes it takes a bit o'work," she nodded tensely at Ella. "Hang on, hang on, almost there. Aye, here it comes!" Even I heard the relief in her voice. "I tell you, for a short spell there, it put my heart crosswise, waiting for the afterbirth to come down."

The tissue now in Sarah's birthing bowl, the waves of pain at last began to subside. My son reclaimed my attention, and Ella placed him back on my chest. I placed one of my fingers near his perfect little hand and he grabbed it and held on for dear life. I started to relax and study this new little life thrust into the world. I bit my lip, guilty I had ever entertained thoughts of not wanting this sweet little being. What a shock it must have been for him to leave such a warm and dark water world and end up cold and naked in a roomful of excited, shrieking people! Sandwiched between the blanket Ella had laid over him and my bare chest, he felt toasty. No longer rooting around, he lay still, observing his surroundings. Even though he had a rather squashed face, I had to admit he was cute. Maybe once I got used to him, things would be all right, after all.

"Almost finished here, lovey, and then we need to get him to breast." Sarah proclaimed.

She completed whatever she was doing down below, wiped her hands on a clean rag and moved toward us.

"Time for your first meal, wee one. Sweetie, can you sit up?"

Ella came over and the two of them helped me into a reclining position propped against pillows.

Too exhausted to care, I think they could have done anything with me.

"So, dearie, you've seen your mam nurse babbies, aye?" she asked as she swaddled my baby boy into the soft little blanket.

I nodded my head, though no longer so confident I wanted to attempt this. It seemed like it might hurt. Sarah did not give me a choice in the matter.

"Let's tuck the little feller into the crook of your arm, like this," and she maneuvered his head into position, "and lift your bosom like so," she lifted my breast to demonstrate, "and tickle his lips with your teat. Aye! He's got it. Good, good."

"Ouch!" I gasped as he latched on and began to suckle with a strength I found surprising for such a diminutive little mite. Thankfully, the pins and needles sensation subsided after a minute and his suckling fell into a rhythmic pattern. A new wave of pain spread its tendrils throughout my lower body. I panicked, "Sarah, I'm still cramping! Is there more afterbirth to deliver?"

"Not to worry lovey, you're feelin' your female organs starting their backward journey to normal size. It may trouble you for a couple 'a days, but it's a good sign things inside are doing what they should."

A greedy baby, he suckled for a long time. What a relief to learn nursing didn't hurt nearly as much as I had feared.

"I'm famished!"

"Aye, well, that's good, darlin' and you should be, after what you've been through today. "Miss Ella, might you round up something for this new mama to eat now?" My sister nodded and left to find me nourishment in the kitchen downstairs.

Soon after, he popped off the breast like a cork from a bottle. I laughed aloud.

"Oh! You're a strong one, aren't you?" I asked him. With awe I realized he had been inside me a short time ago and now, here he was, finishing up his first meal, something which would never happen again.

"Offer him the other teat, now, would you? Here, Missus, I'll help you."

She helped me move him to the other side, where, with a little prodding, he latched, took several gentle suckles and pulled away, sound asleep.

Sarah smiled at the two of us, and I could tell she was proud of our accomplishment. "Here, honey, let me help you into your robe."

"Thank you, Sarah."

"Would you like me to brush out your hair?"

"Oh, yes! Thank you." Elated, yet weary, I accepted her helping hand. This woman was a jewel.

Ella soon returned with some bread, cheese, and my husband.

"My God, Maggie, you've done it!" Sam cried, rushing toward the bed, his face alight. "You've given me a son." Tears filled his eyes as he leaned down, his lips brushing the top of my head. "This is truly the best day of my life!" Quite overcome with joy, he seemed to be dancing without even moving his feet. "Might I hold him?"

"Oh, Sam, yes, of course!" I giggled at his eagerness.

"Come here, my son," as he lifted him from my arms. Sam stared at the sleeping baby, wondering aloud, "And what will your name be, little one? I hear that you roared like a lion when you entered our world." He contemplated our son for a long moment. "I think Leander will suit you."

We had discussed this name earlier. Leander meant "lion of a man," so I had to agree with his assessment. "Sam, Leander sounds perfect. And, his middle name will be Samuel."

Sam smiled at me. He was as happy as I had ever seen him.

12.

Macomb County, Michigan, Summer, 1891. "Oh, Sam, wait, I forgot the bouquet of flowers." In my haste to corral Leander and situate the two of us in the buggy, I had forgotten our gift.

"Tsk, where'd you leave it?"

"On the porch." I refused to let his sullen mood spoil my enthusiasm for our outing. A hot and muggy Saturday in July, I supposed he'd rather stay in the coolness of our barn, communing with Absalom about the cart races tomorrow, than attend a celebration with my family. My social life revolved around an eleven-month-old and occasional visits from my sisters, so I could not contain my excitement at leaving home for an entire afternoon. Sam had developed the mindset I shouldn't leave home without him these days. While unclear to me whether this edict resulted from anxiety about Leander's safety or something else, it was apparent my wings had been clipped. He would *not* entertain discussion on the subject.

Sam's annoyance palpable as he turned the buggy around, the horses retraced their steps up the lane. Despite the tension, I experienced a sense of satisfaction as we came around the corner, bringing our farmhouse back into view. The fresh coat of white paint gave our house an appearance of newness. The seeds I planted around the house had blossomed into multicolored flowers and added to its appeal. I realized that, while not the house of my dreams, I could still be happy living in it for the rest of my life.

The cut flowers were for Papa and Lizzie, who had invited us to join them to celebrate their second anniversary. I had combined wildflowers with purple irises, white daisies and a few early zinnias, along with several pink and white cosmos. I thanked my green thumb for this gorgeous bouquet.

Back on the roadway moments later, we headed to the Perry farm. My heart beat faster in anticipation of spending time with my first family. Even though the ride took less than half an hour, I found it a challenge to keep Leander from wriggling into his father's lap or moving in the opposite direction and falling off my side of the buggy. Sitting quietly was a concept he had yet to grasp.

Now within sight of my childhood home, I could see Eva, Edith and Janie on the front porch and I waved to them.

"Look, Leander, there are your aunties. Can you wave to them?" I helped him move his soft, dimpled little hand up and down.

"Bye, bye."

I chuckled, "No, sweetheart, you mean, hi."

His little forehead furrowed, he repeated in a serious voice, "Bye, bye!"

"Maggie, Maggie!" Eva shouted, "Guess what? I bet you can't guess what?"

Close on her heels as they ran up to our buggy, Edith poked her sister in the back.

"Eva, shush!"

I wondered what that was all about, but shrugged and handed Leander down into Edith's arms. My three sisters took turns holding and hugging and kissing him, while he giggled with delight. We all walked together up to the porch, while Sam tended to the buggy.

Gazing at my sisters, the air hummed with expectancy, making it evident something was afoot.

"We have a surprise for you," confided Eva, "but I mustn't tell."

Leander began to squirm in his Aunt Janie's arms, so she set him down, where he rolled onto his hands and knees and crawled over to the edge of the steps. *What a busy little one.* I stared at his downy blonde hair and chubby little legs.

Before I could intervene, his papa appeared, reached down and swung him up into his arms, lifting him over his head asking, "Hey, sonny, where are you headed?"

Leander chortled, and shrieked, "Dada! Dada!" *Sam was such a good papa. Maybe it was me who caused his moodiness.*

The rest of the family wouldn't arrive until they finished the workday around five, which meant we'd have some special time alone with Papa and Lizzie. We went inside and found the two of them sitting in the parlor on the settee near the window. I handed Lizzie the flowers. "Congratulations on your wedding anniversary!"

Lizzie's eyes lit up, "What a breathtaking bouquet, Maggie. Thank you."

"Thank you, darlin,' the flowers are splendid." Papa's eyes danced, alight with a mirth rarely seen in recent years. He hugged me effusively, and nodded at Sam before extending his hands to gather little Leander into his arms. "How's my wee Leander? Come to Grandada!" *My, Papa was in a good mood this afternoon!* My baby squealed with joy.

I hadn't seen Lizzie in some time, so it was with complete and utter astonishment I watched as she arose, handing the flowers to Janie, a smile on her face as she walked toward me. Like a bolt of lightning, I understood what "the surprise" must be. Lizzie had an unmistakable glow about her, and her waistline revealed an obvious thickening. My mouth dropped open with the realization she was with child, leaving me totally speechless.

Sam saved the day, by proclaiming, "Why, James and Lizzie, I see congratulations are in order!" He reached out to shake Papa's hand.

Several seconds passed before I recovered enough to find my voice, stammering, "Oh! Oh, well, congratulations, this *is* a surprise. But, a nice surprise," I quickly added.

"Why, thank you, Maggie. This is such a joyful turn of events for us. We held little hope, at our advanced ages, of being so blessed, but there you have it. We have more than an anniversary to celebrate today. We expect Christmas joy to come early this year," Papa turned with a flourish and a broad smile, grasping Lizzie's shoulder, pulling her to him. She looked toward him, radiating an undeniable affection. Our family spent a pleasant afternoon together, swapping stories and sharing laughs, with Leander, of course, the center of attention. When it was time to depart, I wished our little family might stay longer and soak up more of Papa and Lizzie's happiness.

Leander lay relaxed across my lap as I nursed him on the way home. I loved the closeness, and early on, I'd found this to be the best way to keep him calm and happy, especially at this time of the evening. Dusk settled upon us, bringing a comfortable tranquility to the ride. Otis, our sweet-tempered Morgan bay, pulled the buggy smartly down the dirt road toward home. Hues of salmon and saffron suffused the indigo of the night sky, framing the twilight-darkened branches of the trees we passed. The sounds of evening swelled into a jubilant chorus of chirping crickets and croaking frogs along the riverbank, with intermittent soft coos of the mourning doves and the occasional trill of a screech owl. My breath caught in my throat; all was right with the world.

Absorbing the news of Lizzie and Papa's upcoming arrival, I concluded that it reflected the resounding success of their marriage. She would celebrate forty years in November, and Papa, already fifty-six, still exuded the energy of a much younger man. He would certainly need it a few months from now. Goodness! It occurred to me Leander would be older than his new aunt or uncle.

"Sam, were you shocked by Papa and Lizzie's news?"

"Hadn't thought much about it."

The topic fizzled. *How dissimilar the thinking of men and women.*

❧

Lucy and Ella had borrowed Louis' buggy and driven out to our farm for a visit on this late-summer afternoon. Amidst the resonant hum of the cicadas and oppressively thick air, we sat on the porch snapping beans from my garden. It would be a busy day tomorrow canning vegetables for the winter season. This task evoked memories of a year ago, when Leander was born. How swiftly the time had passed. I gazed at my adorable child, wearing but a diaper, exploring his world. He had pulled himself to a standing position, using the stairs for support, attempting to work his way along the edge of the house, determined in his efforts to walk. How he had grown and changed in the past year! He was not alone, and I considered how much my views of life had expanded, even as I found myself more tethered to a daily routine. My experiences were immeasurably broadened by this captivating child. How childish I had been! To think I had worried I wouldn't be able to love him. How easy it had been to lay to rest all my fears and insecurities. My heart skipped a beat whenever he reached out his arms for me and I sensed the depth and breadth of his love. Leander's love was pure and without conditions, and I wished my relationship with his father could be that simple and sweet.

My attention returned to my sisters when Ella remarked in a neutral-sounding voice, "Lucy, tell Maggie your news."

"What news?"

"She's begun corresponding with someone."

"Really? Who?" My interested piqued, I opened my eyes wider. Leander babbled, endeavoring to join our conversation. We all turned to him and smiled.

"Well, if you must know, I have met someone."

". . . And?" I prodded for more details.

"His name is William Wolff and he's a long-time friend and former classmate of John Henry's. He was born in Detroit, but grew up here in Mt. Clemens." I digested this information, searching my memory, but finding no recollection of him. This came as no surprise, considering our brother was fourteen years my senior.

"He's lived in Montana for almost a decade."

"Montana? My goodness, what a long way from here! It sounds ever so exotic to say you are corresponding with someone from

Montana! How did you meet a man from Montana? Did John Henry introduce you?" It puzzled me why he would introduce her, and not Ella, to this eligible bachelor.

"Well, while William was here visiting family, he ran into our brother at the mercantile and they thought it would be good fun to renew their acquaintance. Abi didn't feel up to hosting a party, so Louis and Mayme offered. They also invited Ella and me."

Louis had moved home from Detroit to set up shop as a barber and married Mayme this October past. She loved to entertain.

"William sat across from me at the gathering and I now wonder if it might have been a set-up by my devious brother!" Truth be told, I later found out it *had* been a set-up by John Henry, but it had been Ella, after all, that he'd had in mind for this thirty-five-year-old bachelor. Cupid's arrow must have hit the wrong target.

Leander had by now plopped down on the ground next to some flowers near the house, busily examining the brown earth with his fingers. I leaned over, showing him how to move the dirt around with a spoon. He grinned at me, saying, "Mama, mine!" as he reached his hand out for it, eager to scoop on his own. Already a little general with a mind of his own. I smiled, handing it to him.

I turned my attention back to Lucy. "What occupation took him to Montana? Is he tall, dark and handsome?" I grinned, amused at my own levity.

"I'd say he's of medium build, with gorgeous coffee-colored eyes, a marvelous moustache and lots of dark hair. He's got an obvious intellect, which kept me on my toes all evening."

"He's quite handsome," interjected Ella.

"William's a prominent sheep rancher in eastern Montana," Lucy continued. "He delayed his return train ticket last week to spend more time with me! In that time, we've discovered an undeniable mutual attraction to each other. We've decided to begin a correspondence to become better acquainted through the written word."

"There's more," Ella said.

"And . . . ?" Good gracious, my sister was not forthcoming.

Perhaps Ella couldn't tolerate the suspense one moment longer either, as she blurted, "They're officially courting!"

"Oh, Lucy, congratulations! What splendid news."

Her eyes shone. "He is somewhat older than I, and more experienced in matters of the heart. I suspect I'm not his first romance, but I do expect to be his last," she said, in typical Lucy-like fashion.

"Does that mean you'll move to Montana?"

"We are talking about marriage next year, if the courtship proceeds as we imagine. He'll return to Michigan for me and, yes, I *will* be moving. I would miss you both dreadfully, but I've little apprehension, as I anticipate many exciting western adventures. I think it's the opportunity I've been waiting for, these twenty-four years."

I'm positive she was genuinely happy for our sister, yet one look at Ella's downcast eyes revealed to me her lack of enthusiasm for this eventuality.

"Ella, you *will* come by train to visit me in Montana. I won't have it any other way!" Lucy had also noticed our sister's melancholy.

I wondered if Lucy would ever outgrow her bossiness.

13.

Sugarbush Road, December, 1891. While Leander took an afternoon nap upstairs, I positioned myself close to the warmth of the fireplace, using the time to finish up a sewing project for the upcoming addition to the Perry household. With Christmas but a couple of weeks away, they expected the baby any time. Once I adjusted to the prospect of a new half-brother or sister, I felt inspired to sew the little one some new clothes as a welcome present.

"Mama, Mama!" I set aside my sewing and dashed up the stairs. Leander began bawling in earnest the moment he laid eyes on me. He usually awakened smiling, his disposition sunny, so this was unusual.

"What's the trouble, little man? Are you unwell?" Flushed with fever, his cheeks were a bright pink. He patted my breast and whimpered, so I sat down in the rocking chair and offered it to him. He latched and suckled briefly, before pulling off, turning away and screeching, as if in dire pain. *What could be wrong?* Milk dripping everywhere, I continued my attempts to feed him, but to no avail. Perhaps he had a sore throat, making sucking painful. I recalled something Mother had done with my little sisters when they'd had sore throats.

"Let's go downstairs and wet a cloth with my milk for you to suck on instead. You'll find that easier to suckle, sweetheart."

I carried him into the kitchen, sitting him on a chair. I squeezed out milk from my breast onto a clean cloth, while Leander watched in fascination. I offered this to him and he greedily began to suck, along with his whimpering. I was relieved to hear him swallow. He had been such a healthy child, I'd had little experience with illness.

"Is Mommy's little love feeling poorly? Let's go sit together and Mama will tell you a story."

Sam found us still sitting in the rocker when he came in from his afternoon chores. Not seeing any supper preparations underway, he cocked his head, giving me a quizzical look.

"Sam, something's wrong with Leander. He has a fever and won't take any nourishment."

He walked over to where we were sitting and peered into his son's reddened face. "Sonny, are you ailing?"

"He's burning up with fever. Perhaps we could try a sponge bath." This was another remedy I had learned from Mother.

"Good plan, Maggie. I'll warm some water."

We sponged him with the tepid water, and it seemed to help, both with the fever and soothing him.

"Let me hold him for a bit, while you get supper on the table," Sam suggested, wrapping our son in a towel, and lifting him into his arms.

We took turns holding and rocking Leander all evening, as it seemed to be all that calmed him. He was completely uninterested in nursing, and my breasts felt uncomfortably full. I hand massaged them to remove enough milk to relieve the pressure, and offered this to him in a cup. He took a few small sips before turning away, only to begin crying anew.

<hr/>

Rose and violet hues crept across the sky, heralding sunrise. An angry red sun peeped over the horizon, reflecting off the white landscape of winter. A sleepless night sitting in the rocking chair cradling my son had, at last, ended. Exhausted, I felt a mounting sense of panic as, time after time, his attempts to nurse had proven futile, leaving him fussing in my arms.

I checked his diaper, which was mostly dry. I did see a red rash in the folds of skin where the hip met his leg. I undressed him to investigate and found more of the tiny bumps on his chest, neck, and armpits. Oddly for December in Michigan, he appeared sunburned. Sam sat in bed watching me.

"Sam, look at this rash. And, he's still feverish. Perhaps we should fetch Dr. Brockton?" I posed it more as a question than a demand, hoping for a positive response from my husband. He didn't like me to issue orders.

Sam took a long look at Leander and agreed with me. He dressed in haste and was on his way. Fretting, I hoped he found the doctor home and not off on other business. I continued to rock my darling boy, singing to him as he calmed. "Poor little one. You feel miserable, don't you?"

⌇

"Maggie . . . Sam. Leander appears to have a case of scarlet fever," Dr. Brockton explained, after he had done his exam. "I've been seeing it all around the county over the last few weeks."

"How'd he get it, doc?" Sam asked.

"Hard to say, but he was somehow exposed. Maybe someone sneezed or coughed and he happened to be the recipient of these nasty germs. Keep him hydrated and give him warm sponge baths in hopes of keeping the fever under control."

"How can we keep him hydrated," I asked in irritation, "when he won't nurse or drink from a cup? He barely sucks milk from a wet cloth! There must be something else we can do for him?" Frantic, my voice sounded shrill.

"Maggie, there really isn't anything else we can do, but watch and wait. He needs to be isolated, to keep the germs from passing, so I'm going to have to quarantine your house. His tongue already has the telltale white furry coating and in a couple of days will probably start to appear a strawberry red color, and his throat may develop yellowish specks of pus. This is the normal course of the disease. All we can do is wait it out. I should mention vomiting is common."

"What would he vomit, if he can't even eat or drink?"

"Do your best, dear. Keep offering sustenance and continue with the sponge baths. You're already doing all we know how to do."

A terrible thought popped into my head. "Doctor, he won't die, will he?"

His voice grave, Dr. Brockton spoke carefully. "Maggie, I'd be telling an untruth if I said positively 'no.' This disease reacts differently with each person. Since you have still been feeding him your milk, I would say his chances for recovery are quite good, but it would be unethical for me to promise this."

"He can't die. He won't die!" I shouted, suddenly paralyzed with fear.

Sam came over and put his arm around me, as the doctor wrapped Leander in a blanket and handed him to me. I leaned back against Sam, feeling faint, and he helped me to sit down in the rocking chair, where I wept as I rocked my sweet child.

"I'll see you out, Doc."

"As I mentioned, I'll be putting a quarantine sign on your door. I'll check in with you tomorrow, first thing. Please come for me if anything changes."

Morning turned to afternoon, which turned to evening. I did not dress or leave our bedroom. Sam brought me foodstuff intermittently, saying, "Maggie, you must eat a little something to maintain your strength and not fall ill yourself."

I had no appetite, but managed to chew and swallow a few tasteless bites. Convincing Leander to drink something became my sole concern. I had squeezed milk out of my breasts every few hours and he had suckled, albeit weakly, on the milk-soaked cloth, but had vomited more than it appeared he had swallowed. Wrapped in a cloak of dread, I asked myself how this could be happening. I couldn't think beyond the next minute. My baby was alive. I focused on that.

Later, Sam found me asleep in the rocking chair with Leander balanced precariously on my lap. He helped me to stand and maneuvered the two of us toward the bed, where I collapsed, already almost back to sleep. I sensed rather than watched him lay Leander beside me, covering us both with a quilt, before sitting down to keep vigil and leaving only to bring me food and drink or to tend to our livestock. He sat in the corner, rocking back and forth, the creaking of the chair oddly comforting.

I slept for several hours, which gave me strength to face another excruciatingly long night. Leander's restless slumber was interspersed with tearless crying. Terrified, there was naught I could do but hold him and pray. *Oh, God, let him live. I beg you, please, God, let him live.*

Dr. Brockton arrived mid-morning to examine our son. His countenance was grim. "Sorry, folks, but it was an all-nighter for me too, attending a difficult birth," he apologized. "Leander is holding his own, despite the fact he still appears dehydrated. Please continue to endeavor to get fluids into him. That's of the utmost importance."

We somehow endured another day and he slept better this third night, which encouraged me. Perhaps God had heard my prayers. Toward morning, my dear child even tried to nurse, but without much success, maybe because of weakness from a continued lack of nourishment. He did take a few sips of my milk from a cup and didn't vomit, which I found heartening.

We struggled day by day, each much the same as the last. Sometimes Leander would drink a little and not vomit, but just as likely, he'd spit up the little he had drunk. The doctor didn't come by for the next two days, sending word he had taken ill from an inflammation of the lung. We were thankful his illness was not scarlet fever. Nevertheless, his absence all but pushed me over the edge of sanity. By the fifth day, my composure had dissolved. My baby had shown little improvement in his ability to take in fluids. His diapers remained almost dry, with streaks of orange. Even my untrained eye could tell he had lost weight.

Over the past couple of days, terrible thoughts had infected my own mind, notions God had decided to punish Sam and me for conceiving this beautiful child out of wedlock. Worse, maybe it was my penance for questioning whether I even wanted a child. This might be all my fault. *Oh, God, please forgive me for my horrid thoughts and let my precious baby be well. God, I beg you, if you must, take me instead, but let Leander live.* My prayers were ceaseless, and never before or since would I ever feel such desolation as I did that unending week. Leander no longer whimpered, he mewed like a newborn kitten. His suckle had grown so weak, all I could do was dribble milk into his mouth, one drop at a time. Helpless, my angelic, golden-haired child faded before me. Prayers were reduced to rocking and sobbing. I beseeched God to spare him, as I held his dear little self close to my heart.

The sixth day, a Sunday, the Lord's day, dawned clear and cold, a mere ten days before Christmas. Moments after sunrise, Sam found the two of us rocking together, back and forth in an uneasy rhythm. He looked at us and knew. He knew what I didn't yet perceive. He sat down wearily on our bed, covered his face with his hands and began to weep.

Dr. Brockton arrived around midday. When no one answered his knock, he let himself in and came upstairs to find me still in the chair rocking my baby, while Sam sat on the bed, unseeing, both of us inert.

The doctor walked over and reached for my dear child. Not comprehending, I did nothing more than stare at him as he extended his arms for Leander.

With reluctance, I offered my angel to him, and he carried him over to our bed to unwrap the blanket. Leander remained still and so quiet. No whimpers. No cries. Only silence. Dr. Brockton rewrapped him and handed him back to me. I continued to rock.

"Sam," said the doctor, the first word spoken in this room, in several hours. No response. "Sam!" he repeated, shaking Sam by the shoulders. "Sam! Look at me!" Sam gazed up at him with hollow eyes. "You must be the strong one. Pull yourself together. Your wife needs you now more than she ever has needed anyone. You need to go to her."

Sam appeared bewildered.

"Now!" the doctor said firmly. Sam stood docilely and walked toward me. He reached out his hand to help me up. I stood and handed our sweet boy to him, then collapsed in a heap. An intense keening crescendoed from somewhere deep within me, the sound of a wounded animal suffering overwhelming anguish.

I have little, if any, recollection of what happened next. Before he left to inform the undertaker, Dr. Brockton gave me a sedative and later Ella told me I slept off and on for nearly twenty hours, awakening just long enough to sip water, offered by one of my sisters, who took turns sitting with me. I have no memory of how they came to be there, but perhaps Sam had called upon them. When consciousness returned, it was with the realization that my milk had shriveled and my heart had shattered.

Not having the willpower to venture from my bed, I learned from one of my sisters Sam had retreated to his parent's home after the undertaker arrived. He had left instructions for the undertaker to take Leander's body. Somehow he understood I would not be able to bear the sight of our child's tiny body lying in a box inside our home. Three days passed before I saw my husband again, an indescribable act of abandonment.

Arrangements were hastily made with the help of Sam's father, Henry, and the family service was set for December 16 at our house. I had no strength to attend a church funeral, and would have preferred staying in my bed, but the doctor stressed the importance of closure for the health of my mind.

On this most awful of Wednesday afternoons, Ella was helping me to dress in the same mourning clothes I had worn when Mother died. "Maggie, I need to tell you something before we go downstairs."

With effort, I managed to look at her unsmiling face.

"What I must tell you is difficult and unfair." She hesitated and I could do no more than furrow my brow, continuing to stare at her with incurious eyes. Her voice compassionate, the words all came out in a rush, "Lizzie delivered a baby girl in the wee hours of yesterday morning, so I'm uncertain whether or not Papa will be here this afternoon. If he isn't here, I wanted you to understand why."

I nodded my head slowly, remembering a similar numbness in the aftermath of Mother's death four years ago. This felt worse, much worse.

"Maggie, speak to me. Say something," my sister pleaded.

I looked at her. I had nothing to say. Life as I understood it had ended. My child was dead and my husband had abandoned me. God had abandoned me and in some way I understood it to be my fault. I wanted to die, too. I had no reason to continue living.

"Take my arm and stay close as we descend the steps." Ella placed my hand in the crook of her arm and, feeling weak, I leaned in to her as we made our way downstairs and into the front room. Lucy met us on the stair landing and took my other hand.

There stood Papa, Sam and his parents, and others of my kin. I no longer recall who, except for Ella and Lucy, one on either side. The ordeal may have lasted ten minutes or an hour; time moved in a different way for me during those moments. Like the survivor of a shipwreck, I somehow endured the waves of grief besieging my soul.

Neither Sam nor I could face the task, so Henry also selected and purchased Leander's coffin. This little wooden box, bearing his remains, would be placed in cold storage until the ground thawed in the spring, at which time we could have the graveside burial service. I believed this proof that my agony would never cease.

Now that the funeral was behind us, Sam came home, but like me, he was a changed person. We avoided eye contact, our conversations brief and perfunctory. I found this a relief, as every time I looked at him, I began to weep anew. Desolate, we somehow continued to stumble through life, but acted as strangers cast together in an unending sea of wretchedness, suffering a bereavement overflowing with anguish. It is said traumatic events can either bring a couple closer together or drive a wedge between them. In our case, it was the latter.

14.

Winter, 1892. The dark night of my soul. I had no passion for life and scarcely moved from my bed. I felt dead inside, as dead as the leafless trees outside my bedroom window. The ache in my heart was unremitting and intensified by Sam's behavior. He spent much of his time away from our house and I had no inkling where, but suspected he was somewhere drinking liquor, in his own search for solace. It was near midnight when Sam first came back to me. He'd been sleeping downstairs, but on this night he joined me in our bed, seeking the comfort of touch. We were united in our mutual anguish, falling asleep together for the first time since Leander had taken ill. Sometime towards sunrise, he awakened me, caressing me from my slumber. In a kind of languid, dreamlike state of mind, I allowed him to enter me, and fill me with his seed. Afterwards, as I drifted off, some part of my brain questioned if the experience had been real or imagined. When I woke up again, there was no sign of him.

With Sam absent, and overwhelmed by loneliness, I behaved as an invalid, remaining in my bed. Lucy and Ella were bound to return to their jobs and Janie had no means to travel to our farm. Even if she had, Lizzie needed her at home to help with her newborn since both Edith and Eva attended school. And it *is* the women whom we depend upon to sustain us through tragedy, is it not?

Within a few days, Sam's mother, Gertrude, recognized my situation and became my guiding light, as she attempted to lead me from the brink of despair. She faithfully visited several times a week in hopes of raising my spirits and redeeming my existence, bringing me nourishment for both body and soul. Who can fathom what might have happened to me, if not for the many hours she willingly spent at my bedside, reading to me from *Science and Health,* her Christian Scientist guide.

Over the next weeks, I eagerly anticipated her visits, hungry for the sustenance provided by her spoken words and the wisdom of that guide book. Those words offered me hope, when nothing else could.

From these teachings, I learned about the evilness of the material world in which we lived. I learned sickness and death were illusions; that reality was purely mental, and it was *all* good. I began studying in earnest to become a true Christian Scientist. I believed the tenets offered a preventative for ill health, as well as accidents and life's misfortunes, and that if I reached the proper level of consciousness, these woes would cease to exist. It helped me come to terms with my son's death, knowing I need not suffer such despair again. Gertrude taught me that our dear Leander, in his pure and unfettered innocence, would never suffer from sin or the pain and disappointment of life on this earth.

This wisdom was especially comforting during the long and lonely nights, when I awakened after such vivid dreams of him. I could almost sense his presence near me.

One evening as I sat in my chair beside the fireplace reading, with a blanket over my lap, the front door flew open. Sam stormed in, shouting angrily in a drunken tirade.

"There's no arguing, it's your fault! He wouldn't have died if you'd taken better care of him!" He leaned down and picked up a small log from the grate on our hearth, heaving it at the wall. I gathered into myself with a fervent wish to simply disappear, as I crouched low, drawing my knees up under my chin and peering downward.

My heart lurched, yet I attempted to stay calm, realizing this presented an opportunity to employ the new skills Gertrude had taught me. What I had earlier taken for her meekness was actually equanimity achieved through religious beliefs. It was the secret to her ability to deal so serenely with Henry's drinking all these years. I would endeavor to apply the same skills to create my own harmonious household.

I raised my head courageously, but remained silent. For some reason, this action further infuriated him. "Don't look at me like that! It's not *my* doing. If you'd been a better mother, I would still have a son."

I looked back down and bit my tongue to keep from lashing out, then replied in a calm voice, "Sam, I was the best mother I knew how to be. I loved Leander more than life itself. I'd have given my life for him."

"Hah!" This sarcastic reply stung. "Your negligence in keeping him safe brought this tragedy into our lives. I doubt I can *ever* forgive you." He started to take a swing at me, but caught himself and instead stomped back outside, leaving a cold blast of frigid air in his wake.

Trembling, I stood and shut the door, barely holding myself together. He had almost struck me! I bolted up the stairs and collapsed onto our bed. Something in me broke open and my grief exploded with great, heaving sobs and cries, shaking me to the core of my being.

Sam spoke the truth. I had been deluding myself with Gertrude's teachings. If Leander's death had been an illusion, as Gertrude taught, why did I feel such a burden of guilt? No one could deny I had committed an unforgivable sin with Sam, before our marriage. To make matters worse, I had questioned whether I wanted or could ever love my child. How could I not be culpable?

Even admitting this didn't make it easier to accept God's punishment. Religion confused me. How could I ever reach a state of consciousness where all reality resided in my brain and it was all good? It seemed hopeless.

Ultimately, I fell into a dreamless slumber, waking up shivering sometime in the night. I crawled under the covers, still dressed, realizing the emptiness of my soul had filled me with an overpowering sense of self-loathing. No, that wasn't altogether true. I also recognized a tiny, but growing thread of resentment and anger directed toward my husband for his contemptible behavior in the time since our loss.

I stood gazing out the kitchen window the next morning, waiting for the coffee to brew, when an unexpected queasiness overcame me and I rushed out on the front porch in time to retch. Dry heaves left me weak. The instantaneous memory of a previous experience startled me and my head snapped up with shock. *No! I couldn't possibly be with child. Why, Sam and I hadn't even been sleeping in the same bed!* I walked slowly back into the house, uncertain how I felt about this new circumstance. I had assumed my lack of a monthly to be anxiety-induced. Not this! Then I remembered the night Sam had come into our bed. It had been no dream. My mind rushed in all directions as I stoked the fire, wondering where my husband might be.

I found out moments later, when he barged into the house, wrapped in several wool blankets.

"Slept in the barn," he mumbled, as he strode over to the kitchen sink and pumped out some cold water to splash on his face. No words passed between us as Sam poured a cup of coffee and ventured over to stand near me. I held my ground. His hair disheveled and his clothing wrinkled, he looked as though he'd not slept a wink. After a few moments, his weary eyes met mine. "Maggie, I humbly regret my actions this evening past. There was no calling for such shameful conduct. Please, dearest, can you ever forgive me?" Sadness clouded his countenance. He threw aside the blankets and began to pace. My already squeamish stomach tied itself into knots.

"I haven't the slightest idea what came over me, but I blame it on the whiskey. How might I make it up to you? How about I take you into town today to see your sisters? Would that make you feel better?" He stopped before me and smiled a most disarming smile.

Believing it my Christian duty to turn the other cheek, I relented and reached out to him. Still, for now, my news would remain hidden close to my heart.

⁓

The winter wore on, and it became ever more difficult for me to hide the changes beginning to take place in my body. Somehow, I managed to keep my secret deeply buried. Sam's repeated absences made it easier, but I knew it was simply a matter of time before he'd notice the telltale signs.

Even with this new life growing inside me, Leander preoccupied my thoughts. Everything I saw evoked memories of my lost child. My sisters had removed his little cot, clothes and baby toys, but my eyes still imagined him lying beside me in our bed. I imagined gathering him into my arms again, and nursing in the rocking chair. There he was, holding a spoon for the first time, blowing kisses to me, taking his first steps, or sitting in the little tub next to the fireplace having a bath. I beheld his sunny smile, his wispy blonde hair and his bright blue eyes.

I found it impossible to survive a day without his ghost arising vividly before me. The child within me did not seem real, but Leander was still very much a presence in my life. No. That was wrong, the child within me was real and Leander no longer was! Sometimes I lacked the ability to discern what was true and what was not.

Sam and I had forged an uneasy truce. Exercising caution, I was careful not to provoke his temper. I aspired to be more like Gertrude, and learned I was, indeed, quite adept at burying my emotions.

Gertrude and I were sitting at the dining table having a cup of tea, as she finished up our lesson. I had gotten up and dressed today, suspecting she might choose this balmy February day to come calling. Gertrude, outfitted in a black and white wool shepherd checked skirt with a dark bodice, was a trifle taller than myself and slender, with silky blonde hair and light blue eyes. Her fragile appearance belied the quiet fortitude I had earlier recognized, and wanted to emulate.

"And, so, dear Maggie, as Christian Scientists, we do not believe there is either a heaven or a hell. Remember, death is merely a state of mind in man's immortal and eternal life." She smiled. "Leander has simply moved on to the next stage."

At times I struggled, but felt it disrespectful to question the teachings. After all, those explanations had led me out of the dark well into which I slipped after Leander's passing. I was committed to gaining a better understanding of Christian Science, along with coming to terms with this new concept of eternal life.

Gertrude changed the subject, saying "By the way, I was at the mercantile this morning and spoke to Ella." My mother-in-law often brought me news and sometimes a letter when she visited.

"Oh! How is she?" Upon hearing Ella's name, my heart fluttered and I realized how much I missed my sister. I interpreted this as a small step in the direction of rejoining life.

"She appeared to be in fine spirits. She was elated to share the news Mr. William Wallace Wolff arrived back in Mt. Clemens yesterday to claim your sister Lucy's hand in marriage."

"Oh, my gracious. So, it will happen, after all."

"She asked me to let you know and ask if you might feel up to meeting him, should the three of them visit you sometime in the next few days."

I hesitated. Longing to see my sisters, my reticence now had as much to do with my condition as my low mood, not to mention Sam's unpredictability.

"Did she say when the wedding ceremony would occur?"

"Yes, I believe it will be sometime before the beginning of March. Ella indicated they are planning to leave soon afterward for Montana."

"Why, that's in less than two weeks!" This information nudged me and I gave myself permission to feel enthusiasm. "Yes, I would be pleased to have them come calling, if you'd be so kind as to pass it along. Thank you, Gertrude!" It might be my lone opportunity to meet and spend time with my sister and her fiancé. Somehow I would find a way to appear healthy and whole.

My frequently queasy stomach was calm, and I privately celebrated that I had still been able to keep my secret safe. In my quest to accept the reality of being with child again, I wavered between fear and guarded hopefulness. I couldn't imagine ever giving my heart so completely to another human being. It was much too dangerous. Yet, while another baby would in no way replace Leander, there were moments when the thought of it took my mind off the everlasting sorrow harbored in my soul. I could almost, just almost, imagine the feel of a little one in my arms again.

The warmth radiating from our fireplace was substantial, yet I shivered, not from the winter chill, but from the thrill of anticipation. My sisters and Mr. William Wolff would be arriving at any moment! Sam had kindly built up the fire for me and left extra wood in the grate on the hearth, before taking his leave for an appointment in town.

I heard a jingling sound and caught sight of the buggy approaching. We'd had a mid-winter thaw the past week, so most of our snow had melted and the countryside appeared brown and dreary. My heart swelled with gladness that my cheerful mood had nothing in common with the depressing scenery.

"Welcome, welcome!" I called from the porch. I watched as William assisted Ella, dressed in grey winter wool, out of the buggy. Next was Lucy, adorned in a rich maroon-colored hooded cloak with what I guessed might be a white-rabbit fur collar and matching muffler. Her togs were almost certainly a gift from her betrothed. He was taller than I expected, with broad shoulders and as Lucy had described, a bushy moustache. I perceived a kindliness in his well-weathered face.

"Oh, Maggie, how marvelous to see you. I'm glad you have a chance to meet William." She turned toward him and smiled, her green eyes sparkling.

"So pleased to meet you," I said, extending my hand.

"Likewise," he nodded. "I've heard a great deal about you."

I narrowed my eyes, wondering if this was good or bad, coming from Lucy, but decided by his smile it was good, and returned his nod.

Ella gave me a long and loving hug. "I'm so happy to behold a smile upon your face again, dear sister," she said, her voice somber.

"Won't you come in?" We went inside, where in a flurry, everyone removed their cloaks, hats and gloves.

"Where's Sam?" asked Lucy.

"Um, well, I'm not entirely certain, but he had some sort of appointment in town." Given his unpredictable nature, kind one moment and fiery the next, I was privately relieved that Sam would not be here to stir up any kerfuffle.

We gathered around our dining table for coffee and tea. I'd had enough pluck this morning to make a pie with some canned cherries given to me last fall by Lizzie. Everyone remarked how delicious the pastry tasted, which left me feeling satisfied and content, emotions I had not experienced in quite some time.

We spoke of many things that afternoon. William radiated confidence, was well spoken, and exuded a quiet charm. While I believed he and Ella might have gotten on well enough, it didn't take long to realize why he'd been attracted to Lucy. A patient and steady person, he was perfectly content to let Lucy do the talking, enthralled by her vivaciousness and sharp wit. Observing the intensity of his vibrant brown eyes gazing at her, I could tell he worshipped her. A shadow of doubt crossed my mind as I contemplated whether my sister might grow weary of such an earnest man. I shook off my apprehension, once again engrossed in our conversation about the upcoming wedding and the journey to Montana.

"William has told me so much about his ranch. I can't wait to see it. He raises sheep and horses, hens and hogs."

"Hmm. Like the Perry farm," I commented drolly.

Lucy rolled her eyes at me. "Well, of course, it's like the Perry farm. But, it's in *Montana*, sister, where everything is bigger and better. William has told me that on a clear day, we'll even be able to gaze upon mountains from his front porch. There are deer, moose, elk and even bison wandering across his land. It will be spectacular!"

William chuckled at Lucy's enthusiasm. "Lucy, *you* are an extraordinary woman. I can't believe my luck in finding you."

My sister's face turned red. Had his unbridled ardor embarrassed her?

The visit was a rousing success and it was with a certain sadness that I bid them all farewell. Ella and I would both miss our spirited sister, and Ella appeared especially despondent. She would be losing not just her sister, but her best friend and housemate, all at once.

We hugged and said our goodbyes. I stood on the front porch, waving, until the buggy disappeared from sight, thankful that Sam hadn't been around to cause any fuss.

A family affair, we gathered for Lucy and William's wedding at the Presbyterian Church, followed by a celebratory dinner at John Henry's home. Another week passed and they had departed yesterday, on their way to start a new life together in Montana.

Gertrude and I sat at my dining table, visiting. "Maggie, your mood seems rather low today. I wonder if you'd like me to take you into Mt. Clemens tomorrow or the next day, to visit Ella?"

"Oh, Gertrude, that would cheer me so!" She was a perceptive woman, and recognized that fresh air and a change of scenery would do me a world of good.

We decided she would collect me the day after tomorrow, as long as the weather held, and we would make an afternoon of it.

We continued to chat, as I worked up courage to ask something which had been of constant concern. "Gertrude, do you have any notion where Samuel's off to each day? He's seldom home."

"Not exactly, Maggie." She cleared her throat and sighed, "He does seem to spend a considerable amount of time with Henry these days. I believe they're working on some sort of business involving the buying and selling of thoroughbred horses. Perhaps you might ask him about it, child?"

"Yes, Gertrude, I should ask him, shouldn't I?" Inevitably, I needed to have a conversation with my husband, and soon, on more than one topic.

"I think we all deal with loss in different ways and I'd encourage you to be patient and give it some time. Sam can be impulsive and a little temperamental, so my advice is to wait it out. He's a lot like his father."

Well, I supposed this advice about the son from the mother was advice best heeded. If I could just make peace with Sam's inner nature.

"Sam, might we talk?" Still sitting at the table, we had just finished another silent supper.

"What's on your mind?" His eyes narrowed, looking at me over the rim of his coffee cup.

Pondering what might be the safest approach, the words in my mouth turned to ash. I sat riveted to my chair, frightened and hesitant.

Sam made another attempt, "Maggie? What are you thinking about?"

These were the first personal questions I could recall in such a long time, offering a glimpse of the man I remembered and loved. I found a shred of courage. "Sam, I have many matters on my mind and find I'm uncertain where to begin." Would it be better to start by asking where he spent all his time, or finding out how he was coping with Leander's death, or by telling him about the baby? Perhaps it was best to start with good news.

I took a deep breath. "Sam. We'll be having another child, come October."

He stared at me, incredulous. "What? What do you mean *we'll* be having a child? How could that be, when we haven't slept together in months?" His eyes flashed darkly.

"You do recollect that night when you came to me in our bed, yes?"

He backed down. "Oh. Yes, I suppose you're right. I guess it *is* possible."

Had he thought to accuse me of infidelity? "Of course it's possible!" I shot back, my own dander raised. Oh, how I wanted to ask by what means it could be any other way, but chose not to offer any credence to what I could plainly divine he'd been thinking.

His manner relaxed and his mood did a turnaround. "Maggie, what spectacular news!" He stood and walked over to where I was seated, lifted me out of the chair and swung my rigid body around the room. "I'm ecstatic to hear this! Have you been well?"

"No, I have *not* been well. In fact, I have lost weight. I retch and have headaches and often feel unable to cope." I was still hurt from his implied accusation and may have sounded a bit sharp.

"How have I missed this?"

My brows snapped together and I glowered at him in silence.

"Well, I suppose I haven't been here much of late, have I?"

I remained mute.

"Maggie, Father and I are developing a new business of buying and selling thoroughbreds. It might prove more profitable than farming could ever be. For now, we'll both continue farming, as we recognize it'll take a few years to increase our stock and clientele, as well as our reputation for breeding champion cart-racing horses.

Father has taken note of my farming success and has at last been willing to listen to my suggestions and opinions about this new venture. We've had several meetings with the banker, who is prepared to lend us money in the future, should we find it necessary." He smiled a winning smile.

My heart beat faster. These were more words Sam had said to me in over two months and the most animated he had been since last year before our world collapsed. We both had news to assimilate.

"Maggie, this has been one of the more positive ways I've coped with our loss. As I've grappled with Leander's death, I confess some of my other approaches have been less than exemplary."

How could I resist him? I walked toward him and we ended the evening in bed together, wrapped in each other's arms. I marveled that no matter how much anger might pass between us, we always seemed able to rekindle our passion.

Spring, 1892. On a pleasant morning in May, sunshine streamed through the window, gently caressing my face. I sat at the dining table, contemplating planting flowers or perhaps my vegetable garden. Inertia had overtaken any initiative to accomplish either task and I daydreamed, basking listlessly in the sun. I glanced again at the note Gertrude had delivered when she had visited yesterday.

> *May 5, 1892*
> *Mt. Clemens, Michigan*
> *Dear Sister,*
>
> *Attached is a work request from a Moira McGinnis. I am aware how unwell you have been, and found this notice on the board at the mercantile. I am acquainted with Moira and she seems a sweet enough girl, about 17 years, with a hard-luck story. Her papa died last winter and her mama has several younger children. She needs the work to help her family, if you*

are so inclined. Should you wish to meet her, write me a note,
and I will arrange it.
> *Faithfully,*
> *Ella R. Perry*

I might be inclined, but would Sam? My confinement was still some months away, yet we had discussed hiring a girl to assist me. I had begun to put on some weight, though I seldom found food appealing. Headaches plagued me and I developed a painful crick in my back if I stood very long. Perhaps he would allow me some help before my lying in, if it meant better meals than I had been serving. I would approach the topic after supper tonight.

"Sam, yesterday your mother delivered a note to me from Ella."

He looked at me, so I had his attention. A good start. Since our heart-to-heart talk last winter, our affinity for each other had rekindled. With tilling and soil preparation finished, he had hired a man to help with the planting of crops. Farming left Sam so bushed in the evening he often stayed home, acting the solicitous husband, perhaps inspired by my current condition.

"Ella knows a young lady looking for day work, and believes she might be appropriate for our needs."

"What needs are those?"

I think the promise of better meals won him over. He agreed to give her a chance.

"Good day, ma'am, my name is Moira, and Miss Ella tells me you may be of a mind to hire a day worker?"

About my size, but with flaxen, curly hair and striking green eyes, Moira McGinnis wore a plain blue and white gingham chambray frock. She was so thin, I imagined a good gust of wind might blow her away. Could she cook?

"Yes, we *are* considering such an arrangement. Why don't you come in and sit a spell, so we might chat?" That's how Moira came to be a part of our lives.

She cooked, cleaned, did laundry and lent a hand in the garden. We got on fine and I enjoyed her company. She'd had to drop out of school when her father died, to help support the family, not uncommon in this day and age. Sam appreciated her too, particularly with his eyes, which could be found gazing at her when he presumed my attention diverted. This concerned me, but I disregarded it, accepting that this trait of taking a gander now and again the way of most men, especially when a good-looking young lady like Moira was at hand. I noted she didn't pay him any heed, which further alleviated my concerns.

15.

Mid-summer, 1895. Amidst the tumultuous seas of life, I found an island of respite nursing my sweet Helen, just as I had three years ago when my dear son Oscar had arrived. Rocking her gently, pent up anxiety ebbed away ever-so-slowly, replaced by a moment of tranquility. I had come to rely on these fleeting moments of peace as temporary escapes from the increasing volatility of our marriage.

I would not say the change of circumstance arose from any single event, although Leander's death surely seemed to play a part in it. I would describe the changes more as the waxing and waning of an unhurried, yet pervasive, shift in my relationship with Sam. The edges became sharper, the divisions more pronounced.

During these moments of bliss with Helen, the angst subsided. Yet inevitably, the tension in my body reappeared, as uninvited and unwanted memories of strife and conflict once again flooded my mind. *Moira. Oh, Moira.* I rocked and reminisced.

It happened a couple of weeks after the birth of Oscar. Sleep deprived and filled with more than the usual anxiety for this new little person's well-being, I admit to a lack of romantic interest in my husband, which in no way excuses what transpired. Moira had worked for us not quite five months.

"Missus, may I speak to you with frankness?" She approached me in the bedroom where I sat rocking my two-week-old Oscar.

"Of course, dear! What's on your mind?" Her appearance reminded me of a skittish foal, wary and more than a little apprehensive.

"Oh, Missus, I'd hoped this would all blow over, but I'm uncertain if it will and I find I can't go on with things the way they are and . . ." Her words ran together in an outpouring of emotion.

"Moira, slow down! What's happened?" My imagination began to run loops around what I prayed she would not give voice to.

"Ma'am, Mr. Sam has been quite fresh with me."

Serene on the outside, quaking on the inside, I asked, "Whatever do you mean?" I dreaded what words might follow.

"He corners me whenever he doesn't think you'll see and attempts to touch me in private places. Sometimes he tries to kiss me. I've politely asked him to stop, but he won't listen. I can't go on this way, as he is becoming more cheeky with each passing week."

"Each passing week! How long has this been going on, Moira?" I did my best to maintain a calm demeanor.

"For months, ma'am. In the beginning, it seemed no more than a simple flirtation . . ."

Her words called to mind all the times I had caught Sam sneaking a glance at her. Now I heard the bitter truth.

"I really need the job, ma'am, but under the circumstances, I don't see how I can go on working for you. You've been so kind to me and I enjoy our time together and I've already fallen in love with wee Oscar. What, oh what, should I do?" She shook her head back and forth, covering her face with her hands as she began to cry.

"Oh, lovey, come here." I hugged her to me. She trembled.

"Ma'am, I didn't want to tell you and cause any upset in your marriage, but Mr. Sam is getting bolder and I am frightened by what might happen."

"Moira," I said, heaving an enormous sigh, "of course you can't continue on under these circumstances."

How I would survive without her, I did not know, but I would have to manage. Somehow. I made up my mind that the most important qualification for the next girl would be homeliness.

Within the week, Moira gave notice and departed our employ. She told us she'd found employment closer to home, with better hours. I suspected these reasons were just pretense, and while curious to find out Sam's thoughts, I chose not to ask. That incident would turn out to be only the first of many.

Over the next three years, I'd discovered it was of no consequence whether the hired girl was homely or fetching. Sam chased anything wearing a skirt.

In my efforts to outwit him, I'd attempted to hire an older retired nurse to help after Helen's birth. He discovered my correspondence with this woman and, unbeknownst to me, wrote her himself, saying we'd employed someone else and wouldn't need her services.

"Sam! I received a note from the nurse thanking me for considering her. I don't understand. What does she mean she was 'sorry we'd selected someone else?'"

"I'm not having some old battle-ax in our house, trying to take over!" he spit the words at me.

"What are you talking about? She was going to help me with Oscar and the new baby during my confinement." My voice reverberated in my ears.

"Don't provoke me, Maggie!" he warned, with an edge to his voice.

"You just want some young miss you can put your hands all over!"

"What the blazes are you ranting and raving about? You damn bitch."

Without warning, he grabbed me by the hair and shoved me onto the fireplace hearth. Stunned, I instinctively grabbed the first object I could find. My fingers found a good-sized stick of kindling, and I smacked him on the forehead, square between the eyes. He screamed and the wood fell from my hand, clattering to the ground.

After a few brief seconds of shocked silence, Sam gave a roar and lunged after me, his eyes wild. I flew into the kitchen and crouched down beside the table on my hands and knees, tucking my head into my chest, in an attempt to protect my unborn child. Sobbing, I shrieked, "No, no, no! Leave me be! The baby!"

He instantly came to his senses. Without another word, he turned and stomped out the door. I hurried over and latched it. *He'd be sleeping in the barn with our hired man tonight and every night thereafter, if I had my way. Despicable man!*

The next morning, he knocked on our front door, contrite as always after one of his violent episodes. I opened it a crack and peeked out at him. There he stood, staring back at me, his forehead marred by a large purple bruise.

"Oh Sam, I am so sorry." I let him come in.

"Maggie, can we leave it behind us and start afresh?"

I nodded and we discussed it no further. In a stroke of good luck, my sister Janie came to live with us for a time after Helen's birth mid-April. Thus ensued a period of relative peace, as to my knowledge, Sam made no advances on her. Unfortunately, the respite proved short-lived.

"Where are you off to?" I asked Sam, quite nattily dressed for a Thursday evening in mid-summer. I sat on our sofa cradling three-month old Helen, who'd settled in for a nap, while Oscar played near my feet.

"Out." He wore his new sable brushed cotton sack suit, the coat left open, displaying his red silk waistcoat beneath, his four-in-hand tie perfectly fixed. The newly popular newsboy cap, woven with matching tan-colored tweed, set off his ensemble. He was irresistibly good-looking.

"What do you mean, 'out?'"

"Not your concern." He turned on his heel and strode out of the house.

My imagination ran wild.

He stumbled up the stairs to our bedroom around midnight. Sleep had thus far eluded me, so I heard him when he collided with the door frame.

"Hmmph. Damn it."

In his cups again, obviously. I prayed he wouldn't wake the children. He came closer, and I detected an unfamiliar scent.

"Where were you?" I sat up in bed.

"None of your damn business." Other than balance, he held his liquor better than most.

I watched with trepidation as he disrobed, his clothing thrown in a heap on the floor. He lunged for me, the bed frame squeaking as it bounced under our weight. He seized my wrists, pinning them against the mattress and sat astride my prone body. I yanked on my arms, attempting to free them from his grip, shaking my head back and forth and kicking my legs, in a futile attempt to wrest them from him. His vile, whiskey-laden breath, combined with a vague scent of citrus, nearly gagged me.

"No!" I hissed, "No! Please!" I wanted to shout at him, but it would awaken Helen, who lay sleeping in her cradle at the foot of our bed. I well knew her wakefulness would be considered my fault and disrupt his intent. I couldn't risk the aftermath.

He ignored my desperate pleas, as always. Broken, I whimpered as he mounted me, convulsing as he relieved his need within me.

Long afterwards, tired of wallowing in my powerlessness, I pounded the bed with my fists, remembering far too many similar occurrences. One of those had resulted in Helen.

How could something so beautiful result from something so loathsome?

Bile rose into my throat and I sat up and swallowed its bitterness. Now passed out beside me, Sam snored heavily. Oh, how he revolted me! At that instant, something inside me cracked.

With uncommon strength, I savagely pushed and shoved him, until he fell onto the floor, landing with a thud. Unbelievably, he did not awaken.

My heart thumped in my chest as I lay back down. My body calmed, but my thoughts ran amok. *Why did he do this? What had happened to us?* Moving beyond speculation about where he had been, or the fact he had forced himself upon me again tonight, I pondered the course of our lives over the past several years. It perplexed me and left me disheartened. Distracted, I scratched my finger. I'd developed a rash underneath my wedding band not long ago, and it itched incessantly. Life had certainly changed since Sam put this symbol of love and fidelity on my finger five long years ago. I considered for a moment what it might feel like to take it off.

Is this how I will live out my days? I foresaw no solution or salvation, only torment.

Out of nowhere, an evil and shocking idea occurred to me. It would be so straightforward and uncomplicated. *But, no, I couldn't!* It was immoral. *But, it would rid me of him.* I swallowed and picked up his pillow, lying next to me on the bed. Holding my breath, I leaned over the edge of our bed, pillow in hand.

His eyes popped open. "Oh, have I died? My God! Who *is* this radiant vision of an angel floating above me?" He smiled innocently before his eyes fell shut.

Sighing, the moment passed and I regained my right mind. I placed the pillow under his head on the floor and arranged a coverlet over him, before I lay back down, defeated.

May, 1896. "Helen Edith Jobsa! Get down this instant!" I spoke sharply to my daughter, as she teetered on the edge of a kitchen chair in her attempt to climb up on the counter. I rushed to her side at the moment she started to topple off the stool onto the floor, and snared her by the waistband of her pinafore.

The afternoon heat had turned oppressive, leaving us all with sour dispositions. Helen suffered from a heat rash and Oscar was restless. Perhaps my restlessness was contagious? Going on four, he had a sunny disposition and was the apple of his father's eye. But today, he was fretful and whiny. My daughter turned a year old last month and already toddled about unassisted, a bundle of energy, her little hands always searching for something to climb on or a drawer to pull open and empty of whatever contents she discovered within.

Oscar stood in the front room watching out the window for his father to drive up in the buggy. "Mama, I see Daddy coming now, and he has on a frowny face!"

I groaned. I didn't want any part of another of Sam's horrid moods. He leapt off the seat and bounded into the house, the frown replaced by a grin when he laid eyes on his son. "How's my favorite boy?" He grasped him under the arms and swung him high overhead, while Oscar hooted with laughter.

Sam glanced my way with narrowed eyes, speaking brusquely, "Are you ready?"

"Yes, of course," my voice matching his.

"Let's be off, as the list is long." He carried Oscar on his shoulders and I followed them out, with Helen wriggling in my arms.

Not a word was uttered on the ride into town, just two miles away. At a trot, the journey lasted about fifteen minutes. We drove past the cart-racing track on the outskirts of Mt. Clemens. *Oh, how my life had changed in the nine years since Sam's accident at the race.* If I could turn back time, how different my choices would now be.

Sam and his father, Henry, as well as Papa, had enjoyed greater than usual success over the past five years in the cart racing business. In addition to winning at the track, all three of them now bred, bought and sold horses, focusing less on farming and more on the raising of stock. I'd little time or inclination to attend the races, for the simple reason that I could not conceive of watching a race while looking after two busy children. The days of fun and excitement at the cart track were over for me, at least for the present.

I always looked forward to these weekly trips to town, to break the monotony of farm life. Mt. Clemens was bustling for a Tuesday and my heart beat a little faster as we pulled to a stop in front of the mercantile, where we would be doing the bulk of our shopping. Now housed in two adjacent buildings, it had grown in recent years. Sam went directly into the hardware portion of the second building and we dutifully followed. After a time, we migrated into the other room, filled with canned or boxed food, fabric and other more domestic notions.

"Oh, Ella, I'm so happy to see you!" I walked over to where my sister stood near the fabric table, and gave her a hug.

"Hello, you three! Oh, Helen, I think you've grown taller since last I saw you. Come to Auntie Ella!" She reached out to take her from my arms and Helen giggled as she held out her arms to her favorite Aunt. "Oscar, you're looking mighty fine!" Ella leaned over and solemnly shook his tiny hand.

"How are you, dear sister?"

"Working too many hours, between the store and my seamstress business, yet I'm loving every minute of being independent. How are things at the farm?"

I'm married to a drunk who chases after women and scares and abuses me. I have no recourse or place to run. Oh, how I wished I might be honest.

"Fine, Ellie, just fine." I began babbling, "Now that he's gotten the crops planted, Sam's been busy driving Absalom around to various farms to offer stud service. Even though he's now too old to race, Absalom's still earning money for Sam! Sam's acquired quite a substantial number of breeding stock of his own and . . ."

"Well, how about you, Maggie? What's new with you?"

"Me? Oh, getting ready to plant my garden. We are purchasing our seed today," I pointed into the other room of the mercantile from whence we'd come. "The children keep me busy and what with chores, life is very full," my voice wound down to a standstill. I hoped my chatter sounded convincing, while my true mind went along the lines of *please let me and the children come live with you, Ella.*

She stared at me quizzically, but said nothing.

"Maggie, while I'm thinking of it," changing the subject, "the annual church bazaar to benefit the poor is coming up this Saturday. I'd like to invite you and the children for a birthday outing! I thought we might enjoy browsing at the various craft tables, along with the adjacent flea market."

"I'm not sure Ella . . ." I hesitated, "we're so busy . . . yet, I would greatly relish spending the day with you. It would be something gay to look forward to and I'd completely forgotten my birthday. I'll ask Sam."

"Maggie, I'm not inviting Sam. I'm inviting you and the children."

I knew what she meant. I also knew he did not allow me to make decisions without his approval. "Oh! Well, in that case, we'd be delighted to accept your offer." I smiled brightly. This reply carried a calculated risk on my part, but what else could I do? I found it unthinkable to tell her the actual truth.

"Would you need me to borrow Louis's surrey to retrieve you or can you manage to drive your own buggy with the children in tow?"

"We'll be fine. I'll bring ours." Oh dear, I'd now dug the hole even deeper.

"I think I may have a little something for the two of you." Ella again focused her attention on Oscar and Helen, winking at them and moving toward the counter near the cash register. She reached into a large glass jar and pulled out two thumb-sized treats, offering up a coin which she placed on the register. "Mama, I should have asked first, but is it okay to give them each one?" Ella peered at me, wrinkling her forehead.

"Of course. Treats are very special, aren't they children? What do you say to your Auntie?"

"Thank you," Oscar eagerly reached for his sweet.

"Tayu," Helen attempted to imitate her brother, extending her chubby fingers for the sweet treat.

While the children enjoyed their candies, Ella shared some news. "I had a long, concerning letter from Lucy the other day."

"Really? In what way?"

"I am somewhat fearful for her mental state. Relations between her and William appear sound, but she's vexed by the tedium of household chores. I think it's more than that, as she complained of the loneliness living in near isolation out on the prairie, rambling on about the incessant winds. It's unfortunate she's so far away."

I nodded. "I'll write her a cheery letter. I wish there were something more we might do." I remembered Lucy's assurance that marrying William and moving to Montana was the answer to all her life questions. A startling reflection skipped across my mind. Maybe Ella had better sense than either Lucy or me, living life on her own terms, free to come and go as she wished without the complications of a man and a marriage. "Maggie," she said, looking me up and down, as if noting for the first time the old gingham dress that I'd worn for ten or more years, "I think I'd like to sew you a new frock! How would you like that? I'll make a matching one for Helen, to boot."

Ella had found a kind and tactful way of saying I needed some new clothing. Her comments created an almost visceral reaction of exasperation deep inside me. Sam paid no heed to my repeated requests for a new dress or cloak, not caring about the indignity I often felt when we appeared in public.

While often infuriated by my husband, my heart overflowed with love for my sister. I smiled, "Oh Ella, you are so good to us. Whatever did I do to deserve a sister like you?"

"Let's pick out some fabric right now, shall we?"

"Maggie, it's time to move on to the farrier's to see about those new shoes for Absalom," Sam called from the mercantile entryway. He tapped his foot with impatience.

"Well, I'd better not keep Sam waiting," I said, giving her another quick hug, my eyes averted. I would like to believe she glared at him as the children and I made our way toward the exit.

Ella's offer of a new dress was the best chance I'd had for new clothing since Sam and I married. I fumed as I climbed back into the buggy to drive to the farrier on the outskirts of town.

Sam left before nine o'clock Saturday morning astride Absalom to spend the day servicing broodmares, which perfectly suited my plan. I calculated we could take the buggy to town and be home again in time to prepare a simple supper before he returned. So far, Sam hadn't even remembered the day was my birthday.

"Children, we're going on a special adventure today with Aunt Ella."

"Ooh," they cried in unison. "Auntie Ella," Oscar squeaked, "Auntie Ella, Auntie Ella, Auntie Ella!" He turned her name into a little song, as Helen echoed something which sounded like "Oon-ee, Oon-ee."

I chuckled as I finished fitting Oscar's little feet into his hand-me-down shoes. Worn through in places, he seemed not to mind. Helen's tiny slippers were also previously used, but at least had no visible holes. I took a long moment to gaze at the two of them with pride and they returned my gaze, eager for our adventure to begin. I'd dressed my slender, fair-haired Oscar in his best linen blue and white sailor suit. Helen, whose little round face was framed by her russet-colored hair, wore a summery, pale lavender print cotton dress. I was grateful to both Abi and John Henry, and Louis and Mayme, for allowing us to borrow their children's outgrown clothing.

"All right, my dears, time to go!"

Papa taught all his children how to harness a horse to a buggy, so even though it had been several years, it took little time to adeptly finish the task. I tied Oscar and Helen to the seat with one of my shawls and, thus situated, we set off for Mt. Clemens, our carriage pulled by the faithful Otis.

Along the way, I had a serious talk with them. "Children, we are going on a secret adventure. That means we must tell no one, not even Daddy, about our outing today. If you can keep it a secret, I will give you each a sour drop after supper tonight." Goodness, to what depths had I sunk, bribing my children to withhold information from their father? I hoped they would comply, not daring to contemplate the consequences of a loose tongue. I would be reminding them again all the way home later this afternoon.

We arrived at Ella's house mid-morning, and she awaited us with tea and freshly baked cinnamon rolls. "Hello, lovies, I'm so pleased to see you! Happy Birthday, Maggie. How would you like to have a little treat before we leave for the bazaar?" Oh, how I cherished my dear sister's love!

"It's your birthday, Mama?"

"Yes, it is, Oscar." I smiled at my little cherub.

"How old are you?"

"Old enough to be your mama! I am twenty-six."

"Oh." He looked at me with a sudden concern. "That is very old," nodding his head quite seriously, causing both Ella and me to laugh.

As always, my sister and I treasured each other's company. We delighted in watching Oscar and Helen's shining eyes as they sampled the bazaar's enticing fare. Ella indulged them, purchasing small hand-made toys for them to take home.

As we strolled toward the exit, we came upon a seller of used books at the flea market. Our eyes met. "What if we purchased some books to send Lucy?"

"Capital idea! I was thinking the same thing. That may be just the ticket to improve her mood."

Elated to find several appealing titles for our sister at minimal cost, we mentioned our intentions for these books to the vendor and he spontaneously gifted us a couple more. It would be a windfall for Lucy. We laughed as we took turns juggling the books and Helen in our arms all the way back to Ella's.

"Ella, I can't thank you enough for a perfect birthday."

"Oh, don't be silly, sister, it was merely a church bazaar," Ella grinned, "but I'm so pleased you enjoyed the day. Leave Lucy's books with me and I'll get them posted."

She had no inkling of how my world had shrunk. I found such a sense of security and safety with her, I again wished we might stay with her forever.

Loading the children back into our buggy, fear blossomed when I glanced at the sun's point in the sky and realized the time. I had anticipated starting towards home much earlier. On the ride home, Oscar and Helen fell asleep resting against each other. Like transporting two little angels, I smiled with satisfaction at the thought. Today, Ella had given me the gift of lightheartedness and dare I say, happiness, feelings I hadn't experienced for a long while. She might never fully understand how precious her gift was, since she could enjoy these freedoms any day.

I drove down the lane towards our farmhouse with trepidation. As I approached, the barn doors hung open, an ominous sign. I almost hoped it was a thief, as I would rather face a thief than my husband.

It was no thief. Sam must have heard our approach, as he stormed out of the barn and rounded the side of the house as I drove on by. His eyes ablaze with rage, he attempted to grab the horse's harness. I considered turning around and heading back the way I'd come, but knew the strategy would prove futile and possibly dangerous. I envisioned him jumping upon Absalom to chase us down. I pulled the buggy to a halt in front of the barn, said a prayer, and relied on the children's presence to save me.

They awakened, rubbing their eyes, and asked to get down. Sam spoke not a word, so I untied the shawl holding my babies safe to their seats. One at a time, I handed my precious cargo down to him, hoping their touch might calm him.

The three of them stood in silence, peering up at me as I sat frozen to my seat. Seconds passed before Sam seemed to reach a decision. Unexpectedly, he scooped them up, one under each arm, and marched toward our house.

"Mama, Mama!" They clawed at his arms and wriggled desperately, kicking their little legs.

Oscar and Helen's cries startled me out of my stupor and I slid over the side of the wagon to follow. Several steps ahead of me, they disappeared inside and the bar fell into place, locking me out of my own house. Enraged, I kicked and beat at the door, screaming, "Let me in! You devil! Let me in!"

Moments later, the door flew open and he stood ominously before me, the children hidden from view.

"Where were you today?" he asked in a hollow, toneless voice.

"At the church bazaar with Ella. For my birthday," I said, to point out to him what he had forgotten.

"I'll just *bet* you were at the bazaar. I took note of the way you ogled that bootlicker at the farrier's the other day."

"What? What do you mean? Don't be absurd!"

"Don't deceive me! It takes little effort to imagine where you were." He then stepped forward, shut the door behind him, and shoved me backwards. I fell sideways, grabbing for the porch post, missing it and rolling down the steps. Landing on my shoulder in the dirt, I cried out in pain. He followed me and took hold of my other arm to hoist me upwards onto my feet. I twisted away from his foul, whiskey-laden breath.

"Leave me alone," I seethed. "You don't know what you're talking about. We spent the day with Ella at the church bazaar." I repeated this slowly, carefully enunciating each syllable of each word.

"You're no more than a tramp," he snarled. "I could kill you for taking my children into some filthy honky-tonk."

"Poppycock! I presume you're not in your right mind to even suggest such rubbish. They are *my* children too!" I stomped my foot. "You son of a bitch! How *dare* you call me names? *You're* nothing but a vile whoremonger . . . as well as a drunk!" This I added for good measure, and then I slapped him. Hard.

Stunned, he took a step backwards, reaching up to touch the bright red finger marks stamped across his cheek. He pushed me against the porch rail with his other hand. Most certainly drunk, he still had the advantage of simple brute strength.

Mindful that I could *not* physically win this battle, I determined it better to withdraw. I regained my balance and made to move away from him when he lurched forward, snatched me by the collar of my bodice, swung me around and punched me in the face.

"If you conducted yourself properly, I wouldn't have to do this!" He then seized my neck with both hands, choking me. He strangled me tighter and tighter, and I realized I was fighting for not only my breath, but my very life. My vision clouded near the edges, while his putrid breath seared my face.

I couldn't die. My children needed me.

Abruptly, I recalled something my brother James had taught me. With the last bit of strength I could muster, I kneed Sam in his groin. He made a huffing sound, cried out and shrank back, letting go of my neck, hunching forward as he wrapped both arms around his middle, groaning in agony.

Coughing and wheezing, I searched for breath. I turned and lost the contents of my stomach, the spittle dripping onto the red poppies growing beside the house. Still doubled over, Sam backed away from me a few more steps, before turning and making his way crookedly toward the barn. As I lingered in front of the porch, continuing to regain my breath and composure, Sam galloped past me and down our lane on Absalom. I staggered into the house and barred the door.

He'd berated, slapped and pushed me around countless times over the years, but never had I feared for my life. The brutality of his assault had reached a new level and for the first time, I began to question the sanity of remaining.

The next morning, Sam awakened me shortly after sunrise. Startled, I sat up and drew the covers around me, my heart thumping with alarm, aware I had no weapon to protect myself. I subconsciously touched my bruised neck and swollen jaw.

He held a bouquet of iris blooms from my garden as he kneeled beside our bed, caressing my battered face. His mouth fell open. "Oh, look at you, my darling! My heart breaks to see your face and realize how beastly I acted." He paused. Perhaps I looked worse than he had expected. Were his eyes moist?

He bowed his head sorrowfully, "My dearest, I'm here to offer the most humble of apologies. Truly, I don't deserve your forgiveness, but I *beg* you." He paused, considering his words. "No, I beseech you! Forgive me for my deplorable behavior last evening. Please? I implore you to give me another chance. I've learned my lesson. From the bottom of my sorrowful heart, I regret my actions. In fact, I'm thoroughly shamed by them." His face flushed. Staring at him, I spoke not a word.

"It was, after all, your birthday," he continued softly, "and you should be allowed to celebrate. Can you ever, ever see fit to forgive my impulsive and offensive conduct? Oh, Maggie, when I got home and found you and the children missing, I went berserk. You must recognize how much I adore the three of you. My mind conjured shameful visions of you running into the arms of another man and the thought of you with someone else drove me mad. I couldn't bear the anguish this caused me. The longer I waited, the more real my imaginings seemed. I swear to you, as long as I draw breath, such an outburst will never, ever happen again. From this day forward, you will enjoy all future birthdays in whatever manner you choose."

Oh, how I wanted to believe all those flowery words. We had been estranged far too long. Heedless of the past, I latched onto these crumbs, a kernel of hope he had now tossed me.

"I also want to offer you a belated birthday wish." He extended the bouquet towards me, speaking in that suave voice I always found irresistible.

I tipped my head and released a deep breath. Moments passed before I found my voice. In measured tones, I extended an olive branch. "I'm touched. They're lovely." Gazing into his eyes, I murmured, "Thank you, Sam," before reaching up to grasp them. Instead, he set the blooms on our bedside table and moved toward me. Even though I hadn't exactly said I forgave him, my response must have encouraged him enough to feel confident in leaning over, encircling me in his arms and holding me close.

My head resting on his chest, I asked, "By the way, how did you get inside this morning? The door was bolted," I confessed sheepishly.

"Oh, but you left the kitchen window unlatched," he grinned.

16.

Autumn, 1897. "Mama, Mama! Come quick!" Oscar shouted from where he perched near the front window. It was a cloudless Sunday afternoon in September and Sam had already gone to the cart races, leaving our hired man, Joseph, working in the field.

In the kitchen tidying up from our midday dinner, Helen and I rushed over to the window. "Why, it's Auntie Ella and she is riding a bicycle!" My adventurous sister was bumping down the dirt lane toward our farmhouse. She raised her arm to wave. We waved back before scurrying out on the porch to greet her.

"Ella! What do we have here?" I called to her as she whooshed to a stop.

"Isn't this splendid?" she exclaimed with awe in her voice, as she winked at the three of us. "It belonged to Mayme, but she never used it much, so the bicycle is essentially brand new." Never very robust, Louis' wife, Mayme, had passed away last winter from pneumonia. Ella had moved into their home to help Louis look after little Rachel. The most self-sacrificing woman I had ever known, my sister never ceased offering her caregiving ways to our family.

"It's an Overman Safety Bicycle," she went on, "you see there?" She pointed to what looked like a piece of thin metal. "That cover keeps my skirt from catching in the chain, so this machine was built with a woman in mind. You can see the rubber tires even have mud guards to protect my clothes from puddles along the road. Finally, someone has given consideration to a woman's needs!" She laughed, bringing me great delight. With no husband and no children, she had little to inflame her passions, yet paradoxically, seemed so satisfied with life.

"Oh! I almost forgot, I have a post from Lucy." She reached into her skirt pocket and pulled out an envelope, handing it to me, her face beaming.

"From the look on your face, this must contain the announcement we've been waiting for?" I smiled back at her as I slid out the thin sheet of paper.

Mesmerized by the notion of a bicycle, the children listened intently while Ella continued to explain how it all worked and I read Lucy's letter.

> *August 27, 1897*
> *Brandenburg, Montana*
> *Beloved Sisters,*
>
> *William and I are pleased to announce the birth of Grace Estella Wolff, arriving on Friday, August 20 around 4:30 a.m., at our ranch. She and I are both doing fine. I must say, I'm simply glad to be through the whole 9-month ordeal. The baby has a full head of dark hair and vivid blue eyes. William is over the moon, which is putting it mildly. After being married these 5 years, I surmise he had somewhat given up his dream for any children. He is so in love with her, it is quite apparent I have taken a backseat in his affections. He is already talking about her first pony. He will make a sheep rancher of her, no doubt.*
>
> *Please write soon and keep in mind how much I would like for you both to come to Montana to visit.*
> *Affectionately,*
> *Lucy P. Wolff*

I handed the letter back to her, puzzled. "Sounds as though William is perhaps more excited about this than our sister?"

"It appears so," replied Ella, peering over the top of Oscar's head. Much to his delight, she balanced him on the seat. "Oscar, I think it won't be long before you'll be learning to ride this contraption!"

"Come on inside and join me for a cup of tea."

With visitors uncommon, I experienced an unmistakable comfort in bringing out one of Mother's old teapots, which dear Lizzie had given me after she and Papa married. We made ourselves comfortable at the kitchen table, while the children remained outdoors, inspecting her bicycle.

Ella wasted no time in changing the subject, and the tone of our visit turned from joy at Lucy's news to despair, as we began to touch upon my life. "Louis tells me he saw you and the children in Mt. Clemens last week, coming from Dr. Milton's office. Are you ill?"

I had thought about this ahead of time and had a ready reply, in the event a family member spied me in town. "I'm fine. It was but a quick trip to the doctor. I've been having some female difficulties and after what happened to Mother, I wanted some reassurance it was nothing serious. He gave me a potion to help and all is well." Relying on this partial truth, I smiled what I pictured as a reassuring smile.

"Well, Maggie, you may say you are fine, but as I observe your face closely, I see what appears to be a bruise on your chin. When I look into your eyes, I see little but sorrow. How can I not reach the conclusion your words are fraudulent?"

I stared at my hands, unable to meet her gaze. I had experienced such hopefulness last year, that day after my birthday, and had worked hard to cultivate optimism for Sam and myself. But the change proved heartrendingly fleeting, and the downward spiral into our own private hell had continued, with no sign of deliverance yet on the horizon.

"While I find I cannot agree with your choice to withhold a truthful explanation, and as it's not my way to coerce, I'll make a sincere effort to respect your decision to remain silent."

I nodded my head, my eyes downcast, too ashamed to meet her eyes.

She made one last plea. "You do realize you can safely reveal your confidences, and trust they'll go no further? I recognize it sometimes helps to have someone with whom to share your burdens. Moreover, I've sensed for quite some time all's not well between you and Samuel. Does this doctor visit have anything to do with your husband's treatment of you? Maggie! Look at me. This is your sister, Ella, speaking to you. What's going on? Has he been mistreating you?"

So personal, so horrific, dare I give in to her persistence? *Dare I tell her?* Memories of the past couple of months assaulted me.

When at last I lifted my head to face her, I heard how flat my voice sounded, devoid of any vitality or intonation. "Oh, Ella, where do I begin? The story is so ghastly, I'm fearful you'll peg me a loathsome creature."

"Absolutely not. You're my sister. Have you forgotten how much I treasure you? Maggie, you must understand I won't judge you, I love you."

I stood then to see where Oscar and Helen had gotten off to. They'd left the bicycle behind and were busy playing with sticks in the dirt on the edge of the barnyard, well out of earshot. I took a long breath. "Ella, I find I'm a private person, not wanting to put voice to my grievances. Suffice to say, marriage to Sam has had its peaks and valleys."

"That much is obvious."

"Whatever do you mean by such a remark?"

"I've watched you for years, Maggie. You hardly ever show emotion outwardly, yet I know you well and my eyes, heart *and* head tell me all is *not* well between you two and hasn't been for some time."

"An understatement, dear sister, an understatement. You're astute at observing my bruise, a remnant of our last row."

Her gaze was furious and sympathetic at the same time. "Oh, if I were a man . . ." her voice trailed off.

I relented then, surrendering stoicism to reveal the most distasteful of secrets to my sister. "The reason Louis saw me coming from Dr. Milton's office last week was because I knew something was decidedly amiss, necessitating, in my mind, a doctor visit. I really have been having female troubles. For the past couple of months, my monthly bleeding has been occurring almost every two weeks, and in between, my body's been shedding a heavy and putrid discharge. I've had some pain in my lower stomach, much like Mother described. I was frightened, convinced that at twenty-seven, I'm too young to be going through the change of life."

Ella stared at me in shocked silence. I stopped speaking for a moment to take another deep breath and collect myself. "Upon examination, Dr. Milton was reasonably sure that I had a social disease. There was but one way it could have happened. And that one way was through the act of sexual congress with Samuel. He said, 'Mrs. Jobsa, you have a venereal disease called gonorrhea.' He told me I was most fortunate to have had symptoms, as many women have none until too late and in the end, become infertile." I laughed bitterly. "As if I would care about that now."

Both hands covering her cheeks, Ella was shaking her head in complete dismay, horror overtaking her face.

My voice now quivering, my face contorted, I continued. "At least the doctor had knowledge of a recently developed regimen, consisting of an 'irrigation' of my female organ. He reported he's successfully treated some 'painted ladies' using this new procedure. Oh, Ella, how dreadful to be placed into the same category as whores! He regarded me kindly, but I could see the pity in his eyes, which only served to enrage me. He informed me it was 'critical' to treat my husband and advised me not to hesitate 'sending him in.' It took every ounce of my fortitude to remain composed after hearing these words.

"The doctor's wife entertained Oscar and Helen in another room, while he administered the treatment. I tell you honestly, this ordeal was many times more humiliating than fainting at the Avery Hotel. He must have had his suspicions, but the good doctor seemed satisfied to overlook my bruises and I didn't mention them either. I could bear no more of his pity."

I looked down. My words had run dry.

She took both my hands in hers, apparently also at a loss for words. I'm convinced this narrative was not anything near to what she'd expected.

I looked up to see her studying me with a palatable unease, so I tried to reassure her. "Ella, I . . ."

Nothing further was said, as the children came bounding into the house. Taking one look at my weary face, Oscar ran up to me and put his arms around my neck, asking, "Mama? What's the trouble? Are you not quite fine?" Ella released my hands and I hugged him in return, saying in my most reassuring voice, "Oh, sweet boy, Mama is just fine."

Like a spring unwinding, I discovered confiding in my sister had relieved some of my suppressed tension.

"Oh, Maggie." Simple words, spoken with fierce emotion. We continued to stare at each other, our conversation ended.

I chose not to reveal the remaining details of Sam's and my confrontation. Reliving those memories now caused an immediate and repugnant return of the tension I had shed moments before. Shortly, Ella boarded her bicycle to ride the two miles back to Mt. Clemens. With a meaningful look, she promised to come again as soon as she could. The three of us stood on the porch, waving goodbye.

"Mama, can we stay out here and play?"

"Yes, but mind you don't dig up any of my flowers, you hear?"

"No, Mama, we'll be careful." I'd heard that before. Flower-picking often proved too much of a temptation for little hands.

I walked back into the house, the door ajar, so I could hear them. Unwanted memories of the recent grim showdown with Sam summoned my attention.

I had waited until the children went to bed, that evening last week. Sam stayed home after supper, an uncommon occurrence of late, as he typically had "business" to attend to in town.

An autumn chill in the air, he relaxed in his chair near the fireplace, soaking up the warmth, while I sat at the kitchen table doing some mending. I dreaded the unpleasant task of relaying Dr. Milton's advice to Sam. *Why, oh, why did I feel any sense of obligation to him?* If the doctor hadn't been so insistent, I would have let a sleeping dog lie. But for some reason, I harbored a compulsion to do the right thing, despite the inkling I might live to regret my considerate choice.

Sam stood and went over to the sideboard where he kept his whiskey. Not normally one to imbibe, it crossed my mind that maybe tonight some spirits might help to embolden me enough to complete this difficult conversation.

"Sam, might I have a tot as well?"

He arched one brow, looking over to where I sat at the table. "Now, *that* is astonishing! I must say, Maggie, you never cease to amaze me." Shaking his head, he poured me a dram. I stood to retrieve it from him and downed it in one gulp. "Oh!" I gasped, my throat on fire. Much more intense than I had expected, my eyes watered and I coughed.

Incredulous, his eyes narrowed. "What the devil?"

Regaining my breath, I plunged ahead. "You may recall, I'd asked your permission to go into town to see Dr. Milton today to find out why I've been having female troubles."

"Yes? And? What did you learn?"

"I'm not yet going through the change of life . . ." I smiled, as a strange warming sensation pervaded my being. I hoped my smile might bring a little levity to this most serious of conversations. I hiccupped.

He chuckled as we stood facing each other. "All right. That *is* good news."

I stared at him, my face somber.

"So? Is there more?"

"Yes, I'm considering how to tell you." Well, I hadn't meant to say *that* out loud.

"Why? What's going on? Why are you not being more forthcoming? Out with it, Maggie! Is it complications from a miscarriage?" His voice had now taken on a more concerned tone. A good sign. This opening might provide the opportunity I had been awaiting.

Still, though, based on past experience, I hesitated, as I could think of no way to say what needed to be said in a delicate manner. The air became thick with tension.

"Well . . ." I faltered, goosebumps prickling my arms.

"Well, what?" he insisted, his tone now sounding irritated.

Despite my qualms, I forged ahead, "Sam, you gave me the clap and the doctor said it's urgent you seek treatment!"

His eyes opened wide. His body became rigid. In a lightning quick movement, he hauled off and struck me square in the jaw with the back of his hand, using such force it sent me reeling backwards. I stumbled and fell on the floor with a thud, hitting the back of my head against the wall. Dazed, I attempted to catch my breath, rubbing my palm across my now swelling jawline.

"What the hell? *I* gave you the clap? Hah! You've finally gotten caught! Whatever prick's been having his way with you gave *you* the clap, you damn whore!" He spat at me with a savage fury. "Hells bells, Maggie, I can't believe you'd do this to me."

Numb and entirely sober, I sat mutely, holding my jaw. Arguing with him would only serve to further inflame the situation. Dr. Milton would never know what the delivery of his message cost me.

"Stand up and look at me, you harlot!" He walked over to where I crouched against the wall and yanked on my arm, pulling me to my feet.

I pounded his chest with my fists, uttering a strangled-sounding scream. He grasped me by the shoulders and began to shake me, bellowing, "What the blazes have you been up to? Should I find out you've been taking my children along to frequent any low-down, sorry lout in some doggery, I swear to God, you're going to pay! I'd throw you out now, if I could afford to hire someone to tend to our offspring."

Changing course, I closed my eyes and dropped to the ground with a thump, pretending to faint.

"Maggie? Maggie? Answer me! Damn it woman, answer me!" His voice increased in volume.

I remained still. "Son of a bitch," he muttered as he grabbed his hat, and disappeared out the front door.

In agony, I continued to lay on the floor, afraid to move a muscle, in case he returned. Angry tears slid down my cheeks. After what seemed an eternity, I slowly opened my eyes and peeked around the room. Not seeing him anywhere, I cautiously sat up, touching my throbbing, swollen jaw. Several more minutes passed before I stood and made my way to the water pump in the kitchen, where I wet a cloth with cold water to press against my puffy face.

The next day, the children and I drove the buggy to Papa's farm without asking permission from Sam, who had once again ridden away on Absalom. I brushed aside their questions about my bruised face, saying I had accidentally fallen against the kitchen table. They studied me with a watchful silence. I suspected they had overheard their father cursing me and were not taken in by my deception.

We found Papa in his woodshop next to the barn. "Grandpa!" Oscar jumped down and into his Grandpa's arms before Helen and I stepped down from the rig.

"Oscar, my little man!" Papa tousled my son's hair, "And wee Helen, what brings you to the Perry farm today?" He grinned as he picked up my two-year-old and gave her a hug. Then he turned toward me and his face turned ashen when he caught sight of my bruised face.

"Daughter . . . ? What's this all about? What's happened to your face?" Our eyes met and I nodded toward my children.

"Children, why don't we head into the barn and see if we can find the new kitties Mama Cat had last week, aye?" Papa led the way.

They occupied themselves playing with the kittens, while in the shadows of the barn, I spoke in muted tones, vaguely describing Sam's behavior and his violence toward me. I omitted the details of the doctor visit, which I simply could not bring myself to share.

"Daughter, I am aware you can be impertinent at times." His words caught me by surprise, leaving me in stunned silence. "Certainly you must have aggravated Sam to a high degree for him to treat you in such a deplorable manner."

All I could do was stare at him, dumbstruck by his response.

He then reprimanded me. "Maggie, mind your manners! Be respectful and use more prudence in your conversations, as well as actions, toward your husband."

The one-sided conversation soon came to an end. His lack of understanding of my plight offered no comfort, nor did it do anything to relieve my anxiety. In retrospect, I guessed it might have been preferable to speak with Lizzie instead, as I surmised her ear would have been more sympathetic.

"Giddy up," I directed Otis, and we headed home. I laughed disparagingly at myself as we trotted down the road, thinking about that girl of long ago who adamantly insisted she would *never* tolerate an ill-behaved man, the way her mother and mother-in-law had. Ironically, I had ended up like them after all. I now questioned the true love I thought Mother had for Papa, wondering if it had been my imagination, no more than a young girl's fancy. In the end, I supposed both Mother and Gertrude had each concluded they would be better off with a man than without. After all, what other option did a woman with children and no means of making a living have in life? None, really. Although obviously concerned, Ella couldn't provide for the three of us, and if my own Papa lacked empathy, where else could I seek shelter?

"Maggie, close your eyes." Days had passed since Ella's visit and all visible traces of Sam's latest abuse had vanished. I had no idea if he had seen Dr. Milton or not, and as long as he kept his hands from my person, I had no interest in asking. He was now standing in front of me in our kitchen, as I prepared supper. I looked at him warily, wondering what he was up to.

"Come on, Maggie. Please cooperate!" The children were nearby, so I perceived it to be safe. I closed my eyes.

When prompted, I opened them and beheld a dainty emerald encrusted brooch. Sam smiled broadly as he pinned it to my bodice. "This modest bauble is but a small token of my appreciation for all that you do for me and the children."

"Oh! Why, it's beautiful Sam. How nice of you to think of me . . ." My words dangled in the air, disconnected from any real emotion.

This man was so exasperating. Actions such as this left me to question everything I believed to be true. Maybe Papa was right, and it was me who caused our marital distress. Me and the infernal whiskey.

17.

November, 1898. I awakened, disoriented, to the sound of crying babies. *Where was I?* Clarity returned in an instant, and I groaned, remembering the twins. I struggled to my feet, shivering in the November chill and padded barefoot over to the cradle, where month-old Gordon Eugene and Gertrude Elizabeth demanded their due. Hefting one baby into the crook of each arm, I stumbled back into bed, reclaiming the cozy warmth under the quilts. Gordon, impatient, latched immediately and began sucking with gusto, while little Gertrude, more demure, daintily attached to the teat, suckling softly. She had no understanding of her good fortune! It took little effort on her part to obtain the milk, as her brother's keen enthusiasm caused it to flow profusely on both sides.

I lay feeding my babies in the darkness, and my mind wandered. As usual, Sam was nowhere to be found. Even when sober, he seldom noticed the twins, and me, even less. Not overly bothered by this inattention, life progressed more smoothly in his absence. He provided for the children and me, but like a sunflower in autumn, our relationship continued to wither. For a while, I had taken Papa's advice, carefully weighing my responses, in my attempt to avoid any impertinence, but these changes had done little to bolster our marriage. Confused and melancholy, I remained wary of Sam's capricious behavior.

There had been more harrowing episodes, and admittedly, I often lost my temper, making my own bold recriminations in response to Sam's vile accusations. I had picked up some disgraceful language along the way and regrettably, these altercations sometimes happened in front of the two older children. I accepted my share of the blame for our troubles.

Our disagreements led to more instances of physical violence directed towards each other, although my size and strength placed me at a clear disadvantage. Whenever I had warning of an approaching storm, my eye would scan the room for potential ways to defend my person. Provided I could stay out of his grasp, he knew I would no longer hesitate to grab any heavy item within reach, usually a hefty stick of wood, and aim it toward his head.

With utter unpredictability, there had been several short-lived reconciliations, one of which resulted in the sweet babies now snuggled beside me.

Tears trickled down my cheeks as a now familiar, all-encompassing realization swept over me. Imprisoned without choices and tied to my children, with a husband I disliked and a life fraught with peril and instability, I had nowhere to run. My best chance had been Ella, but she now planned to move to Montana sometime in the coming year to be nearer Lucy. She had been talking about this idea for quite some time and it was at last coming to fruition.

"Maggie, since Louis has married Clara, I've decided the time has come for a new adventure." Our brother had remarried a few months ago and Ella had moved out of his house. "If I don't go now, I'll never go." She paused and I sensed her ambivalence. "My heart aches to leave you and the children behind, but I find I'm compelled to do this."

After much reflection, I agreed that, at forty years of age, the time for her to do something for herself had arrived. She had always placed our family first and sacrificed for whomever among us needed her. I could say nothing against her plan. Although I didn't want to, I forced myself to understand. I wished I might flee with her. What a preposterous notion.

Turning my thoughts to my mother-in-law, I knew I would find no respite there. Our visits had dwindled over time, as I found it impossible not to question certain teachings of Christian Science. In the end she had grown tired of my inability to fully embrace the faith, and by mutual agreement, we ceased our meetings to discuss my spiritual evolution.

I also had concerns about where her loyalties would lie, and whether she would offer me refuge during any marital dispute.

Baby-snoring beside me diverted my reflections. Gordon had slipped off the nipple and fallen into a milk-drunk stupor. Typical man, I couldn't help but chuckle. Gertrude also appeared to be slumbering, yet gently continued to suckle now and again. Focusing on Gertrude at my breast calmed me and I drifted off into an unsettled slumber, aware I would soon be awakened for another feeding.

"H-H-heeey!"

Instantly awake, I sat up in bed. *What was that?* Certainly not my babies. It sounded like someone or something wailing. Uncertain how long I had been asleep, I heard the noise again.

"H-h-heeey! Hoo . . ."

Lying back down, I covered my head with my pillow, praying whoever or whatever made the strange sound would go away and not awaken the twins.

"H-h-heeey!"

The yowl did not cease. It came from in front of the house and sounded like a cross between a donkey braying and a drunken Sam. I decided to investigate, tiptoeing to the window.

"Hey, hoo!"

Peering out, I located the source, and it was as I had suspected. Half-sitting, half-sprawling, Sam sat at an awkward angle on the seat of his sulky. It was as plain as the nose on my face that he was dead drunk. I spied another form moving through the shadows toward the cart, and by the light of the moon, I identified our hired man, Joseph, coming to the rescue.

With scorn, I wondered if his job description included helping his tanked up employer out of his racing cart. I watched from my second floor window and knew it wouldn't be easy to transport this stumbling drunk up our front stoop. Joseph quickly abandoned that plan and instead, half dragged, half carried Sam to the barn. A contemptuous "humph" escaped my lips as I walked back to bed and climbed under the quilt for the second time this night, asleep within seconds or at least it seemed so.

Winter, 1899. Sam had driven into town on business this afternoon. With Oscar in school and the other children napping, I treasured the silence. Upstairs sweeping our bedroom floor, I heard, as much as felt, his return. I walked over to the window.

Dashing up the lane in the racing sulky, askew in the seat, Sam snapped the horsewhip, altogether missing the horse's flank. I moved to the side of our bedroom window, concealed by the lace curtain, so if he glanced up he wouldn't see me.

Fear inched up my spine and crept down my arms like hundreds of tiny pinpricks. Foreboding clenched at my insides.

Taking a deep breath, I steeled myself for his arrival. Spying the letter opener on my dressing table, I placed it in the waistband of my skirt, but then reconsidered. Slight of stature, I was no match for his brawn. If he managed to grab the instrument from me, there was no telling what might happen. A wave of nausea swept over me.

I again peeked out the window and shuddered, my heart pounding. With the sulky fast approaching, there was no time to bar the front door. How dare he come home in this condition in the middle of the day!

Terrified, I stepped to the top of the staircase, shaking like a leaf in a windstorm. He flung open the door, staggering into our entryway. I swallowed the lump in my throat, and stood my ground.

"Maggie! What the hell are you doing standing up there?" Disheveled, his fair hair falling rakishly across his forehead, he tossed the sharp words into the air. His piercing blue eyes locked with mine and the hairs on the back of my neck stood on end.

With weak knees, taking one cautious step at a time, I began a halting descent. My pulse raced as I stopped halfway, feeling stronger and somehow larger standing above and peering down on him.

Gaping at me, he hollered, "Damn it woman, get yourself down here this instant and give me a proper welcome home!" He lurched toward the stairway, tripping on the umbrella stand, sending its contents clattering across the oak floor. Remarkably, he regained his balance enough to grip the stair rail, steadying himself and leering at me with eyes ablaze.

I stared back at him, my thoughts tangled, my heart twisted with emotion. Frozen, I was afraid to move forward, yet unable to turn away.

Then, mindful of our children napping nearby, I forced myself down the steps. I held my breath, bracing myself for what I knew lay ahead. Fast and venomous as a striking rattlesnake, he grabbed and overpowered me with his brute strength. With rough hands, he gripped my backside and crushed me fully against his angry, unyielding body.

He pinched my buttocks. Hard. "Ouch! Sam, that hurt!" Any pretense of romance I may have conjured, evaporated.

He pulled away from me. "Let's you and me find a more comfortable place for a little lovin'."

"No, not like this!"

"Don't cross me, you vixen!"

He slapped my face forcefully, and I fell onto the stairs, gasping. Before I could catch my breath, he took hold of me under my arms and dragged me up the stairs and down the hall into our bedroom.

"Sam, please! No, no, no! You're hurting me! Stop! Leave me be!" My face pulsated with pain and I blinked away tears. I pushed against him and attempted to kick him. His unrelenting strength overwhelmed me and he shoved me onto the bed.

"Well, Miss Maggie May, aren't you a wild one? You want a little fight, eh, do you?"

He pinned my arms beside my head with his knees and all my fight dissolved. I choked on snot and tears, as he overpowered me and had his way.

In the aftermath, he left me crumpled in our bed, humiliated and once again broken. Despondent by my powerlessness to escape his advances, I overflowed with a burgeoning fury at his mistreatment. The pattern was monotonously predictable. Just as I'd known what to expect when the sulky came up the lane, I also knew what would happen either later today or at the latest, tomorrow morning. With soberness came contrition.

I had heard it all so many times. "Maggie, oh Maggie, I'm such a louse. You're the *one* woman who can turn me into a decent man. You *know*, without question, you're the best part about me. I'd be desolate without you. I'd just shrivel up and die." His passionate and remorseful pleas for mercy, along with his self-reproach and penitent manner, invariably prevailed on my forgiving nature.

I questioned whether Sam deserved forgiveness, but each time he repented, I convinced myself that he would finally change and the situation would improve. I believed in my heart that by my example, I might make a difference in his life.

On a raw winter afternoon in February, there came a rap at the door. I opened it to find my sister, rosy cheeked and shivering. Inclement weather, including blizzards and high winds, had settled across Macomb County for the past couple of weeks, so I hadn't expected to welcome Ella to the farm.

"Ella, come in this instant! You look half-frozen, but what an unexpected pleasure to see you!"

"Oh my, the temperature out there is cold enough to freeze ice cream hard! Brrr . . ." She uttered this last as she stomped her boots and removed her gloves inside the doorway.

Oscar and Helen ran over to give her a hug and she kneeled down to greet them. School had not been in session this week, due to the severe temperatures.

"Here, let me take your cloak, dear sister! How about a cup of tea? Please, go sit by the fireplace and thaw out your frozen limbs! What brings you out on this bitter day?"

"Maggie, I had the afternoon free from work and thought of you. We haven't seen each other in weeks, so I decided to brave the frigid cold, wrap myself in wool blankets and risk the drive out here. I realize it's easier for me to visit than for you to pack up four children, especially with this current chill."

There was more truth to her remark than she knew. I found no point in sharing that Sam practically kept me prisoner in my own home, seldom giving permission to go out. For now, it was best to simply nod my head in agreement.

"Where are those babies? I've come to hug and kiss them." Her eyes sparkled in anticipation. "Sometimes I ask myself how I can possibly move across the country and leave them behind. I'd like to kidnap and take you all along with me on the journey!"

"Oh, how I wish it were possible," I answered truthfully. "The twins are taking a nap. If they aren't up by the time we finish our tea, we'll go upstairs and wake them, so you can shower them with kisses." She nodded her head and smiled.

Four months old and both angelically chubby, the twins thrived on my milk. Gordon had a twinkle in his merry blue eyes, a sunny disposition and a head full of unruly, curly red locks. Gertrude, also blue-eyed, had silky smooth, flaxen-colored hair and seemed a solemn little soul, quite tentative about life and its perils. I could have called them "day" and "night," as that described how different they were from each other.

The older children, heads together, occupied themselves playing a game of Tiddlywinks while my sister and I sat at the dining table drinking steaming cups of tea. I sensed Ella's mood shift. Soberly, she leaned over to whisper, "Maggie, I'm distressed to hear all the rumors flying about in Mt. Clemens. I'm not one for hearsay, and you know how some people prattle on, but I worry these nasty stories will sully *your* reputation." She paused, before adding, "I find I'm less bothered with Samuel's."

"Whatever are you talking about?" With knots in my stomach, I shuddered, knowing it had been but a matter of time before Sam's recklessness would be exposed.

"Dear sister, I'm wondering if the recent stories being gossiped around town are merely the result of some vile person's ill-will or if there's perhaps some truth to them. It calls to mind your medical difficulty these two years past, and while I had hoped and prayed it an isolated incident, that memory has lately assailed my thoughts. I knew I must have words with you. Have you heard the rumors in regard to Samuel?"

"No. I'm not privy to tales of my husband's behavior, as I do not take many outings these days. With the children and all, you know."

"I don't aim to burden you with accounts of his improprieties, Maggie. I've struggled mightily to do what's proper, but in the end, I believe you should hear it from *someone* and it best be me."

"Out with it, sister."

Her voice even more subdued to protect the children's ears, she said, "He's been observed several times a week leaving various saloons with ladies of the night. On occasion, one of them has been seen driving his sulky about town." She cast her eyes downward, perhaps embarrassed to reveal another of his betrayals being bandied about.

When Ella looked up, she could easily observe that I didn't appear amazed, aghast, hurt or even surprised.

"I am in no way startled by this news, sister, and I doubt you are either, after what transpired two years ago," I muttered. "I've been aware of Sam's comings and goings, arriving back home so soused he needs Joseph's assistance to remove him from the racing cart. Your additional disclosure is not in the least shocking, nor does it come as any revelation. His indiscretions have merely grown more flagrant."

"Have you told Papa of Sam's feckless behavior? Does he have any idea?"

"I've no inkling what he might have heard. He knows Sam has assaulted my person, but he didn't hear, at least from me, anything about his illicit encounters. I went to Papa to show him my bruises quite some time ago. He listened and sent me home with the admonishment to behave myself."

The color drained from her face. "What? He said that?"

I nodded my head.

"Maggie, this is most distressing!"

"It leaves me wondering what I might do. I can't think about my position or I become ill with anxiety. What recourse do I have?"

"Well, you must speak to Papa again. My conscience won't let me even consider a move to Montana this year, leaving you with no confidant, in a conceivably dangerous predicament. I must know you have support, that you and the children are safe."

I rejoiced to hear her whisper those words, yet there was little she could do to prevent any harm caused by Sam's behavior. I couldn't bear that she would again sacrifice herself for our family, so took a different tack. "Joseph assists him to the barn when he arrives home, so no harm comes to me, or the children. I feel secure with Joseph on the property. I bar the door and lock the windows."

She leaned back in the chair and folded her arms.

"Really, Ellie. Please! You must continue to move forward with your plans for Montana. If I'm concerned about the children or my safety, I give you my word I'll take the five of us to Papa's."

She regarded me long and hard, pressing her lips together before countering with, "Yes, Maggie, I believe you, but still, I'd also like your word you will again talk to Papa."

I glanced up to the ceiling in exasperation. "Ella, you know how I dislike airing my dirty laundry to anyone."

"Sister, this is about more than you now. You have four children to consider."

"Well, yes . . . I suppose you're correct in that regard." We stared at each other. "Oh, all right. I see you will give me no rest until I consent. I promise you I'll address the matter once again with Papa."

She nodded her head with satisfaction. I held little hope for Papa's outlook to change, but if my concession helped Ella to achieve her life plan, I would agree to her terms. Our conversation shifted to more cheerful topics and the visit ended after she had spent time holding and admiring both babies.

True to my word, after a spring thaw resulted in a temperature rise unusual for early March, I drove to the Perry farm. Sam had ridden off in the cart soon after Oscar left for school, so Helen, the twins and I dared to set out in the buggy.

We trotted up the rutted lane toward Papa and Lizzie's house, and I gazed out over the fields, beset with memories of times gone by. I wiped away salty tears. Of my original family, only Papa and my three younger sisters were left at home. Most of my kinfolk had moved on . . . Ella and Lucy off to Montana, Louis and James to Mt. Clemens, and me on Sugarbush Road, leaving Papa and Lizzie to farm alone. So much had happened, yet the land remained unchanged. The rich earth slumbered, the fields on the cusp of awakening in a few short weeks, when the breath of spring returned. This I could count on. *Could I bring my children and move home?* I wasn't sure.

By the time I pulled up in front of the house, I had decided this time it was important to include both Papa and Lizzie in the conversation.

"Maggie, how good to see you!" Lizzie had seen us coming up the lane and stood waiting at the foot of the porch steps. "How splendid to see the children. It's been too long! How are you? Oh, look at these twins. They're darling! I'll bet you and Sam are overflowing with joy having these sweet cherubs join your family."

"Why, yes, of course, we're thrilled with Gertrude and Gordon. They're such good babies, but they keep me on my toes, all the same." I forced a smile.

Lizzie prattled on, as she helped me unload the children from the buggy. With each of us toting a drowsy babe, followed by Helen, we made our way inside to the front parlor. Both twins were asleep, so we laid them down side-by-side on the settee.

"Is Papa home today?"

"Oh, yes, he's here. He's out in the barn. I'll go retrieve him straightaway, if you'll keep an eye on Roy." Papa and Lizzie had added to their family with the arrival of Effie May's little brother, Roy, six months younger than my Helen.

He had already grabbed Helen's hand to lead her over to the other side of the room where he played, constructing a tower out of blocks. They continued to build while I waited for Lizzie to bring Papa, contemplating the best approach to my plight.

"Daughter, how grand to see you! It's been too long." Papa looked pleased, as he made his way across the parlor to give me a robust hug. For an older man, he still walked with a spring in his step. I surmised having two youngsters of his own helped to keep him young. Noticing the twins, he exclaimed, "Look at those two sleeping beauties. You've created a fine duet, Maggie." He turned his attention to where Helen and Roy played, calling out "How about a hug, you two?"

After spending an appropriate amount of time on the usual pleasantries, and glad to find both of them at hand, I launched into the real reason for my visit.

"Papa. Lizzie."

They gazed at me expectantly.

"Papa." My voice quavered.

"Maggie, how grim you sound!" exclaimed my step-mother.

I heaved an immense sigh and found my voice. "Well, yes, it is grim. Mostly I'm here because of Ella. She insisted I speak with you before she moves to Montana."

"Aye, daughter? And why would she press you with such a request?"

"I am so unhappy, Papa. Sam is not the man I believed him to be."

"Maggie, is this about his treatment of you again? Did we not discuss this before?" We spoke in hushed tones.

"Papa, I tried to do as you suggested. I really did." With that, I went on to tell them in more explicit detail about the violence, the drinking and the terrible quarrels. I shared my feelings of imprisonment and isolation, along with the paradox of Sam's accusations of immoral behavior and his threats to throw me out. Their faces turned from concern to horror and then resolve.

"Maggie, we'd never abandon you. The tale you've told this morning is highly grievous. I now recognize how unsound was the advice I gave you at our last exchange on this issue. I hang my head in remorse for not hearing your words more clearly. God knows I wasn't the best husband to your dear Mother, may her soul rest in peace, and have long experience with the drink and the havoc it can wreak. This, daughter, goes far beyond a temporary lapse in judgment. I pledge you and the children will always have a place with us, should a time come when the stayin' becomes intolerable." Lizzie nodded her head vigorously in agreement.

At long last I had been heard. Drained, I also nodded my head. The three of us stared at each other in voiceless disquietude. Overcome by a long-sought, overpowering sense of validation and redemption, I then buried my face in my hands, sobbing tears of relief, completely undone. Papa and Lizzie moved as one to surround me with their love, hugging me to them. The children watched curiously from the other side of the room, while the twins continued their innocent slumber. The room fell silent, except for the tick-tock of the grandfather clock.

Summer, 1899. The August day had been hot and slow. After tucking the children into their cots, I sat on the front porch alone, fanning myself, hoping eventide might dispel the stifling heat. Nightfall not far away, the languid chirp of crickets filled the heavy air with song. How quickly time passes. Closing my eyes, I imagined myself a young girl a few miles distant, listening to a similar cricket serenade in a time of few real worries and many dreams. *Where might my children's dreams lead them?* Sighing, I reached for the heart-shaped locket around my neck which held a lock of my firstborn's hair. *Dearest Leander would have been nine years old today.* Unbeckoned tears shimmered on my cheeks, as vivid memories of his sweet, cherubic face flooded my mind. I chastised myself to end this bleak reverie, knowing how the memory led to a sorrowfulness of spirit. I marveled that the mind is such a curious entity, able to travel from future to past without ever leaving the present.

In the fading light, I retrieved Ella's letter from my apron pocket. It had arrived last week. As I set about re-reading it yet again, I acknowledged that while letter-writing in no way closed the distance between us, it softened the ache of absence I suffered for my dear sister.

> *July 17, 1899*
> *Milestown, Montana*
> *Dearest Sister,*
> *Goodness! Where to start? My life has been a whirlwind of activity, which makes it difficult to believe but a month has gone by since I left Michigan. I do offer my apologies for not writing*

sooner. I have written Papa separately, as some of what I will be sharing would best be kept private between us.

The train ride west was magnificent, the land robust with the season's new growth. The prairie itself came alive, with the endlessly rippling green grasses. Living in our forested state of Michigan, you can't begin to imagine the width and breadth of this western landscape.

You will recall Milestown as the town where Lucy and William disembarked from their honeymoon train-ride west all those years ago. I have decided to settle here rather than in Brandenburg, as I will explain in due course.

Lucy did receive my letter in time, which allowed them to meet my train. Oh, sister, our reunion was filled with hugs, laughter, and but a few tears. I met little Grace, a lively toddler with a head-full of curly black hair, nothing like her mother! William welcomed me with a big hug. Once the pleasantries had passed, I quickly perceived the cheerlessness in Lucy's manner and, never one to mince words, she was quick to share her unhappiness when she sensed her husband wouldn't hear.

My, it is a long overland sojourn to Brandenburg, including an overnight stopover at a roadhouse which could use a coat of paint, a scrub brush and some clean linen.

The ranch is magnificent, located near the Tongue River (is that not a strange name?). The vistas from the front porch of the house give the impression you can see forever; the landscape color is distinctive, depending on the time of day. There are few people and many sheep and cattle.

Knowing Lucy and her social nature, I perceive it may be an uphill battle to convince her to stay with her family. Why can she not see how fortunate she is to have not only a loving husband, but also a beautiful daughter? It is difficult for me to fathom her mind-set.

I stayed for 2 weeks and there was no doubt Lucy wished me to stay on. I find I again had to make a difficult choice to leave a sister and chart my own course. There was no viable way for me to earn a living in Brandenburg and my work ethic wouldn't allow me to remain there indefinitely on the charity of my brother-in-law. My internal compass told me my future lies in Milestown, at least for now. Once that decision was revealed, Lucy began to speak to me in earnest of abandoning both her husband and child to move in with me and relive the "good old days" we had in Mt. Clemens. I worry she is not thinking clearly and wonder if the isolation of the ranch has driven her slightly mad. I sincerely believe she needs help, help I am wholly unqualified to offer.

Upon our return to Milestown, amidst hugs and promises to see each other again soon, we bid our farewells. At the moment they turned to leave, as Will grasped Lucy's arm, she gazed at me with the bleakest of stares, causing me some inner panic, as I feared she might pull away from him and demand to stay behind with me. Having plenty of time to consider this matter since, I do pray I am wrong, but recognize a calamity may lie ahead.

On a brighter note, with introductions from William and Lucy, I easily secured a room in the Main Street boarding house in Milestown. Will knows the proprietors and they have given me a good rate. It is clean and well maintained, a relief after that roadhouse on the way to and from Brandenburg. In other good news, the Shore-Newcom Mercantile has work for me, which I consider a good omen indeed that I made the appropriate choice to settle in town. I feel as if I have been accepted into the social fabric with no hesitation, having already become acquainted with several affable women at church and in the mercantile. They have invited me to join both the quilting group and the Ladies Aid Society. I guess what I am saying is I am settling in.

Quite honestly, there is a good chance my "internal compass" may have been weighted in favor of Milestown, which I will now explain. As heavy as my heart feels over the potentially impending disaster with Lucy, my life has taken an unexpected turn I have selfishly decided to pursue. Maggie, on the train out of Chicago, I met an intriguing gentleman by the name of Frank Herman. He has a ranch at the Twelve Mile Dam, south of town, along the Tongue River, up Pumpkin Creek, which I hope to see one day soon.

He was on his way home from Chicago, where he had been meeting buyers at the mammoth stockyards there, making arrangements for the upcoming autumn sale of his spring calves.

He is 42, but never been married; according to him, the "right" woman has yet to come along. He shared this information with a shrewd smile and a wink, and I imagine my face changed several shades of scarlet. We enjoyed conversing and he invited me to prolong our visit by supping with him in the train dining car. Feeling quite blithe of spirit, I promptly put aside any feelings of being a "loose woman," and accepted the invitation.

Since I have been back in Milestown, he has journeyed the 12 miles twice to spend time with me, so we can continue to get to know one another. I have experienced both joy and confusion. Up until now, I've been content as a self-sufficient woman, but meeting Frank has called that into question and I am left wondering if perhaps I have reached a proverbial fork in the road.

In my mind, I can already hear you asking me to tell you more about him. He emigrated with his parents to the United States from Norway when he was but 4 years old, and grew up in St. Peter, Minnesota. He came west with the cavalry in the late '70s and has had all manner of jobs. He has driven a stagecoach, operated a sawmill and is now a rancher. He's fair of hair, with twinkling blue eyes, a tall, lean frame and an easy humor. He has a wonderful handlebar moustache which rivals any I have seen in Mt. Clemens. What he lacks in education, I believe he makes up for in charm, along with a grit and determination to make something of himself. He's worked hard to establish himself as a cattleman and his reputation for raising good beef stock here in eastern Montana has grown over the past 10 years. If I have any hesitation about a future with him, it is the fact he lives out on the prairie, which means, like Lucy, isolated. I am consoled that a dozen miles from town would most likely be easier than Lucy's 44, do you not agree? I ask myself questions such as this as I daydream during slow moments at the mercantile or as I drift off to sleep at night.

Which brings me back to our sister, the other matter weighing on an idle mind. Remember long ago, when I moved to Detroit and we promised to write and share our "heart of hearts?" I freely admit my heart is beset with worry for Lucy. I have a strong sense that I must encourage her to stay the course, as it seems to me she deceives herself, believing she can walk away from her life and feel no sorrow or regret. Forgive me for dwelling on this topic.

Maggie, I think of you often, wondering how things are with Sam. Tell me about the children, as I miss you all so. Please write soon.

> *Your loving sister,*
> *Ella R. Perry*

Each time I read this letter, I again treasured Ella's joyful news about meeting Mr. Frank Herman, yet experienced a pervasive sadness in reading her description of Lucy's travails.

18.

December, 1899. "Maggie, would you ask Mary Jane to spend the night with the children or see if we could leave them with John and Abi on New Year's Eve?" Sam asked at breakfast one early December morning. The local harness racing association had planned a splendid New Year's Eve gathering at the lavish Park Hotel in Mt. Clemens to welcome the arrival of 1900.

Although in the heat of argument, he repeatedly threatened to "throw me out as soon as the children are older," we had formed an uneasy alliance for the sake of those children. I often walked on eggshells to avoid conflict, but for the most part, discretion kept things on an even keel. Leery of his requests or demands, I always looked for hidden meanings in his words.

"Sam, I think it best I stay home from the celebration with the children," I replied tersely, assuming he'd prefer to attend the gala without me.

"Why on earth would you say that? You do realize how important it is for my reputation with the cart-racing association to keep up appearances and attend together?"

Biting my tongue, I refrained from uttering, "And, why would you care about appearances?" Instead, I countered with, "All three of my dresses have been patched so many times, it might reflect poorly on you to be seen with me."

He scrutinized my face, perhaps trying to decipher if this was some type of ploy on my part. "Let me see your clothing."

I brought him my well-worn cloak and gowns, all that was left of my trousseau from ten years ago, and laid them before him on our settee. He examined the garments one-by-one, eyeing them closely.

Unable to dispute my claim, he reached into his wallet and removed a $20 bill. "How has this happened? Why have you let your wardrobe choices become so limited? I want you to drive the buggy into town and find an appropriate gown and cloak to wear to the celebration. Oh, and while you're at it, why don't you go on to your family's house to see about someone to stay with the children?"

Forgotten were all the times he had denied my requests to refurbish my wardrobe.

Like an early Christmas present, this offer lifted my mood and gave me something to look forward to. The following Saturday, the children and I drove into town. With Ella gone, arriving in Mt. Clemens no longer held the same allure, but it was with a certain delight I parked in front of the new women's ready-to-wear store. I had never selected a ready-made gown before and the mere thought of it filled me with happy anticipation.

Sam would approve of the pewter grey A-lined narrow gored skirt I chose, which accentuated my tiny frame. The bodice, a claret-colored moire velour fabric, provided the ideal accent. I also found a reversible cloak made from soft Australian wool, in shades of deep rose and dove grey, and still had enough money left for a coordinating velvet bonnet. My satisfaction with my purchases was cathartic. However temporary, the experience granted me a newfound confidence in my ability to make decisions and a sense of my own power, both sorely lacking in my daily life.

Our next stop was the Perry farm. I'd brought a letter from Ella to share her news.

December 1, 1899
Twelve Mile Dam,
Milestown, Montana
Dear Beloved Family,

I am a bride! Frank and I tied the knot on November 27 at the little Presbyterian Church in Milestown, with my new friends and Frank's old ones in attendance. I missed having my family to witness and share our joy, but held you all close in my heart, believing you will also feel our happiness upon hearing this news.

Lucy and William were not able to attend, due to inclement weather conditions creating impassable roads. Sorely disappointed, we will instead look forward to celebrating with them at a future time.

I realize you may all be of the opinion we have proceeded quickly, but that is because we both recognize we are no longer young. Married life has completely exceeded my expectations and I'm settling in to Frank's quaint ranch house along the Tongue River. Stretching as far as the eye can see, the world is divided into two, creating a panorama of azure sky and a silent, white prairie. I sense otherworldliness in the stillness. Even the deer and antelope move quietly about, nosing through the pristine snow in hopes of finding a few morsels of dead grasses. Their graceful poses or loping gaits across the plains and hills could hold me spellbound for hours on end, yet I stir myself out of the reverie, realizing there is much to be accomplished each day, both inside and out. Frank works hard and some days I barely see him during the day, as he is out feeding his cattle, breaking up the ice in the windmill water troughs or making fence repairs along his property line. I have suggested I join him to be a helpmate, but he insists I stay inside where I will be warm and safe. Given time, I am convinced he will come to learn I am hardy and can be helpful to him. For now, I will enjoy being coddled, an entirely new experience, and use the time to spruce up our house.

Dear ones, rest easy, affirming I am content. My letter comes with a Christmas wish, praying for peace and joy during this season of love.

May you all have a blessed New Year and New Century.

With Tidings of Great Joy,

Mrs. Frank (Ella) Herman

I didn't bring the note she'd included, addressed to me alone.

Dearest Sister,

I include this extra missive to apprise you of the situation with Lucy. Despite the fact we correspond by mail, I have seen her again but a handful of times, when the family has come to Milestown once a month for supplies and William's business. And now I regret it shall be even less, with my move to the Twelve Mile Dam.

During their last visit, she was at once both thrilled and disappointed with me, when I shared the news of my impending marriage to Frank. She acted overjoyed I had found such happiness, even though this information understandably placed a damper on her scheme to move into town to live with me. To my relief, this sort of talk has at last abated in all recent correspondence. I hope she can put aside these notions for good and step forward with her chosen life, for the sake of her daughter.

Write soon and tell me about your life and the children.

Your loving sister,

Ella Perry Herman

The children had been fed, the fire stoked and I was putting the finishing touches on my new ensemble when I heard Sam come in the front door, after having collected my sister. I had high hopes for the evening and couldn't help but feel a flutter of excitement, even if it would be spent with my often willful husband.

"Aunt Janie! Aunt Janie! Come see what we're doing," called Oscar from the corner of the parlor where he and Helen played with his wooden train set, doing their best to avoid the chaos created by Gordon and Gertrude building with blocks in front of the fireplace.

Janie smiled at me as Helen ran over, took her hand and pulled her toward where Oscar sat on the floor.

"We're so grateful you could stay with the children this evening, Janie."

"With Effie May and Roy staying over at Abi and John Henry's tonight and Lizzie and Papa off to the gala, I'm glad not to be home alone. The five of us will have a grand time welcoming 1900, won't we?" She winked at them and smiled.

Always prim, she had never expressed any interest in leaving home, let alone getting married. Both our younger sisters, Edith and Eva, had married, so she was the last of us remaining at the Perry farm. Apparently content to spend time with the youngsters, surely Lizzie and Papa appreciated her, but I couldn't help but wonder if life might pass her by.

Sam stood waiting before me. I found him so appealing in his three-piece suit, with a navy topcoat and cuffed trousers, cut in the new shorter style and crisply creased, both back and front. The topcoat covered a beige waistcoat underneath, left open to reveal his starched white shirt and bowtie. How could he look so engaging, yet act so despicably? I loathed my inability to spurn him.

"Well, Mrs. Jobsa, before we are off to the ball, I have a little something for you, to commemorate these last ten years of matrimony." He beamed and extended a tiny gift-wrapped box. Everyone looked on with anticipation, while I unwrapped it to find a pair of glittering diamond earrings. Dumbfounded, my jaw dropped, leaving me temporarily speechless. Janie gasped.

"Why, Sam," I stuttered, my heart skipping a beat, "I don't know what to say. They're stunning. Thank you."

"Would you do me the honor of wearing them tonight?" How easily he beguiled me, bewitching me with his smile.

Sparkling earrings in place, I kissed the children and with a last glance at them in this century, I took my husband's arm. Like a princess, I walked down our steps toward my awaiting carriage, inhaling deeply of the crisp December air. Once aboard, I snuggled cozily into the wool blankets, and gazed up into the clear night sky. The stars were out full force, lighting our way down the lane. I shivered as Sam reached under the blanket for my hand.

Our moods were ebullient as we bantered effortlessly on the ride to town, discussing the wonder of our children, along with less important, trifling matters. I dared to hold hope in the belief we would start anew with the arrival of the twentieth century.

The sumptuous Park Hotel, built two years earlier and located next to the Park bathhouse, was across the street from the Avery, the site of our wedding reception ten years ago. The hotel had gained a reputation in the township as the most renowned setting for elaborate parties and social gatherings. Our buggy approached the entrance of the opulent three-story building, and my heart beat faster, in anticipation of an enchanted evening. The owners had spared no expense. My first view of the ornate lobby and wide marble hallways filled with promenading couples left me breathless. Arm in arm, Sam and I glided into the ballroom, equally opulent and elaborately adorned. On the other side of the room, I noticed Papa and Lizzie and we strolled toward them.

"Papa, Lizzie, how nice to see you both." Their eyes lit up, as both appeared genuinely delighted to see us. They stood side-by-side, holding hands.

"Maggie, Sam." I hugged them both, and Papa and Sam shook hands. "The harness racing group has gone all out for this soiree, don't you agree?" Papa tipped his head.

"James, by all means. Say, can I bring you something to drink?" Sam had his eye on the table offering two styles of punch, one more dangerous than the other.

"Let me join you in the selection, my boy."

The men returned with our drinks, joined by Sam's father, Henry. "How-do? You dazzle me with your beauty, ladies." Never at a loss for words, that man.

We nodded our thanks and I spoke up, "Where's your lovely wife?"

"Oh, Gertrude's home with a touch of malaise. She insisted I come along without her though, to ring in the New Year." A shiver ran up my spine, as his overly charming smile reminded me unnervingly of Sam. *Was Gertrude indeed infirm or did she simply not wish to participate in her husband's boisterous revelry?*

I redirected my attention to the liveliness of the ballroom. Never had I seen so many gorgeous gowns, or been part of such a jubilant gathering. Sam and I danced, drank champagne--my first since our wedding--and sampled various delectable hors d'oeuvres. The evening proved a grand affair with whistles, horns, fireworks and even the shooting of pistols at midnight.

In the midst of all the fanfare, Sam took me in his arms. "Maggie, I've never loved you more. You radiate such beauty!" He pulled me close and kissed me exuberantly. I laughed and acquiesced, hoping beyond hope our lives might once and for all change direction. Tipsy, I savored the promise of a better future, and this sentiment remained solidly in my mind on the frosty ride home.

Part Three

Finish each day and be done with it. You have done what you could. Some blunders and absurdities no doubt crept in; forget them as soon as you can. Tomorrow is a new day. You shall begin it serenely and with too high a spirit to be encumbered with your old nonsense.
--Ralph Waldo Emerson

19.

Lavina, Montana, October 15, 1941. Deciding a nice cup of coffee would hit the spot, I put fresh water in the kettle to boil and add some ground beans to the muslin bag inside my coffee pot. My son sent me a percolator-type contraption, but the coffee it makes tastes dreadful. I would rather take the time and brew it the old-fashioned way for a fuller and more robust flavor.

Ah, yes, the old-fashioned way . . . standing by the stove, I stare out the window, remembering the first cup of steaming coffee I ever made for Sam. So prophetic! Our future turned out to be as dark as the liquid in that mug. Oh, how clearly I can see now. Mother even tried to warn me. Such a foolish girl, I insisted on moving blindly forward, ignoring all the signs, with no sense of how calamitous life would become.

Losing darling Leander did not help matters. Without that tragedy, would our lives have followed the same course? What if I had not made the desperate attempt to free myself and the children? Would it have altered the heart-rending outcome? I suppose this is unknowable.

Over the years, with the assistance of my ever-expanding faith, I've continued to nudge myself towards self-absolution. As time has passed, I have pondered the unknowable less often, and today, I am resolute. I touch my heart and take a deep breath. I *will* end this reflection and let it go. I have made my atonement and *will* forgive myself.

The whistling kettle draws me back. I pour the boiling water into the pot and decide to dress while the coffee steeps and the pie is baking. After inspecting the contents of my closet, I settle on a blue and white floral print day dress, the perfect choice for today. I'll also wear my pearls. I see no reason why not. Inhaling the mouthwatering aroma of the pie, along with the rich, bold smell of coffee, I brush my thinning hair into a bun, securing it with hairpins. Still in my cotton mules, I traipse back down the hallway toward those beckoning smells.

I savor my breakfast of coffee, toast and a soft-boiled egg. After I finish, I check on the pie. The crust looks perfectly golden, so I lift it out of the oven and set it on the windowsill to cool.

Our interior walls are thin, so I can hear the chattering of the girls as they prepare to open the cafe for the day. Watching out our front room window, it's not long before I see the first customers arrive for a cup of coffee and perhaps breakfast. With the harvest in, the area farmers and ranchers regularly gather at the cafe to shoot the breeze.

Enjoying a second cup of coffee, I read my daily devotionals. Usually Frances and I study together, but with her absence, I've been on my own these past several days.

Like me, my Christian Science textbook is rather worn. Chagrined, I have to admit much of the little book's wear and tear has come from being shoved around in my trunk for years at a time, as I slid in and out of the faith.

I open *Science & Health,* by Mary Baker Eddy and turn to page 491. "Material man is made up of involuntary and voluntary error, of a negative right and a positive wrong, the latter calling itself right. Man's spiritual individuality is never wrong. It is the likeness of man's Maker."

Even though both of us had put our minds to understanding the reason for Frances' malady, in the end, this didn't help her. In truth, that lack of effect sometimes weakens my convictions. I've come to believe some questions have no answer on this plane of existence, so I simply continue to pray for equanimity.

20

Sugarbush Road, Early Spring, 1900. "Mama, why do you cry so?" Oscar stared at me, his blue eyes orbs in which I beheld my own distraught reflection. Four sets of eyes peered at me, slumped in my rocking chair, weeping. While the twins eyed me with curiosity, Helen and Oscar's faces displayed grave concern, as they had rarely, if ever, seen their mother in such a state of complete disarray.

A rage burned within. Visions of shrieking and throwing plates, smoldered beneath my stinging tears. I had reached the boiling point with regard to Sam's continued lapses in judgment. Treading on dangerous ground, I had decided to take a stand. I trembled at the thought of confronting him, but I simply could no longer bear his loutish behavior. It had at last come to this, and the children now witnessed my overpowering dread.

The new year had begun with such promise. Sam occasionally disappeared in the evenings, but his demeanor had been so much more agreeable, I had tolerated his questionable absences--until now. I replayed in my mind our latest exchange at supper last night.

"Frankly Maggie, there are times when I need to get away for a few hours. An evening of cards or conversation with other men improves my attitude on the farm. You should be aware how monotonous farming can be and I find my brain needs company after days of repeated drudgery."

"Sam, can I not help relieve this drudgery? I would be pleased to play cards with you, discuss current events or go into town along with you for the evening. Life for me is often humdrum and tedious as well." I did not believe one whit of his purported "need" to be with other men and had called his bluff.

"Your understanding of my needs is obviously limited." He scoffed as he turned and walked away.

Somehow he had missed the point. Or, had I?

This morning, my heart breaking, I gazed upon my brood. "Oh, children, I love you so. No matter what might happen, I will always love you."

"What do you mean? What might happen, Mama?" asked Helen, alarmed.

In an instant, I recovered and pulled myself together. Sam would return from the fields at any moment and I needed to steady myself. "Oh, nothing will happen, dear one."

❧

"What the hell are you suggesting?" Sam was in rare form, but I was not going to back down. Not this time. The children in bed down the hall, we stood face-to-face in our room.

"I'm not suggesting anything. I'm telling you I found this picture of a hussy in your jacket pocket this morning." I waved the photograph in his face. He swiped at it in an attempt to pluck it away from me, but I prevailed and held onto the incriminating image.

"Oh, God, Maggie, I asked for her picture to bring it home to show to you. I ran into her in Mt. Clemens. She's someone I've known for years and there's sure as hell nothing else to it. I wanted you to see it, as I regarded it a well-done portrait. I hoped perhaps we'd hire the same photographer to have our portraits done. That's all. I don't know why the devil you're so suspicious. Damn, don't I come home every night? Don't I provide shelter, food and all the needs for you and the children? Why can't you ever give me the benefit of the doubt? I don't understand you!"

I supposed there might be some plausibility to the story. Unsure, I wavered. With one glance at me, he detected my indecisiveness and leapt on the opportunity.

His voice calmed, he implored, "Maggie, you must quit jumping to conclusions without knowing the true story. You have to admit, things have been better between us. Stop trying to find fault all the time and start trying to work to make our marriage better, as I've been doing."

Against my better judgment, I relinquished my anger. "Oh, Sam, I'm sorry. I promise to try harder. But, would you make a promise to me you'll stop going into town so often? And, if you do go, you'll take me along? We'll ask my sister to come watch the children. I'd like a night out now and then too."

He sized me up and down, considering my proposal. "Of course. It sounds like an ideal plan." He walked toward me and with some reluctance, I let him take me into his arms, inhaling the familiar scent of leather and musk.

⌇⟶

The agreement lasted a mere four days. We had finished supper when Sam announced he would soon be leaving for town.

"How about if I come? I imagine we can drop the children off with Abi and John Henry for a couple of hours."

"No, this is business and I can't have you tagging along. I may be quite late. Another time."

A predictable response. "But, Sam! What about our agreement? You said . . ."

"Maggie, did you hear what I said?"

"Yes, but . . ."

"The answer is no and I don't appreciate your impertinence!" Noticeably peeved, he went upstairs to change his clothes.

Irritated, I continued cleaning up, while the children played nearby. He came downstairs whistling, his jacket slung over his shoulder. He walked over to me and as he leaned over to give me a peck on the cheek, I turned away. "Fine. Have it your way. Don't wait up. As I said, this business meeting may last into the wee hours."

I intended to wait up for him, but nodded off on the settee, to be awakened when he appeared in the doorway around one o'clock, reeking of spilled whiskey and stale cigars. One look told me he had been drinking and carousing. His bow tie dangled from under his collar, his unevenly buttoned shirt hanging out behind. Ignoring me, he weaved his way across the room and started up the stairs. I followed behind, gagging in the wake of his stench, a silent fury spreading its tentacles from my fingertips to my toes. Once in our bedroom, I ripped at my dress buttons, throwing the gown in a pile on the floor. My fingers shook as I attempted to fasten my nightgown.

He was passed out on the bed fully clothed when I emerged from the dressing closet. I snatched the quilt and my pillow and made a bed for myself on the floor next to my side of the bed, refusing to lie down beside such a detestable man.

Tossing and turning on the hardwood floor, sleep evaded me. Devastated, I realized yet again this scene would always be the story of my life with Sam, trapped in a pit overflowing with anger and fear.

I lay awake, brooding on another notion which had taken root in my mind. There had to be a way out, if only I had the wisdom and courage to find it.

Up at dawn, I had slept little. While buttoning my day dress, Sam awakened. Neither of us spoke. He stripped off his wrinkled evening attire and tossed it on the rocking chair, before pulling his work clothes off the wall peg. Habitually, I picked up his shirt, which stunk of citrus, to determine if it needed laundering. Something caught my attention and my stomach lurched. Perceiving the answer before I asked the question, I asked in a dull, monotone voice, "Sam, what is this?" My back turned to him, I held his shirt up and pulled several long black hairs from the armpit. He paid me no heed. I inspected further and noted the remains of what appeared to be red-tinted rouge on the collar.

It was but one betrayal out of many, but at that moment I decided it would be the last. My face grew hot and my insides writhed. The crumbling inside me was tangible, and my head began to throb. I had reached the end of my rope. I would no longer stand by and swallow the weak excuses thrown in my face. Deep in my chest, my heart convulsed, irreversibly severing any and all ties to this immoral man.

Sam, meanwhile, unaware of this transformation, continued to respond to my question with silence. He stood across the room from me, gazing out the bedroom window.

"Is this what I think it is?" My voice shook with rage as I repeated with more emphasis, "Is this what I think it is?" He remained tight-lipped.

"Sam! How could you? I'm finished with you. This marriage is over! Get out!" I stood to my full height and with a newfound confidence, pointed to the door, "Get. Out!" I'm sure I hollered loud enough to wake the children in the nursery. It certainly got his attention.

"You damn shrew. Shut your mouth! Hells bells, you fly off the handle without even hearing the story. You don't know what the devil you're talking about!"

In five short strides he stood in front of me, leaving me no time to react. Sudden searing pain radiated from my cheek when the force of his blow knocked me backwards toward the window. I grabbed at the windowsill to keep from toppling to the floor. Stunned, I held my burning cheek with the back of my hand and swallowed hard. There would be no tears from me. Not this time.

"This union has reached an end. Find somewhere else to live." How easily these words spilled from my mouth.

"What do you mean, find somewhere else to live?"

"Exactly what I said. Find somewhere else to live. Besides here."

"You can go straight to hell. I live here and I'm not leaving."

I ignored his comment and continued, as if talking to a four-year-old, "You can find accommodation in town or in the barn, because you are never sleeping in our room again. I cannot make it any more plain than that. If you attempt to enter the bedroom, I will report you to the sheriff, citing extreme cruelty."

"Why on earth are you punishing me? You are one cold fish, woman, and for the life of me, God only knows why I married you in the first place!"

Any further words from me would only serve to escalate an already dangerous situation. Arms akimbo, my face throbbing, I held my ground and stared at him in stony silence.

His forehead puckered in frustration. "Have it your way." As he moved toward the doorway he looked back toward me and with a frigid voice said, "Actually, it's a relief, as I can't even stand the sight of you. I find your entire being repugnant." He turned on his heel and stomped down the stairs and out of the house.

Without hesitation, I twisted and tugged at that band of gold encircling the fourth finger of my left hand, and once free, threw it across the room after him. I then crumpled onto the bed, holding my head in my hands, trembling. I had stood up to him with body and soul intact. I began to contemplate divorce, as incredible as that sounded. How could I support my children? Where would we live? My head swirled with emotion and questions. I needed a plan.

Over the next couple of weeks, I bided my time, while contemplating a strategy for our escape. Sam had moved into the barn to bunk with the new hired boy, Albert, leaving the children and me to our own devices. He was evidently and rightfully concerned I might take the children and flee, as the latch on the barn doors now sported a hefty padlock, which kept me away from the buggy and horses. I had searched both high and low for a key to the lock, without success.

I was desperate to send a note to Papa and Lizzie to come rescue us, but could not fathom how to do so. *Might I somehow bribe Albert, perhaps with my emerald brooch or diamond earrings? What if Sam should intercept the note or worse, Albert betray me?* My overwhelming fear of reprisal was far greater than my urge to attempt such a scheme. Since Sam had moved out of the house, he no longer took me along when he went to town for food and supplies. What little contact I had with others was lost. Trapped in Sam's web, I had no way to foresee when someone might drop in for a visit.

During the rest of the month of March, I heard him come home every night near midnight, drunker than a skunk. I couldn't understand how Albert put up with him. In the end, I imagined that's what had driven Joseph away. After days of stewing and fretting, and many sleepless nights, I still had not divined any clear way out. Thoughts of escape tormented me incessantly.

The last day of March, a Saturday, turned breezy in the afternoon, with low lying clouds off to the west. I stood at the window of my bedroom, restless, observing Sam and Albert, tiny figures off working in the furthest field. The twins were napping while Oscar and Helen played in the yard below.

Overpowered by an urgency I could not ignore, all my instincts cried out. The time to leave had arrived. It involved some risk, but without the buggy or horses, my options were limited. I surmised I had a couple of hours or more before the men would return. I likely wouldn't have the liberty to revisit my bedroom, so in haste I gathered together my jewelry, wrapped it in one of Sam's clean handkerchiefs and pinned it inside my skirt pocket, already planning ahead for the time when I would need to sell it.

I called the two oldest into the kitchen. "Oscar. Helen. Mama has to go find Grandada James. I can't take you because it's too far for the twins to walk and I'm not strong enough to carry the both of them and I can't leave them here alone. You'll have to be my brave children and watch over things until I come back for you. I'll run fast and be back as quickly as possible. I want you to stay in the house and keep Gordon and Gertrude out of trouble. Do you understand?"

My four- and seven-year-olds nodded somberly at me, as if they perfectly understood the gravity of the situation. "All right, Mama. Will you be back very soon?"

I tasted my fear and shivered. "As soon as I can, Oscar."

"Mama, I'm scared. Why are you going away from us? Don't go, Mama." Helen started to cry. She grabbed hold of my skirt. My heart fragmented, but I saw no other option.

"Oh, sweet one, I'll be back before you know it and we'll all climb aboard Grandada's wagon and go to his farm. I will run like the wind and be back lickety-split. Maybe even before the twins awaken! I want you both to put on your bravest smiles and wave to me from the window, okay?" I loosened Helen's grip on my skirt.

Because the house and barn were easily visible from the field, I had to sneak out and around the back of the house, through the woods and over the neighbor's pasture to the other side of the road. There would be hell to pay if Sam spotted me. I would run to Papa's, where we would hitch the wagon and return for the children. It was my plan and it had to work. I would will it to work.

I hugged each of my dear, little ones and then walked out the door.

Going the long way around to town cost me precious time and I had misjudged the weather. The wind picked up, pulling ragged, leaky clouds overhead, and a light rain began to fall. The dirt lane soon turned slippery and I fell, landing in the muddy ruts, but didn't stop. I hurried on past Mt. Clemens, running the final couple of miles to the Perry farm, arriving wild-eyed and disheveled only to learn from the hired servant that Papa and Lizzie had taken the wagon into town for supplies.

By this time, crazed with fear Sam had found me out, I sobbed in desperation, "No! No!" The servant reassured me they would soon return, and recognizing something horribly amiss, vigorously encouraged me to come inside to wait and rest a spell. Rather than linger, I knew I had to keep moving, so I returned the way I'd come, at a steady trotting pace, soaked to the bone.

It wasn't long before Papa's wagon came up the road. My hair had loosened from its clip and flew in all directions, my skirt and boots muddied; assuredly looking to them as hysterical as I felt.

"Maggie! My God! What's happened?" Papa shouted, as soon as he was within earshot.

"Papa, oh, Papa! We have to get back to the farm! Now!" I left no room for argument and he helped me squeeze into the buckboard seat, between Lizzie and him. He pulled out an uncommonly used whip and snapped it lightly, directing the horses to a gallop. In breathless fits and starts, I told them my sordid tale, as we bolted down the road toward the farm on Sugarbush Road.

Barreling up the lane to the farmhouse, I sensed trouble before I saw it. We drew closer, and both Sam and Albert stood menacingly on the front porch, my children nowhere to be seen.

"I've half a mind to bring the sheriff over to charge you with abandonment of my children, you good-for-nothing woman!" Sam sneered.

Before I could reply, Papa spoke up. "Well, now, Sam, I don't think my daughter has abandoned her children as she's back to collect them."

"Too late! She's not setting foot on this property again," Sam commanded, talking as if I weren't sitting in the wagon, a few feet away. "If she so much as attempts to take my children, I'll have her charged with both trespassing and kidnapping."

Oscar and Helen stared through the parlor window. I smiled at them, blowing them kisses, which brought relieved smiles to their faces, and they reciprocated in kind.

"Daughter, I think it best we head back to town and hire an attorney, to iron out this predicament. Giddy-up!" Papa called to his horses, and we lurched forward to turn around. I realized the futility of arguing, so sat silent.

Papa's wagon trotted back down the lane, and I turned, aching for what I had left behind. Blinded by tears, my eyes were fixed upon the two small figures in the window, until the sight faded into the ever-increasing distance between us.

21.

Mt. Clemens, Spring, 1900. Martin Crocker, Esq., tamped his pipe bowl, struck a match, and drew in air, soon releasing a cloud of blue smoke which circulated around his head. "Yes, stories about Sam gallivanting around town on the thirty-first with two, er . . . shall I say . . ." and he paused, raising an eyebrow, "women of dubious character, have been circulating all over Mt. Clemens. One of them was even seen driving his buggy!"

With a sinking sensation, I realized that two days had passed since I had last seen my children. I inhaled deeply, finding it difficult to stifle my indignation upon hearing Mr. Crocker's words. I wouldn't put it past Sam, but surely he wouldn't have left them alone to go into town and cavort with filthy whores. Or, would he? I agonized, realizing I had no way to know. With all the willpower I could muster, I squeezed my hands together, gritted my teeth and attempted to refocus my attention on what the attorney was saying.

"Maggie, I believe you have a strong case in your favor. Alice, by the way, include the part about Sam cavorting with the two women the other night. We'll have several witnesses we can call on, in that regard."

Alice, Mr. Crocker's dutiful secretary, nodded her head without lifting her pen from her stenographer's notebook.

Martin Crocker, a middle-aged attorney, well-respected in our township, had a solid reputation for honesty and commitment to his clients. Seated in his wood-paneled office in Mt. Clemens, I had just finished a detailed narrative of my tumultuous marriage to Sam, with

Alice writing down every word. I spared none of the lurid details, from Sam's repeated bouts of drinking to his vulgar accusations, from the stomach-turning violence to the loathsome gonorrhea. It was all there, laid bare for the world to see.

"Maggie, dear, it's my understanding Sam owns the property on Sugarbush Road, free and clear?"

"Yes, Mr. Crocker, as far as I know, that's correct. I believe his father gave him the property years ago, before we married."

"Would I also be correct in assuming there's stock, tools, hay and grain on the property, as well as salable timber?"

"Yes. Why do you ask?"

"Well, in plain language, there have been documented instances of a defendant disposing of his property rather than risk losing it in any sort of divorce settlement. We shall seek a temporary injunction to prevent such action on Sam's part."

While I did not question this advice, I didn't give a damn about the property. All my questions concerned my children. "Mr. Crocker, I'm desperate to see my children! Is there nothing you can do to expedite these proceedings?" Inner turmoil, combined with the pipe smoke, had caused my stomach to become unsettled. It took great concentration to hold my emotions in check, at the mere thought of my absent children.

"All in due time, dear, all in due time. We'll file this Bill of Complaint seeking divorce in Circuit Court, and see what response we receive from Mr. Jobsa or his attorney. We'll ask for temporary alimony of $5 per week during the pendency of the lawsuit, to be paid for the upkeep and maintenance of you and the children, and ask they be turned over to you immediately. It goes without saying we will seek permanent custody as part of the settlement. Maggie, I recognize this is difficult, but we must proceed with caution. And I must recommend you stay away from the farm on Sugarbush Road, as a precaution. Anything you might say or do can and will be used in Sam's defense. Please, you must be patient."

Be patient? I bit my tongue to keep from lashing out at the seeming impossibility of what he asked.

Perceptive enough to realize he had raised my hackles, he added, "We'll hope for an expeditious response from the defendant or his representative. At the moment, I'll need your signature on this deposition." He handed me a pen and in bold script, I signed *Margareta M. Jobsa* to the document. I was officially filing for divorce!

Mr. Crocker stood and signaled our departure with, "I'll be in touch."

He shook our hands, first Papa's and then my own. Somberly, we exited the attorney's office and climbed into the buggy to return to the Perry farm. The absence of conversation left me to ruminate on my own dark thoughts. My stomach roiled with a rising sense of panic, as I wondered yet again who might be caring for my babies. I imagined Sam had told them I had abandoned them. It was not by choice, I reasoned, consoling myself. I hoped and prayed Sam's mother Gertrude, or perhaps one of Sam's maiden aunts, Johanna or Maria, had gone out to the farm. I continued to plot and scheme about ways to rescue Oscar, Helen, Gertrude and Gordon from their father's clutches.

For several days, I did naught but lie sluggishly on the settee in the parlor, imploring sleep to transport me into oblivion as an escape from the constant pain of my heart. Time crept by, with no concern for my grief, one slow minute after the other. I despaired. While no more than a few miles separated us, my four children remained unreachable. Nearly as unreachable as dearest Leander. I tortured myself, questioning my actions over and over. Every moment of every day I agonized over my children. It was a living hell.

"Maggie!" I opened my eyes to find my stepmother inches from my face. "It's high time you get up off the couch and rejoin the living!"

I closed my eyes and turned away from her.

"Maggie!" She grabbed me by the shoulders and shook me. "Wake up! Open your eyes and look at me!"

Startled by her boldness, I reluctantly complied, opening my eyes a crack. "Leave me alone."

"No! You listen, young lady. There can be no greater misery than the forced separation of mother from child! No one knows this better than I. You aren't the only one who has lost children. I'm here to tell you there is no deeper pain. The law gave my boys to that drunkard husband of mine. I'll never forget and I won't ever recover, but I have forged ahead. You must do the same! I stand before you and declare you will make it through this dark time with the love and assistance of your family. Not everyone is blessed to have family nearby." Lizzie finished her tirade with a flourish of her arms.

Astonished by her fervor, I sat up, speechless. Without a word, I stood, walked over to the entryway, grabbed my wrap from the peg and went outside. I trudged through Papa's fields, stopping occasionally to pick up and throw a rock as hard and as far as possible, raging at life, howling at the top of my lungs at its injustice. By the time I returned, I had realized the futility of my behavior. Neither languishing nor raging would ever improve the situation. The truth remained that Sam had the children, and who knew what deceitful ideas he had fed to them. With all my heart, I believed there had to be a way to rescue them. I walked down the hallway and into the kitchen, throwing my arms around Lizzie, where she stood at the sink peeling potatoes.

"Lizzie, you are right." I turned on my heel and went upstairs before she could utter a reply.

Nine days later, on April 11, we had heard not one word from Sam or his attorney. Mr. Crocker summoned Papa and me to his office. He had learned from his sources that Sam had sold a farm horse and worse, had hired some day laborers to begin clearing timber from our property. My attorney did not take this lightly.

"Our next step is to file an amended Bill of Complaint, again seeking divorce and advising the court we've had no communication from either Samuel or his attorney. We'll also command Samuel to halt any further sale or disposal of personal property or timber, and threaten him with a $10,000 fine if he doesn't immediately cease and desist from such activity.

"In addition, we'll petition anew for temporary alimony, custody of the children, and $25 in solicitor fees plus an additional $25 in witness fees. I do believe this time we'll obtain a response relatively soon. Dollar costs customarily receive prompt attention."

Mr. Crocker's office filed the amended Bill of Complaint barely one week later in Circuit Court and the injunction was approved that same day. The court's order elicited an immediate response from Sam, as Mr. Crocker had predicted, and we quickly found ourselves back in his office. Sam's attorney had filed a motion to modify or dissolve the injunction, citing *unreasonableness* and *hardship*. Sam had the audacity to deny all the *material allegations* in my Bill of Complaint, blatantly twisting the truth in his rejoinder to my claims, or *errors*, as he brazenly called them. He admitted being married to me, but that was all he admitted, other than agreeing we had four living children together. He ignored my petition for custody, and accused me of being *unfit* to have such care and custody.

Incredibly, Sam charged me with directing *anger and violence* toward him as well as *extreme and repeated cruelty*, using *profane language* in front of the children and treating them with *cruelty and neglect . . . voluntarily leaving them*. He had the nerve to accuse *me* of deceitfulness, my gonorrheal "illness" brought about by my own *criminal act*. Not only preposterous, I found his denouncements vile. He admitted to *two or three occasions of getting intoxicated* during our marriage, but suggested he was *not in the habit* of doing so. I couldn't help but laugh with scorn when I read that. Under the label of *extreme cruelty*, he even managed to implicate Papa, with the accusation that Papa and Lizzie had *circulated stories* about Sam giving me gonorrhea and *cohabitating with lewd women*, and encouraged me to *desert* him. It didn't end there, but it so incensed me to read the outlandish charges, I tossed the document on the desk in disgust.

"Papa, I'd like to walk home, if you please," I declared as we left Mr. Crocker's office.

"Aye, daughter, I can understand. Blow off some steam for me, too!"

My dignity in tatters, I ran all the way, leaning into the gusting wind and screaming at the top of my lungs. *How dare you, William Samuel Jobsa? How dare you!*

My head spun with schemes for regaining my children, patience be damned. Six days after our meeting with Mr. Crocker, with all the cunning and courage I could muster, I decided to put the best of my plans into action. Dozing off and on, I willed myself to wait in bed fully dressed until the moon rose around 3 a.m. Quietly, I tiptoed out the back door of the farmhouse, down the steps and out to the barn. I felt around in the dark to locate the horse's harness, not wanting to risk lighting the kerosene lamp.

"Daughter, what are you planning here?"

I shrieked aloud in terror, dropping the harness and throwing my arms up before recognizing the voice as Papa's. "Papa! My God! Why, you nearly gave me apoplexy!"

"Jesus, Mary and Joseph! My apologies if I scared you, daughter, but it is the middle of the night, and from where I stood on the other side of the yard, it seemed you might be some sort of intruder."

"What are you doing up and about at this time of the night?"

"Someday when you're older, I imagine you'll learn the answer to that. I didn't want to disturb Lizzie with the chamber pot; she's such a light sleeper."

My ill luck, that he had been outside relieving himself and saw me sneak by.

"Maggie, you've yet to answer my question. What are you up to?"

"Papa, I can't bear it! I want my children! I need to hug them, kiss them, hear their voices, wipe their runny noses, wash their clothes, cook their meals. I want to be a mother again. Please! Let me go.

Without them, my life is worth nothing. This is my chance to regain them!"

"And why do you say this is your 'chance?' What's different about this night?"

"Oh, it makes no difference which night, because most nights, it's the same! I have a hunch Sam will be passed out dead drunk in the barn by this time. Any caretaker of my babes would also be fast asleep, so it is the most favorable time for me to rescue my children, under cover of darkness. Papa, I'm determined to see my plan through to completion."

"Margareta Perry, I do believe ye are daft, woman! Even if Sam is indeed incapacitated, how do you propose to break into the house, collect the four little ones and, as you say, 'rescue' them, without awakening anyone?"

I showed Papa my kitchen knife.

"Holy Mother of God. What are you thinking? Were you going to use that knife to attack Gertrude or whoever might be with the wee ones?" Aghast, he shook his head in dismay, seizing the knife from my grip. "What were you planning to do, if indeed you found success in this venture? Come back here, so the sheriff could show up to arrest you for kidnapping, or perhaps assault? God only knows what might happen if Sam caught you in the act! My dear, darling daughter, your pain's undeniable, but you're not thinking sensibly. That's not the way to bring your children back to you. Come, let's go back into the house and I'll pour you a dram to help you sleep."

Begrudgingly, I followed him back into the house, exasperated and grief-stricken by the powerlessness of my situation.

Two weeks had passed since Papa and I met with Mr. Crocker to discuss my predicament. I labored tirelessly each day, working myself to the bone, falling into bed each night so exhausted I slumbered within seconds. My hands remained busy and so did my head, working out how I might care for and support my children after the court granted my petition for custody. Could we live on $20 a month while waiting for the divorce settlement? I wanted to be certain we would have enough to survive. I was anxious to meet with him again.

On the afternoon of May 8, a cloudy, rainy day, he summoned us to his office. My mood was optimistic, despite the dismal weather.

Mr. Crocker, in his three-piece linen suit, emanated elegance, while I, dressed in the one garment I currently possessed, appeared shabby and unkempt. "Well, folks, in plain terms, yesterday the circuit court judge ruled to modify our injunction. He removed restraints on the sale of personal property except for household furniture and farming utensils. Now, this doesn't concern real property, like the land, timber and buildings. Those are still off limits for him to sell."

Compared to what came next, this quickly became the least of my worries. "This is all well and good, sir, but what about the custody petition?"

"Maggie, your estranged husband's attorney, Mr. Erskine, also filed for their own injunction, which the circuit court has summarily granted."

I narrowed my eyes in suspicion, as I waited for him to continue. He hesitated, so I prompted him, "Go on, if you will."

His voice grave, he spoke in all seriousness. "Their injunction prohibits you from seeing the children, on grounds of abandonment, until matters are settled at the divorce trial."

My ears started ringing, while my body began tingling from my shoulders to my toes. I leaned back in the chair to avoid falling forward into a faint. I must have misheard him. "Excuse me, Mr. Crocker, did you say I cannot see my children?"

"Yes, dear. That is the sad truth."

My stomach tightened as though I had been punched. "How could this be *true*? This is a cruel ploy on the part of my deranged husband to keep me from them! The trial will be soon, will it not?"

"Unfortunately, I must answer in the negative, as we've yet to be given a court date. Justice often moves at a snail's pace, as you are learning. Based on my experience, however, I would presume we'll be on the docket sometime next spring."

"*Next* spring? What are you suggesting? Do you mean in the year 1901?" I cried.

"Yes, Maggie, I'm afraid so. I'll do everything in my power to resolve things sooner, but at this juncture, we haven't been given any sort of firm date. Remember, I did say it's only my best guess, based on my prior experience in this type of proceeding."

I bolted from my chair, leaning forward to clutch the edge of his desk with both hands, and shouted into his face, "No!"

Papa stood and put his arm around me. "Now, now, daughter. Pull yourself together, here." Turning to Mr. Crocker, he asked, " Is there no recourse, sir?"

Mr. Crocker sighed.

We sat back down, and Papa continued to hold me close. Crushed by this news and beyond despair, uncontrollable tears streamed down my cheeks. My head pounded so intensely, I could hardly distinguish his next words.

"Yes, James, contesting their injunction goes without saying. As a matter of fact, my secretary is already drawing up the document. The truth is, not all our current judges think progressively. There are some who see things exclusively from the male viewpoint, believing who better to provide for the child than the father? I'm dismayed some members of the judiciary have not yet joined the twentieth century. It is our misfortune to be at the mercy of whichever circuit court judge reviews the case." He spoke in a soft voice, before adding kindly, "It is only fair that I be completely straightforward with you about such things."

The three of us sat in silence for some minutes. I regained my composure to a degree and looked Mr. Crocker in the eye. Although my voice shook, my resolve was firm. "I believe in justice and no judge worth his salt would keep a mother from her children."

Mr. Crocker raised both eyebrows, offering no comment on my declaration.

Papa kept his arm around me as Mr. Crocker showed us to the door. I was consumed with worry. *A year? How could I make it through a year without my children? How could they make it through the year without me?*

⁓

Mr. Crocker immediately filed paperwork to contest the injunction, but the circuit court judge's ruling was again unfavorable. I was, for all intents and purposes, prohibited from seeing my children until the divorce case was over.

It tormented my soul to watch as Lizzie cuddled Effie May or Roy. I attacked chores with a vigor unseen in the Perry household since Mother had died. I scrubbed floors, cupboards and walls. I cleaned out drawers and closets, and laundered draperies and bed coverings. "Maggie, slow down! You're working yourself to death!" Lizzie admonished.

When housework wasn't enough to settle my bubbling anger, I joined Papa outside, milking cows, feeding the stock and wielding the harrow behind Blackie. My mind raced. *What lies might Sam be telling our children? With his cunning, he was easily capable of turning them against me. Did I believe in my heart he would stoop so low? Sadly, I did. Why, oh, why couldn't I see them? I must get them back!*

My imagination worked overtime. After days of pondering every conceivable possibility for securing my children, the plan that seemed most likely to succeed involved taking them with me to Montana to live with Ella and Frank. I had yet to work out all the details. One afternoon, I walked into Mt. Clemens and picked up a train schedule.

Wretched bad luck. In hindsight, that's all I could call it. It happened one evening in June. Papa joined me where I sat on the front stoop contemplating schemes to snatch my children and flee westward. We sat in companionable silence for some minutes before he handed me the train schedule. "So, are you plannin' a trip then, daughter?"

With those eight words, Papa shattered my dream. Where had he gotten the schedule? In my fog of grief, had I left it sitting out?

How could I tell him yes, I was planning a trip and that plan also included kidnapping my children? My mind swirled.

Caught completely off guard, my mouth opened, but nothing came out. I stared at him and he looked me in the eye. Finally, I managed to stammer, "Yes, well, um . . . I have been thinking a change of scenery might serve me well," crestfallen by my cowardly response.

Papa and Lizzie applauded my "idea" and promptly purchased a train ticket for me. They agreed an extended visit with my sisters might be precisely the tonic necessary to survive the long months leading up to the trial.

I never learned how Papa got ahold of the schedule, but I did wonder if he might have had an inkling of my true plot.

Within a week, Montana-bound and bereft, I sat alone in the passenger compartment of a Grand Trunk Railway car, waving goodbye to the Perry clan standing together on the station platform.

22.

Eastern Montana, 1900. It was midnight, nearly six months later when the train pulled away from the Milestown station. In thirty-six hours, I'd be in Chicago where I would switch trains, boarding the Grand Trunk, homeward bound. Our departure had been delayed by what the porter described as an "unplanned equipment servicing." Peering out the window into the darkness, my own reflection stared back at me. The November snow rose high along the track outside and I shivered, pulling the blanket closer and praying the car warmed up soon. I closed my eyes and leaned my head back against the plush, rose-colored upholstery, replaying the last conversation with Ella in my mind.

"Ella, how can I ever thank you for these past six months? You and Frank took me in at my worst, loved me and made me part of your lives."

"Oh, Maggie! It brought me such joy to have you, and I'm so pleased you've had the chance to become acquainted with my beloved husband these many months. There is no repayment expected or needed. You would do the same for me."

Would I? I hoped she were right. "Oh, dearest Ella, how can I leave you? When shall we meet again?"

"You're always in my heart, little sister. For now, you must go back to Michigan and gather your children. Who knows? Maybe next time, you will all come back to Montana together!"

I loved her sentiment. Moments later, I boarded the train on a frosty, star-filled evening, quite the opposite of the hot, dry, June morning when I had disembarked to find Ella and Frank waiting on the Milestown depot platform.

They had welcomed me with wide, open arms. I hugged my sister to me and burst into tears.

"Oh, sweet one. Life has dealt you some bitter medicine."

"The devil's own luck, I'd say," Frank agreed. He then attempted to cheer me. "A big welcome to Montana, Maggie!" He shook my hand with gusto and a sincere smile, and I noted his yellowed teeth, not quite hidden by an enormous handlebar moustache.

I chided myself for this petty observation and smiled back. "Thank you! I'm pleased to make your acquaintance, sir."

"Pleasure's all mine," he replied in earnest, before turning back to Ella, pulling her close and giving her a small peck on the cheek. "You've a comely sister, dear wife!" Her face reddened at this public show of affection.

I turned my attention to this self-described cowtown, on the eastern prairies of Montana. To my left was a park, and beyond that a line of trees, which might indicate a riverbank. Ahead of me, a few dilapidated houses lined a side street. To the north, two or three blocks from the depot, was the main thoroughfare, extending several blocks east, a church steeple at the furthest distance. One could not call this a bustling metropolis.

Frank noted the direction of my gaze. "Yessum, you're looking at Main Street and where we'll be headed, soon as we load up your luggage on the wagon."

We drove down 5th Street toward Main, with Frank sharing a bit of information along the way.

"Milestown's doubled its population since I moved here ten years ago."

"Exactly how large *is* this 'city?'" I inquired.

"Oh, near on two thousand residents, I've heard tell. Straight ahead you'll see the Leighton Hotel. We'll stop there for a meal before we head on home to the ranch."

The wagon traveled at a steady clip over low, rolling hills. The landscape varied between green grasses, sagebrush, and tawny, sand-colored prairie. In the distance, I spied an occasional bluff. This land afforded a strange, new sort of beauty. I marveled at the vast expanses. And, the sky! Oh, how boundless!

The heat of the day was upon us, and I was grateful for the breeze. All the moisture had been sucked out of the air. I worried my skin might shrivel and flake off. The twelve-mile ride took more than two hours, and at times, the perpetual, rolling movement lulled me to sleep. Gratefully, Ella always noticed and saved me from falling sideways out of the wagon.

Along the way, Frank pointed toward the horizon. "Look over yonder. See them buzzards circling? They're scavengers who've pry found part of a carcass to feed on." Oh, what a wild and sweeping country now surrounded me!

The final two miles led us off the main road, and as we crested the last rise, I spotted a small log ranch house nestled in the hollow before us, with a huge stone fireplace rising up at either end, an old barn and several outbuildings. These structures stood not far from a meandering, muddy river. I gasped, but not from elation. The scene before me appeared rustic, speaking generously. How did Ella manage? I realized her descriptions had been filtered through a set of rose-colored lenses.

Thankfully, Frank took my gasp as a positive reaction, nodding his head with pride. "Yes ma'am, ain't she a sight for sore eyes! I don't never come over this rise without a similar feeling. I'm pleased you're so taken with our little piece a' paradise."

Ella remained quiet. I think she recognized my gasp for what it really meant. Still, I hoped she trusted, as I did, that I would land on my feet, as she had.

Frank beamed as he related that over the past several years, he had transformed the house from one room to three, and even tacked on a front porch. I had to admit, with Ella's magical touch, the interior was quite homey and inviting, easing my earlier concerns. I slept on a cot in the combined kitchen and front room, the lack of privacy nothing new. I settled in and it wasn't long before living and working next to my sister and her husband became the new normal course of my life.

Minutes turned into days, and days into weeks. The ranch chores kept me so engaged I had little time to feel sorry for myself, collapsing into bed each evening and sleeping soundly until morning arrived and we started anew. The hard work hadn't lessened my need for my children, it had simply numbed and distracted me.

I now sat aboard the Great Northern train heading east towards home, and offered up an ardent prayer we would soon be reunited. My heart stirred, igniting anticipation as well as excitement. I pulled a letter out of my satchel and re-read it once again.

> *September 4, 1900*
> *Mt. Clemens, Michigan*
> *Dear Mrs. Jobsa:*
> *In your absence, a petition has been filed in your name in regard to a purported violation of the April 19th injunction filed and approved in the Circuit Court of Judge O'Brien J. Atkinson. We have, on good authority, by Reliable Witnesses, learned that Defendant William S. Jobsa has cut Two Hundred or more cords of Standing timber, contrary to the terms of said Injunction, some of which he has sold in the Village of New Baltimore, and some taken to the City of Mt. Clemens. We are informed he has stated he will "sell all the good standing Elm there is on the farm as well as other timber." Furthermore, we believe several men are now engaged in cutting down trees on said Farm, in which you, as Complainant, have a vested right under the Statutes of the State of Michigan. We wish to make application to the Court to secure an order requiring the said Defendant, William S. Jobsa, to show cause why he should not*

be punished for Contempt for disobedience of the said Injunction. A hearing in regard to William S. Jobsa's alleged violation is scheduled for 10 o'clock a.m. Wednesday, 5th December, 1900 in the Circuit Court For the County of Macomb in the Chancery of the Honorable James G. Tucker. Subpoenaed witnesses will be called to testify in this matter. The presence of Complainant is requested.

Please advise.

Sincerely,

Martin Crocker, Esq.

Finally, after such a dearth of good news, a ray of hope appeared. Sam's flagrant violation of the injunction could prove to be the turning point. With these witnesses, the judge might find him in contempt of the court's order and sentence him to jail.

I dared to hope this would result in me regaining custody of my children. Closing my eyes, I smiled to myself, imagining my four little ones and how they had changed in these past months. Could Oscar now read the little primer he had been working on in March? Did Helen still follow him around and gaze at her big brother with adoration? Perhaps they had begun to squabble like Lucy and me, over some perceived injustice. What were those twins like by now? I imagined them climbing all over and starting to speak. Oh, how I wanted to cuddle up with my adorable Gertrude and mischievous Gordon! I envisioned the four of them running to me, crying out "Mama, Mama!" We would all laugh and fall to the ground as they clambered atop me for hugs and kisses. *Dreams have power. Dreams can come true.*

The train rolled along, and with it the night. The continuous motion lulled me into a fitful sleep.

A familiar, curly, dark-haired child wandered on the bluff above the ranch house, crying out for her mother. Indians rapidly approached on horseback, dust flying. My bones reverberated with the pounding of the horses' hooves, as the scene played out before me. The child screamed, terrified, and my sister, Ella, appeared out of nowhere and raced to her, scooping the child up into her arms. The Indians jumped off their ponies and ran toward the two of them.

Startled awake, I opened my eyes and blinked, feeling disoriented. I glimpsed tiny, flickering lights along the ceiling, and felt the otherwise dark room rumble and shift. Oh yes, the train. As my head cleared, I sat up, rubbed my eyes and surveyed my surroundings. Almost all the other passengers slept, although I noted a couple of men at the other end of the car smoking and speaking in soft tones, the aroma of their tobacco wafting toward me.

I closed my eyes and willed myself to go back to sleep. Minutes passed while my mind replayed the dream. Indians. They frightened me, for no reason I could easily identify. Perhaps it was because they were so different from all that was familiar.

One day when Ella and I stood at the clothesline hanging out the wash, I had glanced up and seen three of them walking along the rise, leading their spotted ponies. Dressed in breechcloths, naked from the waist up, they had long braids and feathers in their hair. I stood transfixed, not knowing what to do.

"Maggie," Ella spoke quietly, "it's all right. Continue on. Everything is all right. They're Cheyenne from the reservation, probably out game hunting. Frank never makes a fuss if they cross his land, so just act normally."

The Cheyenne stood motionless on the rise and watched us for quite some time. Ella continued to hang up the clean laundry, showing no concern. I remained stock-still, unable to do anything but stare back at them, imagining what we might do if they came down the hill toward us. My mind blank, I couldn't think of any action certain to ensure our safety. Eventually they continued on their way. I sat down hard on the ground, shaking, the spell broken.

And now, they visited me in my dreams. Dearest Ella. I yearned for her comfort and mourned leaving her all over again. How I wished we weren't so far apart. *When would we ever see each other again?* I could see how happy she was with Frank, yet I also detected a certain wistfulness. One day last July, I had broached the subject, as we pulled weeds together in the garden.

"Ellie, sharing our heart of hearts, tell me how you really are, as I sense a touch of melancholy lurking behind those sparkling blue eyes."

"Oh, Maggie, I'm delighted with my life! The melancholy, as you call it . . . it's nothing . . ." she trailed off.

"It's nothing, *but* . . . ? Out with it, sister." It was my turn to be forthright.

She brushed the hair off her forehead and looked off into the distance. "Maggie, you know me too well." Sighing, she continued, "We'd so wanted a child, but that has not happened. I'm afraid I'm too old. It weighs on my heart and I can tell how discouraged Frank feels at my inability to give him a son. Sometimes, I can't help but think I've been a failure and a disappointment to him."

"Oh, dear sister, you've been married such a short time. Be patient. I've seen those love-struck eyes of his watching you with adoration and I have witnessed how he treats you with unmistakable tenderness. Perhaps you're mistaken in regard to his thoughts?"

"Perhaps." She looked down at the dirt.

I didn't know what else I might say to assuage her fears, so I moved toward her and hugged her to me, as we knelt that day in the garden.

Shivering, I pulled my blanket closer around me. Enveloped in the inky darkness of the train, I prayed for sleep to return. My mind had other ideas. Concerns and cares of the day always seemed bleakest during this deepest part of the night. A vision of Grace with her curly black hair popped into my head, an unsettling reminder of my earlier dream. From there, my thoughts drifted to Lucy and Will, and my August visit to their ranch. Now wide awake, I revisited the conversation which transpired between Ella and me after I had returned.

"Ella, I'm terribly worried about Lucy's state of mind these days."

"Yes, it also worries me. What was it like, staying with them?"

"Well, I found Will to be an easy-going man, who, by all appearances, adores his wife and daughter. With such a large spread, he's absent quite a lot, so when he is there, he tends to overindulge both Lucy and Grace. Little Grace is winsome and appealing, with all her dark, curly hair and soft brown eyes. I would have to say that she is fairly spoiled by her daddy, yet somewhat ignored by her mother. More worrisome, Lucy doesn't appear to have that maternal quality so necessary to raise a confident child. It's a rather sad situation."

"Did you get a sense of what Lucy might be intending?"

"Not exactly. We skirted around the issue. She complained about Will's absences, but also grumbled that even when he is home, she's bored silly by what she calls his 'insipid temperament.' I think he tries so hard to please her, he's afraid to have the 'wrong' opinion and get crossways with her, so he agrees with everything she says or wants. I wish I could have told him to be a little more fiery and to try to occasionally catch her a bit off-guard. That might add some challenge and variety to what seems a somewhat bland relationship. They even have separate bedrooms."

"Oh, that doesn't sound very hopeful for the future, does it?"

"Who can know what to expect from Lucy? In the back of my mind, I can see her picking up one day and leaving him, alone. I hope I'm wrong, but that's my intuition. My heart breaks for poor little Gracie. I think Lucy treats her too sternly. Far be it for me to give advice on mothering, but I think anyone would agree on the importance of motherly affection in a child's life."

"Why, yes, of course. Heavens, I wish we weren't so many miles apart. I came to Montana believing Lucy and I would be closer, but this is worse than being in Michigan. I must make a better effort to find a way to visit them more often, Maggie." The burden of distance weighed down her thin shoulders.

To this very moment, I wished I hadn't burdened her with the worrisome information about Lucy. Ella had enough on her mind with ranch work, a husband and an empty womb.

The sun finally peeked over the horizon, bringing with it an end to this interminable night. I continued to gaze out the window as the train rumbled steadily eastward. Dawn, with its hues of soft blue, pink and coral, soon gave way to daylight. The muted colors and rhythmic sounds soothed my soul, and I soon fell into a calm, somewhat thoughtless state, which I welcomed. Antelope and deer bounded across the plains and every once in awhile, I spied a tiny sod house in the distance, looking so lonesome in the middle of the flat, vast prairie.

Mt. Clemens, Michigan, Winter, 1900-1901. I returned home, but not to the Perry farm. My first family now lived in an unfamiliar three-story Victorian-style house in Mt. Clemens. Papa had sold the hundred-acre farm in the fall and moved into town. It grieved me to think of someone else occupying our home, the place of so many memories, but he no longer cared to try and manage it alone.

Sitting in the window seat of the upstairs bedroom I shared with my sister Janie, I reviewed my meeting with Mr. Crocker this morning, in preparation for the upcoming court date on December fifth. Our conversation had left me uneasy and anxious.

"Maggie, it's evident the time in Montana sat well with you." Martin Crocker stood, extending his hand to offer me a firm handshake. I nodded in agreement, then sat down across the desk from him. "I've asked you here today to review our plan for next Wednesday."

"All right, thank you."

"You'll sit with me at a table facing the judge, at the front of the room. After His Honor opens the session, the proceedings should be straightforward. We've subpoenaed three witnesses, who will be in the court to testify for your cause. They'll swear under oath Sam is indeed harvesting the timber, selling it in both New Baltimore and here in Mt. Clemens, violating the terms of the injunction. I don't expect the hearing will be long. In my opinion, it's a cut and dried case and he'll likely rule in your favor."

"Will Sam go to jail, perhaps?"

"Perhaps. He will be given a chance to refute the allegations. If he's unable to do so, he'll be found in contempt for violating and disobeying the injunction, and punished by either a monetary fine or jail time."

"Can we request jail time? Could I not claim back my children if he were given a jail sentence?"

"Maggie, slow down. Should he be found guilty, it won't be up to us to sentence him. That is at the discretion of the judge."

Had I misled myself? Had I misperceived the situation? "Mr. Crocker, I don't understand. Surely if Samuel's found guilty, no judge would leave four children with him!"

"Maggie, that's not something we can predict. I believe . . ."

My patience nil, I rudely interrupted him, "Well then, sir, when will we secure a court date for the divorce? I haven't seen my children in almost nine months. There's no justice in this injunction against me. I find it beyond comprehension that a judge would deny a mother visitation. It's not as if I'm a felon or imbecile! Is there nothing to be done?"

"Maggie, as I mentioned to you last spring, some judges in our circuit court view things in a different manner than you or me. If you wish, we can re-file an affidavit seeking visitation, and see where it takes us. Had you disobeyed the injunction against you, as Sam has, there would be no point in re-filing. But I must agree, this current situation is untenable. Depriving you of your children, and denying them a relationship with their mother, is in my mind cruel and unusual and should be challenged.

"We should be given a date for the divorce trial after the first of the year. We're nearly there, so keep your chin up, my dear! We'll go ahead and draw up the necessary papers seeking a reconsideration of the injunction denying visitation. Why don't you plan on stopping back tomorrow sometime to sign the paperwork?"

Two days after the December fifth court date, I again sat in the bedroom window seat, brooding. As I stared at the barren trees lining the streets, I was struck by how well they reflected my emptiness. I had returned from Montana to attend a hearing that might determine my fate, and that of my children. Faith in our cause had kept me sane, as Papa and I sat steadfastly both days outside the courtroom door with our witnesses, waiting for our time in court. The afternoon of the second day, Mr. Crocker came out of the courtroom and approached us. From his demeanor, it was obvious he did not bring good news.

"Maggie, I have been informed that our hearing has been cancelled and . . ."

"What do you mean, it's been cancelled?" I interrupted.

"Simply put, the case now in session will not be finished in time to hold our hearing. It's been rescheduled for January fifth."

What else could go wrong? Another blow to my cause.

Since our witnesses had been held waiting, we could do nothing less than pay them their witness fees. We would petition Sam for another $25 to bring them back in January. At times like this, the court system was almost as frustrating as marriage to Sam.

At last! A ruling in my favor! The Circuit Judge found that Sam had indeed violated and disobeyed the injunction by clearing timber on the property. Sam was given a week to show cause why he shouldn't be held in contempt. I envisioned him sitting in a jail cell, as it was clear he had no way to prove his innocence. The witnesses Mr. Crocker called on my behalf were flawless in their testimony, due in large part to Mr. Crocker's superior ability to draw out the truth. The double-paid witness fees proved to be a worthwhile investment.

When a note arrived from Mr. Crocker the third week of January, I held my breath as I ripped open the envelope. I studied the first part of his memo, but the further I read, the more my heart sank. By hook or by crook, Mr. Erskine had worked a sort of miracle, leaving Sam with a small fine and no jail time for his sale of the timber. Mr. Crocker surmised the ruling involved a bit of "back room shenanigans." After the way Sam and his attorney had manipulated other circumstances to date, this ruling should not have surprised me. Wishful thinking had gotten the best of me. I consciously chose to not let this news dampen my spirit or resolve, because the rest of the dispatch offered hope. Two dates had been set by the court, with my own injunction hearing scheduled for April 5. Deep within my soul, I believed the judge would rule in my favor. The divorce trial was set for April 22. I could finally see an end to this nightmare. I felt it in my bones; 1901 would be a banner year.

Some good news arrived by post today, lifting the spirits of our entire family.

> *February 2, 1901*
> *12-Mile Dam, Miles City, Montana*
> *My dearest sister,*
> *Maggie, I am writing with utter delight and a thankful heart to share the happiest news of my life. Frank and I are expecting a child at the end of the summer. Jubilant, our feet have yet to touch the ground. At first, neither of us could believe our good fortune, but, based on the doctor's experience in such matters, he confirmed our suspicions earlier this week.*

Frank has been treating me as if I was made of the finest porcelain, and I rejoice it is wintertime, when the garden is fallow and less is expected day-to-day. I have waited a lifetime for this opportunity. Bringing a child into the world to nurture and love brings me the greatest of joys.

Maggie, even though you are more than a thousand miles away, I can hear your voice of concern, saying you are worried because of my advanced age and the ranch's distance from town. You can be certain that my excitement exceeds my worry and I savor every moment of this extraordinary experience. I would be delighted if you would share my joyful news with the family.

Please write and tell me about your life and what happened in regards to the court hearing, and if there is a trial date yet or any change in the status of visitation with your children.

Love to You,

Ella R. Herman

23

Spring, 1901.

> *March 15, 1901*
> *12 Miles Dam, Miles City, Montana*
> *Dear Sister-in-law,*
> I am writing this letter to you for my wife Ella, as she ain't able, and she wanted me to tell you the bad news. My apologies for being blunt, but my dear, she lost the baby on Monday of this week and they ain't sure why. Ever since, she has been feeling poorly. I remain worried and hope you might write her a note sometime soon. Could you please tell this sad news to the rest of your family?
> *Most sincerely,*
> *Frank Herman*

I crumpled the letter and stuffed it into my dress pocket, hurrying out the front door of Papa's house before anyone saw me. I vehemently wiped the tears off my cheeks, devastated for my sister and her unbearable loss. Ignoring the well-wishes and greetings of neighbors along the road, I both walked and ran toward a wooded area on the outskirts of town. At a stand of birch trees, I stopped and leaned down to pick up a thick clump of moist earth. I wanted to give the universe a tongue-lashing, but instead, settled for throwing dirt clods at unsuspecting tree trunks, all the while raging at life's unfairness. After exhausting myself, I walked home to share Ella's sorrowful news with my family. And then, I sat to write my dear sister.

⁘

"Maggie! Someone's rapping on the front door and I'm up to my elbows with soap in the washtub and Janie's out back with the children. Could you answer it?" Lizzie called up the stairs, where I worked at stripping the beds in preparation for wash day.

"Be right there!" I scurried down the steps, opening the door to find a messenger boy of not more than twelve, his bicycle leaning against the step post. "Mrs. Maggie Jobsa, please?" he inquired.

"Yes, I'm Maggie Jobsa," I declared, alarmed that someone had sent a note via messenger, hoping it not more bad news about Ella.

He handed it to me and waited, I supposed, for a tip. I found a few loose coins on the glass tray sitting atop the hall sideboard. He nodded and smiled as he accepted my thanks, then turned and bounded down the porch steps, two at a time. The young messenger then leapt on his bicycle and peddled off without a second glance at me, on to his next errand.

With trepidation, I slit open the small envelope and unfolded the note. Looking first to the bottom of what appeared to be a hurriedly drafted message, I saw the name *Martin Crocker, Esq.*, written in his now familiar, spidery script.

> *March 29, 1901*
> *Mt. Clemens, Michigan*
> *Dear Mrs. Jobsa:*
> *Moments ago, I learned from a reliable source that the Mt. Clemens medical examiner was called to the Jobsa farmhouse on Sugarbush Road the day before yesterday to gather the body of a deceased child, and knew you should be informed directly. As your Attorney, I must remind you that you are prohibited, under court order, from visiting the farm and while I cannot tell you what to do, I believe this would be one of those times I would*

choose to look the other way, should you decide to disobey this injunction.

  Godspeed,
  Martin Crocker, Esq.

I clutched the note to my heart and stood, frozen in the doorway. Spring crocus and grape hyacinths blossomed in the yard across the street. A cardinal whistled in the tree beside our house. Wispy clouds floated silently in a cornflower sky. How dare the world appear the same as it had a minute ago, when nothing would ever be the same again? Jolted back to reality, I began to shake uncontrollably. Sam was an abomination. I would kill him.

With my heart pounding and fists clenched, a sound arose from deep in my throat, rising to the surface in a high-pitched outcry, unfettered in its intensity. I slammed the heavy oak door with all my might, and the stained-glass transom above shuddered with fear.

"My Lord, child, what's happened?" Lizzie appeared out of nowhere, grasping me by the shoulders and turning me to face her. She scrutinized my face.

"I will kill him."

"Come now, Maggie, what's happened?" She again asked, attempting to draw me toward her.

I jerked away, inconsolable. "How could he?" A bloodcurdling cry of anguish escaped my mouth.

Lizzie firmly steered me down the hallway and into the front parlor, sitting me down beside her on the settee. As if turned to stone, I stared unblinkingly at the far wall.

"Would you like to show me what was in the note?" she asked kindly, after a few minutes had passed.

I broke into a cold sweat, still fiercely clutching the crumpled paper. I handed it over, emptiness washing over me.

"I must . . . I must . . . oh, my God!" I couldn't think. *Was this true? One of my babies had died?* This must be a horrible mistake. Surely, God could not be so cruel.

Lizzie drove the wagon. I could barely see the road, through my cascading tears. "How could I lose another child? I couldn't. It's impossible. I never should have obeyed the injunction. I should've gone back for them, no matter what anyone said. This is unbearable!" My harsh cries pierced the air as I wailed, railing against even the possibility that Mr. Crocker's words were true. A gnawing pain began to tear at my insides, threatening to rend my heart.

"There, there, maybe it's all a mistake, Maggie." Lizzie did her best to calm me. I continued to keen throughout the longest ride I would ever take. Although my emotions were spent by the time we pulled in front of the farmhouse, knowing my children were within reach called forth a renewed fervor. I slid over the side of the buggy and darted up the steps onto the porch before Lizzie had even stepped down to the ground.

The house was unlocked, and heedless of what might await us, I burst inside. What greeted me was shocking and incomprehensible. How could I begin to describe the deplorable conditions? Shabby? Squalid? Worse than a nightmare. My beautiful home had become utterly unwholesome, a pigsty, so foul smelling that Lizzie and I had to cover our noses to block the stench.

We heard faint noises from above, so we dashed upstairs and discovered Oscar, Helen and Gertrude lying together side-by-side on my old bed, lethargic. They resembled little waifs, sickly, dirty, and sadly unkempt. Weak and emaciated, they could barely focus on my words or comprehend their mother standing before them.

"Mama?" Louder now, "Mama? Is that you?"

"Oh, Oscar, yes! It is me. Oh, dear, oh, dear." I held him to me, weeping. My little girls stared vacantly at me. I scooped them both into my arms as well, holding all three of them as close as possible. I sobbed with abandon, while they appeared listless, showing no outward response to my attempts at comforting them.

Someone had taken a pair of scissors to Gertrude and Helen's hair, cropping it so near the scalp they could be mistaken for boys. This half-hearted attempt to eradicate the lice inhabiting their scalps was a complete failure, as the hair on all their heads looked frowsy and tangled, still crawling with the tiny, unsavory creatures.

I hugged my children while scrutinizing the bedroom. Never would I have expected to witness thus, that a father could stand by and watch his children living amid such decay.

"Maggie, I've searched for any sign of Gordon and found no one else here. I did see astonishingly filthy, bug-infested mattresses and not a sheet or pillowcase in sight." Lizzie gagged.

"Everything in this hellhole is at sixes and sevens, wretchedness beyond my wildest imaginings." I grimaced in disgust. My lovingly hand-stitched bedspread, pristine white when I left, was greasy, grey and dingy. Oh, I wanted to retch!

"My God, oh my God! Where is Gordon?" Was it true? Was my bright, red-haired darling gone? It was beyond comprehension or endurance.

"I can't bear to think of what these children have suffered! I will kill that man when next I lay eyes on him!" I swore at the heavens, as my angels watched me impassively, their eyes dull.

After a time, Lizzie and I helped them to stand and descend the stairway into the kitchen. They were pathetically hungry, so I searched around to find something to feed them. As far as I could tell, they had been living largely upon crackers, all I found in the pantry save for a colony of ants.

By this time, Albert, the hired boy, had noticed our wagon parked in front of the farmhouse, or perhaps he heard my outraged shrieking. He barged into the house, shouting, "Missus! Why are you here? You're not supposed to be here!" He lunged toward us.

"Where is my Gordon? What have you done with him?" I yelled back, in a rage.

"Margareta! Elizabeth! What are you doing here?" Johanna, Sam's maiden aunt, now appeared in the kitchen, arms akimbo, and stood alongside Albert. Before either of us could speak, she pointed toward the front door. "Get out! You have no license to be on this property!"

Hysterical, my hands balled and arms stiff at my sides, I shouted, "We'll get out, but not without my children!"

"You'll do no such thing! I'll call to Sam down in the field and he'll have the sheriff come arrest you for trespassing. You've no business here!"

"Where is my son, Gordon?" I spat at them in my harshest voice.

"Ma'am, he's dead." Albert gawked at me with what might be described by some as compassion. I witnessed a crude young man, devoid of tact.

I dropped to my knees, bawling. My three remaining children, who'd been standing mutely, reacted as though awakened from a spell. Oscar and Helen ran to me, putting their arms around me, crying, "Mama, Mama!" Gertrude hung back, seemingly unsure of whom I might be, a further blow to my already shattered heart.

"Gordon. Gordon. Gordon! My sweet child!" I turned on Johanna with malice. "This is your fault! You've killed my son with your neglect! If he was unwell, why didn't someone call the doctor? Why?" As I challenged her, I gently nudged my children toward the fireplace grate, where I found a hefty piece of wood. Out of my mind, I waved it at her crazily, shouting, "Your fault, your fault, your fault indeed!" A dark thought crossed my mind. *Why, oh, why, hadn't I brought along Papa's shotgun?*

Johanna scowled at me, yet her demeanor softened as she spoke slowly. "Margareta. Please, Maggie. Hear me out." She snatched the stick from me as I collapsed onto my knees, gathering my three protectively into my arms.

"Listen to me. The children had all been ill for several days . . ."

"Why in God's name didn't someone call Dr. Lenfestey?" I asked in a defeated voice.

"Margareta, I must ask you not to take the name of our Lord in vain. And, we did seek the doctor."

"Yes, and I have evidence to show he wasn't sought until after my poor child had passed. What is wrong with you? What is wrong with their father? Johanna! Look at my children! Can you not see they are in dire need of attention? Are you blind? How can you be so neglectful of these innocents? Would you see fit to sacrifice them as well?"

"Margareta," she snapped, indignant. "Have you not learned that as a good Christian Scientist, this illness was naught but a mental error. With great faith, Sam's mother and I have extended many fervent prayers."

"Well, I cannot see how your 'great faith,' as you say, has helped, since my child is dead! Dead! Do you hear me? It's beyond rational thinking that you didn't call the doctor sooner!"

"We deemed the good doctor unnecessary, as it was God's will Gordon not be cured. This material world is nothing more than an illusion anyway, and the dear child has reached the true reality, that of the spiritual world. We rejoice in his release! You should recall this from your own studies of the faith!"

"My own studies of the faith tell me not to stand by in silence and watch someone die, if a healer is nearby. Pray all you want, but there is also a place for a doctor's knowledge and skill! It is *naught* but neglect! His *father's* neglect . . . and *your* neglect!" I exhorted, my vehemence returned. "My other three will soon follow if we don't remove them without delay from this filth and degradation!"

"Maggie is right, Johanna." Lizzie backed me up. "These children are in grave danger of following their brother's path. Please, see to reason and let us take them, clean them up, feed them and nurse them back to good health."

Johanna's anger swelled and she again pointed at the door. "Out with you! This is your last warning!" She moved to where I knelt with my children in the center of the room and peeled them away from me one by one, shoving them behind her. Albert grabbed me by the arm and started to pull me to the door.

"Stop! Release me this instant!" I screamed as I attempted to disengage myself from his grip. I lifted my boot and kicked him in the shin with all my might, and he instantly let go. Lizzie then took hold of me and pulled me toward the door herself.

"Come on, Maggie, we'll get the sheriff ourselves," she blustered.

With great reluctance, I complied. Before we left, I turned once more toward my three little ones, who were crying and bravely attempting to break free of Johanna's firm grasp.

"My dearest children, I shall return for you!" Sobbing, I stumbled onto the porch, guided by Lizzie's steady hand.

In an instant, Albert had barred the door. I hadn't even found out if there would be a funeral.

Lizzie and I decided not to go to the Sheriff first. We remembered him to be a good friend of Henry Jobsa, so thought the better of it, as it would do me no good to be arrested for violating the injunction. Instead, we talked it over and decided a better strategy would be to find Mr. Crocker, so we drove the buggy directly to his office.

"I need to see Mr. Crocker!" I demanded, the moment we burst into the foyer.

"I beg your pardon, Mrs. Jobsa, but Mr. Crocker is in court, and if there is no ruling today, he will also be there on Monday. His first available appointment time is Tuesday afternoon, the second of April, at two o'clock. Would that be agreeable?"

With all the self-control I could muster, I told her it would not be agreeable in the least. In the end, I had to satisfy myself with leaving a written note informing Mr. Crocker of the travesty on Sugarbush Road, and asking if he would please see me at his earliest convenience. Defeated, we went home. The weekend passed as slowly as a crippled snail. I ate little and slept even less. Early Monday morning, Mr. Crocker's messenger delivered an apologetic note stating he wouldn't be available until Tuesday afternoon, so I was left with no recourse but to wait.

Tuesday finally arrived, and Lizzie and I went to Mr. Crocker's office. There, we gave a detailed accounting of our Friday morning visit to the farm. He deposed each of us individually, and after we both swore our testimony to be true, Alice typed it up. Once notarized, it was ready to be filed in circuit court. I reckoned we did well in our descriptions and genuinely believed this affidavit would make a difference in the judge's ruling.

"Maggie, I must tell you the injunction hearing has been postponed and will probably be cancelled, as the divorce trial will presumably be held before the hearing can be rescheduled." He delivered this discouraging bit of news after we had finished our affidavit. Another defeat. How much more could I be expected to endure? "Mr. Crocker, I'm afraid my other three children might be dead by then." My voice quavered. Chiding myself to be strong and not cry in front of him, I begged, "There must be something more we can do!"

"If you truly fear for their lives, we'll request that the sheriff drive out to investigate the situation immediately. Should he find just cause, I will attempt to get an immediate court order to remove the children and place them in your custody."

The next morning, I stood waiting outside Mr. Crocker's office when he arrived at nine o'clock. "Mr. Crocker, what have you heard from the sheriff?"

He unlocked the front door, waving me in ahead of him. "Maggie, the sheriff's report indicated Sam, Gertrude and Johanna were all present when he visited the farmhouse. They welcomed him in and he found the room was in order and the children appeared recently bathed. The six of them were sitting at the table eating a midday meal of, and I quote, 'boiled chicken, potatoes, carrots and turnips.' There was naught for him to do but kindly tip his hat and thank them before taking his leave. I'm sorry, but that leaves us little choice but to wait for the trial."

I couldn't believe my ears. How could this be? Cynically, I retorted, "Are you sure he is truthful? Sam probably paid him to say as much. Certainly that was not what we observed just five days ago." Furious, I could say nothing more without losing my temper.

Mr. Crocker remained quiet while I attempted to regain my composure. Once again, he reassured me we had a strong case, and reminded me the trial would be held in a little more than two weeks. His words did little to assuage my spirits. All I wanted was my children.

24.

April 22, 1901. "All rise for the Honorable James G. Tucker, Circuit Court Judge for the County of Macomb." The judge took his place on the bench and the gavel banged. "This circuit court is now in session."

Seated beside Mr. Crocker at a wide, wooden table in the front of the courtroom, I glanced to my right at the other table where Sam was seated next to his attorney, Mr. Erskine. Sam stared straight ahead, dressed in all his finery, looking every bit the gentleman that he wasn't. The mere sight of him brought my blood to a boil and I wished I might stand and walk over to where he sat and strangle him, or at the very least, spit on him.

As I began to imagine other heinous things I might do to Sam, the judge commenced the proceedings. "In the matter of Margareta Jobsa, Complainant vs. William S. Jobsa, Defendant, who represents said causes?" The attorneys introduced themselves, after which they both gave opening statements. Next, Mr. Crocker presented our cause. He called several character witnesses who could attest to Sam's misconduct in Mt. Clemens, along with testimony from Papa and Lizzie in regard to his treatment of the children and me. After he finished presenting our case, it was Sam's turn to offer evidence refuting our claims. Mr. Erskine boldly stated I had abandoned my children, insinuating Sam the only parent fit to have custody. Surely Sam's lies could not change the powerfully incriminating nature of the evidence against him.

After a midday recess, the court reconvened and each of our attorneys offered closing statements. Although Mr. Crocker sounded eloquent, my skin prickled with foreboding as the judge took some time to make notes. After several minutes, Judge Tucker cleared his throat, banged his gavel, and stated his judgment.

I held my breath.

"In the matter of the cause filed by complainant Margareta Jobsa, this court finds the material facts charged in such Bill of Complaint are true and the defendant William Samuel Jobsa guilty of the several acts of cruelty therein charged in this cause."

I knew it. The judge had ruled in my favor. Victory was mine!

He then proceeded, "It appears to this Court there is nothing affecting the rights of the children mentioned in this case that required the interference of the public, and no reason appearing they were not properly cared for."

I flinched, incredulous. *How could he possibly think they have been properly cared for? One of my children died in that hell house! That damn sheriff.*

"On motion of Crocker & Knight, Solicitors, the counsel for said complainant, it is ordered, adjudged and decreed in this Court that the marriage between the said complainant Margareta Jobsa and the defendant William Samuel Jobsa be dissolved . . ."

My heart leapt to hear I had gained my freedom, but I was leery of what he might say next.

"It is also further ordered, adjudged and decreed that Margareta Jobsa, shall have the custody, care, control and education of the minor child Gertrude Elizabeth Jobsa, aged two years, provided she personally care for, support and maintain said child."

Oh, hallelujah. Thank God. My baby was coming home! I dissolved in tears of relief, joy and thankfulness. *Gertrude will be coming home with me.* I wiped away my tears and stole a look at Sam and his attorney, sitting at the table next to us. Sam's expression was inscrutable. I turned my attention back to the judge, waiting for his next words.

"It is also ordered, adjudged and decreed that the defendant have the custody, care, control and education of the two minor children,

Oscar Henry, aged eight years and Helen Edith Jobsa, aged five years, provided he personally care for, support, and maintain said children."

No! My God, this can't be right. He's made a mistake. Surely he's made a terrible mistake.

I tensed and my legs began to quiver. As I grabbed the edge of the table with both hands, Mr. Crocker must have sensed I planned to stand and try to address the court. He put his left hand on my forearm and his right index finger to his lips, cautioning me to remain quiet. This restraint barely kept me seated. Every fiber of my being demanded I leap to my feet and challenge this feeble-minded judge, who continued to speak. I wanted nothing more than for him to stop his doubletalk and hear me out. Sam, meanwhile, looked smug and self-satisfied. He did not care enough about the children to take good care of them, but he knew that by keeping Oscar and Helen from me, he had achieved the ultimate revenge for my actions in leaving him.

"It is also ordered, adjudged and decreed that the defendant pay to the complainant $1,700 in alimony. The defendant shall pay the costs of this proceeding in the sum of $18.70, along with the complainant's solicitor fee of $50."

"Margareta Jobsa shall release and relinquish all claim for dower and property . . ."

He went on and on. I no longer cared what he said. His heartless ruling had crushed the life out of me. He spoke on about alimony, but I only caught snippets, my mind racing as I desperately searched for a way to right this terrible injustice. ". . . the sum of $1,100 be paid to the complainant . . . delivery of such deed . . ."

I had lost the gist of what he was ordering, adjudging and decreeing. I put my head down on my folded arms, resting on the table. Life as I knew it was over. I had abandoned my children, telling them I would be back for them, and I'd failed. In my mind's eye, all I could see was their tiny, forlorn faces in the window, staring after me.

The judge continued his monologue. ". . . the remaining $600 of said alimony be paid to said complainant in annual sums of $50 per year for twelve years, commencing January 1, 1902 . . ."

"It is also ordered, adjudged and decreed that the children of the parties hereto shall at reasonable and seasonable times be permitted to see each other and exchange visits."

What did he say? They could see each other? What about me? I came to attention, glaring at this abominable judge. He talked on and on, yet I heard naught. Finally, Judge Tucker focused his gaze on the all but empty courtroom, pounded his gavel, and called, "Court dismissed." He rose from the bench and strode imperiously from the courtroom, his black robes swirling around him, as the final bang of the gavel still echoed in my mind.

Stunned. I was absolutely and utterly stunned. What had gone wrong? I continued to sit at the large table, numb to my very depths, as Papa and Lizzie came forward to enfold me in their arms. "It's finally at an end, Maggie," Papa said. "Let's proceed to the farm and collect little Gertrude."

I broke free of their embraces and turned to my attorney. "Mr. Crocker, what happened? Why did the judge take away my children?" My voice was reduced to a pitiful whisper.

"Maggie, I presume the judge had little confidence in your ability to support three children, so he made the fairest judgment possible by giving you custody of the baby. Beyond that, you have received your divorce, along with a good settlement of $1,700."

"I can't believe this! They were living in filth and starving. How could the judge not find just cause to award me my children? This can't be the end of it!"

Mr. Crocker shook his head, as he gathered up his paperwork. "Maggie, under the circumstances, it is my opinion the judgment would be considered fair. In reality, you do not have a way to provide for three children. I consider receiving custody of even one of them a victory."

I could tell his patience with me had worn thin and realized I sounded ungrateful. "Sir, I thank you for all the preparation and time you've invested in my cause. I wouldn't have had a chance without you. Please accept my heartfelt thank you." He nodded in affirmation. Yet, when at last I drifted out of the courtroom, supported by Lizzie and Papa, it was with a sense of crushing defeat. I had lost two . . . no, three, of my children through this ordeal.

I was in such a state that Papa took Lizzie and me back to the house. He then went to retrieve my baby girl, convinced it would be less traumatic for everyone concerned if Oscar, Helen and I did not have to say goodbye to each other again. There was no telling what my reaction might have been, departing the farmhouse on Sugarbush Road for the last time with only one of my children. Already my mind was running through options. There had to be a way to rescue Oscar and Helen. There simply had to be. I could not, would not, accept the fact Sam had retained custody of both.

Gertrude arrived with her meager belongings, the dress she wore and one other, along with a filthy cloth dolly. Stained and grimy, we burned both dresses and found her new ones. Taking away her dolly, the one familiar object she had left, seemed ill-advised. I washed and then rewashed it in scalding water, trusting any miniscule, unseen vermin had met their demise.

Uncertain about the change in her circumstances, my daughter spoke not a word for the better part of that first week. At two-and-a-half, I was sure she felt quite bewildered, wondering what had happened to her older brother and sister, Aunties, Grandma and Papa, not to mention her twin.

"Gertrude, I am your mommy and you live with me now. I love you very, very much. You will see the rest of your family again, I promise. They live nearby and we'll take the buggy and go visit. Would you like that?" She stared at me, her lower lip quivering, tears in the corners of her sad, blue eyes. Within those eyes were the reflections of the children lost to me. I repeated this one-sided conversation many times a day, hoping to ease our mutual pain.

I considered I might be going mad. My two missing children haunted my thoughts relentlessly, day and night. I continued to wrack my brain for ways to reclaim them, legal or not.

"Oskie, Oskie, Oskie!" I jumped in the darkness of our room as Gertrude's cry awakened me out of a restless slumber for the third time this night.

"Little one, it's Mommy. I'm right here. It will be all right." I held her snugly, stroking her hair.

She continued whimpering for her brother, before at last calming and returning to a dream-state, leaving me to ruminate on our future together.

I rocked and sang to her each evening. Despite this, she still cried herself to sleep and often had night terrors, so confused was she by the changes in her little life. I grieved along with her. Not only had I lost my other children, but Gertrude had no memory of me, even though I had both birthed her and nursed her at my breast. In some ways, it felt like I had lost her too.

Each devastated in our own way, I asked myself what would become of the two of us. We couldn't subsist on Papa's charity forever, and the sale of my jewelry could only take us so far. Adrift from my God, I could no longer face Him in prayer. These were my meditations before I received the telegram which would set in motion a chain of events that changed my life path for a second time.

25

May, 1901. "Maggie, the one recourse which might assist you in regaining custody of Oscar and Helen is to prove to the judge you are able to take care of three children." Frowning, I sat stiffly in Mr. Crocker's office.

I nodded my head, recognizing this as a tall order to fill. I stubbornly refused to relinquish my efforts to reunite with Oscar and Helen. I thanked him for his time and drifted home, lost in thoughts of how to accomplish such an undertaking. Walking up the path to the front door, I nearly bumped into the now familiar messenger boy. *What now?*

"Good afternoon, missus." He nodded at me, then hopped aboard his bicycle and rode off before I had had time to inquire about his mission. I rushed up the steps and through the entryway, where I found Lizzie standing in the hallway, holding a telegram addressed to me. Sensing bad news, I tore open the envelope.

> *Mrs. Maggie Jobsa*
> *54 South Avenue*
> *Mt. Clemens, Michigan*
> *Ella unwell. Will arrive Mt. Clemens aboard Grand Trunk, 5/3 16:30.*
> *Frank Herman*
> *Milestown, Montana*

I handed it to Lizzie. May 3 was the day after tomorrow. My mind was already overcrowded with pressing concerns. *Where might I fit another?*

I will never forget the beautiful spring day, warm and breezy, the sky a sea of blue, when my sister came home. Noisy jaybirds chattered in the trees on the outer edges of the platform, filling the silence as Papa, Lizzie, Gertrude and I anxiously awaited the approach of the Grand Trunk.

The train clattered into the station a few minutes early. Frank, his face pinched and drawn, disembarked, carrying Ella in his arms. His eyes met mine and told a story I didn't want to hear. Gaunt, except for a strangely protruding stomach, she appeared listless and hardly recognizable as my darling sister. She had aged a lifetime since last I'd seen her, six short months ago.

We had brought the wagon, with blankets laid out in the back, but Frank refused to lay her down. Instead, with Papa's help, he climbed into the back with Ella still in his arms. No one spoke on the ride back to the house. I supposed we all had the same dire thoughts.

Frank gently carried her upstairs and I helped him to settle her into bed. She opened her eyes and a hint of a smile passed over her face. "Sister." Her voice but a whisper, she grimaced and clutched her bloated stomach. After Frank administered some laudanum, she at last relaxed and dozed off, so we joined Papa and Lizzie in the front parlor.

"Well, folks, these past couple of months have been hard." Frank got right to it. "The doctor don't seem to know what to do to bring her back to health. I hate to say it, but she looks to be slipping away. She don't keep much food down, yet her stomach bulges. Some days she has the fever and acts out of her head and other days, none and she feels some better. On those days, all she talks about is going home. I took that to mean Michigan."

We all sat frozen in place, waiting for him to continue.

"The doctor in Milestown says her ailments are most likely related to losing the baby. She was so sick after that happened and hasn't really felt good since. I do blame myself for getting her in the family way." He cast his eyes downward, unwinding with a deep sigh, his speech apparently finished.

"Well now Frank, it seems to me we ought to take her to the doctor here in Mt. Clemens. Did you have good faith in the doctor?"

"Mr. Perry, not so much. I admit Dr. Redd's experience with women is limited," Frank admitted. "He's done a lot of doctoring for the cavalrymen on the outskirts of Miles at Fort Keogh. The doc thinks she might have an infection in her womanly parts, which causes them fevers she's been having. I sure wonder, and would be grateful if you'd help me get her to a doctor here."

***

"Missus Maggie, Dr. Ferris opined she got herself an infection after losing the baby." Frank chose to share this first morsel of information on the day after meeting with our family doctor. Although most anxious to learn the particulars of this visit, we respected the couple's privacy and waited for Frank to disclose the details in his own time. Over the next several days, various bits and pieces emerged as we sat vigil together at Ella's bedside. Since Frank acted most comfortable around me, I became the conduit for relaying information to the rest of the family.

This day was much like every other day. Frank and I sat on either side of Ella. Holding one of her frail hands, I beheld her sunken eyes, lax mouth and matted hair. She grimaced in her sleep, her discomfort evident. I had nothing left within to offer, as I watched my sister suffering, with a sort of detachment that could not be normal.

Gertrude often played with her dolly on the floor nearby, bringing a touch of brightness and vitality to this otherwise bleak and depressing sickroom. Thankful for her presence, I recognized the spark she generated within my heart. Little by little, we had made progress. I redeemed the title "Mama," and she became my shadow, following me everywhere.

"Sing me a song, Mama." At bedtime, we sat down together in the rocking chair in our room. I smoothed her wispy blonde hair and tucked it behind her ears. She smelled of lavender soap, with skin as soft as velvet. I rocked and sang a lullaby, while grateful teardrops fell softly onto her nightgown.

"Why do you cry, Mama?"

"Because I love you so, little one." At last, I had reclaimed her love.

Frank startled me one afternoon when he broke our typical silence to say, "The infection pry caused scar tissue. I ain't a learned man, so I don't know much about our insides, but the doc says this tissue's gripping her gut tighter and tighter." In a somber voice, he added, "That's choking it so she can't eliminate too often." His face flushed red at revealing so much delicate information, and that ended our one-sided conversation.

At least I now understood why she strained in such horrible pain at those times.

The next time we sat together, I pursued the subject further. "Does the doctor offer a remedy for the scar tissue? Can they not do surgery?"

"The doc said that could be the case."

"So, why does he wait?"

"Well, Maggie. I guess he's waiting for me to decide. It's a risky operation to take out her womb and I could lose her real quick that way. The doc wanted me to think on it a spell. Truth be told, I don't rightly know what to do."

He sounded so forlorn. *What could I offer?* I waited helplessly, while one of the people I loved most in the world battled for her life, waiting, as her husband struggled to make a difficult decision with an uncertain outcome.

In the end, no operation was performed. The oozing, from what the doctor called an "abscess" in her womb, worsened, making it too late to even consider the perilous surgery. This bit of information held no surprise for me. I had been changing the bed linens several times a day, recognizing that since they had arrived, Ella's fragile condition had continued to deteriorate. After Frank shared that there would be no operation, he up and disappeared. Almost twenty-four hours later he returned, forlorn and disheveled, with red-rimmed eyes and a day's stubbly growth of beard. It took little imagination to deduce where he had been. I had witnessed a man in that condition "the day after" many times.

While all the family spent time with Ella, Frank and I were with her most often, either together, or alternating our vigil at her bedside. Hour by hour, she lay motionless on her sickbed, soundlessly fading away. I found her plight beyond all understanding and could not fathom saying goodbye to my beloved sister and confidante. Although her eyes remained shut, I wondered idly what passed through her mind or if she might be able to hear our conversations. I did perceive she knew her time had come.

One day I sat alone at Ella's bedside, Frank resting and Gertrude napping. My thoughts turned to Mother and the pain of losing her so young. This, coupled with the dual loss of my precious Leander and Gordon, awakened long dormant emotions, and I sensed the beginning of a deep fracture in my soul. I cried a river of tears that afternoon, until the landscape of my heart turned as dry as a parched prairie in late summer.

Days passed, and even with strong doses of laudanum, my beautiful sister writhed in pain, moaning, out of her mind, babbling gibberish. A handful of times she opened her eyes and we had brief, yet lucid, conversations.

"Maggie?"

"Yes, dearest Ellie?"

"Maggie, this will be hard for Frank. Promise me you'll help him after I go," she murmured one afternoon as I sat beside her, holding her hand in mine.

"Ellie, don't be foolish, you'll recover with time," I lied.

"Maggie, you're a terrible liar. I recognize I'm dying. Maggie, please say you'll be a true friend to Frank and help him get through this?" She became slightly agitated.

I didn't want her to expend what little energy she possessed arguing with me, so I agreed, although unclear about exactly what she meant for me to do. "Yes, Ella, I promise," I whispered. This appeared to satisfy her as she closed her eyes, relaxed and slipped back into her delirium.

At other times, I was unable to bear her struggle and ran from the sick room, overcome by the stench of death lurking in every corner of the room. The days dragged on, the nights interminable.

"Maggie?" In the dark of night, I startled at her words, having fallen asleep on the floor beside her bed.

"Yes, dearest sister?" I knelt by the bed, taking her hand in mine.

"Will you tell Lucy? I didn't tell her!" She sounded panicked.

"Yes, of course, Ellie. I'll write her straightaway. Rest assured."

She nodded, after which her eyes drifted shut again. I watched carefully to see that she still breathed, and while unsteady at times, her chest continued to rise and fall. The watching had become a new habit for me.

"How fortunate you are to have the gift of little Gertrude in your life." Ella's words startled me awake once again.

"Ella?" Groggy, I again took her withered hand in mine.

"I've watched you with Gertrude . . . uh," she winced.

"Can I get you some medicine, dear sister?"

"No, it will pass." We waited a moment or two before she continued.

"You're a good mother, remember that raising a child is such privilege, you know . . ."

Unable to stop the tears, I nodded, before leaning over to kiss her delicate forehead. "Thank you, Ellie."

On May 17, upon her request, all the family gathered for a few short minutes, surrounding her bed.

"Please, let me hear you sing 'Happy Birthday to You' to Maggie." She spoke haltingly, but clearly, oddly radiant. Gertrude clasped one of my hands, and I held Ella's in my other. I looked around the room at my family singing a happy song on such a sad day, and tears of both sorrow and joy trickled down my cheeks. How could I ever reconcile this incongruity, of the delight I felt at once again holding the hand of my dear child, and the anguish of the impending loss of a once-in-a-lifetime sisterly love?

The next morning, the pain in Ella's stomach returned with such ferocity she needed a double dose of laudanum, and then more, after which she managed to rest more tranquilly throughout the day. By early evening, her breathing was shallower and more labored. Ella languidly opened her eyes and smiled serenely at both Frank and me before imperceptibly nodding her head.

A moment later, as the stars began to twinkle in the heavens, Ella took flight, quietly leaving this world for the hereafter. Surely she had ascended, now a star in her own right, next to Mama, Leander and little Gordon. We remained near her in silence for quite some time, as twilight, with its shadows, was gradually overtaken, and darkness settled upon us.

At last I stood to leave the room, so they might be together one last time, but Frank also stood and moved toward me. Our embrace offered comfort to each other in a time of sorrow, yet I felt a peculiar twinge, leaving me disconcerted.

26.

Windsor, Ontario, December, 1901. Frank and I faced Pastor David Bovington in the tiny church. Also present were the minister's wife, Martha, and a willing congregant, Bertha Johnston, who witnessed our vows. It was midmorning on a dull, overcast Tuesday. The minister made short work of the brief service, and without further adieu, another knot was tied.

Frank and I arranged to catch the Canada Southern Train in the early afternoon, traveling to Niagara Falls for our honeymoon. With more than an hour before our scheduled departure, we stood in the rectory drinking a cup of tea with the Canadians. I practiced an outer serenity, while my stomach churned with apprehension. Frank noticed my eyes glistening with tears and dabbed at them with his handkerchief. "Aw, Maggie, don't cry," he implored in a gentle tone.

"Oh, I love it when a bride cries!" Mrs. Johnston mistook my tears for happiness. *What might Frank be thinking?*

I missed Gertrude. I shouldn't have left her behind. Oh my, what were Papa and Lizzie thinking about Frank and me? It had all happened so quickly. *What impulse led me to Windsor, Ontario on this bitingly cold December day?*

Frank had returned to Montana soon after Ella's funeral and I began a search for employment. Disheartened as door after door closed in my face, Papa and I surmised Henry Jobsa's connections had effectively blacklisted me from securing a job.

To help keep the memory of dearest Ella alive, Frank and I had agreed to correspond with each other. Besides little Gertrude, this correspondence became the only other bright spot in a colorless life.

Letters exchanged between us throughout the summer and autumn had unmasked a compatibility of outlook and disposition that he persuaded me should not be disregarded. If Ella had held him in such high regard, I reasoned, he must be trustworthy and decent. I convinced myself matrimony was a sound decision, and I planned to be a good wife, succeeding where my first marriage had failed.

I also had to admit that loneliness for companionship, as well as the sense of security in knowing Gertrude and I would be supported and cared for, contributed to my decision to accept his proposal. I hoped our union would become more than a purely practical choice. I liked to believe we each shared a spirit of adventure and, in time, we would come to love one another more fully.

We feared family and friends might find it unseemly to wed but a month after the mourning period for Ella had ended, so we eloped. I wanted to bring Gertrude along, but deferred to Lizzie and Papa, who considered it best I leave her with them for the few days Frank and I would be gone.

I had petitioned the court, seeking permission to move Gertrude from Michigan to Montana. The judge agreed, and Sam signed off on it, provided I signed papers agreeing to forego the rest of the alimony awarded in the divorce trial. Although not pleased with this requirement, I did realize it liberated us. Leaving Oscar and Helen behind troubled me far more.

"Is it not incredible?" our seat mate asked, as we removed our cloaks and situated ourselves. While the entire train car buzzed with anticipation, Frank and I stared at her blankly.

"Haven't you heard?" The woman was the epitome of high fashion, dressed in a cinnamon and ecru-colored tweed suit. A red fox fur and a wide-brimmed hat, perched atop rolled mounds of russet hair, completed her ensemble. Frank, himself in a new suit, had wired money to me weeks ago to buy a dress for our wedding. I had purchased a deep violet-colored faille skirt with matching bodice, and a high collared white dimity blouse, feeling quite stylish until I set eyes upon this lady. In comparison, even my velvet hat, trimmed with a satin bow, appeared commonplace. Momentarily taken aback by her attire, I soon regained my equilibrium and shook my head "no," to her inquiry, which wasn't necessary, as she had already found in us a captive audience and continued non-stop with her patter, "Well," she tsked, "I assumed everyone had heard of Mrs. Annie Edson Taylor."

Frank and I looked at each other, raising our brows in wry amusement at her banter.

"Don't you know, Mrs. Taylor went over the falls at Niagara on her sixty-third birthday, this past October 24? The news story said she crawled out of a rowboat and into a barrel, which was screwed shut and set in the river."

"Just like that," she snapped her fingers, "they cast her off, bobbing towards the great falls. Can you imagine such a thing?" She took a breath and we both shook our heads.

"Before she knew it, whoosh, her barrel plunged over the top, straight down into the pool below. It's the first time anyone has ever done that!"

I pressed my hand against my mouth and moved closer. "Someone went over the falls in a barrel?"

"Yes ma'am! It caused quite a sensation, let me tell you."

"Did she survive such a tumble?"

"All said it was a miracle, but she came out of it with nary more than a scrape to her head. Folks say she makes appearances at the falls sometimes, describing her feat. I'm hoping to meet her."

"Well, how about it, Maggie? Is that something you'd like to try?" Frank joked.

How startling! What would cause someone of any age to be so desperate as to crawl inside a barrel to go over the Niagara Falls? There were certainly some curious people in the world!

Night had fallen when the train chugged to a stop in Niagara. I shivered when we encountered the frosty December air. Frank hired a horse-drawn cab to transport us to the Hotel Lafayette. Weary from the train ride, I lay down to rest after we had checked into our room, while Frank went to confirm our meal reservations. The dark paneled walls, along with the candelabra-style chandelier, reminded me of a similar hotel room from twelve years ago, but I quickly pushed aside such memories. Even so, other recollections from the past, some not so pleasant, creeped uninvited into my consciousness. I was relieved when Frank returned to our room sober, and invited me to accompany him to supper.

Never would I seek to compare Sam with Frank in any way other than this, but that night I learned the difference between passion and duty. After a sumptuous meal and faltering conversation, we departed the dining room, each preoccupied by our own thoughts. *Did he already have regrets? . . . Did I?* I glanced at his profile and observed a man with a straight aquiline nose, high cheekbones, bushy moustache and a determined chin. *Who is he, really? Is he truly a good man? Will Gertrude and I be safe with him? What will Montana be like for us?* My reflections began to spiral. In a brief moment of panic, it took all my wits to keep my composure and continue to step in a relaxed manner beside my new husband.

In an almighty effort to distract myself, I turned my attention to what I imagined would unfold after returning to our room. I was not in any way prepared for intimacy with this man, who, in many respects, remained a stranger to me. I also sensed his unease, watching as he all but stumbled at the top of the stairway before fumbling for our room key.

Once in the room, he removed a flask of whiskey from his inside coat pocket, unscrewed the lid with a trembling hand, and took a long draw. "Would you like a swig, eh, wife?" His blue eyes twinkled, teasing, and he extended it toward me.

Calling his bluff, I nodded and reached for the flask, taking a healthy gulp of the fiery, amber liquid. His eyes widened, perhaps a bit nonplussed that not only had I accepted the flask, but had swallowed a generous mouthful. Turns out I *had* learned a few things during my life with Sam Jobsa, things Frank had yet to learn about his new wife.

"Why, Frank Herman, are you nervous?" I spoke with bravado, in an attempt to hide my own trepidation. His hands shook perceptibly. I sat down on the edge of the bed, resigned to getting it over with. "Why don't you come sit down beside me?"

He hesitated a moment before settling himself next to me on the bed. Seconds later, he put his arm around me awkwardly and leaned over and pecked me on the cheek, his bushy, blonde moustache feeling like the boar bristles of my hairbrush. Thrust back in time, I stepped off the train at the railway depot in Milestown and watched as Frank kissed my sister on the cheek in precisely the same fashion. Memories of Ella flooded my mind, obliterating any romantic notions I had cultivated for her husband. No, that was wrong. He was now *my* husband, or . . . was he *our* husband? I chanted *my husband* to myself, hoping to shut out any lingering images of my sister and Frank in an act of intimacy.

Disconcerted, I abruptly stood and went over to peer into the mirror on the wall above the washbasin, where I removed my pearl necklace and matching earrings, an unexpected wedding present from Papa and Lizzie. Frank, who still sat on the bed's edge, grunted as he bent over and began removing his boots. I inched my way around to the other side of the bed and crawled under the covers fully clothed. He turned to glance over his shoulder at me with a puzzled look on his face, as I carefully and inelegantly disrobed, one garment at a time, each piece slithering over the bedside onto the floor, creating a lumpy mound.

Frank watched mesmerized, saying nary a word. Did he feel scandalized by the fact I lay stark naked under the covers, waiting? I turned on my side to face away from him, toward the heavily curtained window. While I could not see him disrobe, I could hear his careful movements as he removed his suspenders. I imagined him loosening his necktie, unbuttoning his stiff wing-collared white shirt and removing his dark wool trousers. Would he next strip off his undergarments? Were they clean or grimy? Would he neatly fold them on the chair or leave them in a jumble on the floor? I did not yet know these details about my husband.

My eyes open a slit, I beheld the slight glow from the room's incandescent overhead light slowly extinguish. The bed creaked as he set his weight upon it and I shivered, although not from the chill, as he pulled the covers aside only enough to slip in beside me. I tensed as he reached for me, both dreading and anticipating his touch, with its inevitable outcome. In truth, I wished to be somewhere, anywhere, else.

Some time later, as he lay snoring beside me, I contemplated our union. I had neither swooned nor cried out, and had seen the act through to consummation with little true emotion. He had not the passion of Sam, but I perceived him as a considerate, if somewhat inept, lover. Exhausted by the sheer effort of it all, I rolled over and fell into a dreamless slumber.

The next morning dawned crisp, the snow sparkling from the reflection of a silvery blue sky. A balcony with a graceful wrought iron railing just beyond our sitting room beckoned me. There I stood, watching the magnificent falls, in awe of the surrounding grandeur, while contemplating the remarkable twist my life had taken. I had to concede I never, ever expected to find myself at Niagara Falls, much less on a honeymoon!

Later, we explored the observatory located atop the hotel's six-story turret, viewing both the American and Horseshoe Falls. The sunshine lured us outdoors in the afternoon, where we walked briskly to the tourist observation platform. After witnessing the thundering magnitude of Horseshoe Falls in closer proximity, Mrs. Taylor's daredevil feat looked to be all the more harrowing and incredible. We were a trifle disappointed when she didn't appear this day, but I decided I rather liked to imagine her in my own mind instead, for she may have fallen sadly short of my expectations in person.

We remained in Niagara Falls for another day, satisfied to spend time within the confines of the hotel, as the weather turned frigid, with near blizzard conditions. I had never experienced electric lights, an electric elevator, hot running water straight from the tap, and our own private bath. I marveled at all these modern conveniences, recognizing I would be leaving such trappings far behind with the move west.

Mt. Clemens, Michigan. A part of my heart would forever remain in Michigan. By early summer, thanks to Mr. Crocker and a compassionate judge, I had been granted visitation rights with Oscar and Helen. Sam hired a girl to help with their care, so finding them clean and well-fed when I visited eased in small measure my broken heart.

Gertrude and I spent a final bittersweet afternoon with the two of them, and I was sick to my stomach the entire visit. "Mama, will we see you and Gertrude again later?" Helen quizzed me as our time together drew to an end. What could I say?

"Yes, of course we will see you again!" I held them both close, praying I spoke the truth. *What on earth was I doing? Why was I leaving them yet again?* My insides twisted into knots and I fought back tears as I gave hugs, long and deep, to my two oldest children. Regrettably, to find security and a new life for Gertrude and myself, I had to let go of the other two. What will become of them? Could I trust that Sam wouldn't mistreat them? Would he turn them against me? Would I ever see them again? *How could I move so far away from them?* If only the judge had ruled in my favor. If only Sam would relinquish custody. If only I could kidnap them. If only.

The day before we left for Montana, I had one more visit to make. A frigid January day, it had begun snowing mid-morning and showed no signs of letting up as I drove Papa's buggy to my destination. I shivered as I tied the horse to the hitching pole, glad I had worn my boots. Pulling my wrap tightly around me, I gingerly made my way down the snow-covered, slippery pathway.

After locating the Jobsa family plot, I knelt in the snow, brushing aside the icy crystals from two small headstones placed side-by-side. I bowed my head, overwhelmed by a familiar, never-ending sorrow. A raw wind pierced the bitter air, blowing snowflakes in my face where they mingled with the teardrops streaking down my cheeks. *Goodbye, dearest boys, eternally in my heart and unceasingly in my mind, I love you both so.* They, of course, didn't ask when I would be back, but I made a covenant with myself that I would return before my life ended to touch each stone again. This was the closest I could be on this earth to my two boy angels, one, a dimpled, blonde cherub, and the other, a red haired sprite with a twinkle in his eye.

Standing, I moved further along the pathway, stopping at a more familiar section of the cemetery. I found her grave and knelt before it, touching my hand to her headstone. *I wish I had some flowers to bring to you today. I've come to bid you farewell and to tell you that you were right. Your advice was sound. The folly of girlish love blinded me. I am starting anew, Mother, and I pray this choice is one of which you would approve. Love has not blinded me this time.* I lingered quietly, listening for a reply. At first, there was nothing but silence, but then I heard the whistle of a solitary scarlet cardinal, trilling affirmation.

I stepped to the right where I found another headstone, the most recent addition to the Perry family plot. *Oh, dearest Ellie.* What might I say? *I have to wonder if this is what you really meant for us to do. What were you truly thinking? You knew the two of us better than anyone, so I hope we're being faithful to your wishes. If I'm not back to see you for a while, it's because tomorrow Gertrude, Frank and I board the Grand Trunk to Chicago and from there, the Great Northern, Montana bound, to begin our new life together.* I patted the top of her gravestone. *I'll give your regards to Lucy, dear sister.*

Part Four

All our choices are made out of either love or fear.
And, fear is often disguised as practicality.
--Jim Carrey

27

Lavina, Montana, October 15, 1941. By mid-morning, I deliver a pie to tempt the lunch crowd, for which I receive a heartfelt "thank you" from the girls. I spend some time tidying up the house, and before I know it, lunchtime arrives and I order up some soup. A few minutes later I hear a rap on the door separating the house from the cafe, and I unlatch it to find Jean bearing a tray of vegetable soup, saltine crackers and a large dill pickle. She must have remembered I've recently developed a weakness for pickles.

After lunch, I lie down on my bed for a short nap, falling soundly asleep in what seems like seconds. Why I can't do this in the middle of the night remains a mystery. A touch of grogginess upon awakening brings me to the kitchen for an afternoon cup of tea. While it steeps, I stare out the window, pleased to see the day still sunny and pleasant. Teacup empty, I decide to walk to the corner and back to soak up a bit of the autumn sunshine. This means, of course, I need to replace my slippers with suitable walking shoes. Rummaging around the floor of my closet in search of those sturdy shoes, I finally find them on top of an old, broken-down pasteboard box. Oh! I had completely forgotten it was back there. When we moved to Lavina, I had tucked it into the closet to sort through later, but that's as far as I had gotten.

Carefully removing the lid, I peer inside. A photo of Oscar and me standing beside his house in Mt. Clemens stares back. Taken on my sixtieth birthday, during my second visit back to Michigan, the image reminds me again how very handsome he is. It pleases me to remember the way people spoke about his kind and gentle nature. I love him so.

Underneath that picture I find a few postcards. Sifting through, I find one from Kirksville that Frances used her artistic skills to colorize. Kirksville took several months of our lives. My daughter had been so courageous.

I pick up the box and settle into a more comfortable position in the chair by my bed. The walk can wait.

Next, I come across some old receipts I must have at one time deemed important. Well, I might as well throw them away now. To this pile, I soon add an old white handkerchief, with the monogrammed initials "WSJ." It was wrapped around a tarnished sterling silver souvenir spoon from Niagara Falls, somewhere I never dreamt I would see, but I did. What a spectacular sight! I also discover a deck of Niagara Falls playing cards, well worn from all the games of gin rummy Babe, Frances and I played over the years. They sit atop a small, white, satin-covered booklet with the words "Wedding Chimes" embossed on the cover in silver leaf, encircled by blue, mauve and white forget-me-not flowers. A knot forms in my stomach. I know its contents, and wonder why I've saved it.

As I unwrap a tiny tissue-covered package, a miniature wine-colored leather purse drops into my lap. Empty now, I recall how it had once held a golden locket engraved with an intertwined "M" and "S." What a silly girl I'd been, in love with the idea of love. It has taken me nearly a lifetime and three marriages to grasp the true essence of love.

I find a picture of me with three of my girls. I would guess it must have been taken back around 1908 or '09. The two little girls wore lacy white dresses, while Gertrude and I had on high-necked white blouses and linen skirts. Both Babe and Gertrude have such elegantly fine facial bone structure. My attention is drawn to another photo from a few years later; the girls are wearing those old black wool stockings, standing beside the house up at the dam with that sweet black and white barn cat. How bow-legged Frances looks!

I stop and examine the next picture, my eyes tearing up as I gaze at Oscar, Helen and the twins. Judging by their size, I think the photo was taken around the turn of the century. The four of them are standing in the field where wild flowers grew, out behind the farmhouse on Sugarbush Road. Oscar, wearing a cap and knee pants with suspenders, has a sweater jauntily placed around his shoulders and stands to the left, while Helen, in her smocked dress (which I clearly remember as being yellow), sports a wide-brimmed hat and stands to the right. The twins, my babies Gertrude and Gordon, stand between Oscar and Helen. They hold hands, both barefoot, wearing matching long-sleeved dresses and hats and eyeing the camera with great suspicion. It was certainly not a happy time, as I can easily see reflected in their expressions. Of all the low points in my life, that may have been the lowest. Tears stream down my cheeks. Maybe all these memories would have best been left alone, on today, of all days.

I sit quietly for another minute, and when I feel calmer, find I cannot resist probing further into the contents of the box. After all, I do have the time.

28.

Twelve Mile Dam, Montana, Summer, 1905. My shoulders ached as I stood over the washtub in the yard and rubbed at grease stains on Frank's work shirt. Back and forth across the washboard, my roughened hands scrubbed the soiled garment, the monotony wearying. For a moment, my gaze lingered on the open prairie, its vastness nothing but a bleak panorama reaching to the horizon. Staring down into the murky liquid before me, I contemplated how I had come to be in this place.

Abruptly, my attention was drawn to Gussie chasing after a squealing two-year-old Frances, as they dashed around the side of our house. Be it a bug or a cow-pie, Frances found everything fascinating and deserving of further exploration.

"Mother, Frances is pulling up bean plants!" Gussie hollered moments later from our vegetable garden. "I told her to leave them be, but she won't mind."

Irked, I took off at a trot to investigate. Sure enough, Frances held several tender young shoots in her grubby little hands when I swooped in and grabbed her under the arms, "Frances! That's a no-no. Come watch Mama finish washing Daddy's clothes."

She giggled and I carried her back to where the tub full of grimy clothes remained untended, silently bidding me to resume the disagreeable task. Gertrude had wandered off, most likely in search of a hiding place where she might daydream unhampered by her little sister. Soon after our move west, we began calling her Gussie, part of my effort to start fresh in our new circumstances. An observant child, both quiet and shy, she had taken to studying Frank and me from a safe distance, watching for signs of an impending quarrel so she could take cover. Memories of her turbulent young life remained all too fresh in her mind.

Perhaps because Frank was already forty-seven when Frances arrived and had never spent time around youngsters, or perhaps a result of his bitter disappointment Frances hadn't been a "Frank," he didn't seem to well tolerate children. The whiskey bottle, his preferred companion, kept him company as I tended the girls. While I did not favor the drink much after my years with Sam, I appreciated that it softened his mind to the chaos stirred up by two energetic little ones. Ella had died before the blush fell off the rose, so surely, she had never experienced the Frank I had come to know. Or, had she? *Oh, Ella, what secrets did you hold close about this man, this land?*

My arms and hands remained on task, while my mind had flown on from Frank and Ella, to memories of Oscar and Helen. All were accompanied by the familiar ache of my broken heart. Covering that heart with a soapy hand, I prayed for the children I had abandoned, and my stomach churned.

I seldom heard news of them or their wretched father. What little I did hear came second-or third-hand, courtesy of gossip my dear stepmother Lizzie overheard at the mercantile or church. A few precious letters, which I imagined Sam's new wife, Fannie, helped the children write, arrived now and then, but with little real news relayed in their childish scrawl. Those beloved children haunted me, day and night. Even though I wrote at least monthly, I loathed myself for leaving them behind for another woman to raise. In response to those feelings of powerlessness, I threw myself into the grueling tasks of maintaining the homestead with an unbridled fervor.

A sudden stillness in the air brought me back to the present moment. "Frances," I called, "where have you gotten off to? Gussie!" Oh, these children!

I squinted against the glare of the fierce sun, searching the empty yard for a sign of my girls. Dancing with abandon, a dust devil swirled in the road.

"Over here, Mama! We're in the barn, watching the kittens play."

Relieved, I called back, "You mind Frances for me while I hang out the wash, you hear?"

"Yes, ma'am."

By the time I finished that chore, the sun had climbed further in the sky, the heat sweltering. Weeds in the garden beckoned, and then, dinner preparations. Frank expected a noon meal when he returned after a long morning out on the range, checking the cattle. I didn't shirk the hard work, but like my sister Lucy, the isolation and bleakness often preyed upon my mind, leaving me blue. There were days I searched in vain for my misplaced sense of humor.

I felt older than my thirty-five years, but maybe that's what happens when you live with an ornery man pushing fifty. Well, I'd made my bed, as they say, and must now lie in it. I could expect no rescue from Papa this time. Unbidden tears dribbled down my dusty cheeks as I recalled the telegram Lizzie sent in early May. A letter with the details arrived a week later. Papa had stepped on a rusty nail and contracted blood poisoning. The cruel infection took his life, leaving us all to mourn his passing. A part of my world ended with his death, the protective barrier cast away. My brothers, sisters and I had now moved to next in line.

Even all these weeks later, I still couldn't envision Papa being gone. I much preferred to imagine him back in Mt. Clemens with those smiling Irish eyes, playing with his children and hugging his grandchildren.

⸙

"You do make a fine pie, Maggie." Frank complimented me after supper one evening, emitting a satisfied belch as he picked at his teeth with a splinter of wood.

I smiled and nodded my head in thanks.

"Headin' to town tomorrow. Suppose you and the girls will want to come along?"

"Yes! I do need some notions and perhaps a few yards of summer-weight fabric. I'd like to visit Lucy, too."

"We'll leave at first light. Be ready, as I'm not gonna wait on you."

The first blush of morning settled upon us as the girls and I waited patiently, while Frank loaded up the broken axle from his disc harrow.

Minutes later, Frank called, "Giddy-up, then!" The wagon lurched forward, Milestown bound.

I held Frances, half-asleep, in my arms, delighting in her sweet smell and the softness of her chubby little arms and legs curled up in my lap. I counted my blessings to have this chance to raise another child, even though living with Frank could at times be unpleasant. I glanced at Gussie, who sat rigidly between us, lost in her own little world. *Did she ever daydream about her brother and sister so far away in Michigan?*

Lucy, as I had predicted, moved into Milestown a year ago, leaving her husband and daughter in Brandenburg. Her decision came as no surprise, although I continued to struggle with the "whys" and "hows" of such a choice. She lived in a small house near downtown and worked at Shore Newcom Mercantile. She was quick to point out mingling with customers suited her better than marriage and child rearing in the "backwoods." I found this comment disquieting, but as my only link to my first family, I appreciated any time together to reminisce and catch up on Michigan news.

"Maggie! Girls! What brings you all to town?" All smiles, Lucy met us in the entryway of the mercantile, where Frank had dropped us off on his way to Miles & Strevell's Hardware store. Lucy's move to Milestown had made a world of difference in both her appearance and her outlook. She exuded an allure and vivacity I hadn't seen in many a year.

"Oh you, know, the usual. A broken axle on the harrow." I smiled playfully, in return. "What news do you hear? Have you had any letters from Michigan?"

"No, but I'm sure Lizzie is quite preoccupied with getting the boarding house up and running, leaving little time to write."

"Of course! I hope it will be a grand success for her. I do wish we weren't so far away. I miss them all so."

"I do too. I dream of seeing Louis again someday," she lamented, before changing the subject. "Maggie, can I help you with anything today?"

I followed her lead. "Well, I am looking for fabric to make some summer wear for the girls. What would you suggest?"

Lucy led the way to the bolts of cloth stacked high on the shelves and together, we browsed through the choices. "My divorce will be final this month," she said. "William, of course, will receive custody of Grace, but will continue to bring her for monthly visitation when he comes to town."

I figured I would never understand my sister. "Are you satisfied with this arrangement, Lucy?"

"Why yes, I'm content. Grace will be much happier on the ranch with her father. They are so much alike."

Wishing it were that easy for me to let go of my children, I frowned.

"Maggie, don't despair! This outcome is for the best. I can move forward with my life."

Whatever she meant by that, I had no idea. Rather than share my true sentiments, I nodded in agreement. "Yes, sister, you can get on with your life."

We completed our business with the purchase of some muslin gauze fabric covered in dainty pink roses, perfect to make frocks for the girls. With promises to see each other again soon, the three of us made way for the wagon, parked a couple of blocks down the street in front of John Carter's Saloon.

Before climbing into the wagon, I peered over the top of the swinging saloon doors and not surprisingly, spied my husband perched on a bar stool, in deep conversation with a rough-looking character. Steeling myself, I stood there for a few minutes, unsure of my intent. I hoped he would glance our way, but when that didn't happen, I decided to forge ahead, a daughter on either side, each holding a hand.

"Frank." I spoke clearly and more loudly than I had intended.

He started and glowered at us. "Maggie, by God, what're you doing in here with the young'uns?"

"Uh . . . I was uncertain if we'd need to board the wagon to wait or how long you'd be."

"Go on with you, this ain't no place for women. Besides, I'm in the middle of a business meeting." He shooed us away with his hand.

My face burned. I turned on my heel and dragged the girls along with me out of the saloon without another word. On an impulse, I walked in the opposite direction of the wagon. We marched toward the Olive Hotel--the old Leighton with a new name--at the other end of the block. My cheeks were red from embarrassment at being spoken to like a schoolgirl, and, combined with my two-year-old's stubbornness in resisting our brisk pace, we attracted the stares of onlookers. We traipsed into the hotel's elegant lobby, Frances screeching like a cat whose tail had gotten caught in the barn door.

"Frances! That's quite enough."

"Shall I swat her, Mother?" asked Gussie.

"No! Listen, both of you! We shall sit down and behave like ladies until your father is finished with his business and we see him come out of the saloon. If you cooperate, maybe I'll offer you a treat." The mention of the word "treat" silenced Frances. Gussie simply looked at me with wistful eyes.

And then, a caprice. "In fact, girls, I've changed my mind. We aren't going to sit here and wait for your dad, after all. Let's walk across the street to the park and pass the time there."

"How will he find us, then?" asked Gertrude.

"We'll keep an eye out for him. Don't worry, we won't lose him." I smiled reassuringly. While part of me wished he might lose *us*, I recognized how frivolous such a notion was.

I found a shady bench and sat down next to another woman. The two girls trotted off to the grassy area near the stream, which ran along the side of the park under old, majestic cottonwoods. I leaned back and looked up at the heavens. This was a much better idea than sitting in the hotel lobby. A few wispy clouds floated high above in an otherwise clear sky. I inhaled the sweet scents of a warm, summer day as Gussie came running.

"Mother, Frances is drinking water out of the stream!" I could always rely on Gussie to tattle. The other woman smiled knowingly, which told me she had experienced the same sort of behavior by her own children.

I rescued Frances from the edge of the creek, unsure how much of the dark and murky water she had swallowed. "Oh, Frances, what have you done?" I shook my head, wiping the dirt from her face and hands.

Less than a week later, in the middle of the alfalfa harvest, Frances took ill. While there is never a convenient time for illness, the worst time is in the middle of cutting, as we struggle to bring in the crop before a rainstorm comes along and ruins it.

"Mother, I think there's something wrong with Frances. She won't get up." Gussie walked into the kitchen as I made the morning coffee.

I finished up with that task straightaway and scurried into their sleeping room. "Mama, no feel good, head hurts," Frances whimpered. Her head did feel feverish.

"Well, sweet one, you can stay in bed today. Mama will be close by, cooking dinner for the field hands and Daddy. Are you hungry?" She shook her head and I left her to rest.

Mid-morning, I brought her some water, along with a bit of bread. I coaxed her to eat, and then felt responsible when she soon retched. Within hours came the dysentery, followed by a general malaise, which continued over the next couple of days. She became noticeably weaker and refused our attempts to take her to the privy.

"Frank, I'm worried about Frances and would like to take her into town to see the doctor. She's dwindling, not keeping down food or drink." I couldn't avoid the terror taking root within me, as memories of Leander invaded my mind.

"Soon as the harvest's in, if'n she's no better, we'll take her in." He walked into the girls' room and with a rare tenderness, gathered her into his arms. "You feeling poorly, little one?"

She nodded, and then cried out, "Owee, owee, hurts!" Even simple movements elicited this uncharacteristic fussiness.

"Mama, me hurt," Frances whined most of the day. My worry over her well-being intensified, and a deep sense of foreboding began to seep under my skin.

That evening, I told Frank, "I'm going to drive Frances to town myself tomorrow. I know the way. Gussie can come along with me."

"Suit yourself. I'd go too, but I've got to finish getting the alfalfa in."

Milestown, Montana. Young Dr. Thomas Archibald MacKenzie had emigrated from Edinburgh, Scotland, to Canada several years ago, and earlier this year to the United States. He had built a steady practice in a town where there had been few doctors. We parked the buggy in front of his office on Main Street, a block east of the Olive Hotel.

"Mrs. Herman, based on what you've told me, along with Frances' evident neck pain, stiffness of spine and extreme sensitivity to touch, I'm led to suspect we're looking at a case of Epidemic Infantile Paralysis, or Heine-Medin disease," diagnosed Dr. MacKenzie in his lilting Scottish brogue.

All I heard was the word 'paralysis.' "Doctor, what are you telling me? My daughter is paralyzed? Whatever do you mean?" My voice was unintentionally sharp. I jumped to my feet, unable to contain a rising panic.

"Madam, please remain calm, as it's likely she'll make a full recovery. Nearly all do. In the unlikely event that she doesn't, she's liable to be slightly affected at most, long-term."

"Slightly affected?"

"Yes, what I mean is perhaps slight muscle weakness or a bit of uneven growth in some of her extremities. We won't know for certain for a few months, but most often, people experience a complete recovery," he repeated. "There are some who believe exercising the affected limbs may help, but we'll discuss that later, after this initial symptomatic period passes."

Stunned into speechlessness, I barely absorbed what he said.

"Mrs. Herman, I think the best we can do is to keep Frances comfortable and not push her to move about. I'd like to admit her to my clinic hospital for a time, to be sure she doesn't become severely dehydrated and so I can monitor her symptoms. She may also be contagious to others. Would that be agreeable to you?"

Words escaped me, but I nodded my head, dumbfounded. He left the examination room to make arrangements, while I held my whimpering daughter in my arms, and Gussie stood silently beside us.

I collected my wits about me enough that when he returned, I asked, "Dr. MacKenzie, how did this happen?"

"Well, Mrs. Herman, it's often spread through feces-contaminated food or water. Are you aware if she's gotten into anything of late, within the past week or two? Did she drink from the horse trough? Or, perhaps attempt to eat something out of the ordinary, as small children are prone to do?"

It hit me like a huge boulder. The stream. Oh, Lord, the water in the stream. I explained what had happened that day in the park.

Gussie cried all the way home, and it caused me to consider how, in a past life, I had left other children behind, crying out, "Mama! Mama! No leave me!" These cries echoed incessantly in my mind. I blamed myself, and specifically my impulsiveness, for Frances' sickness. Had I walked the other way and boarded the wagon, this wouldn't have happened. What would I tell Frank?

"Oh, Maggie! I rightly blame myself for not getting her to the doc sooner." We sat at the table, after tucking Gussie into bed.

"It wouldn't have helped. The doctor told me there's nothing to do for it but wait and see what happens after the disease has run its course," I replied, my voice a monotone. He had said she wouldn't die, or had he? I couldn't recall.

Anxiety and an attitude of "watch, wait and pray for the best outcome" filled our next days. Gussie and I drove the buggy into town several times alone, and once with Frank. We soon developed the ability to predict with flawless accuracy the location of every major bump and pothole along the way. We counted fence posts, birds and clouds. We told stories, recited poetry and prayed aloud for Frances' recovery. Not only did my prowess with a buggy grow stronger during this time, but my resolve to learn how to be more independent blossomed as well. I felt guilty for exposing my baby girl to harm, yet I also blamed Frank for shooing us out of the saloon in the first place.

As the doctor predicted, Frances slowly improved. She remained in Dr. MacKenzie's clinic hospital for over two weeks, after which we brought her home to convalesce. Evidently, she was but one of several children stricken over the summer. We were unerringly faithful to the doctor's therapies, and over time, Frances' limbs regained all their function and we gave thanks for this miracle, believing the disease had not harmed her in any lasting way.

29

Early Autumn, 1909. "Mama! Me want it! Me want it!"

"No, Babe, you already had a cookie. That's all you're getting. Supper will be on the table soon. Go find your sister and play with her, while Mama gets the biscuits in the oven." My voice was soft, yet firm, in the hope of avoiding an all-too-frequent temper tantrum.

If we described Gussie as considerate and Frances inquisitive, Gladys--or Babe, as we called her--would doubtless be labeled strong-willed. Approaching three years of age, we nicknamed her the "little tyrant," based on her steadfast attempts to rule the roost. Oh, what a talent Babe displayed for provoking her daddy!

Frank's disposition became more and more cantankerous, and he displayed increasingly limited patience and a short fuse. Confrontations with his daughters became more frequent, invariably resulting in slapping and sometimes spanking the both of them. I attempted to intervenc, placing myself between the girls and him, though I typically ended up on the wrong side of the fence, with all three of us garnering bruises. The oft-present whiskey served only to fuel his anger.

Whenever Gertrude's highly developed sixth sense detected a skirmish afoot, she disappeared to hide under the bed or out in the barn. Frank never laid a hand on her, but perhaps this was because she wasn't his flesh and blood. I gave thanks that one innocent child could escape his brutality. Years of practice walking on eggshells around Sam made it easier for me to steer clear of Frank's wrath, but his daughters had no such history to fall back on. Besides, they were little children, prone to mischief.

⌒⌒⌒

"Goldarn it, I must have left the receipt in my saddlebag." Frank grumbled as he stood, heading to the barn to retrieve the missing paperwork. He sometimes sat at his desk and managed ledger entries while I made supper.

Dropping spoonfuls of batter onto the biscuit pan, I glanced up in time to catch Frances and Babe moving toward their dad's desk. Where was Gussie?

"Girls, stay away from your father's desk!"

They looked at me and smiled angelically, but continued to sashay in that direction, Babe humming a little tune.

"Gussie, where are you?" No answer.

I set down the bowl with a clatter and dashed over to them, but a moment too late. Giggling, Babe had crawled quick like a bunny from her daddy's chair onto the top of the desk, grabbed his pen and tipped over the ink bottle, causing it to run like a bubbling brook down his ledger page. No longer smiling, Frances reached for the bottle, but this attempt only worsened the problem, as the rest of the ink cascaded down her arm, splashing all over the front of her dress.

"Uh oh," Babe pronounced, matter-of-factly.

"Uh oh is the least of it!" They began crying in response to my sharp voice, realizing they were in hot water.

Frank stood in the doorway. "What in thunderation is going on in here?" He rushed toward the desk to find both his work and his eldest daughter covered in ink.

"Frank, it was an accident! Frances was trying to stop Babe from getting into the inkpot."

He wasn't listening. Fit to be tied, he swooped down, grabbed Frances under her arms, and threw her against the wall. Her lungs made a whooshing sound before she collapsed in a heap, the strength of his blow knocking the breath from her.

"Stop! Stop it, you beast! She's but an innocent child!"

He then yanked Babe, frozen in fear, off his desktop, spanking her soundly as she began howling, as much from fright as from the actual pain of his hand striking her bottom.

Frances lay whimpering against the wall, while Babe scampered off to escape any further attack by her father.

I ran over to Frances and clutched her to my bosom, but not before Frank hauled off and smacked me broadside across the face, yelling, "What kind of mother are you? Your children are wild as Injuns! Get them under control before I do something we'll both regret!" With that, he stormed out.

I helped Frances to her feet and she limped alongside me to their room, where we found Gussie and Babe hiding under the bed.

"Mother, your cheek is all red and there's blood," Gussie observed, patting my cheek softly with her fingers.

My face stung and throbbed. Running my tongue over my swollen lip, the taste of blood mingled with my tears. I heaved a half-sigh, half-sob and offered up a silent prayer to God. This could not go on. Then and there, I resolved to find a way out, but this time, one which included my three daughters. Desperate, I realized that prayer had slowly begun to find its way into my life again, as I sought to heal my personal rift with God and religion. I had only a hazy memory of the calm and serenity that filled my heart whenever I attended services with Sam's mother, Gertrude, back in Mt. Clemens.

During the following weeks, an idea began to take shape. A couple of years ago, the Herman ranch had become a swing station for the Broadus Stage, which delivered both mail and people to outlying areas in the county. The Stage switched out the horses every dozen or so miles, making our ranch a logical first stop after departing Milestown. Housing and feeding the huge draft horses, who ate up to a bale of hay a day, provided some extra income.

The stagecoach traveled the eighty miles from Milestown to Broadus every other day, taking somewhere between eight to ten hours one way. Some days brought only the U.S. mail on board, whereas on others, there were passengers as well. Since the Stage arrived near midday, I had lately considered applying to be a home station, selling hot, home-cooked meals for $1. I would provide something beyond the typical fare of johnnycakes and beans or black bread and watered-down coffee. I speculated this might turn into a money-making venture for me, as word would quickly spread about my tasty home cooking. And no one could resist my pies!

A home station designation would further my plans for a possible future without Frank. The next time we traveled into Milestown for supplies, as was his custom, he dropped the girls and me at Shore Newcom Mercantile before heading off to do his own errands.

"Sister! How are you all faring this fine day?" Lucy stood near the pickle barrel, replenishing the supply of the dark green cured vegetables from a tin container. Although she had remarried last year, she continued to work at the mercantile. Her new husband, a divorcee by the name of Joseph Robinson McKay, was a former state senator back in 1899. Known around town as "J.R.," he had garnered the respect of the community. This gave Lucy a certain elevated status among town folk, one in which she took pride. Based on the reemergence of her vivacious nature, I deduced that J.R., older even than Frank, had turned out to be an ideal match for my sister.

She never spoke of Grace, so I was reluctant to mention her. I contemplated the situation time and again, wondering how a mother could so blithely walk away from her child. Lord knew, not a day passed I didn't chastise myself for leaving behind two children, only to find myself yet again in unhealthy circumstances. The paradox was had I not come west, there would be neither Frances nor Babe. There was no reconciling life's choices and the unpredictability of the results. Perhaps my decision to marry again might be labeled an error in judgment. By any definition, the union was not the marriage of my dreams. Any sense of adventure I previously felt had long since dissolved, the romance never kindled. Clearly, I was not Frank's cup of tea, nor he mine. We may have been brought together by our great love for Ella, but that love had not parlayed into love for each other.

"Lucy, could you mind the girls for a few minutes? I need to do an errand alone."

"How mysterious . . . " She eyed me with suspicion.

"Oh, it's nothing, really. I want to apply to become a home station for the Stage, without having the girls in tow."

She wrinkled her nose. "A home station? Well, now, Maggie, that sounds like a fine plan to keep you busy out there at the dam. I suppose you can leave them, as long as you aren't gone too long. I don't want to arouse the ire of my employer."

"Girls, if you mind your manners for Aunt Lucy, there will be a treat for you when I return." Three smiling faces promised to behave. I hurried out of the mercantile and made my way to the Stage Division Agent's office. In a stroke of luck, I found the agent available to speak with me.

"Mrs. Herman, establishing a home station along the Broadus Stage route has come up in recent conversations with the Division Superintendent." Agent Richard Willson nodded his head before continuing, "Since your place is currently a swing station, it seems a rather natural transition. Lodging would be unnecessary, unless we experienced inclement weather, but I imagine the opportunity for a hot, home-cooked meal would be appreciated. I'll offer up this proposition to my superiors and if there's interest, I'd like to meet your husband to discuss it further and work out a business arrangement." He bent forward and smiled at me condescendingly.

"Excuse me, Mr. Willson, but this doesn't involve my husband. You may work out any possible agreement with me." I smiled sweetly.

"Oh, I see." He paused for a moment and leaned back in his chair, his brows knitting together, the fingertips of each hand creating a steeple under his chin. He regarded me carefully. "Well, now, I'm not accustomed to doing business with a woman." He sat back up, eying me with skepticism. "This will take some further review. Is your husband aware of this proposal?"

"I do not see how that question is relevant to our discussion, Mr. Willson," I replied, peeved by his arrogance, "as I will be the one doing the cooking and housekeeping."

His eyes narrowed as he carefully considered his next words. "Yes, I suppose that is true, but all the same, Mr. Herman should be informed."

"And why, sir, is that?" I asked, my face serene.

He hesitated, and ignoring my question, continued. "Well, then, perhaps you can return to my office at some future date, after I've had a chance to consider and discuss it with the superintendent?"

Exercising great self-restraint, I remained cordial and did not reveal my exasperation with his condescending attitude. "Why yes, Mr. Willson, I believe that's possible. I'll be in touch." We both stood and shook hands.

And with that, we bid each other a good day. Exultant, but fuming, I stormed the two blocks back to the mercantile.

"Did your meeting go well?" Observing the look on my face, Lucy continued, "Oh, maybe not? You look as though you're in a royal snit."

"Men!" I wanted to stomp my foot, but thought the better of it, instead taking a deep, calming breath before explaining to my sister the agent's complete lack of respect.

"Well, Maggie, I think it's a victory he even listened to your proposal. I would find baking pies and cooking for others unappealing, though it sounds like the perfect way for you to earn some extra money." I chose to withhold the fact my plan included more than just earning "extra" money; rather, it afforded a livelihood to help support myself and my three daughters and offer a viable case for gaining custody of my children in a divorce settlement. Determined it would somehow all work out, I also placed faith in the belief Frank would continue to financially care for his daughters.

Snug in their beds, the girls slumbered later that evening when I approached Frank about becoming a home station.

"Well, now, Maggie. That's not a half-bad idea. It'll give us a little extra money to tuck away for a rainy day now, won't it?"

"Yes, Frank, I think it's a step in the right direction." I wondered if he had any inkling then what I really had in mind.

It took several visits over several months and more than one pie delivered to Agent Willson. In the end, we struck a deal for the Herman ranch to be designated a home station, with meal service and lodging on the Broadus Stage route, commencing March 1, 1910.

30.

Milestown, Montana, 1911. Walking down the steps of the Custer County Courthouse, my hands trembled as I looked down at the court's order and reread the words declaring the marriage between Frank Herman and Margareta Perry Jobsa Herman dissolved, effective March 14, 1911. I was elated to have been given custody of my girls, partly because I could prove I had a steady income from the stage line for the past year, but mostly because Frank voluntarily gave up his rights. I marveled at the ease with which we had come to the terms of settlement, so different from my divorce from Sam. The agreement stipulated he would continue to own the ranch. If he died, it would be placed in a trust, with my name listed as beneficiary until our two daughters reached maturity. I would be allowed to remain on the property and receive a monthly stipend for child support. Frank decided he would build a second, smaller house for himself, down the road from the main house. He would manage the ranch and provide for his children, while I would support myself by operating the Home Station for the stage line.

Always better off as friends, I didn't mind him nearby, just not in the same living space as the girls and me. He acted both pleased and relieved to carry on running the ranch, yet not have to live with the four of us. It appeared to me an ideal divorce situation and I believe he was of like mind. The decree also specified the girls could visit him whenever it struck their fancy. I regarded the whole arrangement as being quite modern and forward thinking.

As I had anticipated, our home station soon developed a reputation along the Stage route for outstanding home-cooked meals. I set great store by the fact that virtually every passenger on every coach eagerly entered our dining room, keen to sample my savory meals and pay me $1 apiece to do so.

⁓

Twelve Mile Dam. Sweat trickled down my forehead, dripping into the crevice between my breasts, as the four of us worked to prepare the noon meal on this steamy July morning. A slight breeze rippled the air, carrying with it the song of a meadowlark drifting in through the kitchen window. We expected the stage at the usual time, carrying anywhere from one to five guests. Even without passengers, the driver could be counted upon to eat. I looked up from rolling out the noodle dough and glanced at the windowsill, where I had set two loaves of bread to cool.

Without warning, I found myself face-to-face with a Cheyenne man, as he peered at me through the open window, his head and upper body towering above me. "Girls, I want the three of you to quietly move into the bedroom and get under the bed. Now!" Gussie discreetly slid the knife she was using to chop vegetables into her apron pocket, took Frances and Babe's hands, and as unobtrusively as possible, tiptoed out of the kitchen and down the hall. I peered into his almond-shaped eyes and he boldly stared back, his lips drawn into a thin, firm line. His high cheekbones were framed by long, black hair with a feather twisted into a small braid, drooping onto his chest. He wore a threadbare and white man's dirty shirt, sleeves rolled up to his elbows. I had no idea what he wore below and had no inclination to find out.

"Hungry."

My heart thudded as I gestured with a turn of my head toward the loaves of bread on the sill. He reached out and tentatively picked one up, nodded his head in what I perceived as thanks, then turned and walked away from the house. After a moment, I moved over to the window and looked out. Along the ridge stood an Indian mother and several little ones. Dressed in calico and buckskin, the woman held the reins of an ancient-looking black and white Paint, pulling a travois. I wondered if they came from the reservation and where they might be traveling. Realizing I had been holding my breath, I slowly exhaled and uttered a quiet prayer of gratitude. I was thankful to be in my home with my daughters, and that we need not beg for food.

I watched as the Cheyenne man rejoined the others, and they devoured the bread. Turning away, I sighed, ashamed for not giving them both loaves. When I again turned toward the window, my eyes followed them as they trudged on, disappearing over the top of the ridge on their way to somewhere or nowhere, I wasn't sure which.

I found the girls under the bed, their eyes big as saucers. "You can come out. He's gone."

Frances and Babe remained silent as their sister, shaking with fright, whimpered, "Mother, I was so afraid they'd take us away!"

"Oh, Gussie. It's all right. He just wanted food for his family. They were hungry."

"Did you give them food, Mama?" Frances demanded. "Daddy said never give them food, or they'll keep coming back!"

"Well Frances, that may be true, but we have enough and they have little. Part of being a kind person is to share. You've been taught as much. I was a little scared myself, yet it seemed like the right thing to do."

"Do you think they'll come back and steal us?" Six-year-old Babe stared at me wide-eyed.

"No, little one, I don't think they'll steal you. You'd be but one more mouth to feed!" I smiled, hoping to allay her fears. But despite my bravado, I was not certain my words rang true. In the two years since Frank and I had divorced, there had been other times when seeds of doubt caused me to question the wisdom of living on my own. I wondered if having a man in the house might prove advantageous, after all. Perhaps the pistol Frank had given me should be kept somewhere other than under my mattress.

❧

"Oh, this is gonna be so much fun!" shrieked Babe as the buggy rumbled down the road towards Milestown.

"Babe, it's too early to be so loud. Hush up!" Frances admonished her sister from the back seat, where the girls were pressed together.

I agreed with Frances. The edges of the sun were barely visible, lightly coloring the sky in shades of rose and tangerine, accompanied by a medley of birdsong. We had set out early, aiming to arrive in plenty of time to attend the renowned Milestown Independence Day parade. The hired man offered to do the milking and feeding for the day, making it possible for us all to go, Frank included. Afterwards, the girls and I planned a noon picnic with Lucy and J.R., followed by the afternoon rodeo. Against all odds at their advanced ages, they had welcomed little Perry James in April. I smiled to myself, eager to see them and cradle this new baby in my arms.

People jammed the wooden walkways, making it a challenge to keep track of the girls. We passed several small clusters of people speaking in different tongues, the result of an influx of folks brought in by the railroad in '08. The town had also acquired its share of vagrants, or "weary willies," as they were called. I kept a close eye on my daughters as we strolled down Main Street, searching for a suitable spot from which to watch the parade.

We stood in front of the Foster Building and before long, the mayor and chief of police rode by in a trolley. This signaled the official start of the festivities. Float after horse-drawn float followed, all built by local merchants to advertise their wares, promote some cause, or celebrate our country's birthday. Everyone stared, our eyes as big as saucers, as several automobiles drove by. Such novelties! I questioned whether they would ever catch on, as we all knew horses were much more reliable.

The girls giggled and laughed with excitement as clowns riding bicycles tossed hard candies into the crowd. Predictably, Babe popped up with twice as many pieces as her sisters. Full of spunk, that little gal.

The Salvation Army band high-stepped to a rousing Sousa melody, ahead of three Indian groups replete with dancers in full regalia. Lastly came the cowgirls and cowboys, horses prancing, their leather tack embellished with brass and silver and polished to a brilliant sheen. I identified horses of many breeds and colors, mostly quarter horses but also Appaloosas, Paints and Palominos. Sensing the pomp, they pranced and tossed their manes, to the delight of all the city folk lining the streets. Watching these splendid creatures made my heart ache, since it brought back wistful but proud memories of our cart-racing Standardbreds in Michigan.

Around noon, with the sun at its zenith, we walked over to Riverside Park, seeking shelter from the scorching heat. The lofty cottonwood trees provided welcome shade, and just being near the water provided the respite we sought. Across the river, the bank was lined with teepees of the various tribes. I held my daughters' hands tighter. Distant sounds of patriotic speeches drifted from the gazebo at the other end of the park.

A commotion surrounded us as the competitive Indian dancing got underway. The government had outlawed pow-wow dancing in the mid-1800s, yet the reservation agent always gave special permission for this type of dancing on Independence Day, considering it social, not subversive. The performances were a thrilling spectacle, filled with brightly beaded costumes, sacred feathers, rhythmic singing and drumming, and whirling dancers. Each of the three rival tribes, Northern Cheyenne, Crow and Assiniboine, competed fiercely to be judged "best." The girls begged to watch the performances rather than listen to speeches, and I heartily agreed. Frank tagged along with us, standing off to the side like a bodyguard. We wiggled our way into a spot quite close to the front edge of the circle. After our incident with the bread, I sensed the girls might be a bit wary as they crowded close to me.

Mesmerized by the drumbeat, I tried to follow the dancers' complicated footwork as they whooped and sang out in their native tongue, keeping perfect rhythm in a high-energy gourd dance. I marveled at the intricate beadwork on their buckskin leggings, shirts and headdresses. Around the edge, townspeople threw coins into the circle--the white man's way of showing appreciation. Indian children scooped them up almost before they touched the ground.

"Mama, where's Babe?" Frances pulled on my arm.

"What?" I peered down at Frances, startled out of my reverie.

"I can't see Babe!" Frances yelled over the top of the din. Gertrude was also looking this way and that.

Alarmed, I scanned the throng of people, but found no trace of Babe anywhere within my line of sight. Out of nowhere, Frank appeared by my side. "Frank!" My voice shook. "We've lost Babe!" Earlier, I had been annoyed by his presence, but now I was relieved, although he had no more of an inkling than I did where she was. What kind of parents were we, to lose our daughter in this huge crowd of people?

A frantic search ensued in the vicinity of the dancing, then fanned out to the surrounding areas. Please, God, keep her safe! Let us find her. Terrified, I located a policeman on the fringes of the park, and he joined the hunt.

"Babe! Babe!" We continued to call her name. Nothing. I was sick to my stomach and growing more distraught by the second. After ten more minutes of searching with no success, I considered rushing into the circle to scream for help. What if these Indians actually did steal little white girls?

In a panic, I moved along the edge of the park, hardly able to see straight. I clapped my hands over my ears to block out the ear-splitting racket in the background. In that instant, I caught a glimpse of Babe across the way, darting along the riverbank. I hollered her name, but my words were lost in the cacophony of sounds. In an instant, Frank appeared and chased after her. I gazed heavenward and issued a silent prayer of thanks, breathing a tremendous sigh of relief. With wobbly legs, I ran around the outer edge of the crowd toward them.

"But, Daddy, they were throwing money!" Babe wailed, as her dad swatted her on the backside. She opened her grubby fingers to expose a handful of coins scooped up from the ring.

"Oh, Babe! You'll be the death of me yet!" I shook my head in dismay.

She wailed even louder when we insisted she throw the coins back.

∼

Gussie burst into the kitchen, her words jumbled as she gasped, "Mother, come quick! Something's wrong with Frances!"

I dropped the mending on the table and hurried after my daughter.

We ran up the road where Babe stood crying over Frances, lying on the ground.

"Mama, Mama!" she called. "Frances fell down again and won't get up!"

I kneeled down beside her. "Honey, tell me what happened. Did you trip again?" She nodded her head, her cheeks covered with tears, mingled with streaks of dirt. "Oh sweetie, are you hurt?" Over the years, although a sturdy child, she had become somewhat bowlegged and occasionally went through periods of near lameness, clumsily tripping over random objects in her path. I told myself many children passed through a gawky phase, but in the recesses of my mind, recalled her earlier illness and Dr. MacKenzie's original diagnosis and that terrifying word "paralysis." I brushed that long-ago conversation aside, as always, and peered at my dear child. "Do you think you can stand?"

"Yes?"

It sounded more like a question than an answer, so Gussie and I each took an arm and helped to gather her up. With her legs bowing out, the three of us hobbled to the house, Babe running ahead.

Later, after the girls went to bed, I picked up *Science and Health,* the Christian Science book Sam's mother had given me so many years ago. That small book, along with my King James Bible, accompanied me when I moved to Montana long ago, but lay mostly forgotten until this past year. Although I had fallen away from Christian Science for these many years, after rediscovering the book at the bottom of my trunk and reconciling with God, I recognized how the words of Mrs. Eddy renewed my spirit and decided to once again commit myself to following its principles. Most of them, at least. After losing little Gordon, I could never again forgo medical intervention, as Christian Science dictated, especially when my children were involved. My true motivation involved searching for answers to help explain Frances' recurring ailments. I continued to closely examine the text and ponder explanations. What defect in her physical body caused these afflictions to befall her?

I read the chapter on marriage, and worried that Frank and I had failed Frances by not being divinely-minded enough, resulting in the physical manifestation of disease. I prayed fervently that God correct my thinking. I wondered whether my failure to follow each and every tenet of Christian Science might be a cause of my daughter's problems. Yet, after losing Gordon, I could not and would not ever again deny the power of modern medicine. I was still as confused as ever and suspected that as much as I wanted to believe in it, the little book did not provide all the answers I sought.

Biting my lip, I then distracted myself from such troubling thoughts with a treasured letter tucked into the pages of the little book. The creases were worn from repeated folding and unfolding, and I drew it gently out to read another time.

April, 1911
Sugarbush Road
Dear Mama Maggie,

Thank you for the exquisite locket you sent me for my 16th birthday. It is a fabulous keepsake I shall treasure forever. I celebrated my day with a small gathering of friends and I wish you could have been here. Fannie even baked me a special applesauce cake. Oscar sends his love and says to tell you he hopes to come to Montana someday to visit. Me too! Or, maybe you could come here instead?

Your loving daughter,
Helen Perry

Through these written words, I understood Helen and Oscar had forgiven me, even though I had yet to forgive myself. *Where had the years gone?* Helen's locket was the one Sam had given me on our wedding day, the last piece of jewelry from him remaining in my possession. With that gift, I had hoped to preserve some kind of emotional connection to my oldest daughter's life. Wistfully, I realized that her stepmother, Fannie, knew this daughter of mine far better than I. Having no way to reverse the effects of ten long years of separation, I again experienced a sharp pang, like an arrow piercing my damaged heart.

31.

Eastern Montana, 1912-1916. Over the next several years, the girls and I fell into a rhythm, each responsible for her respective chores, and our household was generally harmonious. They attended the one-room school up the lane, leaving my days empty, except for the Stage coming in three times a week. I had never before lived in such quietude, and for the first time in my life experienced an almost tangible loneliness, isolated in my own mind. Questions about what would happen to Frances and me down the road began to haunt me.

Frank continued to stop by every day to inquire if we needed anything. Our relationship remained affable, and while he managed the ranch, I thrived with my job cooking for the stage line. Because it was convenient, we rode into town together for supplies. This gave me an opportunity to sell our fresh eggs, cream and churned butter to a growing list of well-to-do town folk.

"Maggie!"

In the bedroom changing the linens, I hadn't heard Frank come in. Sometimes I wished he would knock, but after so many years, it seemed certain this habit of entering his former home unannounced would not change.

"Be right there," I called back, leaving the bed for later.

"Remember those folks who homesteaded next to the Porter place, part-way to Miles?"

I walked into the kitchen where he leaned against the table.

"Yes, of course." With a rundown farmhouse and a barn verging on collapse, I had heard that Mr. Adamik struggled mightily to make a go of it in this unpredictable land.

"They're packing it in and going back east. I chanced upon Will Porter a while back and he mentioned they're selling out. I stopped by their place last week and bought their piano . . . for a song!" He chuckled at his own joke.

"Really?" My mouth dropped open and my eyes grew wide at this unanticipated offering. "Frank, how wonderful! The girls will be so thrilled. What a marvelous gift."

"Babe's always singing a tune, so I reckoned maybe she'd like to learn to play the piano, too. Maybe it'll liven up the place a little! So, Leonard's with me and if it's all right by you, we'll bring her on in." I followed him out onto the porch to take a peek at his purchase.

"How do, ma'am." Leonard, the hired hand, tipped his cowboy hat as he hopped down from the wagon seat. Small and wiry, I hoped Leonard was stronger than he looked.

❧

"A piano! Is it ours, Mama? Where did it come from?" The questions flew right and left that afternoon after school. Ecstatic with their dad's gift, Gussie and Babe sprinted down the lane to his place, while Frances hobbled along behind them. I imagine their gushing thank-yous brought a bucketful of happiness into that tiny log house.

Some weeks later, I stood in the kitchen watching them together at the piano, giggling and picking out melodies they had learned at school. I drank in the scene, offering silent, heartfelt thanks to Frank for this wonderful gift. It soon became clear one of them had a definite talent for playing by ear: Babe.

Summer arrived and with it, Saturday night dances. People drove for miles to attend, with our little one-room schoolhouse a frequent venue. For barn dances farther away, Frank insisted on driving the four of us in his Dodge touring automobile, not wanting us to be out late, alone on the dark road in our buggy. We all appreciated the comfort and speediness of riding in an auto.

"Oh, Mama! Can I please sit close by the piano player?" Babe adored these gatherings, not because she wanted to dance, but because she was mesmerized by the music. After spending the entire evening perched on a stool near the band, listening intently, she liked to come home, seat herself at our piano and try to improvise the tunes. I applauded her tenacity.

"Frances, how are you? You look pretty tonight."

"Fine, thank you, Mr. McNeil."

A genuinely nice man, grey-haired Bill McNeil, the square dance caller, always made an effort to converse with my daughter before the dancing began. Not quite thirteen, Frances had become self-conscious. She was afraid to dance because of the weakness in her legs, fearing a fall, and so she preferred to sit near me on the periphery. Older than her years, she loved to watch the goings-on and visit with the elders seated along the sidelines.

Gertrude never lacked for dance partners. I delighted in watching my shy sixteen-year-old daughter's face light up when some handsome young man invited her to take a spin around the dance floor, whether it be a lively reel, a slow Schottische, or a spirited square dance, Over the summer of 1915, one suitor in particular, by the name of Alvin Blum, turned up more often than not.

"Mother, how can you tell if it's true love?" Gertrude and I were in the garden weeding, early one August morning.

True love. Did it even exist, beyond our imaginations? Having failed twice at love, I wasn't sure what to tell her. "Well, Gussie, that's a fine question." Our spades made tiny pinging sounds as they struck errant stones in the moist soil. I stopped for a moment and listened to the song of late summer, a buzzing chorus of cicadas overhead in the towering cottonwood trees. I took a deep breath. What indeed was true love? "Hmm . . . perhaps true love is a bit like coming home to a comfortable place, like this." I spread my arms wide. "Somewhere you can both be yourselves and . . ." I paused, "a place where you're content simply to be together."

Warming to the topic, I had an inspiration. "It means you can trust him not to betray you or your confidences. He's safe and I hope he'd be someone who makes you laugh." I smiled, staring at Gussie before finishing. "Overall, I think it's when you somehow realize deep inside yourself that you want to spend the rest of your time on this good earth waking up next to him, each and every morning."

She smiled back at me and nodded her head. The conversation reached a standstill as we continued pulling weeds in companionable silence. Naive when I married Sam, and misguided when I married Frank, nevertheless, I still believed in the possibility of true love. Just because it hadn't happened yet for me didn't mean it wasn't possible for Gussie.

I sat back on my heels, brushing a few strands of loose hair off my face and remembering the letter from Oscar. It had arrived months ago, back in January, the contents unexpected.

Dear Mother, Helen and I agreed we should notify you Papa passed on November 27, taken quickly, by pneumonia.

At that moment, as it had when my own Papa died, the inevitability of death stared me in the face. I had bravely stared back then, and I did so now, although truthfully, Oscar's words jolted me. I was amazed at my utter indifference toward the man I had once foolishly pledged to love passionately for a lifetime. Through years of ill treatment, our love shriveled and died, much as the pulled weeds beside me withered in the sun. Please, God, I prayed, let my children's journeys be different.

May, 1916. "Stand still!" My patience had worn thin trying to pin up the hem on Babe's dress. "That's fine. Turn just a little. We're almost finished."

"I'm glad, because I'm tired of standing here."

This project challenged both our tempers. At almost ten, Babe stood taller than Frances, a bundle of energy and always in motion.

With but a week until Gertrude's wedding, I was close to finishing Babe and Frances' dresses. I worried about Frances's ability to walk down the aisle without assistance. On good days she walked with but a trace of a limp. On other days she complained of pain in her legs and used a cane.

The doctor could offer no definitive explanation for her symptoms, other than suggesting it might be something called post-polio syndrome. He based this on the recurring weakness she ofttimes displayed. I had my own suspicions, but kept them to myself. It incensed me to remember the abuse she suffered at Frank's hands as a small child, and my powerlessness to stop it. I couldn't help but blame him and his temper for her lameness. In any case, it weighed on me that Dr. MacKenzie had yet to present any therapy or cure for her, leaving us no choice but to live day-by-day, relying on prayer and hope as our only remedies.

I had recently introduced my girls to the Christian Science textbook and Frances in particular appeared to derive comfort from the little book's teachings. We set our sights on reaching a higher level of spiritual consciousness, which we wholeheartedly believed would heal her.

"Mama! Why are you staring at the ceiling? Please hurry and finish!"

My musings abruptly ended, and I returned my attention to pinning up the hem of Babe's gown.

May 27, 1916. The day dawned clear, the air still. Today I would watch as my daughter and her betrothed officially became joined together in holy matrimony. Coffee cup in hand, I turned and beheld my comely Gertrude as she walked into the kitchen, marveling at how she had grown half a head taller than myself. There she stood in her robe, which hung open to expose her silk chemise. She was a fairytale princess, with sparkling blue eyes and light brown hair framing a radiant face. My heart overflowed with joy for her on this special day. Offering the good Lord a swift prayer of thanks for second chances, I was grateful for how far we had been allowed to travel together on life's journey, after such a tentative start. The thought brought a smile of satisfaction to my face.

"Mother, would you help me curl my hair?"

She placed the flat iron on top of the wood stove to heat. Pleased to be asked, I nodded as she pulled out a chair from the table and sat down in front of me.

"Well, Mother, do you have any advice for me?" She turned and looked up at me, a shy smile creating adorable dimples in her cheeks.

I said the first thing that popped into my mind. "Maintain a sense of yourself, so you're not solely reliant upon Alvin."

She turned her head and looked at me, brows raised. "Really? What do you mean?"

"Well, let me think a moment." I carefully brushed her shiny hair while we waited for the curling iron to heat.

"I guess I'm thinking I was so dependent on your papa and it didn't serve me well. With Frank, I was enterprising and had my own income and this offered me a confident sense of self. It also gave me the courage to go it alone . . . not that you'll ever need to," I added hastily.

Gertrude rolled her eyes at me. I guess that wasn't the type of advice she'd expected.

I cherished this wedding as one of the loveliest I'd ever witnessed. Gertrude was dressed in a lacy white gown, with upswept hair and shining eyes that gazed at her beloved, fair-haired Alvin. Sharp and handsome in his pinstriped suit, he was a tall and slender man. I breathed a sigh of relief as Frances, the maid of honor, walked down the aisle slowly, with the aid of her cane, to stand beside her adored older sister. I wondered if she might be asking herself whether she'd ever become a bride.

It took little time to appreciate how much Gertrude had contributed to running the ranch, and how limited Frances's capabilities were. Much of the burden now fell on Babe, who didn't take kindly to this change.

"Why do I have to do everything?" she quizzed me one morning as we stood on the front porch, where I was teaching her how to help me separate the fresh milk Frank had just dropped off.

I ignored her question. "This job takes two people. You know that." Cranking the twelve-inch long cast iron handle on the separator took a certain strength. It had proven too difficult for me to get it started on my own, and it was exhausting even for two to keep it spinning round and round until all the cream had separated out.

"You may recall, Babe, this is one of the ways we earn our living." Sounding a bit more acerbic than I intended, I softened my next words. "And you're aware it helps us afford things like fabric, that we might use to make you a new dress." That quieted her.

In truth, I found it harder to manage all the ranch chores without Gertrude, but that was no excuse for what happened next. Fear? Desperation? Loneliness? Perhaps it was all three, but God alone understands why I took up with a man fourteen years my junior, blind to his true nature until it was too late.

32.

1918-1919. A wet spring created great mud bogs in the road, leading to deep furrows when it dried out. This led to difficult conditions for travelers. The Stage either got stuck in the mire when it was wet, or caught in the ruts when it was dry. On one such occasion, a wheel wrenched free of the axle, causing a minor accident near our ranch. The driver showed up on foot at my door.

"Good day, ma'am. Is this the Stage Line Home Station at 12 Mile Dam?"

I nodded.

"Name's Hankins. I'm the new driver."

He hesitated, so I spoke up. "Yes, what can I do for you, uh, Mr. Hankins, is it? Shading my eyes from the sun, I looked to the road. "Where *is* the stagecoach?"

"Yessum. Well, missus, I've had a bit of a mishap down the way." He glanced back over his shoulder.

"Get on with it, man. Is someone injured? How can I help?"

"Uh, no ma'am, I'm alone today, but the wheel separated from the axle and well, ma'am, is the man of the house around?

"No, there is no man of the house. How can I help you?"

"To be blunt, ma'am, I need some brute strength to put the stage right, to fix the wheel."

"Well, in that case, you'll have to wait until Mr. Herman gets back from riding herd."

"Mr. Herman? He the man of the house?"

"No. Mr. Herman lives next door. I told you there is no man of the house."

He continued to stand there staring at me, and then past me into the house. Remembering this was, after all, a home station, I offered, "Would you care to come inside? I'm getting supper on the table."

"Why, that'd be mighty fine, ma'am. I thank ye kindly."

"Stop calling me 'ma'am.' My name's Maggie Herman."

He looked at me quizzically. "Maggie Herman? That your brother or maybe your father next door?"

"Not that it's any of your business, but Frank is my former husband."

Taken aback, he repeated, "Former husband?"

I sighed, and ushered Mr. Hankins inside.

⁓

His chair tipped back and one boot resting on the edge of the table, Mr. Hankins rolled a toothpick around his mouth. "Yessir, Maggie, you're a mighty fine cook! If it wasn't for your homemade grub, I'd be a scrawny so and so."

I had three other customers from the Stage this day and didn't appreciate his informality. "Mr. Hankins, please take your boot off the table. That's where we eat," I chided him. "And, it's Mrs. Herman to you, sir!"

"Excuse me ma'am." He nodded his head deferentially, grinned and sat up, putting both boots on the floor.

In our usual banter, he complimented me and I then admonished him for some trivial real or imagined transgression.

There was no denying his dark good looks and easy-going charm. He kept me slightly off-balance; I was never sure what to expect in our game of cat and mouse. In all honesty, I had to admit I looked forward to his stopovers. Our repartee broke the tedium of an otherwise drab existence.

⁓

"Maggie, won't you step out with me this weekend? There's a barn dance over at the Tolbert's and we'd make a mighty fine promenade for the square dan . . ."

"Mr. Hankins, you are surely daft! Of course I won't attend a barn dance with you!"

"Maggie, you are the rose of my existence. The why and wherefore that keeps me driving stage is knowing I'll be able to gaze into your enchanting sea-green eyes on the next stopover."

"Mr. Hankins, don't you need to be on your way?" He had no passengers this day and it seemed to me he had overstayed his welcome.

"Fair lady, perhaps you state the truth, and I must take my leave. Be forewarned, I shall return to court you again."

I rolled my eyes and shooed him off. Did I detect a small flutter in my stomach? Nonsense, total nonsense, I quashed the feeling before it could take hold. There was simply no compelling reason to become starry-eyed over this young man, despite his persistence. In fact, I regarded the mere thought as totally preposterous.

It's difficult for me to recall precisely the moment I changed my mind. It crept up on me, in a subtle way. One morning in midsummer, I awakened with the realization that Maggie Herman, a forty-eight-year-old twice-divorced matron, had indeed fallen for this man and his courtly ways. After this insight, little by little, I tossed caution to the wind, allowing myself to warm up to his charm and soak up his flattery, like a parched flower in the rain.

On a sunny, cloudless day in August, midday fast approached and with it, the anticipated arrival of the Stage. The spicy, rich aroma of gingerbread cooling on the windowsill enveloped me as I put the finishing touches on the noon meal. I had topped off my refreshing tomato and cucumber salad with a sprinkling of fresh dill. The shepherd's pie in the oven needed a few more minutes to brown.

Frances was busy embroidering tea towels, while Babe worked in the garden harvesting the last of the green beans.

Did I hear the stage coming? Babe's voice through the open kitchen window soon told me otherwise. "Ma, looks like Gussie coming up the lane!" Frances and I gave each other a knowing glance. I hurried out onto the porch, as Babe came around the side of the house.

"My time grows near, Mother," Gertrude declared as she climbed heavily out of the buggy. "And that bumpy ride didn't help." She scowled at Alvin, who returned the look as he lifted Boyd down. None of us could operate the automobile except Frank. He was off riding herd, leaving Alvin no choice but to drive his buggy into town to fetch the doctor. I hoped they would return straightaway in the doctor's auto.

Smiling, I gathered Boyd into my arms, listening to his baby giggles when I gave him a squeeze and a kiss. He smelled so clean and fresh. It had been a mere sixteen months since Gertrude and Alvin made the same five-mile journey from their farm to my ranch house for Boyd's birth.

"Come in, come in!" I waved Gertrude up the steps to the porch and we all went inside.

"Is it time, then?" Fifteen-year-old Frances called out to her sister from across the room.

Gertrude shivered visibly and nodded before sitting down with a thump on the kitchen chair. "Oh!" She sat up, clutching her big belly and clenching her teeth. "Mother . . ." That was all she got out before gasping, overtaken by the gripping cramps of impending motherhood. Boyd took one look at his mama and began to whimper. I cuddled him close.

"How far apart are your pains, honey?" While inwardly anxious, I knew it was important to stay outwardly calm, for her sake. I prayed the doctor indeed arrived in good time. The role of assistant felt more comfortable, and safer, than that of lone midwife.

Before Gertrude could answer my question, in swaggered Clarence Hankins and two stage passengers, expecting dinner.

"Howdy all!" He tipped his cowboy hat, then removed and tossed it on the table. "Well, what do we have here?" he asked, grinning as he snatched Boyd from my arms and tossed him into the air. Boyd burst into gales of laughter. The rest of us sucked in our breaths at this man's audacity, and all attention turned to them.

"Whee!" Boyd chortled, squealing as he flew in the air. Thank goodness Clarence also caught him on the downward tumble.

"That is my grandson, sir! Kindly put him down!"

"Mo-er?" Boyd babbled exuberantly.

Gertrude continued to observe Clarence, her discomfort momentarily forgotten. It occurred to me she had no notion of who he was or what he might mean to me.

"Gertrude, I'd like you to meet Clarence Hankins, the stage coach driver. Clarence, my daughter, Gertrude, and you've already met Boyd." She nodded at him as he cradled Boyd in one arm, before walking over to place his other arm around my waist. To say my daughter was mystified would be an understatement.

I quickly pushed his arm away and tried to act like nothing had happened. "Won't you have a seat?" I inquired, turning toward the other two passengers who were standing in the entryway gawking, and appearing equally baffled by the events taking place in my kitchen. "Dinner will be ready in a moment." I smiled and bustled over to the oven, removing the shepherd's pie and placing it on the counter. I ignored Gertrude, feeling her eyes boring holes into my back, as I went over to the table and set out the salad. At that moment, she groaned.

"Excuse me, if you will, for a few moments," I said to the guests. "Babe, will you give me a hand?"

We helped Gertrude stand up. Boyd toddled along behind as we walked together haltingly to the girls' bedroom. Gertrude wearily leaned against us, and remained silent as I steered her into a bed.

"Does it hurt bad, Gussie?"

"It hurts off and on, Babe. At this moment, it isn't too bad."

"Well, I'm never having a baby. It looks like it hurts way too much."

"Babe, hush! Gussie, we're close by if you need anything. The passengers won't be here long." I reassured her as I picked up Boyd and the three of us returned to the kitchen. I realized I would have more than a little explaining to do.

Our guests watched in fascination to see what might happen next. "Well folks, as you can plainly see, my daughter will soon birth a baby, so you'll have to forgive me if I'm a bit inattentive today." They smiled and nodded sympathetically, after which I placed the shepherd's pie and gingerbread on the dining table, jumping out of the way as Clarence attempted to pinch my backside. Leaving Frances in charge, I excused myself and went back to face the music down the hall.

"Mother! What in tarnation is going on? Who is that man and why is he . . . ugh . . . ooh . . ." Gertrude's words were lost in a low moan.

"We'll talk later. Right now, we need to prepare for the birth of your baby." I sidestepped her questions for the time being.

Seven hours later, on the evening of August 4, I held my granddaughter for the first time and fell in love with her little rosebud lips and the shock of light blonde hair sticking straight up on top of her head. She stared at me so solemnly, it took me back in time to when I held her mother in my arms. Much like Gussie, it was as if this new little life could peer directly into my mind. I decided she would be a pensive one, this wee girl, May Elizabeth.

❧

"Mother! He's young enough to be your son! What are you thinking?" May suckled greedily at Gertrude's breast.

I opened the curtains and the summer sunshine flooded into the bedroom. "Yes, well, I'm sure it does appear a bit odd, but somehow it works for us. We delight in each other's company and he makes me feel young again!" I smiled serenely as I stared out the window. A cloudless morning, I watched as a lone hawk dipped close to the ground in pursuit of his breakfast.

"Mother! Come to your senses!"

"Oh, Gussie, give him a chance! He brings a light and a joy into my life that has been sorely lacking. At last there is something to look forward to each day besides more hard work!"

"Nothing good can come of this, mark my words."

∽

Milestown, Montana, August 21, 1918. I couldn't help it. When the clerk & recorder asked my age, I told him I was forty. How could I possibly give my real age when Clarence had truthfully answered that he was thirty-four? Completing the marriage license took no time and the civil ceremony barely more. We stepped out of the courthouse as Mr. and Mrs. Clarence Felmore Hankins, and I genuinely hoped that this third time really would be the charm.

I soon learned Clarence had previously been married in Wisconsin back in '06, and divorced not long after. To hear him tell it, she was a witch in women's clothing. "Yessir, Eola was a rattlesnake. Sorry I ever took up with her. She'd get her hackles up and I'd hear them rattles and run for the hills. I was lucky to get out of that entanglement alive!"

I winced as he told this tale and didn't question him any further, not sure I wanted additional details. Besides, I looked at this as a fresh start, so there was no sense in bringing up the past. Clarence, of course, knew about Frank, but for now, I had seen no reason to mention the whole sordid history of my marriage to Sam. Maybe later, when we got to know each other a little better. It struck me how little we actually did know about one another.

"Honey, let's pick up a pint over at the Bison Bar to celebrate tying the knot," Clarence suggested as we strolled arm in arm down Milestown's Main Street, following a celebratory luncheon with J.R. and Lucy. With Frances and Babe back at the ranch with their father,

Clarence and I planned to spend the night in town. As we walked, I caught a glimpse of my trim figure reflected in the glass of a storefront window, happily noting that my new white linen shirtwaist, which I had paired with a flattering navy A-line skirt, perfectly accentuated my frame. I'm quite sure I glowed, so pleased to be on the arm of such a handsome young man. Clarence's suggestion didn't faze me, and I smiled, nodding in agreement. What harm could a bit of spirits cause, anyway?

"Clarence! Stop it! Stop it!" I demanded, giggling. In our room at the Olive Hotel, he chased me around the bed, whooping like a lunatic. I had no idea alcohol would affect him this way. I didn't typically imbibe, but in keeping with the gaiety of the afternoon, had downed a couple of shots and felt lightheaded myself. Only later did I notice the bottle was completely empty. He leapt at me and the two of us tumbled merrily upon the bedcovers. We came together with abandon, clothes peeled off in a flurry, tossed hither and yon.

"Ah, Maggie May, how long I've waited to bed you!" He ogled me and continued his exuberant horseplay, jumping on top of me as I lay prone, pinning my arms to the white chenille coverlet.

"Clarence! Stop it! You're hurting me!" No longer amused, grim scenes from the past flooded my mind and body.

"Aw, come on, honey, let's have us some fun!" He then proceeded to ride me like a pony, but soon collapsed next to me with a thud, passed out. I pushed his arm away and rolled off the bed, my stomach clenched. I looked down and spotted the beginnings of two bruises, one on each wrist. Swallowing hard, I smiled a bitter smile as a familiar heaviness settled upon me.

~

Twelve Mile Dam, Autumn, 1918 – Spring, 1919. 1918 was the first of three years of what later came to be called "the grasshopper plague of eastern Montana." Those pests came by the millions and destroyed wide swaths of crops all over our part of the country. After a wet spring, the summer had turned bone dry, leaving tempers short and tensions high, especially for the dryland farmers. With many of our young men off fighting in the war across the ocean in Europe, we worried about what our world was coming to.

The annual sale of some of Frank's stock in the fall meant money in the bank to buy feed for the remaining animals, come winter. We would weather the plague, but dryland farmers faced a different fate. We watched helplessly as our neighbors' farms withered in the summer heat. We watched cheerlessly as many families relinquished their homesteads in despair that fall. We watched sorrowfully as they packed up their meager belongings and left, finally broken by this unforgiving land. We passed those deserted farms along the road every time we drove into Milestown. How long before these neglected buildings fell into ruins, their stories lost on the eastern plains, the badlands of Montana?

By late fall, Clarence had quit his job with the stage and moved in full-time. Thus began a period of unsettledness for us all. As I once again attempted to adjust to married life, Clarence endeavored to insinuate himself into the daily operations of the ranch. Frank shook his head in disbelief at the entire state of affairs. The girls, specifically Babe, didn't take to my new husband at all and didn't hesitate to tell me about it.

"Mama, that man looks at me funny," Babe repeated again and again, whenever she had the chance. A budding beauty at twelve, boyishly slim with fine-boned features and fair hair, I sensed her childhood drawing to a close.

"Babe, you're seeing things," commented Frances, shaking her head. "He's an old man and you're nothing but his stepdaughter."

Babe stood firm. "No, he looks at me funny."

I did my best to reassure my youngest daughter. But before long, she chose to spend most of her time when not at school with her daddy, and I missed her. I had little time to dwell upon it, with cooking for the stage line, helping to run a ranch, and dealing with Clarence, who turned out to be a handful. Not one to throw in the towel, I found it hard to envision how Frank, Clarence and I would ever reach any sort of harmonious arrangement. "Maggie, I think we should take a trip into town and put your part of the ranch in both our names, just to be on the safe side." Of late, he had taken to meddling in ranch financial affairs.

"Safe side of what?" Puzzled, my eyes narrowed.

"Well, what if Frank challenges us? What if he decides he wants the whole ranch back? We'd hate to end up with a nasty court battle, now wouldn't we, eh? My name on the documents gives us more clout. You know good and well, a man's signature fetches a higher standing in the judge's eyes, too."

"Oh, really?" With an icy glare, I shut down any further discussion on the subject. I did not feel the need to mention that Frank owned the entire ranch outright.

⌐~~~⌐

"Yep, people are droppin' like flies!" The new stagecoach driver sat at our dining table sharing news. "They're sayin' thousands of Injuns down Tongue River way are sick an' dyin' from the influenza and there's nothin' to do for it, 'cept wait and hope it passes."

"I think it's best for us to lay low and avoid going into town 'til this clears up. What do you say, Missus?" Clarence glanced my way.

I nodded in agreement.

I worried over Gertrude, with little Boyd and the new baby, so I had Clarence drop by their place to ask them to come stay with us. They assured us they felt safe staying on their farm, so I left it alone and doubled up on my prayers.

Over the next several months, Clarence made but a few trips into Miles for necessities, and thankfully, we stayed free of the influenza's grip. We heard many thousands of people had died by the spring of 1919, and thanked our lucky stars for the good fortune of not being counted among them.

I began to have my doubts about who the real rattlesnake was in Clarence's first marriage. Peering into the mirror atop Lucy's dressing table, I meekly listened to her lecture as I dabbed Max Factor pancake makeup on the frightful bruise underneath my right eye. In all likelihood it wouldn't do anything for the puffiness, but it might disguise the injury.

"Maggie, you must free yourself of this man! He's nothing more than a fortune hunter, and you're his next prey! Yes, he's charming, handsome and reeks of charisma, but he's not the man for you. I recognized it the day you got married, five minutes after we met him at luncheon. Why, look at you! You have a black eye, and I don't think it came from bumping into a door!" She scurried over and picked up the jar. "Here, let me help you with that foundation."

It was a truth I didn't want to hear. Sighing, I countered, "But, Lucy, he can be so captivating, so irresistible. He flatters me and we share lots of laughs."

"Is that before or after one of his drinking binges?" She stared heavenward. Suddenly, another thought occurred to her. "Lord, I hope you didn't add his name to the trust. You didn't, did you?"

"No, of course not." I hunched my shoulders and slumped into the chair, head in my hands. "How could I have failed at marriage again? What's wrong with me?"

"Maggie, for heaven's sake, it's not you! It's that you keep repeating the same mistake. Don't you see? Sam and Clarence were both cads! All three of them beat you and Frank even abused the girls. It seems to me you'd be better off on your own. Frances and Babe need you alive!" she finished, her old pluck resurfacing.

At the moment I didn't care what happened to me. After a long, despairing exhale, I leaned forward, looked my sister in the eye, and spoke slowly and deliberately. "I suppose you're right, Lucy. He's no good for me and this marriage was a sham from the beginning." Arms crossed, with lips set in a firm line, she watched me as I went on. "It's clear to me all his sweet talking was just an attempt to reach into my pocketbook and get his hands on the ranch. But, oh, how unforgettable to be wooed by such a handsome younger man . . ." My voice trailed off, resigned to the wisdom of Lucy's words.

In the end, I didn't even bother to file for divorce. I promptly moved his belongings into the barn, where he slept for a couple of weeks. Every day he implored me to change my mind, hoping to reconcile and make his way back into my bed. It was Clarence's misfortune that my reserve of forgiveness for despicable husbands had finally run dry.

"Maggie Hankins, don't you know, you're the love of my life! Your eyes at this moment are sparkling like stars, you gorgeous woman, you. Come on, let's put it all behind us, sweep it under the rug and start fresh. What do you say?" He turned on the charm with an ingratiating grin, but I honestly no longer found him appealing.

Finally, I had to stand my ground in the barnyard, pointing Frank's shotgun at him. "Get out! You're not welcome on this property! Jump on your old plug of a horse and vamoose!" I cocked the gun, unwavering in my resolve.

"Aw, Maggie, don't be that way. You know how much fun we have together. Besides, where would I go? You wouldn't turn me out, now, would you? Sweetheart?"

"I would and I am. Go on, get out of here!" I yelled, motioning with my weapon.

He took a few steps toward me. I pointed the shotgun at the dirt in front of him and fired. Buckshot scattered in an uneven line and he jumped like a nervous cat, trying to avoid the spray. I fell backwards and sat down hard on my bum, my shoulder throbbing in pain from the kick of the shotgun, with the beginnings of a bruise that would last near on a month. The shocked look on his face was priceless. I felt more powerful than ever before.

He stomped off into the barn, and I scarcely had time to stand before he trotted out into the barnyard on his old nag, shaking his fist at me and hollering, "You've not seen the last of me, woman!" He then let loose with a string of profanities the likes of which I had never heard, before turning into the lane and riding away.

"Good riddance!" I yelled after him, rather satisfied to have gotten in the final word.

33

Montana to Michigan, 1919. The household soon returned to a state of tranquility. I promised myself that never again would I consider my days dull, realizing what I had previously mistaken for dullness was actually stability. I felt free again, finally rid of that unscrupulous money-grubber. With this newfound sense of peace, I also happily swore off any future involvement with men. Winter passed uneventfully and in due time, spring presented her fickle face, with wind gusts and rain one day and sunshine and budding flowers the next.

The letter arrived in late March. The news delighted me, and it came in plenty of time to plan and prepare. The stage line passengers could get along without home-cooked meals for a couple of weeks and I had more than enough egg and cream money set aside to buy a ticket.

March 15, 1919
Dearest Mother,
It is with great pleasure I announce my forthcoming marriage to Mr. Elmer Beaufait on May 2. This important day would mean so much more were you to attend the ceremony in Mt. Clemens. Please write and tell me you'll come!
Affectionately,
Helen E. Perry Wellman

The piercing whistle and low, rumbling sounds of the eastbound train approached. I tucked the note I'd read so many times back into my purse and waited patiently to board the Great Northern train. I was Michigan bound, my first trip home in more than seventeen years. Helen's first husband, and the father of her daughter Gertrude, had been lost on the battlefield in France. My darling daughter planned to marry for a second time and happily, I would be there to join in the celebration. There would be new family members to meet, including grandchildren Edward and Gertrude. The anticipated bliss of holding Oscar and Helen in my arms once again outweighed any apprehension about seeing them after our long separation.

A recent sadness would also accompany me on this journey, the information reaching me only a few days past. My gentle, unassuming brother Louis had ended his life, leaving all the family stunned by his action. There would be another new headstone to visit in our family plot.

⌒〜〜〜⌒

You can never truly go back. Never. I returned to my original home, my people, and found nothing the same. Everyone had changed. It was no longer the home I had left. In many ways, I was a stranger to the children I had birthed, and all my sorrow at leaving them came rushing back, threatening to drown me.

"Mama, Mama," called Helen, waving from the train platform. It took no effort to recognize her, with her chestnut hair and the strong resemblance to Lucy. I had barely disembarked before my two grown children proceeded to smother me and I melted into their love. What does one say in this circumstance? "My, how you've grown" hardly seemed sufficient.

As I shed tears of happiness, I settled for, "My dream to hold you both has come true! Here, let me look at you." As I drew back to admire them, I glimpsed in a flash all the years I had missed, recognizing them as adults in their own right, grown up without me. Me, a strange and melancholy version of Rip Van Winkle. All three of us spoke at once when, out of the corner of my eye, I caught sight of a man and a woman standing near the depot building, each holding the hand of a toddler and watching attentively. Oscar followed my gaze and addressed them enthusiastically, waving them over. "Elmer, Emma, come meet our mama and, Edward and Gertrude, your Montana Grandma!"

And so began my stay in Mt. Clemens.

"Lizzie?" I burst through the side door of the house on South Avenue and found her in the kitchen taking fresh baked bread from the oven. "It smells heavenly in here!"

"Why, Maggie, is that you? Oh, my heavens! I'd forgotten you were arriving today." She hurried over to where I stood in the entryway and threw her arms around me. I fell easily into the loving embrace of my second mother. Though we had both grown old, time had not diminished my appreciation for her involvement in my life.

"I'll put on the pot for some tea. Go on into the front room and I'll join you in a moment."

The room had not changed at all. It looked tired and dated, and had a palpable emptiness about it. Somehow, irrationally, I had expected to find Papa in his chair reading the racing news. I also half-expected to find Janie in the upstairs bedroom we had shared for a time, but she, too, had moved on, a victim of consumption in her thirty-second year. I confronted the absurdity of my imaginings, lonely to my bones, but reluctantly accepting that they were gone. A mist clouded my vision as I was reminded, yet again, that life is about loss.

Fortunately, life is also about the living, and Helen's wedding brought everyone together. My brain worked overtime to reframe the family I had left, along with new members added through birth and marriage. Exhilarated yet exhausted, I toppled into bed each night all but asleep before my head touched the pillow, but not before wondering how the girls might be faring with Frank, back at the dam.

In all honesty, their faces rarely crossed my mind during the day, so these late night thoughts jarred me, leaving me feeling unsettled and questioning where I truly belonged.

It took little time watching Fannie and Helen together to confirm their closeness. A jolly, heavyset woman, I liked Fannie immediately, and could not fault her in any way for taking the daughter I had abandoned under her wing. I sensed an affinity between us, suspecting being married to Sam had probably not been a nap in a feather bed for her, either.

On the way to the train depot on my last morning, Oscar drove me to the Clinton Grove Cemetery, as my time in Mt. Clemens would otherwise have been incomplete. I kept my promise to once again touch the stones of my two little long-lost angels. My eyesight dimmed by tears, I moved nearby where gravestones had begun to crowd a familiar patch of earth, and kneeled to pay my respects at the Perry plot. So many beloved family members now resided beneath those markers. I sighed with the realization that my life had taken me elsewhere and when it was over, there would be no reunion for me here.

I counted my visit a grand success. The train had traveled a mere ten minutes westward before dreams of a return visit filled my mind.

34.

Twelve Mile Dam, Montana, 1926-1927. "Ma, I've gotten a job!"

Nineteen-year-old Babe drove her daddy's old auto into town every week to make deliveries of our eggs, cream, and butter, and to pick up supplies. On this spring day, it appeared she had found time to pursue employment.

"What do you mean, you've gotten a job? Doing what?"

She handed me an advertising bill. "This was tacked to the mercantile window, so I pulled it down and inquired. Mr. Jensen sent me across the street to Joe Kelly's Cafe. Joe auditioned and hired me on the spot. You remember, he's the fiddle player for one of the local bands, right? They play all summer at barn dances and in his restaurant on Saturday mornings the rest of the year."

I took the bill from her hands.

Wanted: Piano Player for barn dances and other venues, starting this spring.

I was dumbstruck. My daughter had accepted employment playing piano in a traveling band? They had hired a woman? This was a lot to digest. I sat down, rubbing my forehead, and said the first thing that came to mind. "You are aware Joe's Cafe is just a front for the speakeasy downstairs, aren't you? Will they have you playing there as well?" This did not settle well.

"Oh, Mother, I figured you'd say something like that. You're so old-fashioned. It's 1926, for heaven's sake! I'm nineteen and it's time for me to spread my wings and fly a little bit. You were married by this age! I'm not getting any younger," she spat back at me. "Besides, he also offered me work serving food at the cafe. I've already decided to ask Aunt Lucy if I can stay with her and Uncle J.R. until I save enough to rent a place of my own in Miles City."

Milestown had officially become Miles City, to the younger generation. Oh, the naïveté Babe demonstrated, moving on her own into town. It might be true she would only work in the cafe and play piano at barn dances, but something told me she would also be playing in Joe's speakeasy, one of many that had proliferated since Prohibition. Unlike Frances, Christian Science had not become a guiding light in Babe's life.

Neither her dad nor I could talk her out of her plan, and within the week, my strong-willed daughter had packed her belongings. They were now loaded into the old Dodge and Babe sat waiting on the passenger side while Frank turned the crank.

The car grumbled to life, while I watched from the front porch. Babe turned to me and an impish grin lit up her sweet, untouched face. "Love you, Ma. Don't worry, I won't do anything you wouldn't do!"

I did not find her comment comforting.

I could see Frank still shaking his head as they drove off down the road.

With Babe gone, it became harder and harder to keep up with the unending chores. I wondered how much longer I would be able to manage on my own. Frank sent his hired man over now and then, but living on the ranch was becoming ever more challenging. Frances required a considerable amount of caregiving. Even a cane had become useless to help her to move about when her legs refused to cooperate, so we had gotten her a wheelchair. None of us cared to admit it, but for all intents and purposes, she had lost the ability to walk. Mercifully, she could still stand with a cane, otherwise, I'm not sure I would have been capable of transferring her between her chair and the bed or toilet. It was a blessing Frank had added indoor plumbing some years ago.

In the far corners of my mind, troublesome questions had begun niggling at me. For one, I worried about who would care for Frances when I was gone or no longer able. Lacking any obvious answer, I forced myself to bury such musings and then thanked God for my good health.

I awakened with a start. It was pitch dark and someone was pounding on the door. Thank goodness, I was diligent about keeping it locked after Clarence left.

"Mother! Do you hear that? Someone's trying to break in!" Frances' panicked voice called from the room next to mine.

I reached under the mattress and pulled out the handgun Frank had given me all those years ago, and walked warily into the kitchen, hoping I wouldn't have to test my courage and use it.

"Ma! It's me, Ma! Let me in. Please! Let me in."

Babe. What kind of a scrape had she gotten herself into?

"Hold on to your horses, girl, I'm on my way." Setting the gun on the table, I opened the door and she teetered in. Her father's daughter in so many ways, I could smell the alcohol on her breath.

"Babe! What's going on here? Why are you beating on the door at this hour of the night?" I peered around her into the darkness and saw the outline of Lucy's automobile sitting in front of the house.

"It's Hankins, Mama! He's chasing after me."

I jerked my head back and stood before her, arms akimbo. "What? What are you talking about? Hankins?" I trembled. "You mean Clarence?" Feeling faint, my ears buzzing, I sat down hard on the closest chair. "Is he following you?" Oh Lord, I didn't want to have to use that gun.

"Yes, I think he's after me. I'm hoping he doesn't have any means to follow me out here, though. He came into Joe's tonight and walked right up to me at the piano and started sweet-talking me. He had been drinking and I asked him to leave me alone, but he kept at it. Finally, Joe threw him out. Ma, I'm downright scared of that man! I left Joe's later by the back way, and hightailed it back to Lucy and J.R.'s. They're over in Glendive tonight and I didn't want to stay alone, so I borrowed Aunt Lucy's auto." She spoke in a jumbled rush, and her eyes moved to the table where my Colt Derringer rested. "I need a gun!"

What an earful! "Well, this will never do. I won't stand for it." As an afterthought, I confirmed my earlier supposition. "So, you're playing piano in Joe's speakeasy now?"

"Mother? What's going on? Is that you Babe?" Frances was calling from her room. Dazed, Babe helped me up and we walked arm in arm down the hall. The three of us talked until the wee hours of the morning, but reached no definite conclusion or plan of action, other than to talk to Frank come daylight.

In the end, I didn't give Babe my handgun. Frank wouldn't hear of it. By morning, she had calmed down, but it worried me that Hankins had surfaced again. Frank followed her in the Dodge back into town and they went directly to the sheriff's office to file a complaint. What happened next was so baffling, I've yet to unravel her cockeyed thinking.

Several weeks later, I ripped open an official looking envelope from the Custer County Courthouse which had come in the stage mail and was addressed to Mrs. Margareta Herman Hankins. Inside, I found a sheaf of documents. Clarence had sued me for divorce, claiming desertion. This man was certainly touched in the head. I didn't hesitate to sign the paperwork, sending it back to Miles City on the next stage. No skin off my nose if he wanted to spend his money seeking a divorce.

Unremarkably, in July, I received a notice in the mail the divorce had been granted, no contest, and my name had been restored to Herman. Fine and dandy. It pleased me greatly to have severed any remaining ties to that deplorable man.

Babe hadn't been home in the past couple of months, but had sent several notes assuring me of her well-being. Whenever I went into town, I always made a point of stopping to see her at Joe's Cafe, but of late found her rather dismissive and, to some extent, evasive when we spoke.

"No time to talk now, Ma. Customers are waiting," was the usual reply to my attempts at conversation.

I made the best of our abbreviated encounters, ignoring the growing unease in the back of my mind, telling myself next time would be different. Since that dreadful night when Babe had been pursued by Hankins, I assumed he had disappeared again, hopefully for good this time. He had his divorce. Wherever he landed, I only hoped he hadn't found some other poor, unsuspecting woman.

Barely more than a week after receiving the divorce decree, a note arrived in the mail, addressed to Frank and me.

> *Dear Ma and Daddy,*
> *Sometimes we have to do things we realize are wrong, but necessary. I love you both with all my heart and please understand I had no choice. I don't think it will turn out too bad as I'm okay and maybe even having a little fun.*

What on earth? I turned the page over to read the back.

> *Clarence assured me he would kill you, Mama, if I didn't comply and by golly, I believed him. So, while the band did a series of barn dances in Glendive last week, I accepted his proposal and we got married there on the 28th.*

Released from my fingers as if poison, the note fluttered to the floor. I turned to stare out the kitchen window. My senses numbed, I studied a cobweb quivering along the right edge of the window frame. Where had I put my feather duster?

"Mother?" A faint voice called me back. Now, more sharply, "Mother! What's happened?" With a nonchalance I didn't feel, I stooped to retrieve the sheet of paper, turned and handed it to my daughter.

Frances read aloud, her voice sounding ever more incredulous as the words fell from her mouth. *". . . I suspect this may upset you, but I love you too much to see any harm come to you, and like I said, so far, he's treated me fine. Please don't worry and I'll see you soon. Love, Babe"*

If Babe's final sentences were meant to reassure me, they missed the mark. I began shuddering uncontrollably. I had caused this to happen by agreeing to the divorce. *Oh, how could he? That diabolical fiend!* I couldn't find harsh enough words in my vocabulary to describe him. Belatedly, I realized he had made good on his threat. I had not seen the last of him.

Frank was so distressed by the news that he punched a cupboard door with his fist, breaking the top hinge and leaving it hanging at an awkward angle. After he calmed down, we both concluded there was nothing we could do to alter this unsavory turn of events.

Babe's marriage came as a complete surprise to Lucy, as well. Frank drove me into Miles City to talk with my sister and break the news. "Land sakes, Maggie, she's married that scoundrel? She told J.R. and me she planned to be away for a few days, but never in this lifetime would I have expected this. Why, it's the most outlandish thing I've ever heard!" Looking down, she shook her head in dismay. "Somehow I feel responsible, sister. I should have kept a better watch on her . . ."

"No, Lucy, it's not your responsibility. I know firsthand the persuasive powers of that deranged, good-for-nothing Hankins, and I don't blame you. Babe is young and doesn't know what she's gotten herself into. The fault is mine for signing the damn paperwork to finalize our divorce. My intuition tells me she won't be married long, and I pray that is correct. All we can do is bide our time and see what happens next.

My prophecy came to pass. It didn't take long. Shortly after the new year, she showed up at Frank's house. The marriage was less than six months old.

"Maggie, you might want to come on over." Frank stood on my porch early one frosty January morning. "Babe turned up."

Frances and I looked at each other as I gathered my coat, mittens, hat and muffler. Shoving my feet into boots, I wondered why Babe had gone to Frank's house instead of mine. I followed along behind him on the narrow pathway he had cleared between our houses.

The commotion of our entrance awakened our twenty-year-old daughter from where she had been sleeping, camped on Frank's horsehair settee.

"Ma!" she blurted. "Daddy, I told you to leave her out of this!" She was visibly anxious. "I told you what that hateful man said."

"Now, Babe, don't you worry, honey, he's not gonna harm anyone." He looked at me and said, "Seems he threatened to kill you if she come running to your house."

I peered more closely at my youngest daughter, horrified by what I saw. Both eyes were blackened, and bruises, or possibly burns, marked her forearms. Who knew what other evidence of abuse lay underneath her disheveled and wrinkled garments? "Oh, Babe, what has he done to you?" I broke down into tears.

"Maggie, she's safe with us now," Frank reminded me.

"How do you know? Can you guarantee it?" Nausea and hysteria began to wrap their tentacles around me. "I'm going to find the sheriff this minute!"

"No, Ma! He'll kill us all if you do."

"What are you suggesting? We do nothing?"

"Yes. That's the safest plan." Babe answered in a monotone, with a barely perceptible nod of her head. Tears from vacant eyes trickled down her cheeks, as she sat limply, her unwashed hair matted and streaked with dirt.

I pinched my lips together, clenching my jaw. I took a deep breath and released it, then another. "Well, it's not what I'd do," I said, throwing up my hands. "But if you won't file a complaint, I can't do it for you."

"Ma, it wouldn't do any good. It's my word against his, and sure as shootin', he's made up a whole list of reasons why he treated me the way he did."

I could only imagine. And, it was a man's word against a woman's. In the end, we did nothing, and within a couple of weeks, Babe felt well enough to move in with Gertrude and Alvin at their farm. Thank God she wasn't pregnant. As for Hankins, we mercifully never saw or heard from him again.

After seventeen years, my job with the Broadus Stage line ended on March 1, 1927, with the government's introduction of mail delivery by motorized vehicle. After prayerful consideration, it seemed an opportune time for Frances and me to leave the ranch and move into Miles City.

One day after the noon meal, we finished up the dishes and sat together at the kitchen table, each enjoying a cup of tea.

"Well, Frances, what would you think about moving into town?"

Her eyes opened wide. "What? Really? Why?"

I chuckled at her response. "Well, I'm coming up on fifty-seven, you know. And I'm tired. The rigors of ranch work have left me worn to a frazzle."

"And unfortunately, I'm of little help." She looked down at her lap.

Noticing a touch of bitterness, I countered, "Honey, deep in my heart I recognize how narrow the choices must seem for you, living out here in the country."

"But I love it out here, watching the birds and the deer. I'm close to Daddy, too."

"Town offers so many possibilities, sweetheart. We'd have neighbors. We'd be closer to Lucy, and both your sisters, and little Betty and Boyd." I had a hunch this last prospect swayed her over to my side. What I didn't say was that we would also be nearer to a doctor and the hospital.

The first week of March, when spring began offering signs of rebirth, I walked over to Frank's, carefully avoiding most of the mud in the well-worn pathway. "Frank, do you have a minute?"

"Yessum. What can I do for you?" At seventy-one, with a weathered face, deeply lined, and his handlebar moustache practically white, Frank showed his age. Taken aback for a moment, I noticed his hunched shoulders and arthritic hands, as if seeing them for the first time in a long, long while. I pondered how much longer he would be able to carry on managing the place on his own, although this insight did not tempt me to stay. We were, after all, divorced. I was thankful we remained friends, the way it should have always been. But now, it was time for Frances and me to make a new start. It astonished me to realize I had been on the ranch for more than twenty-five years.

"Frank, I've given this a great deal of thought, so don't try to talk me out of it. Frances and I have decided to move into town."

He eyed me circumspectly. "Well, Maggie, I can't say as I'm surprised. I've been half-expectin' this ever since Babe came home all beat up earlier this year. Kinda figured you might want to be closer to her. And, I know how lonely the ranch is for a shut-in like Frances."

35.

Billings, Montana, Spring, 1932. "Mama, it hurts so much, the cramping in my legs won't leave me be."

After five years in Miles City, Frances and I made the difficult decision to move to Billings, a city more than twice as large, two hours west, so she could receive more specialized medical care. After her surgeries back in 1927, Frances' condition had gradually deteriorated. The flares were unpredictable, and when they occurred, agonizing. I marveled at how well she coped with such unrelenting misery.

"I'll go find the nurse." She seldom complained, so this pain must have been excruciating. Once in the hallway, out of sight of my daughter, I stopped for a moment to wipe away tears. I found it difficult watching anyone suffer, but much more so when it was my own child.

She had been a patient at St. Vincent Hospital since we arrived in Billings by train last week. The doctors had not yet been able to work out the best dosage of medicine to relieve her almost continuous discomfort, nor sort out the root of her pain. At times like this, her affliction ruled our lives.

"Oh, Mama, the torment. Could you please read from *Science and Health*? It helps me relax."

"Yes, dear, I have it right here." Under my tutelage, and in opposition to the teachings, Frances agreed with me about the wisdom of medical treatment. Modern science had undeniably come a long way since Mrs. Eddy had her visions, and medicine was firmly rooted in today's world. I knew that Christian Scientists believed prayer to be most effective when it was not combined with medicine, but it wouldn't be the first time I had defied convention. I reached into my pocketbook, pulled out the little missive, and proceeded to read from it until the sedative the nurse had brought took effect and she fell asleep. I beheld my daughter lying in the hospital bed, eyelids now closed over her clear, steel blue eyes. Her thick, dark chestnut hair created a soft border around her face. My beautiful girl, with her full lips and high cheekbones. What were the future prospects for this attractive young woman? I watched the rhythmic breathing of her relaxed body, finally at peace with the pain.

We'd had such hope and trust in the surgeries in Kirksville . . .

"Miss Herman, I'm pleased to report that you're a good candidate for surgery to correct the damage to your legs caused by the infantile paralysis." Dr. Graham directed his remarks to Frances, after conducting a detailed exam of her that spring of 1927. Upon the advice of the doctor in Miles City, we had traveled to the Montana Shodair Hospital in Helena for this evaluation. "I'll prepare a letter of referral for you and send it off to the Kirksville Osteopathic Hospital. After the application is processed, they'll be in touch with you to confirm my recommendation and establish a date for the surgery." He set down the paperwork and leaned forward to ask, "You do understand this unfortunately will not help your scoliosis?"

Frances accepted his statement with a nod.

"Do you have any questions or concerns?"

Frances, her hands clutched together, addressed him with courage. "Nevertheless, Doctor, this is indeed good news! Can you give me some indication as to the success rate? Do you think I'll be able to walk again?"

"Well, Miss Herman, as we've already discussed, it's hard to predict outcomes. You have to realize this is an experimental surgery which has had some outstanding success, but it's never guaranteed."

"I was hoping you'd say there might be a good chance for me . . ." Her voice drifted off.

"Dear, of course there's a good chance for you! Otherwise, we wouldn't bother sending you all the way from Montana to Missouri for this surgery!"

She raised her head, as a smile lit her face and her eyes brightened. Faith makes all things possible.

In the end, we spent over three months in Kirksville. Frances underwent not one, but several surgeries. They shortened the bone in her left leg, to even up the length with her right. They fused joints, and moved muscles and ligaments, all with the goal of restoring movement to her legs. She endured electric shocks, x-rays, splints, and plaster casts, along with complete bed rest, in combination with leg massage and passive motion exercises, always with a lightness of spirit, her mind entirely focused on a positive outcome.

Days melted into weeks and in the end, I detected no real forward progress. Doubts began to seep into my consciousness, but I kept them to myself. By the third month, I had begun to grow weary, my heart heavy. I tried to ignore the tightness in my chest whenever the doctor visited and our options continued to narrow. How did Frances find the fortitude to carry on? And, what had happened to my faith?

By late September, the surgeons had tried everything they could to accomplish a miracle for my daughter. On the day of her discharge, while her caregivers and I clapped and nurses snapped photos, Frances, wearing her new braces and with considerable help, walked triumphantly. This was a major, but short-lived victory, as I helped her out of the uncomfortable braces and back into her wheelchair once we arrived by taxi at the Burlington Railroad station.

While we waited in the depot to board the train, I stared out the window at the granite sky. The crisp golden leaves of autumn drifted downward, landing in silence upon the empty platform. The weather perfectly matched my mounting despondency. Although the hospital would announce another "success," to me, the reality appeared quite different.

Frances kept a stiff upper lip on the long train ride home, quoting her favorite passages by Mary Baker Eddy. "Mama, listen to this...*If the Scientist reaches his patient through divine Love, the healing work will be accomplished on one visit, and the disease will vanish into its native nothingness like dew before the morning sunshine.* Isn't that beautiful? I have a hunch if we spend more time seeking out learned Christian Scientists back in Montana, I can overcome this and walk!"

❧

At the time, I had wished for more of her resolve. Sitting here now in the St. Vincent hospital room, I questioned whether the surgeries failed because her lameness was caused by her father's abuse, and not infantile paralysis. I supposed dwelling on these things got me nowhere. Life would continue to move forward and I would continue to do whatever I needed to ensure the safety and well-being of my daughter.

It was early in the afternoon, so I decided to walk back to my temporary lodging downtown and rest awhile myself. The fresh air would do me good and I would return to have supper with Frances later.

Shivering and pulling my wrap tighter, I walked along 27th Street, wishing I had also worn a sweater on this blustery March day. Obviously a main thoroughfare, I counted nearly two dozen automobiles passing in either direction before I had traveled three blocks. Everyone around me appeared to be in such a hurry. It would take some time to become accustomed to the faster pace of this city, not to mention the noise.

I had left Gussie and her children behind in Miles City. Both in high school now, Betty and Boyd were nearly grown. Even though it had been but a week since we had moved, I already missed them. I held close the years I'd been part of their lives, grateful these memories, tucked safely away in my mind, stood ready to be summoned at will. An unexpected gust of wind stirred up dust in the street and brought my attention back to the present as I hurried through its swirling path.

The presence of an elevator had enticed me to rent a furnished apartment at the Virginia Hotel on Montana Avenue, a twenty-minute walk from the hospital. As I turned from 27th onto Montana, it occurred to me I hadn't yet taken time to explore the surrounding area. Invigorated by my walk, a rest no longer held any appeal, so I went east in the direction of the train depot. Two blocks from our apartment, I spotted a cafe. A large print ad tacked on the inside of the front window caught my eye.

WANTED: Cook--Apply inside

This might be my lucky day, I chuckled to myself as I strode briskly into the St. Louis Cafe. Just past two-thirty, the cafe was empty, save for a man behind the till. Immediately, I experienced an added bonus--the warmth--which caused a pleasant shiver to run down my spine.

He nodded his head, "Take a seat anywhere, Missus, and I'll be with you shortly."

"Oh, I'm not here to eat."

His eyes seemed to say, *you can't come in here and merely take up space*, but his voice, a touch perplexed, uttered, "Uh, well, this is a cafe . . ."

I interrupted him, "Well, yes, I understand that. I'm here to inquire about the job."

"Oh, I see."

I stood straight as he regarded me, and hoped I appeared younger than my sixty-one years. "So, tell me about your skills and why I should hire you."

"Okay, Mr. . . . . ?"

"Lou Franklin's the name."

I blinked and tipped my head. "Lou? As in Louis?"

"Yeah, as in Louis, but I'll tell you, I ain't no saint! My late wife named the place, kind of a joke. Most people think it's named after the town in Missouri, though." He smiled and I noticed a missing front tooth, creating an unwholesome impression. Yet he acted pleasant enough and I knew better than to judge a book by its cover.

The interview lasted long enough for him to hire me.

"The shift'll be five o'clock in the morning until two. Would you be able to start tomorrow?"

"Certainly!" We shook hands before I went on my way, smiling inside and out. Next on my list, but not today, I hoped to find more permanent living quarters for Frances and me. I didn't view the Virginia as a long-term solution. Besides the daily cost and the noise from the railroad and saloons lining Montana Avenue, the place had plainly seen better days.

⌒〜⌒

"Mrs. Herman, Miss Herman." Dr. Louis Allard had smiled kindly before nodding his head and glancing down at his clipboard. He smelled of cigars, which unnecessarily reminded me of Frank. "After careful assessment and monitoring these past couple of weeks, it's our opinion all the surgeries performed on you in Missouri, Miss Herman, will regrettably never aid in helping you to walk again. I'm so very sorry to relay this." He gave us a moment to digest this information.

While I did not find this evaluation surprising, I could tell it devastated my daughter. His news had knocked the wind out of her sails. She grabbed for my hand, squeezing it tight, steeling herself for what might be forthcoming.

He let us down as gently as a doctor could, with the prognosis that unless new treatments for post-polio syndrome became available, her life would likely be spent sitting in a wheelchair.

"Long term, you may suffer from various afflictions ranging from fatigue and trembling muscles and cramps, to pain in your joints, bones and muscles. It is possible the scoliosis may worsen over time.

You might also experience a progressive weakness elsewhere . . . for example, in your arms, and even potential breathing problems. But I want you to keep your spirits up, young lady, because new treatments are being tested daily all over the world and we have every reason to believe a cure will be found within a few years."

Frances stared straight ahead, her face drawn.

Even though he did his best to leave us with hope, the forecast was a large and bitter pill to swallow. My daughter was only twenty-nine years old.

Presently, I sat in the hospital cafeteria, where I had taken cowardly refuge after the disappointing consultation. Chilled, I rubbed my arms. The lone occupant, save for the cashier, I sipped my tea and ruminated about life. In particular, my daughter's life. Frances' fate would prey upon me until my last breath. It troubled me to no end, worrying what might become of my crippled daughter after I died. *Would one of her sisters take her in? Would she wind up in a hospital or a home for the infirm?* I feared my concern over her future had reached the point of an obsession. Too often over the past thirty years, I had awakened in a cold sweat in the dead of night, crying out for my four little children, left behind on Sugarbush Road. Although I had vowed to never abandon a child of mine again, as yet I'd been unable to figure out how to avoid death.

"May I join you?" Startled from these deep thoughts, I glanced up to see a bespectacled older gentleman, also with a cup of tea, standing beside my table.

"I'm sorry, but I think I'd rather be alone for the moment." I looked back down into my cup.

"You sound as if you could use a friend, and I think I may cry if I can't talk to someone." His hands trembled, causing his teacup to rattle, spilling tea onto the saucer.

I wasn't sure what to do. Then, I remembered Papa, the only other man I had ever known to cry. "Oh dear, what's wrong, sir?"

"Would it be okay if I sit down?"

"Please." I waved my hand at the empty seat across from me.

"I don't mean to intrude, ma'am, but a short time ago, I received some bad news and I'm in sore need of some company."

"Would you like to talk about it?" I hoped speaking of his troubles might mollify his distress.

He nodded, while tears welled up in the corners of his eyes. We sat in companionable silence for some minutes, sipping our tea. With thinning, not-yet-grey hair and a slender appearance, he was a tall man, perhaps a foot taller than myself. Impeccably dressed, I judged him to be near my age.

"My wife is upstairs in a hospital room, under sedation."

I nodded, encouraging him to continue.

"She's dying."

"Oh, sir, I'm so sorry to hear that."

The tears started to make tracks down his cheeks. How unusual to see a man cry in public. We again sat quietly for a time, before he added, "There's nothing to be done, so I'm taking her home to die. It's cancer."

"I'm so sorry to hear that." Unable to find fresh words, I echoed my previous ones.

He nodded his head up and down several times.

"My mother died of cancer." I hesitated, and suddenly all the air surrounding me evaporated. I gasped for breath and croaked, "And also my oldest daughter, Helen, this past year." My words came out in an anguished rush. It felt strange to speak them aloud. Why was I telling him this? I didn't even know this man's name.

"So you're familiar with this disease, then?" He perked up a bit and gave me his full attention.

"It's a devastating affliction, truly. I pray they can give your dear wife plenty of pain medication, so she doesn't suffer as my mother did."

"Did your daughter not suffer so?"

I gulped. "I was not there for her passing. I received word of her illness but God did not grant me enough time to make the long train journey to Michigan to say goodbye. It was but a few short weeks after her diagnosis that we lost her." A lump grew in my throat. "But enough about my troubles, sir. I believe you are the one who needs a listening ear today."

Fresh tears trickled down his cheeks as he stared at me, the two of us somehow now bonded by shared misfortune. After a time, he spoke. "I'm very sorry for your losses, ma'am. Thank you kindly for hearing my story." Then, he looked down at his cup of tea, which by this time, must have been stone-cold. "Oh, dear, where are my manners? Name's Oliver Richards, but my friends call me O.C."

"How do you do, Mr. Richards? I'm Maggie Herman, lately of Miles City."

He sat up a little straighter. "I'm not from Billings either. Have a grain elevator and gas pump down the highway about an hour away in Lavina, and a farm between there and Belmont."

I nodded my head. "I've heard of Lavina, but not Belmont."

"Belmont is but a wide spot in the road a few miles from Lavina, so you've not missed much." He smiled. "What brings you to the hospital cafeteria in Billings?"

I spoke of Frances and our move from Miles City. He opened up then and told me about his darling Nettie, and their only child, Helen. A year older than Frances, his Helen, her husband and daughter farmed up north, near Cut Bank. Although the circumstances underlying our conversation were somber, our exchange lifted both our spirits. I chalked it up as a chance encounter with a sympathetic stranger, and didn't expect to see Mr. Richards again.

36.

1932-1935. Frances and I settled into our new life in Billings. After her discharge from the hospital, we moved into a residence on the edge of downtown, a much quieter and more genial neighborhood than the hotel on Montana Avenue. We rented a main floor apartment with an inviting wrap-around porch and easy access for a wheelchair. The distance to the cafe had doubled, but the location made it worth the extra walking time.

It was my day off work and I sat in the living room mending a blouse, thinking it time to start lunch. I heard a loud clatter, and next, a strangled scream, followed by a thump. I hurried into the kitchen. Chicken soup coated the cupboards, the floor and my daughter.

"I hate my life! I hate this chair!" She smacked the icebox with all her might before breaking into sobs of anger and frustration.

"Oh, Frances. Sweet girl." I tried to put my arms around her, but she flung them away and glared at me. She had developed quite a temper in recent months, and there was often no reasoning with her. Calling upon all the patience I could muster, I remembered that everyone handles adversity in different ways.

God had called Frances to bear this burden and she had to come to terms with the fact that she would never walk. Realizing a dream cannot come true, that it will only ever be a dream, changes a person somehow. It certainly changed us both. The sparkle in her bright blue eyes dimmed, and I became more and more preoccupied with her condition.

One day, not long after the chicken soup debacle, I returned from my shift at the cafe and Frances greeted me at the door with a smile. "Mother, there's an ad in the Gazette offering vocational training to learn to hand-color black and white prints. Doesn't that sound like something I might be able to do?" She handed me the newspaper.

There had been so many days of late when nothing seemed to go right for her and she acted peevish or morose. How could I blame her for being down in the dumps? It was heartening to hear her eagerness about something.

"I'm going to write Daddy this afternoon and see if he would consider paying for the training!"

It pleased me to see her face aglow. I agreed on this course of action and she set to work composing her note. Over the years since we had left the ranch, Frances and her father kept up an ongoing correspondence. I sometimes puzzled over why Frances insisted on exchanging letters with him. After all was said and done, I'd come to the conclusion that memories of hard times had faded, replaced by an undeniable kinship between them.

Frank did pay her fees and our daughter put her heart and soul into the training. Considering his treatment of her as a child, I thought it was the least he could do. Her diligence as a pupil paid off. The instructor reported Frances had "exceptional artistic ability," and with this reference she secured part-time employment with two photography studios in Billings.

Despite the hardships brought on by the Great Stock Market Crash of 1929, it surprised us how many people could afford the fee to have their family photos colorized. Her new job provided us some sorely needed additional income, but even more important, it gave my daughter a sense of purpose.

Some months later, as I read the *Billings Gazette*, a death notice caught my eye: "Area Deaths: Nettie Kline Richards, 59, Belmont." Mr. Richards, his daughter and granddaughter immediately came to mind, and I offered up a humble prayer to God. I questioned if it would be considered improper to send a card of condolence and decided it would be rude not to.

Two months passed. I had all but forgotten my gesture of sympathy toward the Richards family when a brief note arrived in the daily mail from Mr. Richards.

> *January 7, 1933*
> *Dear Mrs. Herman,*
> *Thank you for your most gracious letter of condolence. I was touched that not only you remembered my dear Nettie's name, but took the time to send our family such a cordial sympathy card. I will not tell you the ensuing time has been easy, but by the end my cherished wife was in much pain and not herself in any way, and she begged to go. It was with a grief-stricken relief she at last passed on to greener pastures.*
> *Thank you again for your kind gesture.*
> *Regards,*
> *O.C. Richards*

One day in early February, I arrived home from work to find two suitcases on the floor next to the sofa in the living room.

"Hi Ma. Bet you didn't expect to see me!"

Frances looked in my direction and shook her head.

I glanced at Babe and then looked back at the suitcases.

"Don't worry, Ma, it's only until I find my own place. I've decided Miles City is too small for me. I'm tired of working at the cafe and want to try my luck in the big city." Her eyes twinkled.

Always my headstrong child, I walked toward her and embraced her, "Babe, stay as long as you want. It'll be good to have you."

For the most part, the three of us got along fine, although Babe kept late hours, regularly sleeping until noon. With my workday starting at five o'clock, Frances and I arose with the first birdsong. Oftentimes, Babe walked in the door from her night out around the time I put on my coat to leave for the cafe. I had long ago abandoned any notion of attempting to control her actions, and could only pray she didn't end up in another predicament like the one involving Hankins all those years past.

About a month after Babe moved in with us, I bumped into Mr. Richards coming out of the Mercantile.

"Well, good afternoon, Mrs. Herman! Fancy meeting you here. What brings you down to Montana Avenue this fine March day?"

"Why, Mr. Richards, hello! I just finished up my workday at the cafe," I said, pointing to the St. Louis Cafe sign behind me, "and am on my way home."

"You work there? Heavens to Betsy, that café makes the tastiest of pies."

"Well, sir, I do believe those are my pies!"

"Is that so? Well, I'll be. Say, may I offer you a ride? My truck isn't anything special, but it's faster than feet," he chuckled. "At least, a little faster," he added with a smile.

I had been quite firm with myself about never getting involved with another man. With our advanced years, the fact that O.C.'s birthdate was four years before mine made no difference. I found in him everything that Sam, Frank and Clarence had lacked. Genteel would be one way to describe this angel of a man. And, oh, the compassion he displayed toward Frances! She really took a shine to him, too.

In addition to his old Ford truck, he owned a 1930 Ford Model A station wagon. It was easy to move Frances in the back seat and also carry her wheelchair in the back of the wagon. This enabled the three of us to go on adventures together. Frances and I loved to visit his ranch near Belmont, reminiscent of the tranquility we had left so far behind at the dam. We'd often take a picnic lunch and stop along the way at the little community park in Lavina to eat. Afterwards, we liked to stroll down the quiet streets of this tiny burg, with O.C. capably pushing Frances in her wheelchair.

Infrequently, O.C. and I spent time alone, and unfailingly, the same topic came up over and over.

"Maggie, please say 'yes.' Say you'll marry me. You know I'd do anything for you!"

"Anything?" I offered him a sweet smile and a squeeze of his hand.

"Yes, anything! I love you. I love your daughter. We make a terrific family! I'll take care of you both."

Invariably, I answered, "O.C., I love you too, but I'm too old to get married again. What we enjoy is already perfect. I'm content and satisfied, so let's leave it there. Please, let's not ruin it with marriage." I couldn't recall another time I'd had enough confidence to say this with such conviction, sincerely meaning every word.

This exasperated him, but I simply could not bring myself to take the risk of marrying for a fourth time. At long last, I had found a companion with whom to enjoy life. I meant it when I used the words satisfied and content. I also loved it when he held me in his arms, but I didn't believe this to be a mandate that we should marry.

Babe, on the other hand, had different plans with regard to marriage.

"Ma, Clayton and I are planning to get hitched next week." Babe, or Gladys, as she now wished to be called, made this announcement one day in December, 1935. Even more astonishing than her impending marriage, she had renounced the wild life. Despite meeting in a bar, she and Clayton had discovered religion, become teetotalers and committed themselves to the Baptist faith. Gladys played the piano in church these days instead of in drinking establishments. The older I got, the more life surprised me.

37

May 17, 1940. The calendar didn't lie, so I reached the only plausible conclusion: time sped up with each passing year. It had been eight years since I met O.C. in the hospital cafeteria. We continued to be close friends and after I retired, we spent even more time together, often joined by Frances. The two of them planned a party in honor of my seventieth birthday. They decided to hold the party out at the Belmont ranch. O.C. insisted on driving over to Billings to collect Frances and me on the morning of the big celebration.

Soaking up the sunshine, we awaited his arrival on the front porch. We watched two birds putting up a ruckus; perhaps two males arguing over the affections of a lady-bird.

"There he is." We waved to O.C. as he pulled his car up in front of our building mid-morning.

"Happy Birthday!" he called out, as he bounded up the steps with an agility belying his sixty-six years.

"My, don't you both look beautiful this fine spring morning!" Even though I was now much rounder than in earlier years, I did feel pretty in my pink crepe dress. Although older and less fashionable than Frances' dress, it was comfortable, and besides, the color complimented my gray hair. I had to admit, Frances was really dolled up in her smart orange and white-flowered rayon crepe afternoon dress. Oh, how that girl loved bright colors!

Driving up the long hill out of the Yellowstone Valley, sunbeams dazzled us through the open car windows. My spirits rose right along with the station wagon, as we left the city behind to travel across the high plains toward Belmont. Alive with new growth, the rolling hills were a verdant green carpet, dotted with bluebonnets, Indian paintbrush, columbine and purple poppy mallow as far as the eye could see. I had been born in one of the most beautiful months of the year. I breathed in the sweet smell of spring, evoking memories of my youth spent walking the fields on the Perry farm. With a tingling warmth in my limbs, my heart swelled and I wanted to taste the moment, and remember this feeling forever.

"It's a glorious day to be alive!"

O.C. looked at me and beamed, his sunny smile nearly swallowing his cheeks. "I'd like to make a stop on the way to the party, if you wouldn't mind?"

I smiled my consent.

As we passed through Lavina on our way to Belmont, O.C slowed and stopped in front of the little park where we enjoyed picnicking. "Ladies, do you see the empty lot there, next to the park?"

Frances and I nodded.

"Well, I've been considering this for some time. I've decided to make an offer on the property."

"What? Why would you do that?" My daughter quizzed him.

"Because I am going to build a cafe and hire someone to run it. This town needs a gathering place. Somewhere folks can come to chew the fat and eat a piece of pie. Somewhere I can take my two best gals out for a bite to eat!"

"Gosh, that's swell, O.C. I'm pleased for you and can't wait for us to share a meal there." Frances grinned and he winked at her.

He already owned the Texaco Gas Station and the grain elevator up the street. I supposed he'd resolved to become the tycoon of Lavina, population one hundred fifty. I didn't know what to think.

❦

"Welcome, welcome!" O.C.'s daughter, Helen, greeted us the moment we walked into the ranch house. She and her husband

Albert and their two little girls, Zoe and Joan, had moved back permanently last month to help O.C. manage the ranch. Maybe that had something to do with his decision to build a cafe. An energetic man, O.C. preferred keeping busy.

The two little girls were entertaining us by singing, but mostly giggling, a new ditty from school, when I looked up to see an unexpected sight, Gladys and Clayton! They had driven all the way out to Belmont in their old jalopy two-seater.

"Oh, sweetheart, what a wonderful surprise!" I stood to greet them.

"Ma! We couldn't miss this party!" I hugged her to me, delighted to see my "Babe."

My one nervous moment came with the cake. Helen and Gladys wheeled it in on a cart and I feared the whole thing might go up in flames. "Land o' Goshen, there are far too many candles on that cake!"

"Oh Ma, you're still a spring chicken, what are you talking about?" Gladys teased me. We all laughed before she led everyone in a round of "Happy Birthday."

I took a deep breath and managed to blow out a goodly portion of the candles. To my delight, Zoe and Joan helped me blow out the rest. Merriment followed as we cut the cake, each of us savoring every crumb. I rubbed my tongue across the roof of my mouth as the buttercream frosting dissolved, the cake so light and fluffy.

I sat back and watched as my family and O.C.'s laughed and chatted amiably, and I enjoyed a profound sense of fulfillment, reckoning it was a perfect day, on all accounts.

Rather than drive back to Billings, Frances and I stayed the night in Belmont. My first night away from the city in many a year, I lay in the bed next to my daughter, relishing the gift of silence that was only occasionally interrupted by her gentle snoring. Ah, how I had missed this serenity. I relaxed into it, gliding my hand along the smooth bedsheet and luxuriating in its comfortable silkiness. An owl hooted in the distance and the sheer curtains danced with a slight breeze. I shivered, wondering if I should shut the window against the chill. Lacking any inclination to crawl out of my warm nest, I instead pulled the top blanket up closer under my chin.

My body was weary, my mind, restless. Seventy years I had been on this earth. How had that many years passed so swiftly? Inside, I felt seventeen. I had experienced my share of turmoil during many of those years, moving from one crisis to the next. I had never really figured out a way to settle in and savor life. That time had arrived.

My mind wandered to O.C., grateful we had been able to move beyond any talk of marriage. We remained good friends, almost family. I reflected on how much longer our health and agility might last. This circled back to my ever-present dilemma: what would become of Frances?

Frank died last year, and it turned out most of his grazing fee income had remained unpaid. As a result, he had fallen behind paying his taxes. This was not surprising, considering our country's Great Depression, but it resulted in little inheritance for our daughters. Gladys would be fine, but I agonized over Frances's future. I tossed and turned, beset with worry.

All at once and seemingly out of nowhere, seeds of possibility rooted themselves in my mind. But, no, I shook off these seeds. I doubted such a notion could work. Well . . . or, could it? *Was I bold enough to even suggest such an arrangement?* Could the three of us live together? What would O.C. say? For that matter, what would Frances think? Oh dear, were my thoughts completely outlandish? Some part of my mind ignored this brain chatter and raced on, seeds sprouting without permission.

In an effort to quiet my night mind, I forced myself to relax and listen to the stillness. *Dear God, once again, I turn over my worry about Frances to you. Lord, should I approach O.C. with this possible solution? I will trust you to show me the way forward. Amen.*

I lay still, meditating. There was no denying my life had been full of ups and downs. I snuggled deeper into my pillow facing the dark night sky, realizing those ups and downs had made me the woman I was today. In my many years on this earth, I had experienced love and I had experienced loss. Could I endure one more loss? A loss I'd freely give, for the sake of my child? I supposed I could, as I knew, better than many, how to survive.

I began to drift as visions of my dearest sister, Ella, floated across my mind. *How I loved you, dear sister. Though you left this life too soon, I carry you with me in my heart, always.* When we were young women, I worried that Ella's knight in shining armor might never arrive, not realizing my own true knight would take much, much longer.

EPILOGUE

Divine Love always has met and always will meet every human need.
--Mary Baker Eddy, founder of Christian Science

Lavina, Montana, October 15, 1941. With some reluctance, I replace the contents of the paste-board box and set it back on the floor in my bedroom closet. A few items are piled next to me to be thrown away. They hold no special memories for me today and leave me wondering why I kept them in the first place. As late afternoon settles in, I abandon the idea of walking to the corner, even though it would help to pass the time. I return to the front room and instead of sitting in my rocking chair, I choose one of the brown leather couches. Still, the clock ticks too slowly. I banish all unpleasant thoughts, and consider once again what a miracle it has been to meet O.C.

I smile in satisfaction, my mood lifting, as I glance around the freshly painted living room of our new home. True to his word, last year O.C. moved forward with his plans to build the cafe and expanded the project to include attached living quarters. Frances and I gladly left the busy city for the quieter, small town life. It seems the perfect spot to retire.

Tonight, our home will also become O.C.'s home. We've merged our furnishings, in anticipation of his move. In one corner stands the Edison phonograph, housed in a wooden cabinet containing numerous phonograph cylinders. Listening to the recordings of Sousa band marches takes me back to a different time and place. Another corner houses a curio cabinet, filled with trinkets we've collected over time. Fringed hand-knotted throw rugs on the shiny oak floor in front of each of the two couches add warmth to the room. Much of the furniture belongs to O.C., while Frances has created most of the wall art, ranging from framed needlepoint to tapestry, along with colorized pictures and paintings. With his son-in-law taking over the operation of the ranch and the gas station and elevator only a couple of blocks away, everything has fallen into place.

Who would have imagined a seventy-one-year-old woman would feel as giddy as a teenager the day they put up the new sign, *Richards Cafe*, out front? O.C. hired someone to manage the restaurant and although we have our own kitchen, we also have the option of ordering meals if we aren't in the mood to cook. The staff welcomes my fresh pies, whenever the urge strikes and maybe those pies will put Richards Cafe on the map. Situated on the trucker's route between Billings and Great Falls, we are hopeful the cafe will be a success.

As I continue to wait, I think back to the day last year when O.C. lost his composure upon hearing my idea of joining our family. In the end, he agreed to give it some consideration, especially after I reminded him of his frequent statements that he would do "anything" for me.

Frances chided me, "Mother, what are you thinking, for heaven's sake?"

In time, they both came around.

Not without some misgivings, I pray earnestly my heart will prove to be as practical as my head. Can he love her as he had loved me? What will our families think? Will people be shocked? Will they think I forced him to do this? Will we be shunned for all living together? Will he want to care for an invalid or will he expect me to continue doing so?

Panicked and anxious, I know they will arrive at any moment. I wonder what tonight will be like. For that matter, can I face them tomorrow morning at breakfast? Will my daughter be able to face me? Can I stop wanting him as my own knight?

As the sun begins to set, I sense, as much as hear, a car engine switch off out front. At last, the wait is over. Shakily, I arise from where I've been perched in contemplation on the couch, and walk over to open the door. My heart swells as I watch O.C. walk around to the other side of his auto, open the door and lift out his bride, my daughter, Frances. She puts her arms around his neck and he leans in close to give her a kiss. All smiles, they look up and notice me. I wave to them and step outside. They beckon me toward them and I welcome them home from their honeymoon with an embrace.

Afterword

I've been asked if O.C. really married Maggie's daughter, Frances, and if the three of them lived together afterwards. Yes, they did. It really happened. People ask me, "How?"

How *did* Maggie resolve her feelings for O.C.? How did Frances and O.C. reconcile their relationship? Lost to the ages, sadly, no one is left to answer these questions.

Author's Notes

My mother was May Elizabeth or "Betty," as she came to be called, born at the Home Station in 1918. My grandmother and Betty's mother, Gertrude or "Gussie," was the child Maggie brought with her to Montana in 1901, after she married Frank Herman.

In 1997, an inspiration took root in my mind. Always eager to hear stories from the past, I determined the time was ripe for someone to gather our family narrative and promptly elected myself to the position. I planned to compile a memory book for my parents and my children, complete with all remembered family lore, along with pages of old pictures. Well aware many memories had already vanished with the deaths of other family members, there was no time to lose.

Over the course of several visits, I spent hours interviewing Mom and Dad, the only elders of my immediate family still living. I asked them to share every story and memory they could recall, recording it with a cassette tape player and microphone. Next, using my computer word processor and a lot of patience, I painstakingly transcribed all their words.

My maternal Great-Grandmother Maggie's story, above all the others, stood out, leaving me to wonder if I might be able to find more information about her life. I decided to pursue locating a genealogy group in Mt. Clemens, where Maggie lived the first thirty-one years of her life.

An internet search led me to the Mt. Clemens, Michigan library, where I was directed to a volunteer, Ann Faulkner, who, like her mother before her, did genealogy research in her spare time. We struck up an email relationship and over a period of months, she uncovered a number of documents. These included the paperwork from Maggie's divorce filing, the transcript of Sam and Maggie's divorce trial, hand-written depositions given by Maggie and Lizzie, as well as census information. Ultimately, these became the basis of this novel. I owe Ann a huge debt of gratitude, because without her determination and doggedness to keep digging, I believe Maggie's story would have been lost to the ages, buried somewhere in a pile of microfiche or old manila folders, sitting in a dusty corner of some government office building's basement.

I condensed and incorporated this rediscovered information into my family booklet project. With the help of the local print shop, I printed and bound several copies of "Remembering The Early Days" and passed them out to my family in 1998. Lingering in the back of my mind, however, was Maggie. Without a doubt, my great-grandmother's story emerged as the most intriguing. I never let go of the thought to expand her history into book length, believing it had the potential to be transformed into a compelling story of one woman's survival in a time when women had few rights.

Life intervened, the years passed and my idea lay fallow in my frontal lobes. A few months before the January 2014 release of my first book, *Somebody Stole My Iron: A Family Memoir of Dementia,* I was at last ready to begin writing Maggie's story.

Late in 2014, in hopes of tying up some loose ends, I wondered what the chances were Ann might still be volunteering at the library in Mt. Clemens. What were the odds I would find her again after more than seventeen years? I wrote to her old email address. The email didn't come back as undeliverable, but then, neither did a reply. Two weeks passed. I emailed again and this time I received a prompt answer. Yes, Ann, told me, she still volunteered as a genealogy resource, receiving up to seventy-five requests a day for information, hence the time it took her to respond to me. She well-remembered me and we started up another correspondence.

Since I already had plans to visit my oldest daughter and her family in Lansing, Michigan in the coming year, it seemed only fitting to combine a trip to Mt. Clemens. Before lunching together that day in late January, 2015 and for old time's sake, we spent a couple of hours searching through old file folders and microfiche scouring for any additional information on the Perry and Jobsa (aka Jobse) families.

Maggie Perry Jobsa Herman married and divorced three times between 1889 and 1919. While divorces did occur during that period in history, three divorces was unusual, but it was not unusual for women to lose custody of their children in a divorce settlement. Men were the preferred custodians because both society and judges deemed them better equipped to financially support children. It did not seem to matter if said men were proven drunkards, philanderers and/or abusers.

Maggie, O.C. and Frances continued living in Lavina and operating Richards Cafe for many years. As a small child, I remember Mom (May Elizabeth "Betty"), Granny Gussie (Gertrude) and me visiting the three of them in Lavina, never having a clue, until I was much older, about the unconventional backstory.

Maggie took flight from this life on August 26, 1959, at the ripe old age of eighty-nine. O.C. passed away in 1967, after which Frances, who by now was known around town as "Queenie," hired caregivers so that she might remain in Lavina, operating the cafe. Eventually, after essentially losing the use of both arms, as predicted by Dr. Allard in Billings back in 1932, she moved to a nursing home in Miles City to be nearer her sister, Gertrude, and beloved niece, Betty. Frances Herman Richards was released from life in a wheelchair on September 22, 1988.

Betty inherited the cafe and sold it on a contract for deed more than once, but through a series of missteps, the cafe kept returning into the family fold. After Betty's passing in 2008, it was my turn to inherit the slowly crumbling cafe. Sadly, it was not long before the cafe fell on hard times and closed its doors forever. In 2015, the property was sold to the father-in-law of O.C. and Nettie's great-great grandson. Viewed in a certain light, this somehow completes a circle.

After writing Maggie's story, I must admit to tears when the building came down, but "remember" the words I gave to Great-Great-Great Grandma Fries: *It's not what happens in life, but what we do with what happens.* The plan is to build a new coffee shop, welcoming back all the nearby farmers and ranchers who haven't had a place to congregate since the cafe closed in 2011.

Oh, and, Maggie's knack for making piecrust survived, to be passed along to a fifth generation, my daughters.

Acknowledgements

Posthumously, to my fourth cousin Brian Perry Ziel (descendant of Maggie's older brother John Henry), who shared the family history with me way back in the late 1980's and ignited a quest to learn more.

To Ann Faulkner, the persistent genealogist who kept digging deeper, finding me newspaper clippings, affidavits and the trial transcript.

To my family and friends, who supported and offered feedback, encouraging me to keep after it.

To my daughter, Jill, who hung in there with me during all those first *very long* drafts and asked the question: "Is this a family history or a story about Maggie?"

To my friend and fellow author Jean Lee, for her insightful comments and ability to ask the right questions, threshing out the grain from the chaff.

To my friend and editor, Karen Jarussi, for her editing skills, keen intellect and ability to untangle my phrases into plain English.

To my daughter-in-law, Kylee Bodley, for her thoughtful content editing, strengthening a young Maggie's voice.

A sincere and grateful "thank you" to my beta readers: Amie McGraham, Megan Nyquist, Marianne Sciucco, Diane Powers and last, but certainly not least, my patient husband, Lionel Tapia.

To my readers: If you enjoyed Maggie, would you mind taking a minute to write a review on Amazon? Even a short review is helpful, and I'd be ever so appreciative.

About The Author

Vicki Tapia lives in south-central Montana with her husband and mini-Schnauzer. She is the mother of three and grandmother of eight.

After both her parents were diagnosed with dementia, she began a diary to help her cope with the day-to-day challenges of caregiving. Her journal morphed into *Somebody Stole My Iron: A Family Memoir of Dementia*, published in 2014 by Praeclarus Press. This memoir was a finalist in the 2015 High Plains Book Awards.

Long intrigued by stories of her great-grandmother, Vicki has continued writing about the generations of her family in her second book, *Maggie: A Journey of Love, Loss and Survival.* A tribute to the intrepid life of her great-grandmother, *Maggie* was written in remembrance and recognition of a time when women had few rights. It represents every woman of any era who survived abuse, deep loss and became a survivor; an example to others.

Learn more at vickitapia.com